MOLOKA‘I

MOLOKA'I

ALAN BRENNERT

THORNDIKE PRESS
A part of Gale, a Cengage Company

Copyright © 2003 by Alan Brennert.
Thorndike Press, a part of Gale, a Cengage Company.

ALL RIGHTS RESERVED
Thorndike Press® Large Print Historical Fiction.
The text of this Large Print edition is unabridged.
Other aspects of the book may vary from the original edition.
Set in 16 pt. Plantin.

**LIBRARY OF CONGRESS CIP DATA ON FILE.
CATALOGUING IN PUBLICATION FOR THIS BOOK
IS AVAILABLE FROM THE LIBRARY OF CONGRESS**

ISBN-13: 978-1-4328-7225-0 (hardcover alk. paper)

Published in 2020 by arrangement with Macmillan Publishing Group,
LLC/St. Martin's Publishing Group

Printed in Mexico
Print Number: 01   Print Year: 2020

FOR THE PEOPLE OF KALAUPAPA
and
FOR EDGAR AND CHARLOTTE
WITTMER
my 'ohana

OCEAN

PACIFIC

TERRITORY
of
HAWAI'I

NI'IHAU

KAUA'I

O'AHU

Area of Detail

MOLOKA'I

LĀNA'I

MAUI

KAHO'OLAWE

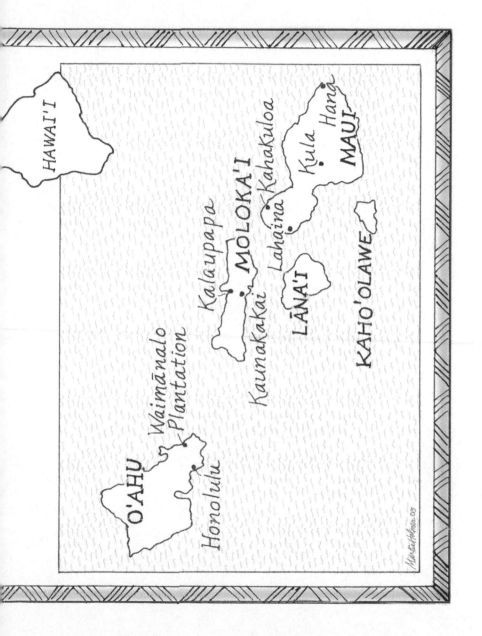

■ ■ ■ ■

PART ONE:
BLUE VAULT OF
HEAVEN

■ ■ ■ ■

CHAPTER 1

1891

Later, when memory was all she had to sustain her, she would come to cherish it: Old Honolulu as it was then, as it would never be again. To a visitor it must have seemed a lush garden of fanciful hybrids: a Florentine-style palace shaded by banyan and monkeypod trees; wooden storefronts flourishing on dusty streets, cuttings from America's Old West; tall New England church steeples blooming above the palm and coconut groves. To a visitor it must have seemed at once exotic and familiar; to five-year-old Rachel it was a playground, and it was home.

Certain things stood out in memory, she couldn't say why: the weight and feel of a five-cent *hapa'umi* coin in her pocket; the taste of cold Tahiti lemonade on a hot day; palm fronds rustling like locusts high above, as she and her brothers played among the rice paddies and fishponds of Waikiki. She remembered taking a swim, much to her

11

mother's dismay, in the broad canals of Kapi'olani Park; she could still feel the mossy bottom, the slippery stones beneath her feet. She remembered riding the trolley cars with her sister up King Street — the two of them squeezed in amidst passengers carrying everything from squid to pigs, chickens to Chinese laundry — mules and horses exuberantly defecating as they dragged the tram along in their wake. Rachel's eyes popped at the size of the turds, longer than her arm, and she giggled when the trolley's wheels squished them underneath.

But most of all, most clearly of all, she remembered Steamer Day — because that was when her father came home.

"Is today Steamer Day?"

"No." Rachel's mother handed her a freshly cooked taro root. "Here. Peel."

Rachel nimbly stripped off the soft purple skin, taking care not to bruise the stem itself, and looked hopefully at her mother. "Is tomorrow Steamer Day?"

Dorothy Kalama, stern-faced at the best of times, shot her daughter an exasperated look. "How do I know? I'm standing lookout on Koko Head, that's where you think I am?" With a stone pestle she pounded a slice of peeled taro into a smooth hard paste, then shrugged. "Could be another week, anyway, before he comes."

"Oh, no, Mama." They'd received a letter from Papa exactly five weeks ago, mailed in Samoa, informing them he'd be leaving for home in a month; and Rachel knew for a fact that the crossing took no more than a week. "Two thousand, two hundred and ninety miles from Samoa to Honolulu," she announced proudly.

Her mother regarded her skeptically. "You know how big is a mile?"

Rachel thought a moment, her round chubby face sober in reflection, then stretched her arms as wide as she could. Dorothy laughed, but before she could respond there was an explosion of boy-noise from outside.

"I hate you! Go 'way!"

"*You* go 'way!"

Rachel's brothers, Benjamin and James — Kimo to everyone but Mama, who disapproved of all but Christian names — roughhoused their way up the front steps and into the house. The sparsely furnished wood-frame home was nearly one large open room: living and dining areas on one side, stove, sink, and cupboards on the other; a tiny corridor led to a triad of tiny bedrooms. Pummeling each other with pulled punches, the boys skidded across a big mat woven from pandanus leaves, Kimo's legs briefly akimbo, like a wishbone in mid-wish.

"You're a big bully!" Ben accused Kimo.

"You're a big baby!" Kimo accused Ben.

Dorothy scooped up two wet handfuls of taro skin and lobbed them at her sons. In moments the boys were sputtering out damp strips of purple taro as Dorothy stood before them, hands on hips, brown eyes blazing righteously.

"What's wrong with you! Fighting on the Sabbath! Now clean your faces and get ready for church, or else!"

"Kimo started it!"

"God don't care who started it! All He cares about is that somebody's making trouble on His day!"

"But, Mama —"

Dorothy hefted another handful of taro skin, and as if by *kahuna* sorcery the boys vanished without another cross word into their shared bedroom.

"I'm done, Mama." Rachel handed the peeled taro to her mother, who eyed it approvingly. "Well now," Dorothy said, face softening, "that's a good job you did." She cut the taro into smaller pieces, pounded them into paste, then added just the right amount of water to it. "You want to mix?" she asked Rachel, whose small hands dove eagerly into the smooth paste and kneaded it — with a little help from her mother — until, wondrously, it was no longer mere taro but delicious *poi.*

"Mama, these shoes are too tight!" Rachel's

14

sister Sarah, two years older, thumped into the room in a white cotton dress with black stockings, affecting a hobble as she pointed at her black leather buttontop shoes. "I can't feel my toes." She saw Rachel's fingers sticky with *poi* and reflexively made a sour face. "That looks lumpy."

Dorothy gave her a scowl. "Your head's lumpy. Rachel did a fine job, didn't she?" She tousled Rachel's long black hair; Rachel beamed and shot Sarah a look that said *ha!* Dorothy turned back to Sarah. "No sandals in church. Guess your toes just gonna fall off. And go get your hat!" Her hobble miraculously healed, Sarah sprinted away, though not without a parting grimace at her sister, who was enthusiastically licking the *poi* off her fingers.

It was a half-mile's walk to Kaumakapili Church, made even longer by the necessity of shoes, and Dorothy did not fail to remind her children — she *never* failed to remind them — how fortunate they were to worship at such a beautiful new church, opened just three years before. Its twin wooden spires — "the better to find God," the king had declared upon their completion — towered like huge javelins above their nearest neighbors. The spires were mirrored in the waters of nearby Nuʻuanu Stream, and to the devout it might appear as though they were pointing not just at heaven but, defiantly, at hell as

15

well, as though challenging Satan in his own domain.

As Dorothy joined with the congregation in singing "Rock of Ages," her children sat, in varying degrees of piety, in Sabbath School. In her kindergarten class Rachel drew Bible scenes with colored crayons, then listened attentively to her teacher, Mr. MacReedy, a veteran of the American Civil War with silvered hair and a shuffle in his walk courtesy of a round of grapeshot to his right foot.

" 'And in the fourth watch of the night,' " Mr. MacReedy recited from the Book of Matthew, " 'Jesus went unto them, walking on the sea. And when the disciples saw him walking on the sea, they —' "

He saw that Rachel's hand was bobbing in the air. "Yes? Rachel?"

Soberly, Rachel asked, "Which sea?"

Her teacher blinked. "What?"

"Which sea did he walk on?"

"Ah . . . well . . ." He scanned the page, vexedly. "It don't say."

"Was it the Pacific?"

"No, I reckon it wasn't."

"The Atlantic?"

"It don't matter, child. What's important is that he was *walking* on the sea, not *which* particular sea it was."

"Oh." Rachel was disappointed. "I just wondered."

Mr. MacReedy continued, telling them of

16

how Jesus bade Peter to walk onto the water with him; how He then went to a new land; and how, "when the men of that place had knowledge of him, they sent out into all that country round about, and brought unto him all that were diseased; And besought him that they might only touch the hem of his garment: and as many as touched were made whole.

" 'Then Jesus went thence, and departed into the coasts of Tyre and Sidon. And behold, a woman of Canaan came out of —' "

Rachel's hand shot up again.

Her teacher sighed. "Yes, Rachel," he said wearily.

"Where's Tyre? And — Sidon?"

Mr. MacReedy took off his reading glasses.

"They were cities. Someplace in the Holy Land. And before you ask, 'Canaan' was an old name for Palestine, or parts of it, anyway. That good enough for you, child?"

Rachel nodded. Her teacher replaced his glasses and continued chronicling Jesus' sojourn. " 'And Jesus departed thence, and came nigh unto the sea of Galilee . . .' "

Mr. MacReedy paused, peered over his glasses at Rachel and said, "I would infer, if anyone's interested, that this is the selfsame sea the Lord walked on a bit earlier."

After church came Rachel's favorite part of the day, when Mama stopped at Love's

17

Bakery on Nuʻuanu Avenue to buy fresh milk bread, baked that morning. Love's was a cathedral of sugar, a holy place of sweets and starches: pound cake, seedcake, biscuits, Jenny Lind cake, soda crackers, cupcakes. Sometimes the owner, Fanny Love, was there to greet customers; sometimes it was her eldest son James, who with a wink and a smile would slip Rachel a cookie or a slice of nutcake and announce, "You're the twenty-eighth customer today; here's your prize!"

Sometimes Mama would buy day-old bread rather than fresh, or as now, try to haggle some leftover New Year's cake for a few pennies less. Even at her age Rachel understood money was often a problem in her family, and though she rarely wanted for anything of substance she knew Mama worked hard to stretch out the money Papa left her; particularly now, eight months after they last saw him.

That night, as every night, Mama stood by Rachel's bedside and made sure she said her prayers, and Rachel never failed to add one of her own: that God help Papa come safely across the sea, and soon.

Honolulu Harbor was a forest of ship's masts huddled within encircling coral reefs, a narrow channel threading through the reefs and out to open sea. Unlike picturesque Waikiki to the east — a bright crescent of sand in the

18

lee of majestic Lē'ahi, or "Diamond Head" as the *haoles,* the white foreigners, had rechristened it — the harbor was an unglamorous collection of cattle wharves, trading companies, saloons, and the occasional brothel. On any given day there might be up to a hundred ships anchored here: barks, schooners, brigantines, cruisers, and more and more, steamers — their squat metal smokestacks proliferating among the wooden masts, an advance guard of the new century. Yet the arrival of a steamship was still exciting enough that whenever one was seen riding the horizon, CLOSED signs sprang up in store windows across the city and men, women, and children thronged toward the harbor to greet the incoming ship.

Rachel, perched on her mother's shoulders, peered over the heads of the crowd surging around them and thrilled to the sight of the SS *Mariposa* steaming toward port. A pilot boat met the steamer and guided it through the channel; then as the ships drew closer to shore the Royal Hawaiian Band, which was gathered at pier's end, struck up the national anthem, "Hawai'i Pono'ī," composed by King Kalākaua himself.

As the *Mariposa* eased into its berth beside a mountain of black coal, Rachel caught sight of a sailor tossing a thick hawser off the deck and onto the dock. He was a stocky Hawaiian in his young thirties, his thick muscled

19

arms tanned by the blistering sun of even lower latitudes. "Papa!" she yelled, waving, but Papa was too busy helping tie up the ship to notice. It was only after all the passengers had disembarked and the cargo was on its way out of the ship's hold that Rachel at last saw her father walk down the gangway, a duffel bag in one hand, a big weathered suitcase in the other.

Henry Kalama, a happy grin on his broad friendly face, hefted his suitcase as though he were about to throw it. " 'Ey! Little girl! Catch!"

Rachel giggled. Henry ran up and Dorothy gave him a reproachful look: "Good-for-nothing rascal, where you been the last eight months?" And she kissed him with a ferocity that quite belied her words.

"Papa!" Rachel was jumping up and down, and now Henry scooped her up in his big arms. " 'Ey, there she is. There's my baby!" He kissed her on the cheek and Rachel wrapped her arms around his thick neck. "I missed you, little girl," he said in a tone so gentle it made Dorothy want to cry. Then he looked at his wife and added, with exaggerated afterthought, "Oh. You, too."

"Yeah, yeah, same to you, no-good." But she didn't object when Henry kissed her again, still holding Rachel in one arm, the five-year-old making an *Eee-uu* face. Dorothy lifted her husband's duffel bag with one hand, slipped the other around his waist, and the three of them started through the crowd, a winch's chain chattering above them as it yanked an enormous crate into the air.

"You sell the other *keiki*?" Henry asked, noting the absence of his older children.

"In school. Rachel oughtta be, but —"

"Where'd you go this time, Papa?"

"Oh, all over. One ship went to Japan and China, this one stopped in Australia, New Zealand, Samoa . . ."

"We got your letter from Samoa!"

On short notice Dorothy organized a feast to celebrate Henry's return. Dorothy's brother Will brought twenty pounds of fresh skipjack tuna he'd caught in his nets that morning; Henry's sister Florence made her best *haupia* pudding, rich with coconut cream; and Rachel helped her mother and Aunt Flo wrap ti leaves around the fresh beef and pork Papa bought at Tinker's Market, the first meat they had seen in weeks.

Friends and family crowded into the Kalama home that night, laughing and eating, singing and talking story. Rachel sat, as she often did at such gatherings, on the lap of her tall, rangy Uncle Pono — Papa's older brother, Kapono Kalama, a plantation worker in Waimānalo. " 'Ey, there's my favorite niece!" he would say, hoisting her into his arms. "You married yet?" Rachel soberly shook her head. "Why not?" Pono shot back.

"Good-looking girl like you? You gonna be an old maid, you wait much longer!" When Rachel did her best not to laugh at his teasing, Pono resorted to tickling — and as she curled up like a snail in his lap, giggling uncontrollably, he'd say, "See, pretty funny after all, eh?"

Later, Henry's brood gathered round as he handed out the presents he never neglected to bring home from faraway ports. They were modest gifts, befitting a seaman's wages, but Papa had uncommonly good taste and always chose something to charm and delight them. Dorothy was presented with a pretty string necklace beaded with dozens of small, imperfectly shaped pearls, each plucked from the ocean floor by native divers in Rarotonga. Sarah was thrilled to receive a pair of silver earrings from New Zealand, though the silver in them probably wouldn't have filled a tooth. Kimo got a box of Chinese puzzles; Ben, a picture book from Tokyo, and another from Hong Kong.

Rachel knew what Papa had brought her, of course. What he always brought her: a doll from one of the countries he'd visited. Already she had a *sakura-ningyö,* a "cherry doll" from Japan; a pair of Mission Dolls from China; and a rag baby from America, purchased on Papa's last trip to San Francisco. What would it be this time? Rachel could hardly contain herself as Papa pulled the last gift box from his suitcase.

"And this one's for Rachel," he said, "from Japan."

Rachel was crestfallen. She already had a Japanese doll! Had Papa forgotten? Trying not to betray her disappointment, she tore the lid off the box, stripping away the tissue paper enfolding the doll. . . .

That is, assuming it *was* a doll. Rachel stared in confusion at the contents of the box, which appeared to be . . . an *egg.* A large wooden egg, no neck, a fat body, a bundled scarf and winter clothes painted on — Humpty Dumpty, but with a woman's face. Hilda Dumpty?

Rachel was surprised at how heavy it was, and entranced by its odd appearance. "What *is* it?" she asked.

Her father scolded, "But you're not done opening the present!" He pointed at the egg. "Hold the bottom with one hand, the head with the other. Then pull."

Rachel did as she was told — then jumped as the egg popped apart, and a second egg fell out! This smaller one resembled a man with a painted-on farmer's outfit; but when Rachel began examining it her father wagged a finger: "Still not finished!" Rachel pulled apart the second doll to discover yet a *third* one, a young girl-egg this time.

Everyone laughed at the expression on Rachel's face as she kept finding littler and littler dolls growing younger and younger, seven in all — the last an infant in painted-on swaddling, made of solid wood.

"They call 'em *matryoshka*," Papa explained. "Nesting dolls. From Russia."

"But you said they were from Japan."

"I *got* 'em in Japan. Japan's next door to Russia. You like?"

Rachel beamed. "They're beautiful, Papa."

That night Rachel carefully weighed where to place the nesting dolls on the coffee-crate shelf that held the rest of her collection. Farthest to the left was the cherry doll, a beautiful Kabuki dancer in a green silk kimono, holding a tiny fan. Next to her were the Chinese Mission dolls: a yellow-skinned *amah*, or nurse, carrying a little yellow baby on her back. And lastly, the rag doll from America, a cuddly infant with a sweet moon-like face, which Rachel sometimes took to bed with her. She remembered then what Papa had said about Japan being "next door" to Russia and she placed the *matryoshka* beside the Japanese cherry doll, then stepped back to admire her collection.

Behind her, she heard a familiar voice. "She fits right in, eh?"

Rachel turned. Papa was standing in the doorway. "Your Mama says you got to say your prayers and get your sneaky little hide into bed."

"Sarah's not in bed yet."

24

"She will be after her bath."

"Will you sing me a song first?" This, too, was old custom between them.

Papa smiled. "Prayers first."

Rachel hurried through her evening prayer, then eagerly jumped into bed. Papa closed the bedroom door, pulled up a chair beside her, and sat. "So, which one you want to hear?"

Rachel thought for a moment, then announced, " 'Whiskey Johnnie.' "

Her father glanced furtively toward the closed door, then back to Rachel. "How 'bout 'Blow the Man Down'?"

" 'Whiskey Johnnie'!" Rachel insisted.

Papa sighed in surrender. He leaned forward in his chair and in a deliberately low voice began to sing:

"Oh whiskey is the life of man
A Whiskey for my Johnnie.
Oh I'll drink whiskey whenever I can
Whiskey, Johnnie.
Bad whiskey gets me in the can —"

A Whiskey for my Johnnie! Rachel joined in. Together they sang two more stanzas, until Rachel burst out giggling and Papa, also laughing, patted her on the hand. "That's my chantey girl," he said with a grin. He kissed her on the forehead. "Now go to sleep."

Rachel's eyes drooped closed. Snug beneath

her woolen blanket, she slept soundly that night — dreaming she was on a schooner plying the sea, bound for the Orient, destined for adventure.

Closer to home, Fort Street School was a big one-story house surrounded by a whitewashed picket fence, arbored by the leafy umbrellas of tall monkeypod trees, with a long porch and white wooden colonnade that would not have looked out of place in southern Virginia. The morning after Papa came home began as usual with the students reciting the Lord's Prayer, then in chorus singing *"Good morning to you"* to their teacher; after which they opened their Tower grammars and followed along with Miss Wallis as she recited the alphabet. But in what seemed like no time at all another teacher, a gray-haired Hawaiian woman, appeared in the classroom doorway.

"Miss Wallis? A moment, please?" Normally quite unflappable, today the older woman looked wan and shaken, almost as if she were about to cry. "Students, I have a . . . an announcement. It is with great sadness that I must tell you that our king" — her voice broke as she said it — "King Kalākaua . . . is dead."

She seemed about to elaborate — then, unable to go on, simply said, "Under the circumstances, Principal Scott has dismissed classes for the day." And she hurried on to the next classroom, the impact of her news rolling in wave after wave through each grade of the primary school.

Students slowly filtered out of the schoolhouse. Rain was falling in a gray mist, the skies seeming to weep along with the people Rachel encountered in the streets. Stunned and grieving, they gathered in small groups from which rose a spontaneous, collective wail unlike anything Rachel had ever heard before — a deep woeful cry that seemed to come from a hundred hearts at once. Its raw anguish frightened her, and she ran home to find both Mama and Papa in tears as well. Rachel, for whom death was still just a word, tried to comfort them, though not quite understanding why: "It's all right, Mama. Don't cry, Papa." Dorothy took her daughter in her arms and wept, and soon Rachel began to feel that she should be crying too, and so she did.

The king had left in November on a goodwill trip to the United States — Hawai'i's most important trading partner and the homeland of most its resident foreigners — and for weeks his subjects had been awaiting his return aboard the USS *Charleston* from San Francisco. But this morning the city's official lookout, "Diamond Head Charlie," spotted the *Charleston* steaming toward Honolulu with its yards acockbill, its flags at half-mast . . . which could mean only one thing. The news was telephoned from Diamond Head and quickly spread across the city like a shadow across the sun; the festive banners and bunting put up in anticipation of Kalākaua's return were quickly torn down and replaced with solemn black crepe.

The king's body lay in state in 'Iolani Palace for the next fifteen days, during which time nearly every resident of Honolulu, and many from the neighbor islands, came to pay their respects. The Kalamas were six among thousands who queued up outside the palace for hours so that they might be able to briefly file past their monarch's casket.

The king had succumbed, it was now known, to a *haole* sickness called Bright's Disease. Old-timers in the crowd found this a melancholy echo of what had befallen Kamehameha II and his queen, both of whom had died after contracting measles on a trip to England. The first of the *haole* diseases had sailed into Hawai'i on the smiles and charm of Captain Cook's crew: syphilis and gonorrhea. Others soon followed: cholera, influenza, tuberculosis, mumps, diphtheria. One outbreak of smallpox alone took six thousand lives. Hawaiians, living in splendid isolation for five centuries, had no resistance to these new plagues that rode in on the backs of commerce and culture. Before Cook's arrival the native population of

Hawai'i was more than a quarter of a million people; a hundred years later, it had plummeted to fewer than sixty thousand.

Kalākaua's people were mourning more than the passing of their king.

No one understood this better than Henry, who in his lifetime had now seen the deaths of four kings. As he and his family finally entered the palace they heard choirs chanting dirges, the ritual laments echoing throughout the vast ornate halls. But in the flower-decked throne room, a dignified silence prevailed. Flanking the coffin were twenty somber attendants holding royal staffs that looked to Rachel like spindly palm trees sprouting feathers instead of fronds. The casket, carved of native woods, was adorned with a silver crown and draped with a golden feather cloak, bright as sunlight. As the Kalamas approached it they now saw, behind thick plate glass, the familiar whiskered profile of David Kalākaua, his head pillowed, looking as if he were merely asleep.

Tears sprang suddenly to Henry's eyes. He thought of the prophecy — made over a century ago by the high priest Ka'opulupulu, who told the ruler of O'ahu that the line of kings would come to an end at Waikiki, and that the land would belong to a people from across the sea. O'ahu was soon conquered by armies from across that sea — Maui and, later, the island of Hawai'i — and now Henry wondered if he were seeing the other half of the prophecy coming true, if soon there would be an end to the line of kings.

As they passed by the casket Henry and Dorothy each grazed the tips of their fingers against the glass, until the grief of those behind them pushed them on, and out.

On the 15th of February, a somber Sunday, the king was finally laid to rest, beginning with a simple Anglican ceremony inside the throne room, as outside a long line of citizens, again including the Kalamas, stood coiled around the palace. At the conclusion of services a long procession of mourners left ʻIolani Palace on a solemn march to the Royal Mausoleum in Nuʻuanu Valley. In years to come Rachel would remember only a few of these hundreds upon hundreds of marchers: the torch bearers representing the symbol of Kalākaua's reign, "the flaming torch at midday," now quenched; the king's black charger, saddled backward, the horse's head bent low as though it too understood grief; pallbearers carrying the king's catafalque, flanked by two columns of brightly plumed standard bearers; and the carriages bearing his widow, Queen Kapiʻolani, and his sister Liliʻuokalani, now Hawaiʻi's first reigning queen. The moment the king's casket left the palace grounds the air was shaken by the guns of the battleships *Charleston* and *Mohican* in the harbor, firing a cannonade in salute, along with a battery emplacement atop Punchbowl Hill. At the same instant, church bells all across the city tolled at once. Rachel clapped her hands to her ears; the noise was almost too much to bear, but she would never forget it, its violence and its majesty. And when the last official members of the cortege left the palace grounds, the procession was joined by those dearest to the late king — his subjects. Hundreds of ordinary Hawaiians who stood twined around the palace now took up the rear of the cortege, a human wreath slowly unfurling itself as the procession wended its way into the green hills above Honolulu.

Rachel understood only that death was a kind of going-away, as when her father went away to sea; but since her father always came back she could not imagine the king would not as well. And so as his casket receded into the distance she raised her hand and waved to him — as she did her father when he boarded his ship and it sailed out onto the open sea, disappearing over the edge of the world.

That moment came, as always, too soon. Papa was home only six weeks before he had to ship out again, this time for San Francisco and, after that, South America. But because he spent so much time away from his children, Henry always did his best to cram six months' worth of activity into the breathless

31

space of one or two, taking them fishing for shrimp in Nu'uanu Stream or riding the waves at Waikiki. The latter had to be managed with stealth and discretion, since Mama had accepted the missionaries' proscription against surfing, seen as a worthless, godless activity; Papa would spirit the children away on some pretext, recover his big redwood surfboard from its exile at his friend Sammy's house, then, one child at a time, paddle out beyond the first shorebreak and instruct them in the ancient art of "wave sliding."

Another day Papa packed everyone up in their rickety old wagon and took off up a winding six-mile road to Mount Tantalus overlooking the city. The road meandered through bowers of stooped trees bent low over the dirt path, the foliage at times so thick it seemed they were driving through a tunnel of leaves, the air sweet and loamy. At a lookout high above the city they sat and ate a picnic supper; Rachel peered down at the green V of the valley, at the doll's houses of Honolulu spread out below that, and at the long sweep of coastline from Diamond Head to Kalihi Bay. Thrilled and amazed that she could see so much all at once, she gazed out at the thin line separating blue ocean from blue sky and realized that somewhere beyond that were the distant lands her father knew — the lands of cherry dolls and *matryoshka,* moonfaced rag dolls and little yellow *amahs.*

The day he left, the whole family accompanied Papa to the harbor — Rachel up front in Mama's lap, Ben, Kimo, and Sarah riding in the back of the lurching wagon. Papa tied up at the Esplanade, his children putting on a brave face as they escorted him back to the SS *Mariposa,* all of them quietly determined not to cry.

But almost as though someone were taking their secret thoughts, their hidden grief, and vocalizing it, there came — from the pier immediately ahead — a terrible, anguished wail. It was not one voice but many, a chorus of lament; and as the cry died away, another promptly began, rising and falling like the wind. It was, Henry and Dorothy both knew, not merely a wail, but a word: *auwē,* Hawaiian for "alas." *Auwē! Auwwayy! (Alas! Alas!)*

It sounded exactly like the cries of grief and loss that Rachel had heard the day the king had come home. "Mama," she said, fearfully, "is the Queen dead, too?"

"No, child, no," Dorothy said.

Moored off Pier 10 was a small, decrepit interisland steamer, the *Mokoli'i.* A distraught crowd huddled behind a wooden barricade, sighing their mournful dirge as a procession of others — young and old, men and women, predominantly Hawaiians and Chinese — were herded by police onto the old cattle boat. Now and then one of the people behind the barricade would reach out to touch someone boarding the ship: a man grasping for a woman, a child reaching for his mother, a friend clasping another's hand for the last time.

"*Ma'i páké,*" Kimo said softly.

"What?" Rachel asked.

"They're lepers, you ninny," Sarah admonished. "Going to Moloka'i."

"What's a leper?"

Someone in the crowd threw a flower *lei* onto the water, but contrary to legend, it was not likely to ever bring any of these travelers back to Honolulu.

"They're sick, baby. Very sick," Mama explained. Rachel didn't understand. The people didn't look sick; they didn't look much different than anyone on the other side of the barricade.

"If they're sick," Rachel asked, "why isn't someone taking care of them?"

No one answered her; and as that word, *leper,* hung in the still humid air, Dorothy dug her fingers into Rachel's shoulders and turned her away from the *Mokoli'i.*

"Come on. Go! Alla you, go!" Henry and Dorothy shepherded their children away from the pier, away from the hapless procession marching onto the grimy little steamer, away from the crowd that mourned for them as though they were already dead; but they couldn't escape the crowd's lament, the sad chorale which followed them like some plain-

34

tive ghost, all the way to the *Mariposa.*
Auwē! Auwwaay! Alas, alas . . .

CHAPTER 2

1892

Waimānalo Plantation, twenty miles up the twisting windward coast from Honolulu, lay spread in a horseshoe valley at the foot of the imposing Ko'olau Range — high jagged peaks with faces like those of worried old men, deep vertical furrows worn by the passage of time and water. Thousands of acres of taro, maize, and sugarcane fanned out from the base of the mountains, the property of a half-Scottish, half-Hawaiian nobleman; cradled among the fields were the sugar mill, ranch buildings, and laborers' camps, the latter segregated by race.

It was suppertime in the camps, and the smell of baking bread and roasted pork, of cabbage and sweet potatoes and fresh fish, hung in the air around the big brick communal ovens. Just as pungent was the smolder of sugarcane as *lunas* — overseers — supervised a rare afternoon fire, burning away the sword-shaped leaves to harvest the cane itself.

36

Children raced and played, weaving among women cooking and men, their backs aching and their hands coarse, returning from a long day in the fields.

The young man in the brown suit and hat walked alongside but apart from the weary column of field hands; his collar, cuffs, the crease in his pants were as crisp as a new dollar bill. He walked briskly, but not so briskly that he didn't have time to smile at little *keiki* or give a friendly nod to women as they pulled steaming loaves of bread from the ovens. No one failed to smile back, less from *aloha* than fear.

He stopped at one of the small plantation cottages, a well-kept house painted forest green with white trim and squatting on a raised slatted foundation several feet off the ground. He climbed the steps to the tiny porch, knocked on the door. It was a few moments before the knock was answered, and when the door opened he faced a short, stocky woman squinting nervously at him: "Yes?"

The man tipped his hat to her. "Health Inspector Nakamura. Sorry to bother you at dinnertime, but could I please speak with" — and here he consulted a notepad in his hand — "Kapono Kalama?"

Margaret Kalama shook her head. "Not here."

"Is he still working?"

"I don't know," she said. "I don't know where he is."

Inspector Nakamura glanced inside. A boy and girl sat at a small table, their eyes big with fear, their dinners going untouched. "May I come in?" he asked.

"If you want," she said, not pleased about it.

There wasn't much to see. A small living area, a bedroom in which both adults and children slept with a single window looking out on the back yard. The mattresses, covered with bedsheets made from hundred-pound sugar sacks, lay flat on the floor with not an inch below to harbor a body. He opened a closet, saw only clothes, shut it. As he walked back into the living room, he smiled at the children: "Please. Your food's getting cold. Go on, eat." He noticed there were four place settings, four hot plates of cabbage and fish and fresh bread.

On his way out he handed Mrs. Kalama a business card and said, "Please tell your husband I'd like to see him at his earliest convenience." As the door closed on him he hurried down the porch steps, checked the wash house — all five compartments, one for each family, were empty — then entered the back yard where the Kalamas kept ducks, chickens, rabbits, and a small taro garden. He noted the way some of the taro plants, right under the bedroom window, had been stomped flat; noted too the footprints in the soft red earth. He followed them out the yard and down a dusty corridor that bisected the cane field; after twenty feet the tracks veered off into the cane, disappearing amid the closely planted stalks.

It was harvest time and the cane was at its tallest, standing almost six feet high. A man could, and often did, hide in the thicket of cane for days if he had to. Nakamura frowned. He was certain Kalama hadn't had time to get very far, but searching the thicket would be a long and no doubt fruitless task. Trying to enlist assistance from the plantation workers would be useless: no one would aid him, he knew, except perhaps the Scottish *lunas*.

He stood there considering his choices, listening to the faint rustle of cane stalks in the breeze, breathing in the sweetly acrid smell of the cane fires.

And then he smiled.

After a brief conversation with the overseers, the inspector climbed atop the miniature saddle-tanker locomotive used to ferry the cane across the plantation. From up here he could see the entire breadth of the cane field. Now too he saw a *luna* directing his men to set a fire in the center of that field; saw the first lick of flames consume the green swords of the leaves; and watched as a thick pillar of brown-black smoke rose into the sky.

In no time at all the radius of the fire had expanded a good fifty feet, a swath of flame and smoke marching to the sea. Not long after, Nakamura heard coughing from deep inside the cane thicket as the smoke enveloped it, and then the frantic rustling of stalks as someone rushed to escape the oncoming blaze.

Nakamura jumped off the locomotive and raced down the perimeter of the field — just in time to see a lanky, frightened Hawaiian man come stumbling out of the cane, coughing and wheezing. Nakamura jumped him; the man went down, offering no resistance.

Pono lay on the ground, half blinded, the tears in his eyes not from the smoke but from the thought of what he was about to lose. His cheek had been abraded by the bramble of cane, but the livid red blemish beneath his left eye was a wound of a very different sort, and a mark — permanent and ineradicable — of his shame and his fear.

Papa had come home from South America in time for the Christmas of '91, bringing with him the usual fine assortment of gifts (including, for Rachel, an Argentine peasant doll from Buenos Aires). There had been a feast on New Year's Day at Aunt Florence's; Rachel was disappointed when Uncle Pono didn't tease and play with her but sat by himself in a corner, seeming withdrawn and depressed. And then in April came the shocking news that Pono had been arrested as a leprosy suspect and sent to the Kalihi Receiving Station on the western flank of Honolulu, where his case was to be "evaluated." For a lucky few, this could mean a diagnosis of some unrelated, relatively benign disease like scabies or scrofula; for most it meant being branded a leper, forcibly detained in the hospital at Kalihi for months or years, and ultimately, exiled to Kalaupapa on the remote northern tip of Moloka'i.

Rachel understood only that Uncle Pono was sick in the hospital, but when she asked if they could go see him, her mother snapped out a brusque *"No"* and changed the subject. Henry Kalama did visit his brother at Kalihi, but no one considered, for reasons obscure to Rachel but obvious to all the adults, bringing children along . . . even if it had been allowed.

Everyone in the *'ohana,* the family, pitched in to help provide for Pono's wife and children, who were not only deprived of husband and father but of his income as well. Margaret and the children went to live with Pono's sister Florence and her husband Eli; Dorothy's brother Will, the fisherman, helped out with a portion of his weekly catch; and Dorothy and Henry lent what small financial assistance they could, even as they struggled to come to terms with what had happened to

Pono. That first night Rachel and Sarah could hear (through the walls, thin as a ginger cracker, separating the girls' room from their parents') the sound of their father weeping for the older brother who had taught him how to swim and how to surf; weeping as if for one already dead. And the girls cried as well, for Uncle Pono and for Papa, so obviously in pain.

Before any of the children left the house after hearing the news, Mama took them aside and cautioned, "You don't tell nobody about this, understand? Not your friends, not your teacher, not Mr. MacReedy at church, *nobody.* You don't even talk about it to *each other,* you understand?" The children all nodded. Mama added, "Or *else.*" They nodded again, and true to their word they didn't even talk about it among themselves, though not out of fear of what Mama might do to them. No, it was the fear they saw in Mama's own eyes that cowed them into silence. They had never seen Mama truly frightened before, never imagined it possible; and as that was far more terrifying to contemplate than any disease, they were only too happy not to speak, even to think, about poor Uncle Pono and this terrible thing called the *ma'i pākē.*

Papa shipped out again in June, but out of concern for Pono he signed on for a shorter stint, a voyage of five months rather than

42

eight or ten. For Rachel life went on as before, though over the summer relations with her sister became more strained than usual, a result of what came to be known as "the soup trouble."

Playing in the back yard with her friends Aggie and Elsa while Mama and Sarah were out, Rachel thought it might be fun to play at cooking dinner. The big steel tub Mama washed clothes in made an excellent saucepan; an old broom, a fine stirring spoon. She and Aggie filled the tub with water brought bucket by bucket from the cistern, and then Rachel considered what kind of "soup" to make.

She knew not to waste food, so each ingredient for Mama's chicken stew had to have its own pretend equivalent. Rachel chose two pair of her own white socks, each rolled into a ball and looking, sort of, like a peeled Irish potato. (She threw in a pair of Papa's brown socks to represent the local sweet potato.) A handful of Mama's green silk handkerchiefs, bought by Papa in Hong Kong, made convincing enough cabbage leaves, particularly when wet. Sarah's yellow felt hat was an adequate summer squash, and a pair of her bracelets, made of orangish *koa* wood, bobbed on the surface like sliced carrots. Aggie kicked off her sandals and dropped them into the mix, where they doubled nicely for boiled chicken legs.

43

Elsa added a pinch of garden soil as a condiment.

They were enthusiastically stirring their "soup" when Mama and Sarah came home from the grocer's. Sarah let out a shriek when she saw her felt hat swirling beside Aggie's dirty sandals; Mama expressed little appreciation for her handkerchiefs' resemblance to cabbage; and Rachel was rewarded with a couple of swats across her behind and no dinner for the night. "I should make you eat your own soup!" Mama threatened, but didn't. Rachel was baffled; she'd thought she was being so responsible, not using real food, only clothing that Mama would eventually wash anyway! Couldn't anybody see what a good job she'd done?

In retaliation the next day, Sarah stripped all of Rachel's dolls of their clothing and played mix-and-match with them: the *sakura-ningyö* was wearing an Argentine peasant's outfit, the Chinese *amah* had apparently taken up *kabuki* dancing, and the rag baby from America was buck naked with its swaddling wrapped like a turban around its head. The baby the *amah* had been carrying now dangled like a tassel from the window curtains.

The soup reached a boil, so to speak, a few days after the start of school. The students were spilling out of the schoolyard, Rachel and Aggie already headed down Fort Street, giggling and talking, when Sarah began pacing them. Slowly Rachel became aware that her sister seemed to be juggling a pair of Easter eggs as she walked.

Easter eggs? In September?

"Hey," she called to Rachel, "you think these'd break if they fell?"

Not eggs. *Matryoshka.* Sarah had two of the nesting dolls and was doing a pretty fair job of keeping them both aloft as she ambled along. Rachel attempted to grab them but Sarah just weaved away:

"Let's make an omelet," she taunted. "A *pretend* omelet." She let one of the nesting dolls fall, then caught it just in time. "Oops!"

"Gimme those!" Rachel yelled, making another lunge for her sister. This time Sarah couldn't weave away in time and Rachel collided with her; the two of them went toppling into the street and the nesting dolls flew from Sarah's hands like skeet shot into the air.

In moments they were kicking and scratching and biting each other, tumbling around in the dusty street like rabid cats; classmates cheered them on, until the sounds of battle reached the schoolhouse and a young teacher came running out to pull them apart, not without some effort.

"Stop it! Stop this at *once*!" The teacher pulled Rachel to her feet, then Sarah, interposing herself between the combatants. "What started this!" she demanded to know.

45

"She took my *matryoshka*!" Rachel cried.

"She used my hat in her soup!" Sarah accused.

The young woman stared blankly at them. "I have *no* idea what you're talking about," she said, "and I don't care! Young ladies, especially sisters, do not fight like cats and dogs in the street." The teacher was obviously an only child. "Are either of you hurt?"

Their clothes were filthy, their noses runny and their hair a mess, but otherwise they seemed intact. "If I catch you fighting again, I assure you, you'll both live to regret it! But for now the worst punishment I can think of is to send you home to explain this to your parents."

With a glare she sent them on their way. Sarah shot her sister a last withering look, crossed the street and soon vanished from sight. Rachel retrieved her scuffed nesting dolls and straggled home, where Dorothy took one look at her and nearly had a stroke: "Rachel! What is it, what happened?"

"Nothing, Mama. I just got in a fight."

Dorothy grabbed a clean towel, wet it; she hoisted Rachel into her lap and wiped at her daughter's dirty face. "Who? Who'd you fight with?"

Rachel shrugged. "Some *wahine* at school."

"What's her name?"

"Nobody, Mama. It don't matter."

Dorothy sighed, wiped Rachel's nose.

"You're one beautiful mess, you know that? One beautiful —"

Dorothy felt something wet fall on her foot, unexpected as a drop of rain on a sunny day. She looked down and saw blood trickling down the back of Rachel's leg.

"Stand up," Mama told her. "Turn round." Dorothy lifted Rachel's skirt. She had scratches all over her legs and on the back of her left thigh there was a patch of pink skin the size of a half dollar with a nasty bleeding gash in the middle. "Rachel! How come you didn't tell me?"

"Tell you what, Mama?"

Rachel craned her head around and saw the cut for the first time. She was surprised to see it, but felt no pain; it was like watching someone else bleed.

"Okay, this gonna sting a little." Dorothy carefully dabbed at the wound, cleaning out the dirt and the small particles of stone in the cut. But Rachel didn't flinch. "You okay, baby?"

"I'm fine, Mama. It don't hurt at all."

Dorothy examined the cut. Not very deep, probably wouldn't even need stitches, but . . . She dabbed at it again, almost trying to provoke a response from Rachel, but not a twitch of pain wrinkled the girl's face.

"You tell me you don't feel that?" Dorothy asked.

Rachel proudly shook her head. "Uh uh."

Anxiously, Dorothy put the tip of her finger against the rosy skin surrounding the wound, pressing her fingernail ever so slightly into the flesh. "How about that? You feel that?"

Smiling, Rachel shook her head again.

Dorothy dug her nail into the skin on one side of the cut, then the other. Rachel made no response until her mother reached a point outside the rose-colored blemish. "Ow! *That* hurt."

As Dorothy bandaged the cut, she told herself, There's nothing to worry about; maybe she pinched a nerve, like Henry did that time he hurt his back, that's all it is. She gave Rachel some candy; the thought of punishing her for getting into a fight never even entered her mind.

That night, after Rachel had thanked God for somehow distracting Mama from punishing her, she lay in bed wondering where Papa was now, what stars he saw in the sky, until she heard her sister's voice, softer than usual. "Rachel?"

She turned on her side and looked across the room, lit only by a stipple of moonlight through lace curtains. "Yeah?"

"You didn't get hurt, did you?"

"Not much. Just a little cut. How 'bout you?"

"Uh uh."

Sarah didn't say anything more, the moon rose higher and the room fell dimmer, and soon they were both asleep. Dorothy, however, was not resting nearly as well.

She gave Rachel's cut two weeks to heal, then one morning before school took her daughter aside, away from prying sibling eyes, and said, "Let me see that cut again, okay?" Trying to conceal the anxiety in her voice.

"It's better, Mama." Rachel lifted her skirt as Dorothy examined the site of the wound. The cut was healed but the pink blemish remained; and now it seemed flaky to the touch. Rachel didn't notice the worry in her mother's face; nor did she see the small pin her mother quietly extracted from a pincushion, the tip of which she now touched to the rosy spot on Rachel's thigh.

Rachel didn't notice that either. Queasily, Dorothy put a little more pressure on the pin.

Rachel said, "How does it look, Mama?"

Dorothy lightly poked the pin all over the blemished skin — not hard enough to puncture it, but enough that Rachel should have felt the pinprick. "You . . . feel that, baby?"

"Feel what, Mama?"

In desperation Dorothy jabbed the pin into her daughter's flesh. A tiny bubble of blood erupted from the skin, but Rachel didn't flinch — didn't cry out — didn't even realize she *had* been pricked.

Dorothy felt light-headed; faint. She struggled to keep her voice calm and her hand steady. "Needs . . . a little more time to heal," she lied, applying a fresh bandage, one that covered the entirety of the blemish. "You just keep this on, understand? Keep it on." Rachel promised that she would, and within minutes was off to school.

Dorothy was not a woman easily brought to tears, but now she sat in the empty house and wept freely. This couldn't be, not her Rachel, she couldn't have the *ma'i pākē* — could she? Could it be something else, anything else? Wedded to her grief was a terrible panic: if only Henry were here, someone to share the anguish and the shock, someone to help her figure out what to do next. But Henry would not be back for another month, and something, she knew, had to be done in the meantime.

If she brought Rachel to a *haole* doctor, and if it was leprosy, the doctor would report it to the Board of Health. That left a *kahuna* as her only recourse — but as a Christian she had been told that *kahunas* were charlatans, ignorant holdovers of a heathen religion. She was a good Christian woman who loved her church, who wanted to believe and to embrace its proscriptions.

Yet she loved Rachel too, and if a heathen could save her daughter's life — save her from banishment . . .

There were *kahunas* who were also Christians — who had reconciled the old ways with

50

the teachings of Christ the Savior — and it was to one of these that Dorothy went, a thin, bony old man named Ua. She told him about the blemish on Rachel's skin, its color and insensitivity to pain. She told him about Pono, and tears welled in her eyes as she spoke. Ua put a comforting hand on hers and said, "Don't worry." He got up and began taking down jars from a shelf, jars filled with leaves and powdered herbs and other, odder things Dorothy did not recognize.

"This," he explained, showing her cuttings from a plant with oblong leaves, yellow flowers, and narrow seed pods, "is used to clear disruptions of the skin. I've had good results with it." He put them in a large bowl along with four sea urchin shells, a teaspoon of salt, and papaya and *kukui*-nut juices. Then he picked up an empty jar and got to his feet. "Excuse me. One more thing I need." He left the room, calling out a name; Dorothy watched as a little girl appeared, took the empty jar, then hurried away. She returned minutes later, the jar filled. As Ua reentered and poured the yellow fluid into the bowl there was no mistaking the familiar pungent smell.

"Has to be from a child, you see," Ua said by way of explanation. "No good otherwise." Dorothy smiled uncertainly, watching as he pounded the ingredients together into one pulpy mix, like some strange *poi*.

51

He wrapped the pulp in coconut fibers and squeezed the juice into another jar, which he now presented to Dorothy. "Apply this to the blemish three times a day for the next five days," he directed. "Pray each night for the Lord God Jehovah to add his love and power to this medicine, and at the end of that time the blemish should be gone." Dorothy took the jar and gratefully paid him his two-dollar fee — a great deal of money, but if this worked it would be worth ten times that, a hundred times!

Dorothy dutifully prayed and applied the medicine to Rachel's blemish — in the morning, after she came home from school, and at bedtime. Rachel blanched at the smelly concoction and soon learned to hold her breath when it was time for an application; even as Sarah and the boys began to wonder how bad this cut could be if Mama were still treating it weeks later and coddling Rachel like a baby.

At the end of five days, miraculously, the blemish disappeared and Dorothy thanked God for His goodness in saving her daughter. She sang joyously in church that Sunday; the tension in the household, which Rachel could detect but not understand, dissipated. After church Mama stopped at Love's and bought Jenny Lind cake for everyone.

Two weeks later, the blemish reappeared.

Ua gave Dorothy another remedy, this one

made from the yellow, milky sap of the Hawaiian poppy. She applied it twice a day, but not only did the blemish not go away, at the end of a week's time Dorothy could see that along the edges of the pink skin a small reddish ring, like a crater of flesh, was beginning to form.

Dorothy's despair deepened; she spent each day in a state of frantic worry and helpless depression. She prayed to God for mercy for her child, but there was only one prayer he answered: at the end of October, Henry came home.

After the initial shock and grief and disbelief, Henry knew exactly what had to be done.

"We need *ho'oponopono*," he said, and Dorothy knew he was right.

Ho'oponopono meant "setting to right," but it was more than a word, it was a process — part of family life in these islands for centuries. Hawaiians believed that physical problems were often the result of interpersonal relations that had gone wrong, and *ho'oponopono* was designed to expose the underlying causes. Sometimes a *kahuna* led these gatherings, sometimes a family elder; for reasons of discretion it was decided that Henry's father, Maka, frail but clear-headed at seventy-two, would be the group leader.

Rachel, Sarah, and their brothers understood little more than that Rachel was sick —

though Rachel swore she didn't *feel* sick — and that this was being done to help her. In addition to Rachel's immediate family, the other participants included Margaret, Will, Florence and Eli. The family gathered in a rough circle on the floor of the Kalama home, and Grandpa Maka opened with a prayer:

"Lord God Jehovah, creator of all things, listen to this humble, loving appeal from Your children. Spirits of our ancestors, join with us in finding the cause of Rachel's illness and setting it to right."

Maka began by asking each of Rachel's siblings if they were bearing any anger toward their sister. Kimo and Benjamin both looked startled and confused by the question; no, they each said, why should they?

"And you, child?" Sarah squirmed under Grandpa Maka's calm gaze. "She ruined my hat," she said finally. "She's always doing *something.*" Out came the litany of Rachel's transgressions against Sarah. Maka listened patiently to them, then said, "Do you know what *kala* means?"

Sarah frowned. "To forgive?"

"More than that: to let go. And when you forgive your sister — when you let go of your anger — you forgive yourself as well."

"But my *hat* —"

"Is the love you felt for this hat more important than your sister's life? What if your anger is what's sickening her? Do you still

54

want to hold onto it so jealously?"

Sarah thought about that, then shook her head. "No," she said. "Not if . . ." She looked at Rachel. "I don't want you to be sick, Rachel."

"So can you *kala* your sister?"

With apparent sincerity she said, "Yes. I *kala* Rachel."

"Rachel, do you *kala* Sarah?"

"Yes."

"Good." Maka nodded. "It's good that Sarah owned up to her anger, and that she was able to let go of it. But . . ." The grandfather's steady gaze swept across them all. "I wonder that something so easily forgiven could be the cause of so grave a sickness. Does anyone else here feel that there is something unsaid? Something to do with Rachel, that needs to be set right?"

Silently the adults searched for an answer in each other's faces, until one of them finally spoke up.

"I do," said Henry.

His father nodded his approval. "Go on."

After a moment's hesitation Henry said, "Before Rachel was born, I had a dream." That piqued everyone's curiosity: dreams were often as significant as the waking life. "I dreamt Dorothy and me were on a mountaintop. Lying on our backs, looking up into the sky, me stroking Dorothy's stomach, feeling our little girl kicking inside." He smiled; Dorothy looked surprised and touched. "It was a bright, clear day. The sky above us was blue and forever, and I looked up at it and thought: *Aouli.* 'Blue vault of heaven.' Just came into my head: *Aouli.*"

There were murmurs from the other adults, confused glances among Rachel and her siblings. Grandpa Maka just nodded. "An *inoa pō,*" he said. To the puzzled children he explained, "A 'night name' — a name found in a dream. It comes from the next world, and once the name is spoken, it must be bestowed on the child."

He turned again to Henry. "You knew that, didn't you? That the name must be given, or the child will sicken, perhaps even die?"

Rachel felt suddenly afraid. Was she going to die? Was that what this was about?

"Yes," Henry said. "I knew."

"But you kept the dream to yourself."

"Yes."

"Why?"

Henry looked down. "Because I knew how my wife felt about such things," he said, startling Dorothy. "The old ways, the old language . . . She wanted all our children to have Christian names, to celebrate Jehovah."

Dorothy pointed out, defensively, "It's the law. The king decreed it, that every child have a Christian name!"

"Is Kimo not Kimo despite what is written on his birth record?" Maka turned to Henry.

"This is why Rachel is sick. Because you heard her night name and you ignored it. If she is to be well, she must be given her *inoa pō.*"

That night some roasted pork, coconut pudding, baked fish and a little *poi* was burned in a fire in the Kalamas' back yard — a sacrificial offering, given up to God or gods, as the family prayed. At the feast that followed, Grandpa Maka spoke aloud his granddaughter's new name for the first time: "May the Lord God and our ancestors be pleased. Let us eat, drink and celebrate the health and long life of this girl, Rachel Aouli Kalama!"

The family applauded and cheered; and Rachel basked in the love and concern she felt from all around her, even Sarah. Though she only vaguely understood what had happened here today, she knew that all these people had come here to help her, and that pleased her. She turned the new name over in her mind: *Aouli.* She didn't feel like an Aouli, she felt like Rachel. But why couldn't she be both? She smiled to herself, starting to like the sound of it, and she thought, Everything will be all right. Her left foot was starting to itch and she reached down to scratch at it, but she knew in her heart that all would be well; that with so many people around her, loving and praying for her, everything would turn out just fine.

CHAPTER 3

"Our Father who art in Heaven, hallowed be thy name. Thy kingdom come, thy will be done —"

Along with the rest of her class, Rachel spoke the prayer as automatically as she could count to ten, but her mind was elsewhere — mostly on the various indignities she had lately been forced to suffer. It was bad enough that Mama refused to remove the bandage on her thigh, long after the cut had healed; bad enough that she also made Rachel wear frocks with long frilly skirts; but now, the supreme embarrassment, her mother actually insisted that Rachel wear *shoes* to school. She tried to tell Mama it wasn't necessary, that the itching she'd felt in her left foot had gone away — she no longer felt anything in that spot, nothing at all — but Mama wouldn't listen. "You're gonna wear shoes or your backside is gonna be as red as your foot!" she warned, Rachel grudgingly submitting. And if it wasn't enough that Rachel's feet were suffocating, her friends

seemed to delight in teasing her about it —
accusing her of putting on airs — and had
lately even taken to calling her "Little Miss
Shoe."

*"Good morning to you; good morning to you
—"*

Today the second-graders were singing a
greeting not just to their teacher, Miss
Johnson, but to a visitor — a blank-faced
haole in a business suit. It was not the man's
first visit to their classroom, nor would it be
his last.

"Class," Miss Johnson said, "you remember
Inspector Wyckoff from the Board of Health.
Please sit quietly at your desks and hold out
your hands as Mr. Wyckoff passes."

As usual the man made his way down the
first aisle, surveying the hands presented for
his inspection. Sometimes it was just a quick
glance, his gray gaze sweeping once over a
child and then on to the next; at other times
he might take a student's hand in his, noting
the color and texture of the skin, turning it
over to study the palm; and only then he
would move on.

Rachel watched as the inspector — *bounty
hunter,* some whispered — stooped to examine a bruise on a boy's knee. Now Rachel
began to feel self-conscious about her own
blemish, hidden beneath bandage and skirt.
As Mr. Wyckoff probed the child's bruise
with the tip of a pen, drawing a wince from

him, Rachel thought about the red spot on her foot and how the strap of her sandal didn't seem to chafe there as it did her other foot. By the time the inspector reached her she was nervously tapping her foot against the leg of her desk; as he took her hand he looked up, sharply. "Please don't do that," he said in a flat tone that instantly froze Rachel's foot. His gaze lowered again to her hands. He turned them over, first the left, then the right; carefully scrutinized the bed of her nails; and just when his interest was beginning to alarm her, he looked up — and smiled! "Long life-line," he said, tapping a finger on her palm. "Means a long life, eh?" Rachel didn't know what to say to that so she just returned his smile. He gave her back her hand, moved on, and she exhaled in relief. There was obviously nothing wrong with her after all!

The inspector continued without incident until he came to Harry Woo in the back row. He gave Harry the same scrutiny he'd lavished on Rachel, then went a step further. He reached out, took one of the boy's earlobes between his fingers, and pinched. Rachel winced, but Harry didn't. Mr. Wyckoff asked for his name and address — the class shuddering as one — and jotted the information in a small notebook. When he had completed his inspection of the class he thanked everyone for their cooperation, smiled at Miss

Johnson, and left.

The next day Harry Woo did not come to school; nor the day after; nor for the rest of the term. After the third day Rachel asked one of her classmates where he was and the girl whispered back, "He has the separating sickness." Rachel thought of Uncle Pono, of the bandage on her thigh, and then did her very best not to think about it anymore.

When Papa came home again in October it was a source of amazement to his children that Mama actually succeeded that first Sunday in dragging their father into church. True, he did stifle the occasional yawn, but he came quickly awake when the minister launched into that week's sermon, titled "Leprosy and the Hawaiian People." Henry and Dorothy tried not to show more than casual interest: since Pono had lived in Waimānalo, no one here suspected the Kalamas had a relative in Kalihi Hospital.

A full-blooded Hawaiian in his fifties, with a fringe of graying hair and a white beard, Reverend Waiamau was a charismatic preacher who began by detailing the history of the disease in Hawai'i: how it may have come from China (hence *ma'i pākē,* "Chinese sickness"); how Hawaiians seemed to be particularly susceptible to it; and how in 1865 the foreigners in His Majesty's government convinced Kamehameha V that unless something were done the scourge would be the death of the Hawaiian race. The result was an "Act to Prevent the Spread of Leprosy," mandating the arrest of all suspected lepers, and even (for the first eight years) confiscation of all their worldly assets to pay for the costs of exiling them to Kalaupapa.

Soon the disease would earn another name as well: "the sickness that tears apart families."

"Some say the *ma'i pākē* affects our people so disproportionately," the pastor said, "because we Hawaiians value family and community so much that we would rather shelter a leprous friend or relative than see him cast out of our midst. Others simply blame bad hygiene — too many hands eating from the same calabash.

"But perhaps there's more to it than that." He fixed his congregation with a sober look. "There are those, indeed, who say leprosy is more than a physical ailment; it is a moral disease as well.

"Some medical men — including the former physician for the Moloka'i Leprosarium, Dr. George Fitch — believe that leprosy is actually a fourth stage of venereal disease. The syphilitic becomes, in time, the leper. Syphilis was the great scourge of our nation in the early years of this century; and now this disease born of impurity and immorality may have festered into an even deadlier plague, one that threatens our people with extinction!"

As the pastor's voice grew in intensity, his parishioners shifted uncomfortably in their seats, but they hung on every word, none more keenly than Dorothy.

"Could this be the true source of leprosy? Not bad hygiene, not leprous touch or breath. *Unchastity. Immorality.*" His voice fairly boomed now. "Too long have we turned away from the sin and vice in our midst, condoning it by our silence and inaction! And now its offspring comes — grown like a mold from the culture of our lust and laziness — and my children, it comes to kill us! To burn the very memory of us from the earth as lava boils away the sea, and if we let it happen, then we *deserve* it!

"Will you let it happen? Or will you show the sinner there is no place for him in society? More important — will you acknowledge and repent the sin in your *own* hearts, and cast it out even as we must cast out the leper? To save our nation, will you first save your own souls?"

His flock responded with enthusiastic cries of "Yes!" and "I will! I will!" And as Dorothy joined in she began to understand the guilt and shame she was feeling; began to see what God was trying to tell her, the message he had writ plain and which only now she began to comprehend.

In the weeks to come she and Henry would argue more than in all their twelve years together. Rachel and Sarah, lying awake in bed, didn't understand all of the shouted words in English and Hawaiian that bled through the bedroom wall, but the tone of them was painfully clear.

"He's your brother! That's all I'm saying."

Henry was adrift, confused at the bitterness in Dorothy's tone. "So?"

"So, this didn't come from *my* brother."

"How the hell do you know that?" Henry asked, irritated. "This sickness, it hides in the body a long time. How do you know Will doesn't have it, too?"

"Because he doesn't!" she snapped. "Will is a good man, a moral man!"

"And Pono isn't?" Henry said in disbelief.

"Pono's a dog. He flirts with any *wahine* he sees — even me, his brother's wife! Margaret says he's slept around plenty on her."

"That's between Margaret and Pono," Henry said, reeling. "And we don't know for sure it came from Pono! Maybe it did, maybe it didn't!"

She gave him a stink-eye look, cold and direct, and Henry was wounded to see the anger in once-loving eyes.

"Maybe it didn't," she said flatly.

Something about the way she said it rankled Henry all the more. "What's that supposed to mean?"

"I'm just agreeing. Maybe it came from somebody else." She kept on giving him the stink-eye. "Lots of leprosy in those places you go to, eh? Shanghai. Hong Kong. Lots of cheap *pākē* whores with dirty *kohes.*"

Henry was stunned, as much by her use of the word for a woman's private parts as by her accusation.

"That's got nothing to do with anything," he said. "Eight, nine months I'm away from home, maybe once or twice I get lonely, it doesn't mean anything!"

"I see you get the *pala,*" and here she used the Hawaiian word for gonorrhea, "but it goes away and I think, 'It doesn't matter. Forget about it.' Reverend Waiamau, he's right, we look away when we shouldn't."

"You think I'm a leper?" Angrily he stripped off his shirt, threw it aside. "You know my body — you seen any sores?" He yanked off his pants, one leg at a time, stood naked before her. "You see any now?"

"Like you say," she replied, unimpressed. "It hides in the body."

They looked at each other, and there seemed to be nothing more to say. Henry pulled on his pants, stalked out of the bedroom and curled up on the mat on the living room floor. But he couldn't sleep, and after an hour he slipped quietly into his daughters' room and stood by Rachel's bed, watching her sleep. Moonlight, through lace curtains, fell in bright freckles across his daughter's face, as though prefiguring what was to come for her. Henry's eyes brimmed with tears. He dropped to his knees, knelt beside Rachel, and prayed as he scarcely ever had before. Dear Jesus, he said, please spare her, spare my daughter. If I've sinned, punish me, give me the leprosy, not her. It's not fair!

But as with the handful of other times he'd spoken to God, he could not tell whether anyone had heard. He knelt at Rachel's side a long while, pleading for mercy, trying to will the sickness from her body into his; and when he finally grew sleepy he went back to the bed he shared with Dorothy and he touched her on the hip, that tender graze that always meant *I'm sorry.* But if Dorothy felt it she didn't show it; and Henry knew then that this trouble would not pass as others had before.

Two weeks later, the truce between Sarah and Rachel came to an abrupt end, and over nothing in particular; it was a conflict born of no true anger, ending only in grief.

Rachel's classmates continued to taunt her about her fancy shoes. "Going to the *opera* house?" they'd say, giving limp-wristed "society" waves. Or, "Every day Sunday for you, eh Rachel?" And then they'd curtsey and dissolve into gales of laughter. Each day another barb, a different quip, until Rachel was tempted to cast off one of the hated shoes and toss it at the next person who crossed her.

One day at recess, Rachel was running across the schoolyard when Sarah, passing by, said mildly, "Hey. Your laces untied, Miss Shoe."

Rachel came to a skidding halt, glaring at her sister. "Don't *you* call me that, too!"

With sudden inspiration Sarah said, "If the shoe fits . . ." And she giggled mightily at her joke.

"Stop it!" Rachel cried out. "Don't *call* me that!"

"Call you what, Miss Shoe?"

Rachel, furious, made a headlong dash at her sister and gave her a push. "*Stop* it!"

"Hey!" Sarah nearly lost her balance. "*You* stop it!" And she pushed Rachel back. Their classmates gathered round: this looked promising.

"Then *you* stop calling me that!" Rachel warned, and gave her sister another shove.

"I'll call you whatever I want!" Sarah yelled, and reciprocated.

"I hate these shoes! I hate *you!*" With one furious lunge, Rachel sent Sarah hurtling backwards into the trunk of a tall monkey-pod tree. Sarah yelped in pain, then angrily leaped forward and gave Rachel an equally rough shove, yelling, *"Leave me alone, you dirty leper!"*

67

The words had barely escaped her when Sarah knew she'd made a horrible mistake. No one had ever spoken the word at home, but by its very absence Sarah had known what must be wrong with Rachel. And as she stood there looking at her sister, she felt as someone might after they'd accidentally cut themselves with a knife, or worse, cut someone else: that certain knowledge that they'd done something terribly wrong, and could not take it back.

Rachel was also hearing the word, in connection with herself, for the first time; and all the silences, all the sad looks, all the tension and whispered prayers were suddenly encapsulated in that one dreadful word: *leper.* Tears sprang to her eyes. "I'm not," she said softly. "I'm *not.*"

Now Sarah began to cry as well. Unable to look her sister in the eye, she bolted away — out of the schoolyard, down Fort Street, out of Rachel's sight.

With everyone in the yard staring at her, Rachel ran to the nearest refuge, an outhouse — ran in and stayed there, sobbing, until recess was over. She forced herself to march back into the classroom and sit calmly down at her desk. For the next three hours she sat staring straight ahead at the chalkboard, her skin crawling as she felt the eyes of her classmates upon her, seeing her in a different way than they had just an hour before, and when the school day was over she ran outside and threw off her accursed shoes and ran, and in the running felt a kind of release. She didn't go home at first but used her only nickel to ride the trolley from one end of King Street to the other and back again, as if she might never see this street, these horses, these wonderful cars again; and when at last she did go home, she found Health Inspector Wyckoff waiting for her.

Mama was with him, and Sarah, both weeping. Sarah kept saying, "I'm sorry. I'm sorry. I didn't *mean* it," seeking an absolution she knew she could never accept. Papa was there too, and the minute Rachel rushed in he scooped her up in his arms and held her tight, kissed her and said, "It's all right, baby. Everything's gonna be okay."

Inspector Wyckoff had the decency not to say anything as first Henry, then Dorothy, embraced their little girl; and when they were finished Wyckoff looked at Rachel and said with a sigh, "Come along, child."

Rachel fought back tears. "Where?"

"To take some tests. To see how sick you are. And if you're not, why you'll come right back here, I promise."

"I'll go with her," Henry said. Wyckoff started to object, then thought better of it and just nodded.

Mama and Sarah followed them outside,

Papa lifting Rachel up onto the seat of Mr. Wyckoff's carriage before sliding in beside her. Neighbors drifted out of their houses to watch in nervous silence. Dorothy gave her daughter a last kiss: "We'll come visit soon as we can, okay, baby?" Rachel nodded, trying to be brave; Papa put his arm around her as Wyckoff snapped the reins.

Dorothy and Sarah, still weeping, watched the carriage go; when it was lost from view Dorothy glanced up and for the first time noticed her neighbors gathered in knots on their doorsteps. Their eyes looked away as they quickly retreated into the safety of their homes; and Dorothy, hot with shame, knew that nothing would ever be the same again.

It seemed a long carriage ride down past the harbor to Kalihi, a marshy triangle of land jutting into the sea west of the harbor. A thick grove of algaroba trees obscured the Receiving Station from the sight of both tourists and residents who didn't wish to be reminded of its presence. But even without the trees it would scarcely have attracted much attention: it was nothing more sinister than a neatly landscaped complex of dormitories, cottages, schoolhouse, hospital, and an infirmary, encircled by a tall wire fence.

The iron gates swung open to admit them and Henry struggled to maintain his composure as the carriage, coming to a halt, was quickly surrounded by curious patients. Most appeared normal, a few merely tattooed with florid spots on faces or arms, but some . . . some of the faces were pocked with ugly sores, some were as bulbous and knobby as a coral bed, while others were mercifully bandaged like mummies.

"*Papa,*" Rachel cried, clinging to his shirt, "don't leave me here, don't make me stay!"

"It's okay, baby, Papa's here." He lifted her up, cradled her in his arms and carried her through the crowd. Rachel buried her face in her father's chest to blot out the monstrous faces all around her.

Wyckoff led them to the infirmary, where he was presented with the ten dollar fee the government paid him for each leprosy suspect he apprehended — and where Henry was required to leave his daughter in the care of a smiling nurse. "You come with me now, Rachel, all right?" the nurse said soothingly. "Your daddy can see you after you've taken your test."

"Papa, don't go." She wouldn't let loose of his hand.

"It's all right, baby. You go with the lady, okay? I'll be right here, I'm not going anywhere."

Reluctantly Rachel let go of her father and followed the nurse down a long corridor and into a small room. "I need you to take off your clothes now, Rachel." Rachel did as she was told and the woman helped her into a

71

white hospital smock, a bit large for the six-year-old. Rachel hardly noticed as the nurse dumped the old clothes into a waste basket.

The door to the room opened and a *haole* doctor entered, barely acknowledging Rachel's presence before he took a scalpel to the red-ringed sore on her thigh. He punctured the insensate skin and scooped out a bit of fluid, which he placed on a glass slide, then scraped a shaving from the rose-colored patch on Rachel's foot.

"Can I go home now?" Rachel asked the nurse hopefully.

"Now some other doctors want to see you." Rachel's gown nearly slipped off as the nurse prodded her out of the room; the woman laced it up tighter in back, then led Rachel down another corridor to a windowless room bright with white tile and the harsh glare of electric lights. The nurse led Rachel to a small platform in the center of the room where a triumvirate of doctors stood before her, making barely a glimmer of eye contact.

One of the doctors nodded to the nurse, who undid the back of Rachel's gown and allowed it to drop to the floor. Rachel stood naked as the doctors made a slow circuit around her, pointing out the ridged sore on her thigh, the beginnings of another on her foot. They poked at her body with metal instruments, seeming to see her not as a six-year-old girl but as a teeming culture of *bacil-*

lus laprae in the shape of a six-year-old girl. Rachel stood there for twenty long minutes, burning with embarrassment, until at last the examining doctors were satisfied and left, and the nurse slipped Rachel's gown back on. "There. That wasn't so bad," she declared.

She smiled, opened the door, and Rachel shot like a bullet down the hall.

She heard the nurse behind her calling her name, which only spurred Rachel on. Tears obscured her vision; she barely saw where she was going but didn't care. She knocked over a cart, saw glass bottles go smashing to the floor, but kept on running. Around a corner, down another hall, weaving between two doctors staring at her in confusion, then another corner and straight into the path of a woman in a hospital gown. Through her tears Rachel saw the woman's face, cratered and oozing pus, and Rachel screamed. In her frantic rush away from the woman she collided with a young girl no older than herself, and she too had a face like a raw wound, and Rachel's shrieks now seemed to fill the building.

Then the nurse was suddenly grabbing her and Rachel was fighting with all her strength, pummeling at the woman with her tiny fists, when she heard a cry. *"Rachel!"*

Papa came running up. The nurse released Rachel and Henry gathered her up in his arms. "Papa's here, Papa's here," he said, holding her tight, and Rachel's screams turned to sobs; it broke Henry's heart to feel her body quake and tremble with such fear. He glared at the nurse. "What the hell'd you do to her?"

"Nothing! The doctors examined her, that's all —"

"I want to go home," Rachel begged, "please Papa, take me *home* —"

"Rachel," he said softly. "Rachel, listen to me, listen to Papa." He took her by the shoulders, made her look into his eyes, and Rachel quieted. "You're a sick girl, baby. We want you to get better. And the only way you're gonna get better is to stay here."

"I want to go home!"

"I know you do. And —" He told himself that it was possible, that it *might* happen. "You will. When you're better. But right now, you gotta be brave and stay here a while, you understand? Your Mama and me, we come visit you every day, I promise. Okay?"

Rachel, calmed as always by his presence, slowly nodded. Henry smiled. "Good girl! Now you go with this lady, and Papa'll see you tomorrow, all right?"

He gave her a hug, and Rachel was taken to a room in the isolation ward where, she was told, she would be spending the night. She was relieved that she had the room to herself, no monsters anywhere in sight. She gratefully donned pajamas and crawled into bed, trying to find the most comfortable spot on the lumpy straw mattress. The nurse left and Rachel was alone — the first time she had ever been truly alone in her life. She didn't much like it.

Later another nurse brought her dinner: some dry fish, rice with gravy, and *poi,* with chocolate cake for dessert. Rachel ate the cake first, then the *poi,* the rice, and the fish; and as the sun set outside her room she took refuge in sleep, transported in her dreams not to China or India or far Ceylon, but to her own room in her own house in a time before all of this.

The next morning, after breakfast, another nurse appeared in the doorway and announced, "Time for your first treatment." She gave Rachel a pill to take, then off came the pajamas, on went the hospital gown, and Rachel was again taken down a long hallway to another tiled room. But instead of a panel of prying doctors inside there was what looked like an enormous bathtub. The water was hot and had a nice smell, which the nurse said came from "mineral salts and herbs." It was called "the Goto treatment," she explained, named after a Japanese doctor who was trying to find a cure for leprosy, and Rachel would have to soak in this tub twice a day for half an hour. She splashed around happily for the first ten minutes; after that the novelty wore off and she was sweaty, wrinkly, and bored.

After the Goto bath she was given more medicine. They called this one a "beverage," but it had a foul bitter taste befitting its origins, a kind of Japanese tree bark. She got dressed in a brand-new blouse and skirt and was moved out of isolation and into the girls' dormitories, clean institutional rooms smelling of strong medicinal soap and — something else. Something the soap couldn't quite mask, a heavy, sickly odor Rachel didn't recognize.

She was distressed to learn that she would have to share a room with another girl, but before she had time to think about this she was told she had some visitors and was taken by a guard to a long narrow visiting room. On one side of the room was a bench, on the other a table and chairs, between them a wire mesh screen rising from floor to ceiling. And waiting on the bench were Mama and Papa! Ecstatic, Rachel ran toward them, her fingers poking through the holes in the wire screen — only to find herself pulled back by the guard, who warned, "No touching allowed!" The words were like a knife in the heart for both parents and child. From now on all their visits would take place at a small remove, only words allowed to pass between them, and Rachel would come to ache for her mother's kisses, for the comforting warmth of Papa's chest against her.

The guard stood outside as Papa haltingly explained to Rachel that the tests she took the day before had come back positive. "That means the leprosy germ is inside you. But they're gonna try and force it out, with those baths and the pills they give you. You take 'em after every meal, just like the nurses tell you, okay?"

Mama was pretty quiet, for Mama, letting Papa do most of the talking; Rachel asked if she could have one of her dolls to sleep with, and Papa promised to ask about it. Then Mama finally spoke, telling her that Sarah wanted to come but the doctors here wouldn't let her. "She's so sorry, baby," Mama said, "she didn't mean to do it."

Rachel wasn't so sure of that. All she said was, "How long do I have to stay here?"

"Two, three months, maybe," Papa said, repeating what the doctors had told him, but not believing it himself. "Long enough for the treatment to work."

By the end of the visit Mama looked sadder than Rachel had ever seen her, and said in a small voice, "I love you, baby."

"I love you, too, Mama," Rachel said, and then the nurse took her back into the dormitory and Dorothy began to cry.

Meals were no longer a private catered affair; Rachel had to eat in the cafeteria with the other *keiki* and the moment she entered

77

she wanted to dash out again. At the tables and in line to get food were dozens of boys and girls, and many of them, like Rachel, showed few outward signs of their disease; but many more did, and Rachel shrank from them as she would a ghost. Smiles appeared on tumorous faces as the children tried to chat with her, but Rachel just looked away, scooped her noodles and *poi* from the steaming vats of food, then sat by herself in a corner, wondering fearfully if *she* would look like this someday.

It was like that everywhere: Kalihi's tiny school boasted a curriculum of horrors, boys with earlobes drooping like taffy, girls with deep scores in their young skin like wizened gnomes with bright shiny hair. After school she met her roommate Francine, a young Hawaiian girl with short pixieish hair, who asked Rachel if she wanted to go play in the recreation yard; but though Francine had smooth unblemished skin, her left hand was starting to contract into a lobster's claw and Rachel looked away, shaking her head. "I don't feel like it."

"Come on," Francine said, reaching out to nudge her on the arm, "they got volleyball, and badminton, and —"

When Francine's clawed hand touched her, Rachel screamed and flung herself onto the bed. Francine looked at her sadly — seeing, perhaps, her own first day here — and let her be. Rachel lay on the lumpy mattress and wept, ignoring dinner, refusing her Goto bath, crying herself asleep before the light had even faded outside the window.

When she woke it was evening. She was still alone in the room, a faint electric light spilling in from the hall. She was hungry and lonely and afraid. She longed for Mama and Papa; it hurt so much to think she couldn't call out for them in the middle of the night. She started to cry again, then jumped as she heard a male voice.

" 'Ey, you!"

She looked up and saw a man standing in the doorway. His face was pitted with sores, his ears were strangely misshapen, and he leaned on a cane. Rachel shrank back onto the headboard of her bed.

"You hear 'bout the clumsy little girl who broke the wind?" he said, and took a step inside. "On account of she had Portagee *bean soup* for dinner!"

As he laughed at his own rude joke Rachel saw past the sores on his face, and she beamed with delight.

"Uncle Pono!"

She jumped out of bed and raced across the room toward him. " 'Ey, there's my little favorite," he said, squatting down to embrace her. "My *special* girl." Rachel wrapped her arms around him, cried with joy and relief, and scarcely noticed that there were tears in her uncle's eyes as well. It didn't matter that his face was pocked and his ears looked strange; it was her Uncle Pono, he was holding her, and nothing else mattered. And would matter less and less, from that moment on.

CHAPTER 4

1892–93

The day after Rachel's arrest, Dorothy and Henry came home from visiting their daughter at Kalihi to find a bright yellow sign nailed to the fence surrounding their house.

QUARANTINE NOTICE
This house has a communicable disease,
LEPROSY,
and is subject to Fumigation.

The following Sunday in church it was as though the family were surrounded by a bubble of air that pushed away anyone who strayed too close: friends and neighbors of long standing greeted them at a comfortable distance, smiling hello but always somehow on their way elsewhere. Parishioners beside whom Dorothy had sung for twenty years now sat two pews behind her, or three ahead. Children stared at her with a mixture of confusion and fear, and once Dorothy overheard a mother whisper to her little boy,

"That family's dirty." As though their home were a filthy breeding ground for leprosy germs.

Dorothy was mortified, but she told herself this would pass in time, and for now she must swallow her anger and her hurt and remember Christ's admonitions that "ye resist not evil: but whosoever shall smite thee on thy right cheek, turn to him the other also." And so the more they avoided her, the more she tried to engage them in conversation. The greater the fear in their eyes, the louder she sang the hymns, to show them all how deeply she believed, how fervently she held Christ in her heart.

For the annual Christmas bake sale, raising money to buy gifts for sick and underprivileged children — including those at Kalaupapa — Dorothy baked, as usual, an angelfood cake with passionfruit filling and sweet coconut icing. She brought it to church and gave it to Mrs. Fujita, the sale organizer, who held it in her hands as though it were an unexploded artillery shell . . . then slowly handed it back to Dorothy. "I'm sorry," she said. "We can't take this." Dorothy stared at her, uncomprehending, until she added, "For . . . sanitary reasons."

The words stung Dorothy as nothing else had. She blinked back tears and quickly left. She walked the ten blocks to her home carrying the cake in her hands, as though she were taking it to a party, as though she were not dying inside; only after she hurried past the yellow QUARANTINE sign and into the house did she put the cake down and allow herself to weep.

She continued to love and worship Christ in her heart, but after that Dorothy stopped going to church.

That Christmas was a cheerless one for Rachel. Oh, the staff at Kalihi tried to make it a festive enough day for the patients, and Mama and Papa came and brought her a new doll as a Christmas gift; but once their allotted time with her was up, Rachel cried out for them to stay longer and had to be dragged out of the visiting room. At supper, Uncle Pono's attempts to cheer her up only made her sadder. She cried herself to sleep again that night, her doll lying forgotten on the bed beside her. Had she not been lost in her own grief and homesickness, she might have noticed that not all the girls on the ward had visitors that day, and fewer still had Christmas presents.

With his world coming apart as if it were a *matryoshka* — each new horror splitting open to reveal yet another nesting inside — Henry decided he could no longer afford to spend long months at sea away from his family, and so took a job as a stevedore at Honolulu Harbor. He worked from seven in the morning to five in the afternoon, and thanks to the harbor's proximity to Kalihi he could visit Rachel each evening, unless he had to work an extra shift or Dorothy needed him at home (less and less, these days). Sometimes Pono would hobble into the visiting room with Rachel — the *maʻi pākē* having caused wasting and contracture in his left foot — telling jokes, tickling his niece under her arms. And in those moments Henry actually envied his brother for being a leper — for being able to touch Rachel, to make her laugh or wipe away a tear.

One evening in January, after Rachel had returned to her room, a more subdued Pono quietly asked his brother, "Henry. You seen my *keiki*?"

"Yeah, sure, last month, at Eli's."

"They okay?" Pono said wistfully. "I ain't seen them in so long."

Over a year, Henry realized. He tried to imagine not seeing Rachel for an entire year.

"Yeah," Henry said. "They're good. Florence and Eli, they're taking good care of them."

Pono nodded. "Florence, she's a good sister," he said, then added, "And you been a good brother, Henry."

With difficulty Henry said, "You been a good brother too, Pono. And a good uncle to my Rachel."

Pono's eyes reflected both guilt and shame. "Better uncle than a husband, 'ey?" he said gloomily. Then, "You know leprosy is grounds for divorce?"

"Margaret won't divorce you."

Pono laughed, not a happy laugh.

"Minute I go to Moloka'i, she'll file. You watch."

"Who says you're goin' to Moloka'i?"

Pono pulled a wrinkled sheet of paper from his pants pocket. Since he couldn't pass it through the wire mesh separating them, Pono held it up for his brother to read. It was a letter on Board of Health stationery, and informed Pono that on January 15, 1893, he would be transferred from Kalihi to Kalaupapa on the island of Moloka'i.

Henry hung his head and began to cry.

Rachel was no less upset by the news. When at breakfast the next morning her uncle told her, she too cried, but they were angry tears. "No! It's not fair!"

Pono shrugged. "Not fair we got leprosy, either. It just is."

"I won't stay here, I want to go with you!" She pushed away her tray of *poi* and eggs; it went skidding across the table and onto the floor.

Pono calmly picked up her discarded breakfast, then turned to Rachel and said gently, "Now how you gonna do that? You're gonna get well, grow up, get married — they don't send healthy old married ladies to Moloka'i, 'ey?"

85

He smiled and wiped a tear from beneath her eye. "You do me a favor, though. Whoever you marry — no matter how handsome he is — you stay my special girl, okay?"

Rachel agreed that she would, then ran weeping out of the dining hall.

Henry visited Kalihi the night before his brother's departure for Kalaupapa, but at Pono's urging neither he nor Dorothy ventured to the wharf that day to see him off — for fear that if Henry's employers saw that he was related to a leper, they would fire him. It had happened before.

The day after Pono's departure, shortly before five in the afternoon, Henry Kalama's world split open like a *matryoshka* yet again.

There was always a great clamor at the docks — the groan of winches and cranes, the blast of a ship's horn, shouts and curses in half a dozen languages — so when Henry, clocking out for the day, turned to leave, he hadn't heard anything that might've prepared him for what he now saw: four boatloads of American sailors, rowing ashore from the USS *Boston* moored in the harbor.

Henry had seen American soldiers before, but never so many: three companies of bluejackets, one of marines, a hospital unit, even a corps of musicians. And the troops now landing at Brewer's and Charlton's wharves were bristling with weaponry. Each man carried a rifle and double cartridge belt, and the artillery unit was bringing ashore Gatling guns and a pair of revolving cannon!

The soldiers quickly formed a single column and began marching off the docks and into downtown Honolulu. Unlike most American sailors Henry had known, these offered no friendly smiles, no boyish waves — they walked ramrod-straight, rifles resting on shoulders, in parade formation.

A young man lounging at the dock reminded Henry there had been a public rally that day in support of Queen Lili‘uokalani, who wanted a new constitution. The old constitution had been forced on King Kalākaua by *haole* vigilante groups, and had stripped the monarchy of much of its power — and most Hawaiians of their right to vote. "Maybe things get ugly," the young man speculated. Had the Americans been called to help keep the peace?

As he watched the troops march away, Henry's disquiet grew. Unlike most Hawaiians, he had traveled far and wide; had witnessed the might of great navies. The more he saw of the world, the more he realized how small and vulnerable these islands truly were. And he was only too aware that the twenty-six-inch guns of the American warship in the harbor could have quickly leveled most of downtown Honolulu.

Henry followed the troops up Fort Street.

At the corner of Fort and Merchant a marine company was detached to guard the American consulate, the remainder of the troops turning right onto Merchant Street. In minutes they were marching into Palace Square. This was where the rally was to have been held, but it was empty now; clearly the Americans were not here to quell a riot.

Glancing toward 'Iolani Palace, Henry saw Queen Liliu'okalani herself standing on a balcony, watching the troops as they passed by. They gave her a respectful salute, the flag bearers drooping their colors, the musicians delivering four short ruffles of their drums. The queen was a large, sturdy woman, but standing there on her balcony she seemed to Henry quite fragile.

He found himself thinking, *And the land shall belong to a people from across the sea.*

The Americans marched on under a light rain, finally encamping beneath the sheltering trees of an expensive house. There the soldiers laid aside their rifles and began to look and act more like the Americans he had known — smiling, laughing, rolling cigarettes. A *haole* woman came out of the house and served the troops lemonade and bananas, as if they were on a picnic. And on the grounds of the nearby Hawaiian Hotel, the Royal Hawaiian Band began its weekly Monday night concert and Henry could hear the familiar, comforting melody of "Pua Alani" under the patter of rain.

Henry told himself he was being silly; surely the Americans were simply here on some sort of maneuvers. He caught a trolley going west on King Street, toward Kalihi, and put everything but Rachel out of his mind.

The next day, the shocking news radiated across the city: the queen had been deposed.

Immediately after Lili'uokalani's call for a new constitution, a small coterie of white businessmen had formed a Committee for Safety — their own. Fearing that a more powerful queen might threaten their property and business interests, they dedicated themselves to her overthrow. They would have been easily overwhelmed by the Queen's Royal Guard had it not been for the collusion of the American Minister to Hawai'i, John Stevens, who landed troops to "prevent the destruction of American life and property," though there was no such property anywhere near where the troops were deployed.

Before the Committee had time to rearrange the furniture in the Government Building, Stevens formally recognized the Provisional Government. That night, on the reasonable assumption that her Royal Guard was outnumbered by American forces, the queen reluctantly surrendered.

In the days after the coup, there was little

practical difference in the way people lived their lives. Streetcars ran on the same schedules, stores kept the same hours, the price of a shank of beef remained the same. At a public meeting at Kaumakapili Church, Reverend Waiamau suggested that nothing important had been lost, and in the long run Hawai'i had much to gain from the new status quo. Henry argued that what they were in danger of losing was their very history: for what were the *ali'i,* the royalty, but the Hawaiian people's living kinship to their own past?

Most people thought the whole thing would simply blow over. Henry's own father reminded him of another coup — engineered by a rogue British consul, not unlike this man Stevens — which overthrew the king when Maka had been a small boy. (Assignment to Hawai'i seemed to bring out the worst kind of colonialist megalomania in foreign diplomats.) When word of that coup reached England, the British government wasted no time reversing the consul's actions and restoring the Hawaiian monarchy. "The same will happen this time," he assured Henry. Surely, he maintained, as great and freedom-loving a country as the United States could not allow such a flagrant miscarriage of justice to long stand.

Rachel never stopped missing her Uncle Pono, but she made other friends at Kalihi,

90

especially Francine, whose pixieish looks belied the heart of a true hellion. Once Rachel overcame her dread of her roommate's clawed hand, the two became fast friends and partners in crime, principally frivolous escape. One evening at the height of summer, the air as thick with mosquitoes as with humidity, Rachel and Francine sneaked past the night watchmen, climbed the six-foot wire fence behind the hospital, and took a refreshing dip in Kalihi Bay. Their absence was discovered almost immediately (it wasn't hard to follow the sounds of splashing and giggling) and they were confined to their room for a week. But this didn't discourage them from other excursions over the fence, such as the occasional trip to buy ice cream; and they began to accumulate a disquieting number of black marks on their record.

On a particularly hot, muggy day in July, as Rachel and other *keiki* kept cool by tossing handfuls of drinking water at each other, a group of adult inmates listened to a riveting newspaper account from the island of Kaua'i — where a leper named Ko'olau and his family had successfully evaded capture by hiding in the thickly wooded Kalalau Valley. When Deputy Sheriff Louis Stolz finally tracked them down, Ko'olau told him he would only go to Moloka'i if his wife and child could accompany him. Stolz flatly refused, despite the fact that there was a long custom of allowing

91

healthy spouses (though not children) to go to Moloka'i as *kōkuas* — helpers. The family fled again into the lush recesses of the valley. When police pursued them, Ko'olau shot Stolz dead with his rifle, wounded two other officers, and inadvertently caused the death of a fourth.

When the man reading the paper finished, there was a long silence. Then an elderly man spoke up, saying, "Why didn't I think of that?" — and everyone within hearing roared with laughter.

The Goto treatments helped heal some patients' sores, but Rachel showed no particular improvement; the sore on her thigh was still there, as was the one on her left foot, but at least she got no worse. In November, after a year at Kalihi, it was time to reevaluate her condition. Once again Rachel was told to take off her clothes and put on a gown, then brought into the white-tiled examination room, this time to face just one of the doctors who had conducted her initial exam. "Please remove the patient's gown." As it fell around her feet Rachel tried to give him the stink-eye, but his gaze never met hers — it just tracked across her body as a butcher might inspect a spoiled cut of meat. The nurse jotted down his comments as the doctor noted dispassionately, "Female, Hawaiian, age — seven, is it? — eyebrows intact, no sign of alopecia. Face not affected. Open your mouth, please." He stuck in a tongue depressor and peered inside. "Slight thickening in roof of mouth, extending back to soft palate. No indication of tubercular-leprous vegetations. Hold out your hands?"

He looked over her hands, still free of blemishes. "Hands, fingers, appear not to be affected." He examined her feet, poking at her left foot with a sharp needle. "Small patch of scaly dry skin on left foot, with anesthesia." He worked his way up to the spot on her thigh. "Red ringed tubercle on inside of right thigh, skin thick, anesthesia present. Genital development," and here he put a gloved hand between her thighs, "appears to be normal." He palpated her groin, and Rachel flinched.

"That hurts!"

"Skin of the groin shows some sensitivity," he noted, otherwise ignoring her discomfort; Rachel jerked away.

"Stop it!" she yelled.

"Please stand still," the doctor responded curtly, reaching again for her groin. Angrily, Rachel reached for *his* groin — grabbed and squeezed, as he had done to her.

The doctor howled so vigorously that Rachel immediately let go and jumped back a good two feet. He doubled over in exquisite distress, and the nurse, deciding on her own initiative that the examination was over, threw Rachel's gown over her and hastened her out of the room.

She was taken back to the dormitory and never heard another thing about the incident, but less than a month later her parents received a terse letter in the mail:

BOARD OF HEALTH

November 10, 1893

Dear Mr. and Mrs. Kalama:

You are advised that at a regular meeting of the Board of Health, held on November 7, 1893, after a full assessment of your daughter's records it was decided that continued treatment is no longer of any benefit to her, and voted that she be transferred to the Leprosarium on Molokai.

She is to be transported by steamer SS *Mokolii,* leaving at 5 P.M., November 30, 1893.

By direction of the President and the Executive Officer, Board of Health,

William O. Smith

Henry and Dorothy went at once to see the head administrator at Kalihi; but though he grudgingly agreed to postpone Rachel's transfer until after Christmas, he coldly insisted she must and would be transferred to Moloka'i. Whether it was true that the treatments were ineffective, or whether Ra-

chel was being punished for troublesome
behavior, they couldn't tell; all that was
certain was that in less than two months' time
their little girl would be on her way to the
open grave known as Kalaupapa.

At home that night they argued as vociferously as ever. "Seven years old, she can't go
alone," Dorothy said. "I'll go with her; *kōkua*
her."

"You got three other kids to take care of,"
Henry said. "I'll go."

"And who's gonna work, put food on the
table?" Dorothy asked. "Ben and Kimo and
Sarah, they're gonna go hungry 'cause their
papa's gone to Moloka'i?"

In the end, the bleak truth was that neither
of them could go, even if the government allowed it, which, as Ko'olau could have told
them, increasingly it did not. The only consolation — more consolation than many a family had — was that Pono was already on
Moloka'i. His heart breaking, Henry wrote
his brother to ask if he would take care of
Rachel.

Henry barely slept that week. He walked
the house at night, looking at Rachel's dolls,
her toys — knowing that he would never see
his daughter here, in this house, ever again.
He wept inconsolably, mourning a girl still
alive, wishing that his skin would erupt in
hideous sores so that he might yet accompany
her to Moloka'i. He loved all his children,

95

but now he was forced to admit to himself that he loved Rachel best, and that rended his heart even more.

The next day they went to see her, Rachel and her parents separated as ever by the wire mesh barrier as a guard stood outside, and Henry told her the truth.

"I'm so sorry, baby," he said. "The Board of Health says you gotta go to Kalaupapa."

Rachel stared at him, not quite comprehending.

"Are you . . . coming with me?" she asked.

Henry wanted to die. "No, baby, I can't."

Rachel's eyes went fearfully to her mother. "Mama? Will you go with me?"

Fighting back tears, unable to speak, Dorothy shook her head.

"You said I was gonna stay here till I was cured, then go home!" Rachel accused, and her father sagged in his seat, feeling now the full weight of his lie.

"I know, honey," he said softly. "I'm sorry."

Dorothy found her voice. "Your Uncle Pono's there, Rachel. You'll live with him, he'll take care of you."

"And we'll come visit you, soon as we can." The administrator had assured Henry that visitors were allowed, if not exactly encouraged, to go to the settlement.

Rachel tapped new depths of fear as she realized she might never again see the two people she loved most in the world. "I don't want to go!" she cried out tearfully. "Mama, Papa, don't make me go!"

Rachel sprang out of her seat and hurled herself against the wire screen, her fingers desperately grasping the wire mesh. Dorothy ran to her, fingers closing around her daughter's; Rachel pressed her face against the screen and her mother kissed her as best as she could. The guard rushed in to separate them, only to be blocked by Henry Kalama's imposing figure and dissuaded by the cold fury in his eyes. "Leave 'em be," Henry warned, and after due consideration the guard backed off and left the room.

Henry and Dorothy touched their daughter the only way they could, through the wire barrier. They wept with her and told her they loved her; that they would always love her; and that someday, maybe, somebody would find a cure for the *ma'i pākē* and she could come home again. Rachel's face was pressed against the screen and Henry managed to get the tip of one thick finger through, to stroke her cheek. "We come visit you as soon as we can," he promised. "And I'll bring you a new doll, all right?"

Rachel sniffed back her tears long enough to ask, "Can I bring my dolls to Kalaupapa?"

Henry nodded. After several more minutes the guard meekly opened the door and told them he was sorry but their time was up, there were other families waiting to use the

97

visiting room. Rachel was returned to the dormitories and fell sobbing onto her bed. Francine comforted her, telling her everything would be all right, that her Uncle Pono was waiting for her, and besides, "I'll probably go Kalaupapa too, pretty soon. You wait for me, okay?" Rachel smiled and nodded, and it was only the thought of Pono and Francine being on Moloka'i that allowed her to sleep, however fitfully, through the night.

On December, after a thorough inquiry into the overthrow of the monarchy, U.S. President Grover Cleveland concluded that American troops had been wrongfully deployed on Hawaiian soil. "The military occupation of Honolulu by the United States was wholly without justification," the President said. "The Provisional Government owes its existence to an armed invasion by the United States."

But though Cleveland attempted to bluff the conspirators into surrendering power and returning the queen to her throne, it was only a bluff. A single armed battalion, backed by the guns of the USS *Boston,* could have handily defeated the Provisional forces and restored the monarchy; but no such battalion ever landed. Though the United States did reject annexation of Hawai'i under the circumstances, the Provisional Government would soon grandly declare itself the "Republic of Hawai'i" — a republic in name only that existed only against the day America might accept its jilted suitor.

So as he prepared himself to lose a daughter he cherished, and mourned a marriage painfully bled of love and affection, Henry Kalama grieved too for the loss of his country, his kingdom, now just a kingdom of the heart.

Two days after Christmas, Rachel and some thirty other patients were transported by wagon from Kalihi to Honolulu Harbor. A few of them were as old as sixty years; none was younger than Rachel. Some held the entirety of their worldly goods in worn carpetbags, while others had more substantial belongings in the cargo hold. Henry made certain that the steamer trunk containing Rachel's dolls was safely stowed aboard the *Mokoli'i:* he did it himself. And then he waited at the wharf until Dorothy, Ben, Kimo, and Sarah arrived, and he didn't care that his fellow stevedores were staring at him, wondering what he was doing, and wasn't that the leper ship, the dirty steamer that carried dirty lepers to Moloka'i?

As the harbor came into view Rachel tried to be brave. She swallowed her fear and, when the wagon came to a stop, took a deep breath and followed the other patients onto the pier, even as the crowd on the other side of the wooden barricade gave up the terrible and familiar moan Rachel had first heard years before.

But in that collective wail Rachel heard some distinctive voices, and now she saw, on the other side of the barrier, Mama and Papa and her siblings; and seeing them, Rachel's resolve crumbled, her tears flowed. The police herded the patients along, discouraging contact with friends and relatives. Already the first of the exiles were being taken up the gangway and onto the ship. Rachel, adults towering on every side of her, could barely make out her family and felt suddenly afraid; she had to see them one last time! She began pushing her way through the mass of people, struggling to get closer. "Let me through! Let me *through*!" she cried out, barely able to see past the barricade of her own tears; she shoved and elbowed her way over, until at last she broke through the bulwarks of leprous flesh and saw them, saw Mama and Papa and Ben and Kimo and Sarah pressed against the wooden fence. When they saw her their hands shot out, they called her name, their bodies strained against the barrier. The crowd surged behind Rachel, she was propelled forward like a speck of foam on a billowing wave; her hand reached out, the tip of her fingers just grazing Mama's palm as she passed, the human wave carrying her away. Rachel would cherish that last touch for years to come, remembering the warmth of her skin, the way her big fingers almost closed around Rachel's, and the desperate love in Mama's face as it was stolen away from her.

■ ■ ■ ■

Part Two:
The Stone Leaf

■ ■ ■ ■

CHAPTER 5

The *Mokoli'i* shuddered as it pitched down into the face of a ten-foot wave, white water crashing over its bow and engulfing the pilot's cabin. For a moment the moon and stars appeared only as bright refractions in an explosion of foam; then, almost as soon as the sky cleared, the little steamer was lifted on the next swell, the wave rolling beneath it like lava squeezed from the cracked earth.

Inside the ship's cabin the crew and paying passengers were shielded from the cold, gusty spray of the Kaiwi Channel, but the same could not be said for the thirty-odd men, women, and children huddled in a wooden pen in the stern, not far from a similar enclosure holding twenty head of cattle. One man, sick to his stomach as were they all, heaved through the wooden slats of the pen. The bluster of the wind, the frightened lowing of the cattle, the tortured groans of the hull amounted to pure bedlam.

Rachel barely noticed any of it, and not just

because she was insulated by the press of bodies on every side of her. She paid little mind to the deck bucking beneath her like a maddened mule, or even to the stink of feces and urine that the exiles were forced to void where they sat. She was simply numb, her mind having absorbed all the fear it could, like a sponge saturated with water: after a while the fear became a constant, cold companion, a simple fact of existence.

She couldn't tell where she was going or where she had been; for ten hours all she'd been able to see was the starry arch of the night sky above. When she dozed, she dreamt that she was clinging to a piece of driftwood, floating ever farther from her family; then she would wake, and the reality, horribly, would be no different from the nightmare. She forced herself to stay awake until the stars were wiped away like letters on a blackboard and the bright moon became a pale ghost of itself.

First light fell on calmer seas, and now, through a bright morning haze, the exiles glimpsed land off the port side. Moloka'i. It was not a name spoken lightly in these islands. Sometimes it was called "Moloka'i of the potent prayers," known for centuries as the home of powerful sorcerers capable of praying men to death, of sending giant fireballs hurtling across the sea, fiery planets of destruction seeking out hapless victims.

Today the island was still an object of fear and fascination; but for very different reasons.

The cattle were quieting, the rumble of the engines now louder than the bluster of the wind. A few passengers, bound for the gentler shores of Maui, cautiously ventured out of the cabin, gazing curiously at what lay ahead.

The Kalaupapa Peninsula was a nearly flat, triangular promontory, shaped rather like a leaf, spat into the sea by a volcano which was now a spent crater at the center of the triangle. Six square miles of land — a dry plain, nearly treeless, matted with brown wintry grasses.

And rising up behind this stone leaf were the walls of a prison.

The huddled exiles gazed up, taking in the towering *pali* that rose so impossibly high above the peninsula: a sheer vertical cliff, green and densely wooded, reaching two thousand feet into the sky. Waterfalls spilled like tears down its face. It could scarcely be imagined anyone in the most robust health scaling its heights, much less the sick and the weak. The high sea cliffs tapered into the distance on both sides of the peninsula, extending the prison wall for nearly the entire length of North Moloka'i, precluding any hope of escape. The exiles gave up a collective sigh as they sailed into the shadow of the *pali,* standing like a judgment before them, immense and final. *Auwē! Alas!*

All around Rachel people began to stand up, their lament sounding in her ears. Despite her fear, Rachel felt a tickle of curiosity. She got to her feet, tugged at a man's pant leg. "Can I see?"

The man grunted and picked her up. Suddenly aloft on his shoulders, Rachel gasped as she looked up.

She saw what the others saw, and yet did not.

Rachel saw the lush green *pali* soaring high into the sky — bigger than anything she had ever seen, more beautiful than anything she could have imagined. She felt some of what she'd felt atop Mount Tantalus, but this was something more, something that reached inside to penetrate her cocoon of numbness and fear. Much later she would learn the word for it: *grandeur.* There was a grandeur to the *pali* that awed and moved her, and for the first time in days she actually felt something other than terror and loneliness.

A few hundred yards out the *Mokoli'i* cut its engines and rode in on the swells, tossing anchor and beginning the laborious task of landing passengers and cattle. The latter found themselves rudely dumped into churning surf and expected to swim to shore, herded by *paniolos* — native cowboys. Three of the cows evidently decided to swim back to O'ahu and were never heard from again.

The steamer's human freight was brought

ashore in rowboats bearing four or five passengers at a time. Rachel was in the third boat; in the distance she saw clusters of white, green, and red buildings scattered across the stony peninsula like bright coral heads on a rocky seabed. But as the landing drew nearer, so did the faces of those waiting on shore: a man whose features were nearly obscured by a moonscape of tumors; a woman whose deeply scored skin had the hard glossiness of a varnished wooden idol. For every person of normal appearance, Rachel saw two more whose faces looked as cracked and hard as the shell of a *kukui* nut.

Yet she wasn't as frightened as she had been that first day at Kalihi. Everyone in the crowd, despite the grim corruptions of their flesh, was smiling broadly — even those whose mouths were distorted into something Rachel would never have imagined *could* smile — their sometimes fingerless hands waving gaily at the incoming ship. Those ruined, gay faces somehow lessened Rachel's fear, more so when she spotted one face in particular.

"Uncle Pono! Uncle Pono!" Rachel waved joyously, and the thought draped itself around her, warm and comforting as a favorite blanket: she wasn't alone here.

Soon the waves were jolting the rowboat against the landing dock; a sailor from the *Mokoli'i* lifted Rachel up and onto a rusty ladder, which she quickly scrambled up. The moment her short legs touched land, Rachel ran into her uncle's welcoming arms. Pono scooped her up and cried, " 'Ey, look, it's my favorite niece! Fancy meeting you here!" Rachel wrapped her arms around her uncle's neck and wept with relief.

Pono wiped away her tears, and as he turned slightly Rachel now saw that he was standing alongside someone else: a woman almost as tall as Pono himself, in her fifties, with long gray-flecked hair, her only evidence of leprosy a contracture of her left hand.

"Rachel, this is my friend, Haleola. She's a *kahuna lapa'au* — a healer. You get sick, she makes you better."

Rachel sensed at once a calmness, a composure about the woman, quite unlike Mama's more mercurial temperament. Haleola smiled kindly and said, "*Aloha,* Rachel. Your uncle's told me all about you."

Rachel had never seen a real *kahuna* before. "You make sick people better?"

"I try."

"Can you make me and Uncle Pono better? So we can go home?"

Haleola said sadly, "No, I can't. I'm sorry."

Ambrose Hutchison — a part-Hawaiian patient who served as resident superintendent, second only to the head *luna,* R.W. Meyer, who lived on "topside" Moloka'i —

110

wandered over with an open ledger in his hand:

"Pono, what is it about you? You attract all the prettiest *wahines*." He winked at Haleola, then smiled at Rachel, pen poised to write. "And what's your name, miss?"

"Rachel Kalama," Pono answered for her.

"Rachel *Aouli* Kalama," she corrected him.

"Ah! Yes. *Aouli,*" Pono said, then muttered under his breath, "For all the good it's done you."

"And your age would be . . . twenty-eight? Twenty-nine?"

This drew the expected laugh and the scolding response, "Seven!"

"My niece," Pono said proudly. "She's come to live with her uncle!"

Rachel caught a glimpse of the first cargo — boxes, crates, bags — being brought ashore, and called out with the urgency of childhood, "My dolls! I need my dolls!"

"We'll get them, Aouli," Haleola said, and her use of the name somehow pleased Rachel. Ambrose excused himself to check in more arrivals, and ten minutes later Rachel's steamer trunk was lifted out of a rowboat and onto dry land. Between Pono's limp and Haleola's clawed hand, they had a time of it getting the trunk into Haleola's old wagon; but soon Rachel was snuggled up against her uncle, absorbing his familiar warmth and smell, as Haleola, at the reins, navigated the

111

narrow streets of Kalaupapa. It looked much like any little village in the islands: a general store, a butcher shop, several churches, even a Young Men's Christian Association. The homes were all neatly painted wood-frame houses, many bordered by little gardens of taro and other vegetables. But then Haleola turned onto a larger road, one which seemed to take them *away* from the settlement, and Rachel nervously asked her uncle, "Why are we leaving?"

"Oh, this is Kalaupapa. I live in Kalawao."

"When the government first started sending people here," Haleola explained, "the settlement was on the other side of the peninsula. Back then they thought cold weather was good for people with leprosy, and you can't find any place on Moloka'i colder than Kalawao! Except it turns out cold weather's *not* good for us, in fact it makes us sicker . . . so once the government buys up all the remaining land here, we'll all move to Kalaupapa."

Rachel was relieved. "How long have you been here?"

"A long time. Since eighteen hundred and seventy. My husband, Keo, was a leper, and I came to take care of him. By the time he died, I had the disease myself."

"It's nicer here than they said it would be at Kalihi," Rachel noted with surprise.

"Oh, it wasn't always so nice! When Keo

and I first came, the steamer landed us at Kalaupapa, so we had to walk three miles in the rain, to Kalawao. Thirty sick, hungry, tired people, and we had to walk! Keo said, 'How perceptive of them to notice that we needed the exercise!' " She laughed fondly. "Keo was quite an amusing fellow."

Pono whispered, "Not like me," and Rachel giggled.

"Then when we got to Kalawao, we were told there was no place for us to stay — we'd have to build our own houses out of grass. And until our first allowance of *poi* and meat arrived, we ate wild bananas, peas, even fern roots."

Alarmed, Rachel asked, "Do I have to eat roots?"

Haleola laughed and assured her she would not.

She didn't tell Rachel about the rest of that first day: how in Kalawao they passed a man wearing a kerchief, pushing a wheelbarrow filled with what looked like rags. But there was something about the way the rags jostled as the wheelbarrow bounced along, something that made Haleola stop and look back. At the threshold of a tiny shed, the man tipped the wheelbarrow and shook out its load: not rags but a man in ragged clothing who moaned as he tumbled through the doorway! When Haleola rushed over and demanded to know what was going on, the

113

kerchiefed man just shrugged and said, "It's the *end-of-life.*" Here the sickest people were discarded and left to die — unattended, and in utter squalor. Prostrate in their own filth, with neither blankets, food nor water, in a windowless room fetid with the stench of their own sores.

No, she would not tell Rachel about that.

"Do you have any *keiki*?" the girl asked hopefully.

Haleola nodded. "Three boys. Liko, Kana, and Lono. All grown up now, with children of their own."

"Can I play with their *keiki*?"

"They're not here, Rachel. They're back home, on Maui. I haven't seen my boys in twenty-three years."

Rachel could barely imagine the span of time, let alone the rest of it. "You haven't?"

"Coming to Kalaupapa is very expensive, Aouli. There's the steamer fare, and visitors have to bring their own food, enough to last two weeks. It's more than most poor families can afford."

"But don't you miss your boys?" Rachel asked.

"Yes," Haleola said softly. "I miss them very much."

Kalawao was markedly older than its sister village on the western shore, but though the wood-frame cottages were a bit dilapidated, the residents — many of them quite disfigured — sat outside, playing cards or working gardens, much as people did in any rural village in Hawaiʻi. Pono's house was a one-room plantation-style cottage even smaller than the one his family had lived in at Waimānalo. Rachel was ravenous after her long trip, so Haleola cooked a midday supper and they feasted on grilled fish and roasted coconut. Uncle Pono joked and sang (badly off-key), and for the first time in days Rachel felt safe and relatively happy. But as the fear that had kept her awake ebbed, exhaustion overtook her, and before it was even six o'clock Haleola suggested it might be time for bed.

When Rachel reached into her steamer trunk for her bedclothes she felt something unexpected. She pulled out a doll she'd never seen before: a handmade girl with a round face and long black hair, wearing a dark green dress with a long *kapa* skirt. Around her neck was draped a fragile *lei* strung with tiny shells, and pinned to her front was a handwritten note: *Love you, Papa.*

Rachel was delighted, but as she gazed at her new doll it made her sad to realize that her home was now one of those faraway places across the sea. She tucked the little *wahine* under her blanket with her, cradling it in her arms like a memory, and was instantly asleep.

Haleola noted the affection in Pono's eyes as he pulled the blanket up to cover his niece.

"She's very sweet, your Rachel."

Pono nodded. Haleola saw too the yearning this child evoked in him: "Have you heard from them? Your *keiki*?"

He shook his head. "Not lately. Their mother don't write too good, you know." It was always "their mother," never "Margaret," since the divorce decree. As though the speaking of her name were an entitlement he no longer deserved.

They agreed it was best she sleep at her own home tonight, so after a kiss goodnight Haleola set off on the short walk to her cottage. There was no sunset here in the long shadow of the *pali;* at three o'clock in the afternoon the sun was stolen over the top of the westernmost cliffs, and with it what little warmth it lent to Kalawao. Illuminated by oil lamps and torches, the village seemed even more remote and abandoned than it did by day; the *pali* was nearly invisible in the gloom, a deep well of darkness on every side. As she walked, Haleola heard evening come to Kalawao: as warm air fled the cooling earth, the wind rose up the face of the *pali,* making floorboards creak, windows rattle, causing tin cans to clang against one another and empty bottles to chime. Had she not heard these sounds every night for the past twenty-three years, Haleola might have thought them caused not by wind but by the passage across the plain of the *huaka'i-pō* — that ghostly procession of dead chiefs and warriors who marched across mortal terrain to the place on the shore where their souls would make the leap to the next world.

The night brought other sounds to Kalawao as well: the rowdy laughter of men and women consuming illegal "swipe" alcohol, and from behind closed doors, the sounds of appetite and thirst, desire and consummation. The sounds of people whose bodies might have been failing them, but would not fail, at least, in this one thing.

When she reached her house, Haleola stopped and looked back at the oil lamp burning in Pono's cottage. She thought of Rachel, of the supper she'd cooked for her and the laughter they'd shared, and felt almost as if she had been transported back to the days when her sons were small and the young family grilled fish caught off the Maui coast. It was a feeling she had never dreamed she would recapture. This little girl's smile had brought her something old and new, something lost and impossible. She watched as the oil lamp in Pono's house was snuffed out, and found herself looking forward to tomorrow.

Haleola was up at dawn to start her morning rounds of friends and neighbors who had need of her. Mrs. Pohaku was too stiff and pained with neuritis to work her garden, so

Haleola gathered some taro and sweet potatoes for her and then rubbed a salve made from guava leaves into her aching joints. Harriet Chu's asthma was greatly improved since taking an herb which grew abundantly here on Moloka'i. José Dominguez was running a high fever; Haleola gave him some tamarind seed to reduce his temperature and chopped 'awa root to help him sleep, but sadly she held out little hope for recovery. Few patients died from leprosy itself — most, weakened by the disease, were easy prey to other sicknesses like dysentery or pneumonia. Haleola had been performing tasks like these since before the Board of Health saw fit to assign — thirteen years after the settlement's founding! — a resident physician. But then as now, she whose name meant "house of life" often found herself a helpless attendant in this house of death.

Later, as she and Pono and Rachel sat on the steps of Pono's house enjoying a breakfast of eggs and *poi,* Haleola glanced up to see Ambrose Hutchison approaching the house — and alongside him one of the Catholic Sisters of Charity.

Haleola had known Ambrose long enough to recognize his unease. The sister was young, her delicate features starkly framed by her black and white veil; her expression, it seemed to Haleola, was that of a woman trying very hard to think only pleasant thoughts, and not succeeding.

"Good morning, Haleola. Pono." Ambrose smiled at Rachel, but Haleola had no trouble reading the distress behind the smile. "Did you . . . sleep well, Rachel?"

Rachel nodded, too busy eating her *poi* to do more.

"Pono, Haleola, this is Sister Mary Catherine, from the Order of St. Francis. Sister, this is Kapono Kalama, his niece Rachel, and Haleola Nua."

The nun smiled with what seemed genuine warmth. "*Aloha,* Rachel. Welcome to Moloka'i."

Rachel, still chewing, mumbled a hello around her food. Sister Catherine laughed, a girlish laugh. She couldn't have been more than twenty-two years old.

"Pono, I'm sorry about this, but . . ." Ambrose sighed. "I'm afraid we have to take Rachel with us."

Pono didn't quite understand. "What do you mean? Take her where?"

"To Bishop Home. She has to stay there, Pono; she can't live with you."

Pono jumped to his feet, glowering at Ambrose. "Why the hell not! She's my niece!"

Rachel put down her food, listening with alarm to the raised voices.

Ambrose said, "The sisters prefer that all girls under the age of sixteen reside in their care, at Bishop Home."

"For their own protection," Sister Catherine added, but this only inflamed Pono even more:

"My brother asked me to take care of her!" he shouted, and the sister flinched, lapsing back into silence.

Now Rachel began to cry, and Haleola squatted down to hold her. Pono glared at Ambrose. "You happy now? Maybe you like to sneak up behind her and say 'Boo'? Yeah, look, she ain't nearly scared enough!"

"Damn it, Pono, I don't —"

"Ambrose, there must be some mistake." Haleola's tone was calm and conciliatory. "Why don't we go speak with Mother Marianne?"

She can't be more stubborn, Haleola told herself, remembering earlier times on the island, *than that old mule Damien.*

Kalawao in 1879 was little changed from the village Haleola and her husband, Keo, had first come to nine years earlier. Life was still hard. The Hawaiian government provided each resident with a subsistence diet, but food shipments from Honolulu were subject to the weather and often delayed by storms or high surf. The sum of the average patient's worldly goods was little more than a blanket, a pot and pan, a knife, a spoon, and an oil lamp. And though there were now four churches on the peninsula, there were still many exiles whose only creed was "In this place there is no law" — who abandoned all pretense at civility, as civilization had abandoned them. Why fear retribution for theft, for rape, when there was no punishment worse than the one to which they were already condemned?

And then there was "the crazy pen."

The ramshackle grass house on the outskirts of town was a home for no one and everyone — a place for dancing, drinking, and losing oneself in the moment, because in Kalawao moments were all anyone could count on. A fire blazed outside as around it women danced the *hula:* not the decorous *hula* performed for kings and queens but a wildly sensual dance marked by a lusty gyre of hips.

In those vanished days, Haleola would sometimes watch from the distant shelter of a pandanus tree. She had no desire to join in, to drink from the calabashes of beer or to feel the rough hands of drunken men on her body. She was here for the *hula,* and for the prayers, spoken over a makeshift altar inside the house, which preceded it:

"Collect of garlands, Laka, for you!
Heed our prayer, 'tis for life;
Our petition to you is for life."

How many Hawaiians these days even knew

the *hula*'s patron goddess and her two faces, gentle Laka and fierce Kapo? Yet in exile these people danced to Laka, turned their damaged faces to her, as two-fingered musicians magically coaxed rhythm from homemade drums. So loud were those rhythms that Haleola was oblivious to the sound of hooves until they were almost upon her. A black horse galloped past her, and Haleola's spirits sank as she saw its rider yank on the reins, bringing the horse to a stop.

Father Joseph Damien de Veuster, thirty-nine years old and almost alarmingly robust, quickly dismounted, grabbing his walking stick from where he had lashed it to his saddle. He waded into the crowd outside the crazy pen, brandishing his cane like a sword, scattering the revelers.

"*Pau ia!* Be done with this!" The stocky, broad-faced man in the flat cleric's hat struck a grazing blow of the cane to a man blocking the entrance, then stormed inside. "Go to your homes!" he commanded in competent but undistinguished Hawaiian. His cane lashed out, overturning the calabashes of beer. "Are you men, or animals? God judges not the beast because it knows no better, but God's judgment *will* be made on you, and you, and you!" Most revelers fled; an unlucky few felt the sting of Damien's cane across their backs or hindquarters. The priest stepped up to Laka's altar, brought his stick down onto the altar draped with *maile* vines and smashed it to pieces.

Haleola was baffled by this man — the same she had seen earlier that day, cutting two-by-fours amid the skeletal frame of a dormitory for Kalawao's orphaned children. This "Kamiano," as he was called, built houses for the sick, dressed their sores, comforted the dying. What kept him here on Moloka'i, year after year, a healthy white man tending to lepers? And why did he care if people on their way to the grave drank beer and danced the *hula*?

Haleola turned away in disgust, joining the disgruntled revelers as they straggled back to Kalawao.

Keo was just awakening when she got home, and in the morning light she saw and grieved for the changes time and disease had wrought. His body, once strong and lithe, was now frail and enfeebled; his face, always more endearing than handsome, had been savaged by the *ma'i pākē,* his mouth little more than a gash in ulcerated flesh, the disease having stolen his once impish smile. Keo's had been the smile of a trickster, a rascal. Her parents hadn't liked him, they thought she deserved better, but she'd known she could not have found any better husband, anywhere, than her Keohi. And as the young rascal became a successful merchant and devoted father, she took pleasure in reminding her parents that she had been right.

But Keo could still smile with his voice. "Ah, it must have been quite the night at the crazy pen," he said, amused. "Did you dance the *hula*?"

"Oh, yes. I was shameless. The men could not keep their eyes off me, I was so sinuous and beautiful."

She laughed, but Keo did not. He said simply, "You are. You are beautiful," and the love in his voice almost made her cry.

At breakfast she fed her husband with her hands, scooping *poi* with two fingers. The ruined borders of his mouth closed on them, his tongue licking off the paste.

But he was oddly silent between bites, and when he was finished he said, matter-of-factly, "Last night I heard the drums of the night marchers."

Haleola laughed to dispel the fear that rose in her: "You heard the drums of the crazy place, silly old man."

But Keo just shook his head.

"I saw their torches in the distance. I heard their drums," he insisted. He added quietly, "I have heard them every night for the last week."

He raised the stump of a hand to her cheek. "I love you, my wife. I'm sorry I was not strong enough to resist this disease. I'm sorry that it brought you here."

She took his hand in hers. "Stop it. I'm the

kahuna, and I say you're fine."

Keo laughed, but by evening he was feverish, alternately sweating and chilly. When tamarind seed failed to reduce the fever, Haleola tried the sap of a hibiscus tree; but Keo's skin remained afire.

In desperation she sought out the settlement's new physician, Dr. Emerson, who accompanied her back to the house but refused to enter it, standing in the doorway and examining Keo from a distance. He gave her something he called salicylic acid, but this too proved no help.

Keo was semiconscious and she was holding him, telling him she loved him, when another figure appeared in the doorway — knocking, in *haole* fashion, on the door frame.

She was surprised to see it was the priest, Kamiano.

"May I come in?" he asked in Hawaiian.

"My husband is very sick."

"I know," Damien acknowledged. "Would he . . . like to receive the sacraments?"

"We are not Christian."

"It's never too late to come to God. I can baptize him now, before . . ."

"No, thank you," Haleola said coldly.

The priest took a step inside. His tone grew more emboldened. "For your husband's sake, consider. Would you deprive him of the joys of heaven?"

125

Haleola ignored him. Damien's tone became harsher. "Would you condemn him to everlasting perdition?" he asked. "A moment in hell contains a thousand tortures. Is that what you want for your husband — eternal torment? Because make no mistake," and here his voice fairly boomed, "that is precisely what awaits him if he dies a sinner!"

Something cold and angry broke loose inside Haleola.

"My husband is a good man!" she cried, as vehemently as Damien. "An honest, loving, decent man! He gave me three beautiful sons — sheltered us with his tenderness — never let us go hungry or homeless! And now you tell me he's a 'sinner,' that he's going to burn in some fiery place forever, you dare to tell me that?

"If that is your God, Father Kamiano, your Jehovah, who would condemn a kind and tender man to hell for the sin of not believing in him — then I shall follow my Keo to hell, as I followed him to this one, and together we spit on your God and his heaven!"

She spat enthusiastically at his feet, and for once in his clerical life Damien was speechless.

"Leave our home! Leave my husband to die in peace!"

Damien looked at her evenly and honestly, nodded once, then did as he was asked.

Keo died within the hour.

Haleola prepared his body for burial in the traditional manner, wrapping it in layers of *kapa* cloth, and dug a grave behind their house. She placed into the grave a haunch of the roast pork that Keo enjoyed so much, as well as some items of clothing; then called out to his ancestors, *"Haku, Ano, 'eia mai kou mamo, Keohi."* (Haku, Ano, here is your descendant, Keohi.) Tenderly she placed Keo's bundled body in the grave, his head aligned toward the east, and said, "Keo, here you are departing. Go; but if you have a mind to return, here is food, here is clothing. Come back, and know you are always welcome in my heart."

She closed the grave over him, burned a small piece of sandalwood, and spoke a last prayer: *"Aloha wale, e Keohi, kāua, auwē."* (Boundless love, O Keohi, between us, alas.)

That night she couldn't sleep, and went outside to take in air sweet with the fragrance of the pandanus fruit that grew near the *pali.* At the edge of a bluff she looked down at foaming surf breaking violently on jagged rocks, as it always did at Kalawao: never a gentle meeting of land and sea, always a noisy thrashing, as if in restless sleep.

She heard footsteps behind her, and a moment later she heard someone speaking utilitarian Hawaiian: "My condolences. For your husband."

She turned. Damien's voice was no longer

a thundering bludgeon, but soft and subdued. "He must have been a fine man, to have been loved so much."

The hellfire preacher was gone and in his stead was the builder of orphanages. "You must understand," he said. "Christianity is an evangelical religion. It is our duty to share the glory of it. If I allowed someone to die without repentance, it would be as if I saw a man trapped in a burning house and made no effort to save him."

Haleola shook her head. "Your religion is all about being miserable, and wretched. Ours had time for play, and joy. How is this an improvement?"

To her surprise, Damien laughed — a very warm, very human laugh. "Well, it's not *all* wretchedness and sin," he said, "but if all you know of it is my talk of fire and brimstone, I can see how you might think so."

Not wanting to like this man, Haleola said sharply, "You come here to show us the error of our ways. You treat us like children."

He laughed again.

"But you *are* my children!" he said cheerfully. "Had I stayed and served in my native Tremeloo, my congregation there would have been no less my children." He smiled. "Why do you think they call us Father?"

Haleola sighed. She almost preferred the bombastic, righteous Kamiano — with him, at least, you could win an argument. She searched his face for some clue to this man. "I came here to *kōkua* my husband; I couldn't have done anything else. But why did you come?"

"Like you. To *kōkua.*"

"And to save our poor wayward souls?"

He shrugged. "I'm a practical man, Haleola. It's true, I want to save souls. But it's a poor church that cares only for what happens to a soul after it leaves this life. If I can provide some comfort, some ease of life for those about to lose theirs, how could I hesitate to try?"

"Aren't you afraid," she asked, "of becoming a leper yourself?"

Damien paused, then answered quietly, "Sometimes I think I already am." He added, "But if God chooses for me to share the burden of leprosy with my children, then I will rejoice in it. Whatever God does is well done."

After a moment Damien bowed his head respectfully and left. She watched him go, then turned back to the sea. Far down the coast she saw the flicker of torches, heard the distant sound of drums blown up on the wind. It was probably the bonfire at the crazy pen being lit, the *hula* drums being sounded; but Haleola chose to believe it was the marchers of the night, come to take Keo to the *pō,* the world beyond. "Come back," she told him, softly into the wind, "if you are of a

129

mind to." But he never did.

Fourteen years later, a lanky man with a similarly impish smile had landed at Kalaupapa, his cane digging into the hard ground as he limped up the rocky embankment. As he reached the top, he straightened, looked around, stabbed the tip of his cane into the earth as if planting a flag and announced, "I claim this land in the name of me, and hereby declare myself a Provisional Government!"

Everyone at the landing — including Haleola and Ambrose Hutchison — laughed. The man gave his name to Ambrose as Kapono Kalama, "but you can call me President Pono."

Ambrose smiled. "Do you have a place to stay, Mr. President?"

Pono said, "Why, I thought I'd just seize *your* property."

Haleola smiled to recall it. She was still gazing at Pono, thinking of the ways he was like Keo and the ways he was not, when Ambrose's wagon arrived at Bishop Home. St. Elizabeth's Convent, a modest one-story white building with green shutters, was home to the Franciscan sisters. Behind it stood four pleasant, whitewashed cottages, two of which served as dormitories for leprous girls — many of whom, clad in identical wine-colored dresses, were out playing kickball on the lawn. They quickly encircled the wagon, eager to meet the new arrival. Sister Catherine suggested that perhaps Rachel would like to play with them while Pono and Haleola spoke to Mother Marianne. As Rachel kicked the ball back and forth with the other girls under Catherine's watchful eye, another nun — older and considerably less friendly — took Pono and Haleola to the convent. They couldn't enter, of course, but the sister showed them to lawn chairs and a table, where they were shortly joined by Mother Marianne Cope — a small, handsome woman with a serene smile. She turned to the nun who had brought them. "Sister Victor, would you mind bringing some tea and honey for our guests?"

Sister Victor, it was apparent to all, was not pleased at the request; she gave her Mother Superior a sullen nod, then disappeared, grumbling, into the convent.

Mother Marianne wasted little time getting down to business. "Inasmuch as you've been here less than a year, Mr. Kalama, perhaps you weren't aware that we at St. Elizabeth's have been charged by the Board of Health with the safekeeping of all leper girls under the age of sixteen, even as Brother Dutton cares for the boys.

"Mrs. Nua, I gather you've been at the settlement almost from the beginning. You've certainly seen what can happen to children in Kalawao — forced into servitude, into prostitution, abused or violated . . ."

"Kalawao is a different place than it was twenty years ago," Haleola pointed out.

"Not different enough, I'm afraid. Men and women still brew and consume vast amounts of alcohol. The dreadful *hula* is still danced, and promiscuity has not, alas, gone out of style."

Just then Sister Victor returned carrying a serving tray holding three teacups, a jar of honey, and a pot of tea. She half-placed, half-dropped the tray smack onto the table, jostling the teapot precariously.

"Tea," Sister Victor said brusquely, then turned on her heel and vanished back into the convent.

Mother Marianne winced slightly. "My apologies for Sister Victor. She's been feeling out of sorts for . . ." With a rueful sigh: "About two years, now."

She poured each of them some tea — their teacups were different from hers, no doubt only for lepers — then picked up a slip of paper she had brought with her. "Perhaps this will help. Mr. Kalama, do you read English?"

Pono nodded tightly and took the paper. At the top of the page were the words *Rules and Regulations for the Bishop Home;* the first paragraph read:

The "Bishop Home" has been established

for girls of all ages and unprotected females, married or unmarried, who, having contracted leprosy, have become helpless and have no relatives at the Settlement able properly to care for them.

The nun helpfully pointed out the third paragraph.

It is compulsory for girls arriving at the Settlement under the age of sixteen years to enter the Home, unless they have parents, near relatives, or guardians at the Settlement who are competent to, and who will take proper care of them.

"Ah!" Pono said, seizing the opportunity to produce his own document. "It's very clear, then! My brother Henry asked me to take care of her. Wanted her to live with me. Right there, see what he says to me?"

The Reverend Mother scanned Henry's letter. "Yes, I see."

"It appears to me," Haleola said, "that that letter makes Pono Rachel's guardian."

"Yes," Mother admitted, "that clearly *is* her father's intention. However, as you see, the rules plainly require *'relatives or guardians . . . who are competent to, and who will take proper care of them.'*"

Pono bristled at the intimation. "You think I can't take care of my own niece? That I'm too sick?"

"Mr. Kalama, I'm sure you love Rachel. But as much as you love her and might try to protect her, could you watch over her every moment of the day? Could you guarantee no evil-minded man would force himself on her as she plays by the *pali*?

"Here she would be shielded from all that. By removing her from day-to-day contact with immorality and paganism, we save both her body and her soul."

There it was: Kamiano's favorite word. She means me, Haleola realized. Not just who I am, but . . .

"By immorality," she said, "do you mean Pono and me?"

Mother Marianne looked genuinely regretful. "I'm sorry," she said. "But the blunt fact, Mr. Kalama, is that you *are* a married man. And you are currently living in an unchaste manner with a woman not your wife. That is not, in all candor, the sort of moral influence which I can call proper and competent to care for Rachel. And I would be remiss in my duties if I allowed Rachel to live with such an influence."

"My wife divorced me!" Pono snapped. "I had nothing to say about it!"

"The Church," she reminded him, "does not recognize divorce."

Haleola spoke up, carefully considering her words.

"Do you wonder, Sister, why so many at Kalawao are . . . 'unchaste'? It's not hard to understand. A woman feels a man inside her and feels life. The act they engage in is the one from which all life springs, and for that moment they can feel that *they* are living, not dying." She looked the nun squarely in the eyes. "Would you take that away from us too, Sister? As everything else has been taken?"

Mother Marianne's cheeks were pink with embarrassment, but her composure did not slip.

"God has not been taken from you," she replied evenly. "By forsaking the pleasures of this world, you assure yourselves the joys of the next."

Her tone was not harsh; it was even gentle, in its way. Pono, sensing the nun's intractability, said, "Can I at least *see* my niece occasionally?"

"Of course. You may visit her anytime you wish."

She smiled and stood, the discussion clearly over. As Haleola walked away with Pono, she had already resolved to help him compose a letter to the Board of Health contesting the convent's claim on his niece — even as she wondered how on earth they would explain this to Rachel.

"Did you like playing with the other girls?" Haleola asked her when they returned to the front lawn. Rachel nodded enthusiastically. "Well, good. Because you're going to stay here with them for a while."

"But I don't want to," Rachel said without a moment's hesitation. "I want to go back with you and Uncle Pono."

"Oh, you'll see plenty of us," Haleola said, hoping that wasn't a lie, "but . . ."

Pono said, "It's just for a little while," but Rachel recalled how she was supposed to have been at Kalihi only a little while too. "Nobody wants me!" she said angrily.

Haleola took her hand in hers. "*We* want you, little Aouli. We do! But so do the sisters. They think you'll be happier here in these nice houses, with other little girls to play with." Out of the corner of her eye Haleola saw the young sister, Catherine, watching, a look of what seemed honest pain on her face.

"We'll come visit tomorrow," Haleola promised. She and Pono each hugged Rachel, kissed her on the cheek, and turned to go.

But the sight of their imminent departure panicked Rachel, and she ran screaming after them. She grabbed Pono by the leg, clinging to him desperately: "No! Please! I'll be good, don't *go!*" Her heart breaking, Haleola bent down and wrapped her arms around the frightened girl. "Ssshh, sshhh," she comforted her, even as Pono gently stroked the girl's face. "We'll be back, Aouli. I swear it, I swear it on my husband's grave." She held her until the tears ran their course and Rachel's fear abated . . . then reluctantly handed her over to Sister Catherine, who gently took her by the hand and led her away. Rachel turned around for one last glimpse of her uncle, watching as he and Haleola got into Ambrose's wagon, the ocean framed behind them, rain clouds gathering like smoke above the water — and as the wagon rattled away down the dusty road, Rachel was stubbornly determined that she would hate it here.

CHAPTER 6

Sister Mary Catherine Voorhies was grue-somely ill. She had spent the better part of an hour here in the infirmary, dressing the sores of leprous girls and women, outwardly exhibiting nothing but compassion and good cheer. With thick swabs she cleansed pus from ulcers as though she were polishing tableware, scooped maggots from dead flesh like ants, snipped away skin as if cutting cloth for a dress pattern. She smiled into ravaged faces, said prayers with the devout or the merely frightened, made small talk — "talked story" — with all of them, and somehow managed to keep the bile from rising too far up her throat. As if the sight of worms infest-ing a living person's body wasn't enough, the uniquely nauseating smell of the sores — the death-gasp, as it were, of millions of leprosy bacilli — nearly made her gag, her esophagus constricting against her will. It was only then she allowed herself a moment's relief. Walking across the room for a bandage she didn't need, gratefully stealing a breath of fresh air from an open window, she would then return to work before anyone could guess how weak and frightened she truly was.

With each new patient she was convinced that her strength would give out and she would be forced to surrender the contents of her stomach — as she had, to her mortification, on the steamer trip from Honolulu two weeks before. If there was anything less decorous than a vomiting nun, she was hard-pressed to think of it.

There had been nothing in the life or experience of Ruth Amelia Voorhies, of Ithaca, New York, to quite prepare her for what she found on Moloka'i. Her father had owned a bakery and her family had enjoyed a relatively comfortable, uneventful existence — right up until the day Harold Winchell Voorhies shot himself in the head with a pistol, for reasons unknown. He left his family financially sound but otherwise sundered. Ruth's mother never stopped blaming herself, for what she didn't know; her brother's anger fell on everyone but the cause of it, forever beyond his reach; her sister Polly, two years older, became pregnant by a married man and was sent away to relatives in Albany, where the child was given up for adoption.

Ruth grappled with her grief in her own way, her parish priest showing her the balm and comfort of God; within a year she had entered the novitiate. After taking her vows, she served two years in the Motherhouse in Syracuse before volunteering for the third contingent of Franciscan sisters bound for Hawai'i.

Before coming to Moloka'i she thought she knew something of pain and suffering.

She knew nothing.

She finished bandaging a young woman's sores, then vigorously washed up with carbolic acid. Her hands looked almost as red and raw as a leper's. She took a deep breath of air from the window above the sink and felt a little better. She reminded herself that St. Francis himself had been afraid of leprosy; and despite, or because, of that fear, he had kissed a leper's face.

She forced a smile and turned to the next patient, a girl of perhaps fifteen who held out a bandaged arm. "Hello," the girl said shyly.

"Hello. I'm Sister Catherine. Forgive me, but I'm afraid I don't know everyone's name yet."

The girl's face was free of blemishes; it was hard to imagine there was anything wrong with her. "I'm Noelani."

"A pretty name for a pretty girl. Shall we get that bandage changed, Noelani?" She started unwrapping it, folds of cloth coiling on the floor at her feet.

But as the last swath of linen dropped away,

it revealed not an ulcerous sore but a ring of dead flesh, black as char, surrounding a gaping cavity in the skin . . . exposing the raw, corded muscle beneath.

Catherine let out a horrified cry.

She didn't know which was worse, the sight of the wound or the realization that she had just revealed herself as a fraud. Immediately Sister Leopoldina was at her side:

"Oh! Sister," she said, putting a hand on Catherine's arm, "I'm sorry, did no one tell you? It's gangrene, the poor dear cut herself and didn't know it — they can't feel it, you know, it became infected and Dr. Oliver dressed it himself. I'm so sorry, you should have been told!"

Catherine felt the bile rising in her throat and feared that this time she would not be able to keep it down. "I'm sorry . . . may I —"

A quick nod from Leopoldina sent Catherine rushing outside. She ran behind the cottage, dropped to her knees . . .

But nothing happened. Her nausea abated; she breathed in the fresh ocean breeze and felt a bit calmer.

"Sister Catherine?"

She looked up. Sister Victor, of all people, was gazing down at her, a frown amplifying her normally sullen expression. "You look dreadful," she said bluntly.

"Thank you," Catherine sighed. "That had

somehow escaped my notice."

Face softening, Sister Victor bent down beside her. "It's difficult, isn't it?" she said with atypical gentleness. "At times almost more than one can bear."

Relieved to hear this echo of her own fear and doubt, Catherine asked, "How *do* you bear it?"

Sister Victor's lips pursed in an unhappy smile.

"Like this," she said. "Like you're bearing it now."

Catherine got shakily to her feet. "How long have you been here, Sister?"

"Two years. Heaven help me, it feels like twenty."

Leopoldina now appeared from around the corner of the infirmary. "How are you feeling, Sister? Can I get you anything?"

"No, I'm all right. I'm sorry, Sister, I shouldn't have left like that."

Leopoldina smiled with her usual cheer and kind-heartedness. "Nonsense, nothing to apologize for. Why don't you go to the convent and lie down for a while?"

"No, I'm fine. I'll be right back in, just give me a moment." She gave what she hoped was a reassuring smile and watched Leopoldina disappear again around the building.

In a low voice Sister Victor said, "I think she'd smile like that even if she were sitting in a boiling pot, being picked at by cannibals."

Catherine laughed despite herself. "That's terrible."

"You see, Sister? That's all we have to do. Learn how to smile in the cannibal pot, and life would be so much easier." She patted Catherine's shoulder, went on her way.

Catherine took a deep breath of the briny air, then returned to the horrors inside the pleasant little whitewashed cottage. Somehow she made it through the rest of her shift, and was puzzled when at the end of it Leopoldina took her aside. "Sister, I'd like to show you something."

"I know what it can be like here, for a newcomer," Leopoldina said as they crossed the lawn to the cottage that served as the girls' dining room. Inside three young girls sat at an expensive Westermeyer piano, pecking out simple tunes on the keys. "Mr. Stevenson bought this for us," Leopoldina explained, and indeed Catherine had already heard of the visit to Moloka'i, five years before, by the famous English writer Robert Louis Stevenson. He'd played tirelessly with the girls, talked story with residents — endearing himself to everyone with his openness, humor, and the simple respect he afforded the lepers, whom he treated as people he wanted to get to know and not as objects of fear, pity, or revulsion.

143

As Leopoldina rummaged for something in a cabinet drawer, Catherine watched the three girls somehow making music with hands whose fingers were being slowly stolen away, the bones resorbed back into their bodies. But they giggled as they poked out off-key renditions of "Chopsticks" and "Frère Jacques," and Catherine marveled at their perseverance and good cheer.

"Ah, here we are," Leopoldina said. She handed Catherine a slip of paper. "This was written for us by Mr. Stevenson while he was here." On the paper were penned eight handwritten lines:

To see the infinite pity of this place,
The mangled limb, the devastated face,
The innocent sufferers smiling at the rod,
A fool were tempted to deny his God.

He sees, and shrinks; but if he look again,
Lo, beauty springing from the breast of
    pain! —
He marks the sisters on the painful shores,
And even a fool is silent and adores.

"When we first saw this," Leopoldina told her, "I said to Mother, 'Why, it's beautiful! It's lovely, isn't it?' "

"But Mother looked uncomfortable; embarrassed. 'Yes, of course, it is,' she replied. 'But . . .'

" 'But what?' I said. 'Isn't it flattering?' "

" 'Mr. Stevenson is a dear man,' Mother finally said, 'but we're not the ones to be flattered.' And she bid me to look out on the lawn at the leper girls who were running on lame feet, playing croquet with crippled hands.

" 'There is beauty,' she said, 'in the least beautiful of things.' "

The girls' dormitories, Rachel was aggrieved to discover, were not bleak prison cells but clean, cheerful bungalows providing shelter — or as Mother Marianne would have had it, sanctuary — for some eighty girls and women. The walls were whitewashed and hung with dozens of pictures in a variety of frames, the beds neatly made with frilly comforters; at the head of each bed were private altars of cards, letters, photographs, dolls. Rachel immediately became the center of attention among her new roommates.

"Hi, I'm Emily, who are you?"

"You're Rachel, right? You kick pretty good."

"That's my bed, you can't have it."

"Wanna play marbles?"

"What toys do you have?"

Rachel stubbornly resisted all attempts to get her to play, or anything else that might contradict her single-minded dislike of this place. Sister Catherine issued Rachel a wine-colored uniform and assigned her a bed; Rachel refused to put on the uniform and only grudgingly accepted the bed when the groundskeeper, Mr. Kiyoji, came in with her steamer trunk and needed someplace to put it.

Emily, half-Chinese and half-Hawaiian with a long cascade of black hair down her back, bounced gregariously onto Rachel's bed. "So where you from?"

Rachel grudgingly admitted she was from Honolulu.

"Ooh, big city girl! I'm from Kapa'a. On Kaua'i."

There were only two girls who hadn't approached Rachel, both bedridden and asleep on the other side of the room, and now her curiosity got the better of her anger. "Are those two real sick?" she asked Emily.

Emily gave them a sad glance. "Yeah. That's Josephina. And Violet." She added in a low tone, "They won't be here much longer."

Rachel wasn't quite sure what she meant by that and didn't inquire further for fear Emily would tell her.

One of the sisters now entered the room and announced that it was time for class; a collective groan went up as the girls assembled in a ragged line for school.

Class was held only three hours each day. The books were old and had DISCARD stamped in red ink on the inside front cover;

the crayons were neither as plentiful nor as colorful as those provided at Fort Street School; and the classroom lacked even a globe of the world! After school came lunch, and after lunch there were chores to be done — sewing, washing dishes, mopping floors. This did nothing to endear Bishop Home to Rachel. After chores the girls were allowed to play, but because of the worsening storm they had to do so inside. Rachel used the time to unpack. Her roommates, all enthusiastic collectors of dolls, gathered round to admire hers. Rachel reluctantly accepted their compliments and let them examine her *kabuki* dancer and Mission dolls and *matryoshka.*

By the time the girls finished dinner, the storm had become quite frightful: the wind howled around their dormitory, uprooting shrubs and snapping off tree branches, which then slammed into the side of the cottage so loudly that Rachel jumped and screamed.

"It's okay," one girl assured her, "it's just the devil-winds."

" 'Devil-winds'?" Rachel repeated, eyes wide.

"Ah, they just call 'em that 'cause they're so nasty," Emily said. "Come in alla way from the Pelekunu Valley."

"Last year a devil-wind ripped a porch roof clean off!" someone else added gleefully. The walls of the cottage groaned under the howling onslaught of wind. The constant howl, the alarming sound of branches snapping in two like breaking bones, terrified Rachel.

Then to make matters worse, after lights were snuffed out for the night her roommates decided that this was the *perfect* time to tell ghost stories in the dark.

"There's a *hala* tree in Kamalo," a girl named Hazel intoned with the requisite quiet dread, "and a long time ago, two *keiki,* boy and a girl, used to play under it, and talk about how they were gonna get married when they were older. 'Cause they loved each other very much, you know?

"But then the girl's family had to move — on account of their taro farm was flooded and no good — to O'ahu, where her papa could get work. Well, she tells her boyfriend and he's real sad. After she leaves Moloka'i, he cries, night after night, to think he'll never see her again . . . and late one night, while everybody's asleep, he takes his sister's jump rope and he brings it to the old tree, ties one end around his neck and the other to a branch — and —"

She made an upward yanking motion with her fist that made Rachel jump, then opened her hand and slowly moved it back and forth, miming the swing of the boy's body.

"After that, whenever anyone plays under that tree . . . they start choking. They grab themselves, like this" — her hands closed around her own throat — "and they fall to

148

the ground, like something's strangling 'em!

"Soon as they're taken out from under the tree — they stop choking. They're fine, like nothing ever happened. Pretty soon no one goes near the *hala* tree 'cause they know about the choking ghost, 'ey? Except . . .

"Years later, a lady comes to Kamalo. Says she grew up there; says she's looking for a boy she used to know. Lonely lady. Never married. Somebody tells her, 'The boy you seek is under the *hala* tree at the edge of town.' The people who tell her, they follow to make sure she's okay, to pull her away if she starts choking. But she sits down under the tree, leans up against the trunk, closes her eyes. No choking, no strangling. The people see a smile come onto her face, and they hear her say, 'Oh. Oh, how I've missed you!' And then nothing else for maybe ten minutes. Then she opens her eyes, gets up, and leaves.

"Nobody ever chokes under that tree, ever again. A week later, somebody sees a story in the Honolulu paper 'bout a lonely old woman who came home from a short trip . . . borrowed a jump rope from a little girl next door . . . and next day they find her hanging inna kitchen, and her face looks like this."

Hazel contorted her face into a death's-head grin, and half the girls, including Rachel, screamed — even as the other half giggled appreciatively at a fine tale well told. But before anyone could start another Sister

Albina stalked in and put an end to talking story for the evening.

Rachel couldn't sleep for fear a choking ghost might slip under her bedcovers and strangle her. She'd heard ghost stories before, but before she could always call out for Papa or Mama, and Papa would come and comfort her or Mama would walk in and snap, What silliness is this! Get to sleep or I show you something *really* scary!, and either way Rachel felt better.

But Papa wasn't here, or Mama, and all at once Rachel felt their absence so keenly that she began to cry. She wept into her pillow to muffle her grief, but as she lay there half-sobbing, half-suffocating, she heard a whisper.

"Rachel?" Rachel turned over, found Emily standing at her bedside. "You okay?"

Rachel wiped her nose, nodded. "Guess I got scared."

"It was just a story. You know, for fun."

"Yeah." Rachel looked at her a moment, then said, "How long you been at Kalaupapa?"

"Year and a half."

"Your mama and papa, they ever come to visit you?"

To Rachel's surprise, Emily laughed. "Who cares? Not me," she said indifferently. "My papa, he used to hit me for every little thing. Broke my nose once, right here; see?" She pointed, went on cheerfully, "I go to Kalihi, they take care of me, nobody hits me. I come here, we get good food, the sisters look after us, the sores I get ain't half as bad as the ones my papa'd give me. Happiest day in my life was the day I got leprosy." She gave Rachel a sisterly pat on the arm. "See, it's not so bad here."

As Emily returned to her own bed, Rachel reached out and grabbed her newest doll. She hugged it close, feeling the rough *kapa* skirt against her skin like the stubble on Papa's face when he kissed her.

The next day was clear and bright when Haleola and Pono arrived for a visit. Rachel was ecstatic to see them, and more than a little surprised. So was Haleola: she had half-expected to be barred from Bishop Home by Mother Marianne, but found that none of the sisters were anything but cordial to her. Perhaps they didn't know that Haleola was such a promiscuous siren, and a *kahuna* to boot!

Pono drew Rachel into a croquet game on the lawn with the other girls, but he put a bit too much elbow into his first swing and sent the ball hurtling through space and off the convent grounds. The girls cheered as it disappeared from view and Sister Leopoldina had to go chase it down. Haleola thought this a dull and somewhat pointless game, even for

151

haoles, but she dutifully knocked the ball through the wire hoops. Rachel's team might have won had it not been for Pono, who, having gotten rousing cheers and laughter on his first try, couldn't resist getting more: this time the ball went crashing into the side of the convent, narrowly missing both a window and Sister Leopoldina. Haleola snatched the mallet away from him. "The object of this game," she snapped in whispered Hawaiian, "is not the killing of luckless nuns."

The afternoon went by pleasantly enough, though Rachel cried again when her uncle and his friend had to leave. Back in Kalawao, Haleola helped Pono compose a letter to the Board of Health requesting that Rachel be allowed to live with him, as well as a letter to Henry Kalama suggesting that he write the Board as well. Although the letters would go out on the next steamer, it might be weeks before any response came from Honolulu. In the meantime she and Pono tried to visit Rachel as often as they could, always under the watchful gaze of one of the sisters.

The day the steamer left with his letters, Pono was complaining of a heaviness in his limbs common to many leprosy sufferers; Haleola made an herb tea to bolster his strength and they agreed she should go alone to Bishop Home that day. There she found Rachel and a dozen other girls about to leave for the beach — one of many excursions the sisters organized to relieve the tedium of life at Kalaupapa. It was being led by Sister Catherine, who saw the crestfallen expression on Haleola's face and invited her to join them: "I could use another eye or two on this group." Sister Victor was to have assisted her but was in one of her "moods," as Mother called them, stubbornly refusing to leave the confines of her room.

Catherine took them up the coast to Papaloa, a sandy fringe of beach bordering the settlement's many cemeteries. Some girls wore flannel bathing suits with skirts and pantalettes; most merely stripped down to their underclothes. They danced around lapping waves, built sandcastles on the beach, or body-surfed the waves. Even Rachel was enjoying herself; Catherine clearly saw that the only moments the girl seemed at all content were those spent in Haleola's or Pono's presence. Rachel triumphantly rode a big swell, waving to Haleola, only to be dumped moments later into the churning surf — but wasn't under long before popping out again, wet sand matting her hair.

Catherine loved the ocean too; the girl called Ruth would have liked nothing more than to join them. Her habit couldn't have been any more cumbersome than those bathing suits! But of course it was out of the question and she had to be satisfied to watch — just as well, since she could be more vigilant

153

out of the water than in it.

A terrifying thought came to her, then: what if one of the girls got into trouble? A muscle cramp, an undertow? Then she *would* have to go in after them. What if she couldn't save them because she was flopping around in a sodden habit? Suddenly she no longer took delight in the girls' play; she wanted them all out of there, now, this instant!

Haleola read the panic in her eyes and said, "Don't worry. *Keiki* here learn to swim before they walk."

Catherine blinked in surprise. "Am I so transparent?"

"Clear as water," Haleola said, and her smile made Catherine smile as well.

"Well," Catherine sighed, "at least it's safer than croquet." This brought a hearty laugh from Haleola.

"I understand you knew Father Damien," Catherine said, and Haleola nodded. "What was he like?"

Haleola thought about that a moment, then replied, "Very . . . stubborn." Catherine laughed at this. "It's true, he was the first to admit it. He'd say, 'Oh, I'm just a stubborn Belgian,' when he was fighting with the Board of Health or his superiors in the church — trying to get lumber to build new houses, or more taro, or medicine." Haleola paused. "Kamiano, he did great good for the people here," she said at last. "No one can dispute that. He was a good man, a kind man.

"But you know, so was my husband Keo. So were hundreds of other men who lived and died here. Yet sometimes it seems the world is more moved by the death of one white priest than by the passing of hundreds, thousands, of Hawaiians. Everyone knows Damien's name now, but will anyone remember these girls, other than you and me?"

Catherine watched ten-year-old Lucy race past and into the sea, the water hiking up her baggy pantalettes to reveal legs riddled with sores. Rachel got dunked by another wave but quickly surfaced again, a beard of sand stubbling her chin.

"If only the sea could just . . . wash it all away," Catherine thought aloud.

Rachel ran back into the surf, paddling out to the first set of breakers.

"It does," Haleola said. "For a while."

After half an hour, a waterlogged Rachel returned to shore where Haleola agreed to help her make a sandcastle. Looking for just the right real estate on which to build, Rachel's eyes popped at something she saw.

"What's that?" she cried out, running on ahead. When Haleola caught up, Rachel was already poring over the odd assortment of stones she'd found: some long and flat, some thick and squat, none more than six inches high, arranged in a kind of diamond pattern. Even Rachel could see that their shapes were

155

not natural, that people had chipped away at them to create miniature bricks, slabs, pillars.

"Ah," Haleola said, "it's a *heiau*. A shrine." Rachel still looked puzzled. "A holy thing, like an altar in a church. People prayed here."

"What's it doing by the ocean?"

"Fishermen built it here to pay respect to the gods of the ocean. Ku'ula was the greatest, he had dominion over all the gods of the sea."

Rachel frowned. "Mama says there's only one God."

Haleola sat down beside the ruins of the tiny shrine and smiled. "Well, maybe now there is. But not so long ago, people here prayed to lots of gods. There was a god of the sea; a god of mountains; a god of mists, and rain, and wind. There were even gods for things that you couldn't see: a god of healing, a god of sleep."

"Why so many?"

"Well, each was responsible for different things. For instance, La'ama'oma'o was a goddess of winds and storms. If a fisherman was going out on a cloudy day, he might pray to her to grant him safe passage around a storm. If he needed to feed his family he'd pray to Hinahele or to Ku'ula to put many fish in his net that day.

"There's a story about Ku'ula," Haleola said, "from my home, Maui. It was said that from time to time a god would assume human form and live among us here on earth. One of these was Ku'ula, who a long time ago lived on East Maui, where he was caretaker of a fishpond."

Rachel said, "I saw fishponds in Waikiki!"

"Ah, good. So you're an expert. Well, Ku'ula, he was the best fisherman in all the islands. His pond was always full of fish; his village never went hungry.

"But some people can't stand anyone having something they don't, and one of these was a chief named Keko'ona — who lived right here on Moloka'i. This chief was a man of great power, and his body could take on many shapes. One of these was that of an eel — *three hundred feet* long!"

Rachel's eyes widened. "Really?"

"He was horrible to see," Haleola said. "A huge black body speckled with white — a mouth as big as your head, with teeth like a saw blade! He swam across the channel between Moloka'i and Maui, his tail whipping from side to side with such ferocity he sent waves crashing to shore — swamping beaches, overturning canoes, drowning men, women, children!

"Finally he reached Ku'ula's pond, which teemed with fish. The giant eel wriggled through a narrow inlet into the fishpond, opened his huge mouth, and greedily ate everything in his path. In less than half an hour he'd eaten *every* fish in the pond!

157

"He was very pleased with the evil he'd done, and it tasted good too, but when he tried to leave the pond . . . well, can you imagine what happened?" Rachel shook her head. "He'd eaten so much that he could no longer get through the inlet and back to the ocean!

"He tried to hide in a deep hole, but Ku'ula baited a huge hook with roasted coconut meat — so delicious he knew the greedy eel wouldn't be able to resist taking it. Keko'ona's jaw clamped down on the coconut meat and the hook tore a bloody hole through his lip. He thrashed helplessly, trying to throw off the hook . . . but the hook was attached to two strong ropes and at last the eel was dragged to shore. And before it could change shape, Ku'ula smashed a rock into its head, shattering its jaw!"

Breathlessly, Rachel asked, "Did he kill it?"

"Yes he did. Ku'ula's people gutted and ate the eel; the only things left were the shattered bones of its jaw. Ku'ula turned the jaw to stone, and you can still see it today near the shore, the great mouth with its jaw gaping open, forever hungry.

"And that, little Aouli, is why Ku'ula was the god of all the fish in the sea and why men prayed to him."

Rachel was duly impressed, and after they had completed their sandcastle she returned to the ocean, though not to body-surf. Now she lay face down on the water's surface, drifting on the currents, floating like a mist above a silent forest of coral; and whenever she saw the shadow of a crevice in the coral she would poke a piece of driftwood into it like a spearfisher going for her prey. The first, second, and third pokes met with no resistance; but on the fourth try something gray and fast erupted from the hole, water churned and teeth flashed, and Rachel swam for shore faster than she ever swam in her life, propelled by equal parts fear and excitement, terror and delight.

She returned to Bishop Home to find an envelope bearing three letters, fresh off the latest steamer.

Dear Rachel,
   Mama said I should write and tell you how sorry I am for what I did and how I didn't mean it. I cried so much the day you left. Everybody looks at me in school and nobody wants to eat with me. Becky Thornberry said mean things to me and I hit her and she started screaming because I touched her and they sent us both home for the day. I hate it here now, we may go to a different school next year. Well that's all, I hope you are O.K.

Your sister,
Sarah

The other two were both penned in Mama's careful, missionary-taught cursive:

Dearest Rachel,

Mama misses you so much, she thinks about you all the time. James and Ben miss you too, they send you their love. I know Uncle Pono is taking good care of you so I don't worry. Remember to say your prayers at night and put all your love and trust in the Lord God Jehovah, He will put all things to right.

Love,
Mama

Mea aloha, Rachel,

Did you find the doll in the trunk? I hope you like it, when you look at it think of your family here in Honolulu. How do you like living with your Uncle Pono, I bet you are laughing all the time with him around.

Papa's got to ship out on a steamer next week but I promise to write you from every place I visit. When I get back Mama and I will take the steamer to Kalaupapa to see our baby. I miss you so much little girl. But when I get lonely for you I'm going to sing that song you like so much, and when you get lonely for me you do the same, O.K.?

Papa

Then at the bottom of the page, a hastily scrawled P.S. in Papa's own simple block lettering:

Don't sing that song to nobody but Pono, O.K., baby?

Rachel read the letters and then read them again. Halfway through a third time, she heard a thin little voice say, "You got letters?"

She looked up. Most of the girls were out playing; the question had come from one of the two bedridden girls, the other, Josephina, being deep in a sound sleep.

Rachel went to the girl, saw her face up close for the first time: nose and lips swollen to twice their normal size, skin pocked with raw red sores. She thought of the girl she had seen her first day at Kalihi, the one who made her scream and run; but this one filled her with no fear, only sadness. "Hi. I'm Rachel."

"I'm Violet." She smiled, then asked shyly, "Can I read them? I don't get letters."

Rachel handed them to her. Violet read Dorothy's letter first, then when her eyes had reached the bottom of the page she started again from the top, and only then moved on to Henry's. She smiled with a kind of wistful pleasure; and when she'd read both letters twice over she looked up at Rachel and asked, "What song?"

Rachel hesitated, remembering her father's admonition, but decided he wouldn't mind her making this one exception. In a low voice she sang a chorus of "Whiskey Johnnie" and Violet's eyes widened in delight; she clapped and laughed so much that Rachel sang her the next three verses.

Rachel kept her company a while longer, until the other girls began to drift back into the cottage and it was time for chores. She made a point the next morning to spend some more time with Violet, but when she got back from school that afternoon she saw that Violet's bed was empty, the mattress stripped of its linens. And as the days went by without Violet, Rachel understood what she couldn't comprehend at the king's funeral — feeling an absence even worse than that of her distant family, an absence that was like a sore that wouldn't heal.

CHAPTER 7

At breakfast, after morning Mass, Sister Victor shared a table with Catherine in the convent's dining room and apologized for "abandoning" her the day of the beach trip. Over a meal of tea and hardtack biscuits she owned up to her "black moods" and how at times they so overwhelmed her she couldn't bear to see another human face: "I know what Leopoldina calls it. She says I'm 'sulking' — as though I'm a truculent child! But I swear, I just can't get out of bed. My nerves are so raw, I feel as though the slightest stimulus would be intolerable."

It was storming again outside, the windows rattling with each chilly gust of wind; Catherine cupped her hands around her tea, grateful for its warmth. Only she and Victor lingered over their breakfasts; the other sisters had already begun the day's chores. Sister Mary Victor Macardle took a sip of tea. Her eyes were downcast; there was none of her usual sullenness in her face, only weariness.

"Back in Syracuse I worked with Mother for nine years, in St. Joseph's Hospital," she said quietly. "I spoon-fed children weak with scarlet fever and typhus, and never thought twice about it. I assisted doctors in surgeries, amputations, and never had so much as an upset stomach over it.

"Mother once told me I was the best nursing sister in the hospital," she said, more pain than pride in her voice. "She commended me many times."

"Dear God," she said with scant reverence, "how I hate Hawai'i! Had I stayed in Syracuse I'd be enjoying the fruits of a life well spent — the esteem of my colleagues, and not their contempt."

"Sister," Catherine said, "we don't —"

"You do. Even *I* do." Almost from the moment she arrived on Moloka'i, she admitted, she had been seized by a bleak despair which rarely loosened its grip on her. There had been no shortage of death and disfigurement at St. Joseph's, so at first she failed to understand why the lazaretto should affect her as it did. But at St. Joseph's, whatever the horrors she saw in the course of a day, all she had to do to escape them was to step outside. There was a whole other world just beyond the hospital walls: the clatter of streetcars, the comfort of crowds.

But here at Kalaupapa all was leprosy: leprous sores to be cleaned and dressed, leprous children to be schooled and fed. Leprosy was woven into the fabric of their daily lives, a black thread that could never be cut. Even the fissured heights of the *pali* seemed to look down on her with the attenuated, leonine features of a leper's face.

"It got so I couldn't bear touching the poor things, let alone dressing their wounds. Isn't that odd that I should be so frightened — I who had no fear of tuberculosis or typhus?" She smiled wanly. "Mother saw what was happening and put me in charge of housekeeping for the convent instead. But then she asks me to serve tea to lepers and I want to run, I become angry and sullen, I . . ."

"Sister, we're all afraid of it. Remember how you saw me the other day? Down on my knees outside the infirmary?"

Victor nodded. "Yes. But you went back in."

"Because of what you told me."

Victor shook her head. "No. Not because of me." Her body sagged under a sudden weight; her gaze seemed to turn inward, eyes fixed on something beyond Catherine's sight.

"Isn't it strange," she said, not quite addressing Catherine, "how one so afraid of contracting a fatal malady . . . should so earnestly wish for death, as well?"

There it was, just as she herself had described it: the descent into a black mood, like a swimmer sinking into tar. She made the sign of the cross but it seemed rote, affording her no real comfort.

"Sister —" Catherine started to say, but Victor abruptly pushed aside her teacup — and stood up.

"I'm sorry," she said, no longer able or willing to look Catherine in the eye. "I shouldn't be burdening you with this. Forgive me, Sister." She turned to go.

"Sister, wait!" Catherine stood, but her companion was already on her way out of the room. Night had fallen on her again, and she hurried into her private darkness.

Catherine sat down again, listening to the stutter of rain on the roof, wondering at what point rational fear of contagion turned to unreasoning dread, and whether she would know it when she came to it.

She dressed sores for the next hour and a half, projecting even more false cheer than usual. When she was finished she scrubbed her hands until they hurt.

Helping Leopoldina clean the dormitories while school was in session, she entered the cottage for the youngest girls and found two of them still there. Josephina was abed and asleep, as usual; it wasn't expected she would live to see spring. But sitting listlessly on her own bed, fully clothed, was the normally quite energetic Rachel Kalama.

"Rachel, why aren't you in school?"

Rachel just shrugged.

"Aren't you feeling well?" Catherine asked.

Rachel shrugged again. "I guess."

Catherine sat down beside her. Rachel's face, usually so animated, seemed so languid, her eyes dim. Catherine started to reach out to feel her forehead . . .

And hesitated — just for a moment, but long enough to startle and dismay her. She forced herself to press her palm against Rachel's forehead. There was no fever but for the one Catherine felt in her own cheeks.

"Rachel, is something wrong?"

The question hung in the air for a moment before Rachel blurted out, "Did Violet die?"

Violet? the nun thought, for a moment unable to place the name; and then she remembered. The little girl by the window. They had laid her to rest the other day, Father Wendelin and Mother Marianne her only mourners.

Catherine nodded. "Yes. I'm sorry, she did."

Rachel took that in, thought a moment, and asked, "What happens to you when you die?"

"Why, you go to Heaven. To be with Jesus." When Rachel didn't respond Catherine nervously filled the silence. "Don't feel badly for Violet, Rachel. She's happy now. God called her to Heaven."

Rachel said, "Why?"

Catherine blinked. "Why what?"

"Why did God call her to Heaven?"

The question startled Catherine. "Only God knows that, Rachel. But I'm sure He had a good reason."

Rachel persisted: "Why can't we know what it is?"

Catherine's pulse quickened.

"Well, we . . . we will, someday," she said. "When God calls us to Heaven, too."

"Why can't we know now?"

Catherine took a breath. "Because we can't."

"I think God is mean," Rachel said angrily, "to not tell us."

Catherine flinched. "He's not. He —"

"He killed Violet!" Rachel shouted. "I *hate* him!"

As if she were merely an observer, Catherine watched herself lash out and slap Rachel across the face — hard.

"Don't say that!" she cried, and even Rachel could hear the panic in her voice. "Don't ever say that!"

Tears sprang to Rachel's eyes, but the hurt inside her was far worse than the stinging of her cheek. She ran. Out of the dormitory, into the rain, without a look back.

The awfulness of what she'd done now came home to Catherine; but she felt anger too, a storm raging within her as violent as the one outside. The voice of remorse told her to go after Rachel and apologize, but another voice said, *No excuse for it, got what was coming,* and then she heard Rachel asking *Why? Why can't we . . .* Shut up! she commanded the voices, stop it! She ran from the cottage and into a wet wind, her skirt billowing as she dashed across the muddy lawn to the convent. She tore into St. Elizabeth's, ignoring a greeting from Sister Albina, hurrying to the tiny one-room oratory that was their chapel. Inside she slowed her pace as she approached the altar, dropped to her knees. She crossed herself and began to pray.

Praise the Lord, O my soul, in my life I will praise the Lord: I will sing to my God as long as I shall be . . .

She fairly shouted the prayer in her head, seeking to drown out all but the psalm she conjured from memory.

Blessed is He who hath the God of Jacob for his helper, whose hope is in the Lord his God: who made heaven and earth, the sea, and all the things that are in them . . .

The babble of confused voices grew weaker, softer. She took a deep breath, finding solace in the words.

The Lord looseth them that are fettered: the Lord enlighteneth the blind. The Lord lifteth up them that are cast down: the Lord loveth the just. The Lord keepeth the strangers, he will support the fatherless and the widow . . .

Anger and doubt erupted again like lava, emotions entirely inappropriate for this place, this act. She sprang to her feet and bolted from the chapel, startling a sister about to

169

enter, and retreated to the safety of her room. There she fell again to her knees, knitting her hands together in a tortured mimicry of prayer. Whenever she felt the anger bubbling up she would stop, take a few minutes to compose herself, then start again; but though the anger slowly cooled she found that oozing up between the words of contrition and adoration was a troubling fear. Fear of herself and what she was capable of, what she had done to that little girl; and fear that perhaps Sister Victor was right, that contagion was all around them.

Rachel fled into the pouring rain, her only thought to put as much distance as possible between herself and Sister Catherine. The wind lashed her hair around her neck as she raced between buildings; she was relieved to see on glancing back that the sister was not pursuing her. She took refuge behind the girls' dining hall, under its scant overhang and behind a waterfall of rain sluicing off the roof. She drew her chin up to her knees and allowed herself some tears. She hated this place — hated the rain and cold and wind. She hated it because Mama and Papa weren't here, and because Uncle Pono was but she couldn't live with him. And because people died here, and now she knew what that meant.

She sat and she cried, thunder booming in

170

the distance, and after a while heard someone call her name. She looked up. One of the sisters stood aghast on the other side of the curtain of rain: "Child, what *are* you doing out here! Have you no sense?" She grabbed Rachel roughly by the hand, mistaking the tears on her cheeks for rain, and led her back to the dormitory where she made Rachel towel her hair and change into dry clothes. The sleeping girl, Josephina, was still dozing her life away, and all at once Rachel wanted to go to school.

As she listened to arithmetic lessons she had already learned at Kalihi, she looked out the window and imagined the outline of O'ahu behind the clouds bunched on the horizon, and wondered if Sarah and Ben and Kimo were in school right now. She would have given anything, any number of days of her life, just to hear Sarah call her "Little Miss Shoe."

The rain wore on. When afternoon came and there was no sign of Haleola or Pono, Sister Leopoldina suggested that the main road was either flooded or too muddy to navigate. But Rachel wasn't so sure. Uncle Pono hadn't been to Kalaupapa all week and whenever Rachel asked about him, Haleola just said he was tired. Rachel was becoming adept at sensing when something was going unsaid by adults: it was as if there were an invisible object sitting amid their visible

171

words and Rachel was learning to judge its shape and size by feel alone.

"If Uncle Pono's sick, can't *I* go visit *him?*" Rachel insisted, but Leopoldina just shook her head and Rachel had to spend the afternoon inside, playing with dolls. During dinner the rain finally slacked off. As Rachel left the dining hall she was preoccupied, thinking of Pono; only when she nearly bumped into her did she realize that she was face-to-face with Sister Catherine.

"Rachel?" The guilt in the nun's face was apparent even to a child. "May I speak with you a moment?"

Rachel gave her a sullen shake of the head and strode past her. The sister looked even more hurt, but Rachel found it hard to care. No matter what Sister Catherine was feeling, at least *she* could leave here anytime she wanted!

Haleola placed a jar under the latest leak in Pono's ceiling, less than half a foot from the bed on which he lay. The resident physician, Dr. Oliver, sat on a small stool by Pono's bedside, palpating his patient's groin. "When did you first notice it was painful to urinate?"

"Last year," Pono told him. "Middle of June."

"I gave him some herbs," Haleola said, "and it went away for a while."

"When did it start again, Mr. Kalama?"

"We're gettin' pretty close, Doc, you can call me Pono."

Oliver smiled. "When did it start, Pono?"

" 'Bout a week ago. And it comes out this funny color. Pink, kinda smoky."

The doctor nodded again, examining Pono's abdomen. Haleola watched nervously. When Oliver first arrived at Kalaupapa she had heard rumors about his sobriety, or lack thereof, but in his two years here she had never seen him touch a drink, and he certainly seemed sober enough now.

The *haole* stood. "Well, Pono, it appears you have an infection of the kidneys. As inconvenient as it may be, I need you to drink as much water as possible." He took a small bottle from his medical bag. "Salicylic acid, for the fever. And complete bed rest is essential."

"Hell of a rest I'm gonna get," Pono said with a wan smile, "getting up to piss every half hour."

"Ah, well, we in European medicine have a marvelous invention for that," Oliver said, picking up one of the jars on the floor. "We call it a bedpan."

Pono laughed as he took the jar. Haleola made sure he took one of the doctor's tablets with a glass of water, as Oliver disinfected his hands with a splash of carbolic acid from his medical bag; then she walked out onto the porch with the doctor and asked, "What kind

173

of 'infection'?"

Oliver shrugged on his overcoat, his cheery tone turning grim. "I'm not sure. But I've seen this before with leprosy — malaise, fever, blood in the urine, discomfort in the loins — the disease weakens the body's defenses, makes one more susceptible to other infections."

Haleola nodded. This idea that sickness was the result of tiny, nearly invisible creatures swarming in the blood would have seemed ridiculous but for the fact that Dr. Mouritz had once shown her, under a microscope, the pink, tube-shaped "bacteria" discovered to be the cause of leprosy by the Norwegian scientist Gerhard Hansen. There were, Mouritz believed, three forms of the disease: one which attacked primarily the skin, and which spread rapidly and horribly throughout the body; one which attacked the nerves, progressing more slowly and with less deformity; and certain borderline cases, a mix of the two. Haleola had the neural form; Pono, unfortunately, the former.

Dr. Oliver said, "I *have* seen this sort of kidney infection spontaneously remit — clear up on its own."

"And if it doesn't?"

He frowned. "Complete renal failure is not uncommon either. See to it he rests, and takes plenty of water."

"Thank you for coming," she said, "in such

miserable weather. Will you be able to get back to Kalaupapa?"

"No, I'll just wait out the rain. Plenty to keep me busy in the hospital here."

"How is Napahili?" Dr. Oliver and his wife Ho'opi'i had a young son, Richard Napahili Oliver. She expected the mention of him to lighten Oliver's grim expression, but it only seemed to darken it.

"He's fine, I suppose. I hope." He gazed into the gray heart of the downpour and said quietly, "I pray to God I made the right decision, bringing him here." Haleola didn't know for certain what had brought the doctor to Moloka'i, but she'd heard rumors that he was enormously in debt from a failed plantation on the Big Island, and the position of settlement physician did pay $250 a month.

"We do our best to isolate him from any possible contagion," Oliver said fretfully, "but there's still so much we don't know about this disease. Is it transmitted by touch? By breath? By sexual congress? Who's to say the air, or the very soil beneath our feet, isn't a source of contagion?"

Oliver forced the guilt and apprehension from his voice and smiled tightly. "Well. You know where to find me. Call for me if there's any change." He tipped his hat to her and dashed through muddy streets to the Kalawao hospital.

Not trusting herself yet to present the best

175

face to Pono, Haleola stood outside listening to the drumming of the rain on the roofs of the aged buildings around her. When the time came to move to Kalaupapa, she would miss Kalawao. There was a stark splendor to this craggy coastline, enormous waves crashing white against black rock, sprays of foam exploding in the air like fireworks. Even the *pali* was often in motion here, boulders dislodged by rain or wind tumbling down its face. In Kalawao only two things were truly stationary: two small islands, 'Ōkala and Mōkopu, standing offshore. Mōkopu was long and humped; 'Ōkala was pointed, like the tip of a spear thrust up out of the ocean. Both were covered with a green mantle of fan palms. Centuries ago, for sport, Hawaiian men would braid together those palm fronds and leap from the islands' summits, the leaves slowing their descent into the water as they glided down like birds. No one lived on the islands; they didn't evoke the friendly reassurance of neighbor isles like Maui or O'ahu, but they had weathered the storms and seas of centuries, and they were a comforting link to a time when men flew like birds, a time before leprosy.

She went inside to find Pono fast asleep. Haleola pulled his blanket up to his chin and put a hand to his forehead: he was still feverish. In his sleep he muttered Margaret's name. Haleola kissed his brow, sat down by his bedside, and re-read a letter which had arrived yesterday but which she had yet to show him.

R. W. MEYER, ESQ.
KALAE, MOLOKAI

Mr. Kapono Kalama
Leper Settlement, Kalawao, Molokai
February 1, 1894

Dear Mr. Kalama:

The Board of Health has forwarded your letter of 29 December 1893 to me, as their agent here on Molokai and as Superintendent for the Leper Settlement.

Additionally, I am in receipt of a letter from Mr. Henry Kalama on the same subject.

While I appreciate and commend your feelings for your niece Rachel, I trust implicitly Mother Marianne's judgment in all matters relating to the welfare of minors at the settlement. She has only the best interests of the poor afflicted children at heart, and you can take comfort in the knowledge that it is your niece's health and safety that is uppermost in the minds of the Board of Health and its agents. What you may miss in the way of day-to-day contact with your niece will be rewarded a hundredfold with the preservation of her physical and moral well-being.

I am communicating these sentiments to your brother in Honolulu as well.

Yours Sincerely,

R. W. Meyer

That evening, after Rachel's rebuff, Catherine retreated again to her room and to her private, troubled devotions. For the hundredth time she asked forgiveness for striking Rachel, but her prayers continued to be anxious and uncertain. When, after half an hour, there was a knock at her door, she was relieved to answer it.

Sister Victor stood in the hallway, her hands buried in her robe. "I hear you've been having a bad day."

Catherine started. "Why do you say that?"

"Oh, the usual convent chatter. A person craves a little quiet in the privacy of their own room and everyone gets to talking."

"Talking?" Catherine was mortified to think her sisters were gossiping about her, but Victor just smiled: "Don't worry, you'll get used to it. Let's take a walk."

On their way out Catherine imagined that everyone they passed was staring at them, thinking them crazy malcontents. She barely noticed that her friend was leading her off the convent grounds and toward the beach.

"I like walking by the ocean," Victor said, obviously in better spirits. The light of a crescent moon leaked out from between storm clouds. "Especially after a rain."

"What are they saying about me?" Catherine asked.

"Does it matter?"

"Yes!"

"They think you're excitable. You were seen running out of the chapel."

"Excitable or unstable?"

"*I'm* unstable. You're merely excitable." Sister Victor sat down in the lee of a large sand dune that blocked their view of the convent — and the convent's view of them. Catherine sat beside her.

Sister Victor reached into the pocket of her robe, and to Catherine's surprise pulled out a small bottle with a long fluted neck — and two water glasses! She handed a glass to a puzzled Catherine, who asked, "What's that?"

"Mr. Kiyoji calls it *ume sake,*" Sister Victor said, planting her glass in the sand as she uncorked the bottle. "Plum wine. Relatives send it to him from Japan."

As Sister Victor started to pour, Catherine demurred: "Sister, our vows —"

"We took vows of chastity, poverty, and obedience. Which one of those precludes a sip of wine?" She added confidentially, "Father Wendelin has cases of zinfandel shipped in from California, and I assure you

179

it's *not* all for sacramental purposes."

After a moment Catherine said, "Well . . . just a sip." Victor poured a splash of golden liquid into the glass. Catherine took a sip and found that it was deliciously sweet, almost like fruit juice.

"Why, this is quite light and refreshing, isn't it?" She took another sip. "And I don't taste much alcohol."

"Um," said Sister Victor, topping off Catherine's glass, then filling her own. "So. What did happen today?"

Catherine blushed. "I . . . lost my temper with one of the girls. That's all." She didn't elaborate and Sister Victor didn't inquire further. Catherine took another taste of wine. "You know, this is really good," she said.

She gazed out at the waves breaking close to shore, their foaming crests luminescent in the moonlight. She thought of Rachel and the other girls swimming out there and felt a warm glow in her stomach at the memory.

After a moment she said, "Sister?"

Sister Victor was in mid-swallow. "Hm?"

"Why do you suppose . . ." Catherine hesitated, took another sip of wine, then asked, "Why does God give children leprosy?"

Sister Victor thought a moment and replied, "Why did He visit troubles upon Job?"

"To test his faith, of course. But these are children! Why do they need to be tested? And even if they did . . ." She was feeling emboldened. "What kind of God would inflict such a horrible death — a horrible life — on children, just to test their faith in Him?"

Her cheeks felt hot; in fact, she was perspiring.

Sister Victor refilled her friend's glass and said quietly, "Have some more wine, Sister."

But Catherine was feeling unbearably hot. She took another swallow of the cool drink but it didn't seem to help. Nothing would, she suspected, except . . .

Catherine got to her feet.

She felt dizzy; the world swayed as if it were a top spinning on a table of night. Surprising even herself, she threw off her veil and felt the cool night air on her head.

Sister Victor blinked like a bird. "Sister? What —"

Catherine began removing her habit, the heavy robe and long skirt heaping around her ankles, and now stood on the beach clad only in her underclothes, much to Victor's dismay: "Here, now — what are you doing? Put that —"

Catherine ran down the beach, the sand wet and cool beneath her feet, the water lapping at her ankles. A wave crashed into her, cold and hard like a rebuke, but she kept on running and after a few moments the chill seemed merely bracing. She was chest-high in the ocean, now, and with a sense of exhilaration felt the rocky bottom slip away

181

beneath her; all at once she was floating, suspended in space. She laughed as a wave rolled over her, soaking her short brown hair, the salt stinging her eyes. Giddily she lay back on the pillow of a wave, stretched her arms out on either side of her, and let the cradling surf take her wherever it wished. The sweet cleansing water washed over her, soaking through her cotton underclothes, making them billow in the water like the wings of a jellyfish. It felt just as wonderful as she imagined it would from shore.

She waved at Sister Victor, beckoning her to come in too, but the older woman remained resolutely on dry land.

"Sister Catherine!" She sounded more than a little panicky. "Please, come back!" Catherine ignored her. She stared up at the sky and smiled. Haleola was right: for a while, at least, the ocean washed everything away.

It took Sister Victor half an hour to lure Catherine out of the water, during which time she disposed of the wine bottle by tossing it far out to sea. When Catherine finally stumbled out of the surf — pleasantly exhausted and still thoroughly besotted — Victor coaxed her back into her habit and veil. They sneaked into St. Elizabeth's via a back door, only a trail of droplets betraying their passage. The water would dry up, but if anyone saw them —

Catherine started to giggle.

Sister Victor clapped a hand over her friend's mouth and propelled her down the corridor and into her room. Once prone, Catherine collapsed into a dead sleep. Victor undressed her, tucked her in, and with the relief of one who had managed to stuff the genie back into the bottle, quietly closed the door behind her.

Catherine slept well, but woke badly.

She opened her eyes shortly after dawn, sunlight stabbing through the window curtains. She sat up. Her head throbbed as if it had been used as a croquet ball.

Oh my Lord, she thought as dim memories of the night before came floating back to her. She now realized with dismay that the only thing less decorous than a vomiting nun was a drunken nun.

For a time it seemed she might well be both, but somehow she managed to quell her nausea. It took half an hour for her to approximate her normal demeanor, and she was ten minutes late to Mass. In chapel Sister Victor scrupulously avoided her gaze; as Catherine knelt, she silently offered a prayer of contrition to the Lord. But as ashamed as she was of her inebriation, she couldn't quite bring herself to repent the dip in the ocean.

Later, at breakfast, a slightly more composed Catherine noticed that Sister Leopoldina was missing her usual smile and good cheer today. "Something wrong, Sister?"

Catherine asked as she poured herself a cup of black coffee.

Leopoldina nodded gravely. "One of the girls ran away last night."

"Wilma? Hazel?"

"No. Younger. You know Rachel Kalama?"

Catherine felt the blood drain from her face, and without a word of explanation to Leopoldina she threw down her breakfast and ran from the dining room, to be sick.

CHAPTER 8

She had to see Uncle Pono. Something was wrong and no one would tell her what, so she'd just have to go see for herself, that's all. And if nothing *was* wrong, well, the sisters would come for her and she would be punished — but she would still have seen Uncle Pono. It was only three miles from Kalawao to Kalaupapa; it couldn't take more than an hour to get there on foot. Why, she'd walked farther back when she and her brothers would go to Waikiki to play!

True, the nuns peeked in with annoying regularity every hour, but that still gave her an hour's head start, assuming they even noticed her absence before dawn. Rachel waited until midnight — when Sister Albina poked her head inside, satisfied herself that all was well, and withdrew — then sprang out of bed, dressing as quickly and quietly as she could. She stuffed her dolls under the bed covers; the lump they made under the blanket wouldn't pass close inspection, but it was better than nothing. She opened the nearest window, careful not to awaken her roommates, and climbed up onto the window sill. She swung her legs over; pushed herself off; and dropped to the ground.

She was out.

It was as exciting as if she were stowing away on a boat to Hong Kong. Quietly she closed the window behind her, thrilled with her own daring.

But as she turned away from the window, she was startled by the profound darkness in which she now found herself. The sky was clouded, starless — as though an earthen bowl had been lowered over the peninsula — land, sea, and sky congealing into one great inky mass. She couldn't even tell in which direction she was looking!

She fought off a surge of panic, remembering that the window looked down on the convent's back lawn. And as her eyes adjusted to the gloom she began to make out a few flickering lights — oil lamps burning in nearby houses. Using them as faint stars to guide her, she hurried across the lawn — it was sodden and muddy, as her sandals rapidly became as well — and onto what the sisters referred to as "the Damien Road," the road to Kalawao.

She was excited again; the darkness, broken by an occasional light on either side, was now a friend and conspirator. After a few minutes she looked back and saw only a faint glow from the convent behind her — and, thankfully, no sign of Sister Albina taking up the chase.

But the road was even muddier than the lawn, and the farther she went, the deeper her feet sank into it. The mud oozed between the sandal and the heel of her foot, weighing down the shoe as she tried to take another step; after five minutes she decided she'd make better time barefoot, so she slipped off her sandals and carried them.

Soon the last lights of Kalaupapa were behind her. On either side of the road she could make out faint impressions of tumbled rocks and spiky lantana scrub, but that was all. She had never been afraid of the dark, but then she had never known a dark like this before. It seemed as if the only thing in the world she could truly see was the wet, shifting ground beneath her feet.

And it was *cold* — as cold as mud could get without actually freezing. She saw now how a wagon wheel might become hopelessly mired in this, and wondered if Sister Leopoldina had been right — maybe this was why Haleola and Pono hadn't come. Maybe she should turn around right now, hide her muddy clothes, and sneak back into bed; with luck no one would know she had even been gone.

She turned to look back, but now there was

187

only a black void behind her; even the small length of road she had just traveled had been swallowed up by the darkness.

She told herself that if she went back somebody was likely to see her, or at least find her dirty clothes. She would be punished, and have nothing to show for it. If she kept going, she'd eventually get to Kalawao and at least have the comfort of a few hours with her uncle.

She felt the sting of Sister Catherine's hand across her face, then turned and continued down the road.

After ten more minutes the mud was ankle-deep. Her feet were growing numb with cold and the wind was picking up, gusting like a blade through her light dress. She had "chicken skin" — goosebumps — and not the good kind you got from a ghost story. Each step took more and more effort; she was tiring already and hadn't even covered that much ground. She picked up her pace. . . .

She slipped, pitched forward, and fell face down into the road.

She wasn't hurt, but got a nice mouthful of mud. It tasted even worse than it smelled. She lay there coughing and spitting it out, then slowly got to her feet. Her entire body was plastered with mud; it covered her like a cold, heavy, foul-smelling suit of clothes.

She sank back down into the mud and

started to cry. She wanted to go home. She wanted Papa to come pick her up out of the mud, she wanted Mama to yell at her for getting her clothes dirty. She wanted Uncle Pono! It wasn't fair. Why couldn't the nuns just let her live with him, why did she have to *do* this in the first place?

Then when she had cried herself out, she picked herself up and stumbled on.

She felt like a storm cloud so sodden with rain it might burst at any moment. She had no idea how much time had gone by: one stretch of road looked no different than the last. For one awful moment she wondered if she were walking in a circle; could she even tell?

And then up ahead she finally saw something other than rocks, mud, and bramble.

On her left a narrow trail, splitting off from the main road, cut through the lantana. Rachel rushed toward it, nearly slipping again in her haste; she stood at the trail head, looking up. . . .

Into more darkness. All she could make out of the trail was the next three or four feet. She tried to think: when they'd left Uncle Pono's, she remembered, the wagon *had* traveled a little ways on a smaller road before turning onto the main road to Kalaupapa. So if this was that small road . . . it might lead straight to Uncle Pono's house!

She stood there, trying to decide which way

to go. The wind cut her, and it was starting to rain again.

Papa, where are you? You'd know which way to go!

She felt another lick of rain on her cheek . . . then turned onto the narrow trail.

After several minutes she realized the trail was sloping gently upwards, and the rain grew so heavy that she was forced to take refuge in the surrounding lantana scrub. The shrubbery did afford some shelter, but it also gave off a vile smell; the leaves were prickly and painful, and when the rain eased up after ten or fifteen minutes she was only too happy to continue up the trail.

The higher she climbed, the bigger breaths she seemed to take. Now she started to notice debris scattered along the trail: a broken calabash; a spent shell casing from a rifle; a bandanna, caught on the branch of a shrub, flapping like a flag in the wind. She stared joyously at the bandanna — just a few more minutes and she'd be safe and warm in Uncle Pono's house, she knew it!

She trudged ahead. Then, all at once, she stopped.

It was still as dark as the inside of her mouth, she could barely see a foot in front of her . . . but some sense other than sight caused her to halt.

She wasn't alone. Standing there, staring blindly into the dark, she heard the unmistakable sound of someone, something, drawing breaths from the same air as she.

Frightened, she spun around, probing the darkness for some glimpse of . . . what? She didn't know, and something stopped her from calling out.

The breaths she heard were deep and ragged, and they were growing louder. Or maybe closer.

She didn't move, but heard the rustle of lantana scrub and then the squishing of soft mud being trod underfoot.

She searched the dimness ahead . . . and saw, low to the ground, a pair of shiny little eyes flashing in the dark.

Rachel screamed.

The eyes jumped forward, out of the darkness.

She leaped aside as a wild pig three feet tall charged her, black and horrible. It snorted ferociously, its snout missing her by inches as it stomped past.

Rachel ran shrieking up the trail, her feet barely finding purchase on the slippery ground, her heart pounding as she imagined the pig snapping its jaws at her heel.

In truth the animal gave up the chase much sooner than Rachel stopped running. When she finally realized that the pig wasn't pursuing her, she paused a moment to catch her breath — then for good measure kept on running.

She was startled when, a minute later, the trail suddenly came to an end: it sloped upward, culminating in a rocky lip of some kind. She had reached the top.

But the top of what?

Cautiously she climbed the last few feet of the slope and steadied herself on the edge of whatever it was she had found. She felt a little dizzy, as she had on Tantalus; she peered down but saw largely darkness.

Largely, but not entirely. Below and to the right, no more than a hundred feet away, there was a light.

A light burning in a house. And beside the house a horse was tied to a post, and beside the horse . . .

Rachel could barely contain her excitement. She charged over the lip and called out, called for help.

In a moment she needed it: carelessly she tripped over a tree root and went tumbling down a slope. Something sharp raked her left leg as she fell, and the thick trunk of a *wiliwili* tree rudely stopped her descent, the collision knocking the breath from her. She lay splayed against the tree, blood pooling beneath her leg, too dazed to even think about getting to her feet, and she wept out of humiliation as much as pain.

After a minute she heard the sound of leaves being crushed underfoot — the pig again? She was relieved when she saw the figure of a man towering above her, dim against the tangled darkness of tree limbs and night sky. Then he spoke, in a harsh rasp, like paper being torn: "What in hell?" Rachel wasn't scared, she'd heard voices like his at Kalihi; the leprosy tumors sometimes grew in a person's throat, giving the voice a husky edge.

He stooped down to get a better look at her. He was an old man, older than Haleola, his bald head brown as a coconut, his face a mass of tumors. " 'Ey," he said, "what do we got here?" He looked at her querulously and smiled. "How is it a pretty little girl like you comes falling out of the sky onto an old *wili-wili* tree?"

He moved closer. Rachel flinched and shrank back.

"It's okay," the man said, as gently as his raspy voice would allow, "I ain't gonna hurt you." He saw her injured leg, reached out and touched it tentatively. "Nasty cut," he said. "I fix you up, all right?"

He slid his hands underneath her back. Rachel let out a little yelp of apprehension as he scooped her up in his arms. He didn't seem very strong, though, and his arms quaked as he lifted her; Rachel was afraid he might drop her, but he managed to carry her over to the tiny grass house, lit from within by the flicker of a paraffin lamp. Inside, there wasn't much furniture, just a mattress, a chair, a table.

Winded by the exertion, the man rested a minute, coughing a horrible racking cough. When he recovered he had her take off her wet clothes, all except her underwear; wrapped her in a dry towel; then had her step out of the underwear as well. He laid her on the mattress and said, "Now let's take a look at that leg."

Judiciously he examined the gash below her knee and then wet a rag with water from a jug. "This is gonna hurt a little." It did. Rachel winced as he swabbed dirt and blood from the cut, then bandaged it with a clean rag.

Finally working up the courage to speak, Rachel said quietly, "Thank you."

"You can thank me tomorrow," the man said, a comment Rachel didn't understand. "You got a name?"

Rachel hesitated, then told him her name.

"I'm Moko," he said. "Get some sleep. We'll talk some more tomorrow, okay?"

He covered her with a worn, dirty blanket and she suddenly realized how good it felt to lie down, to be warm and dry. She closed her eyes and fell quickly asleep.

When she woke the lamp had gone out and hazy light filtered through the windows. The storm had passed, and she was alone. Her clothes, draped across the foot of the mattress, had been washed and dried in the sun.

She slipped them on, and not long after, her rescuer entered the house, carrying an armful of papayas.

"You hungry?" The moment he said it Rachel realized she was ravenous. She consumed three whole papayas and washed them down with a big glass of milk. She thanked him for breakfast, then asked, "Do you know my Uncle Pono?"

The old man thought a moment. "Pono . . . Pono . . . he live in Kauhakō?"

She told him her uncle lived in Kalawao, and for a moment Moko seemed surprised. He rubbed his chin thoughtfully and finally said, "Pono . . . sure, I know him. He don't live too far away."

Rachel was delighted. "Can you take me to him?"

"Better see if you can walk first, okay?" At his urging she got up, and though her leg was bruised and achy, she was able to walk around the room without difficulty.

"Good," he said. "Let's go outside." She followed him out the door and into the cool morning.

Rachel's mouth opened in amazement.

They were standing fifty feet below the upper rim of an enormous crater, shaped almost like an egg, two thousand feet long by fourteen hundred feet wide. It wasn't simply a barren, rocky pit, but a green thriving world bursting with color and life. The slopes and floor of the crater were thickly forested: *wili-wili* trees blooming with bright red tiger's-claw flowers; ironwoods carpeting the ground with feathery needles; Chinese banyans and Christmasberry trees, the last of their ripe red fruit spoiling on the ground. Nearly the entire bowl of the crater was overrun with some sort of vegetation. A handful of houses clung to its upper slopes, each surrounded by terraces of taro, sweet potato, sugar, beans, whatever would grow. Most houses had a horse outside; a few, like Moko's, boasted a cow grazing in a field.

In a hushed voice Rachel asked, "What is it?"

"Kauhakō. Used to be a volcano. Long time ago."

Fearfully, Rachel said, "Is it gonna blow up?"

Moko laughed, a laugh that degenerated into a cough. "No, no, not any more. See, in here, we're protected from the winds, the crops flourish. Lotta work, though."

He stooped down again to look her in the eye. "Now, you remember what I told you yesterday? How you could thank me today?" Rachel nodded uncertainly. "Well, you can do it by helping me carry some water from my well to the house. Can you do that?"

"But I want to see my Uncle Pono," Rachel said.

"You will. But first you do this for me."

When she didn't respond he pointed down to the center of the crater floor, where hazy sun gleamed off the mirror of a small lake. "You see that lake down there? They say it's bottomless, that it goes straight down to the center of the earth. Thousands of years ago the people who used to live here buried their dead in that lake. That's how this part of the island got its name. Makanalua — that means 'the given grave.' " He added, "And that lake is where they put little girls who didn't do what they were told."

Rachel gasped. She tried to imagine falling all the way down to that lake — so much more frightening than her little spill down the crater's slope! Terrified, she meekly followed Moko to the well, quite a distance away. After he pulled up each pail of water Rachel dutifully hauled it back to the house, where she poured it into a cistern before returning to get the next bucket.

By the time she had carried back ten pails of water she was growing tired and thirsty, and Moko let her drink some of the water and decided they had enough of it. "Can I see my Uncle Pono now?" she asked, but the old man said, "Gotta eat first, don't we?" and led her to a vegetable patch where he showed Rachel how to harvest taro by grasping the stems below the heart-shaped leaves and yanking the purple tubers from the ground. "Do you know how to make *poi*?" he asked.

Rachel nodded, enthusiastic at the thought of eating some. "I watched my Mama!" So they spent several hours cleaning the taro, boiling it in a pot under a fire out back, then slicing and pounding the cooked taro. It was a hard work, and Rachel's hand began to cramp from so much kneading.

But the *poi* tasted good, and when Moko asked her if she'd ever milked a cow, Rachel was taken with the novelty of the idea. It was fun for a while, but her hands were throbbing again at the end of it. She inquired again about Uncle Pono, but the sun had long since vanished below Kauhakō's western rim and shadows were swallowing up the crater. "We go tomorrow," Moko promised, and as the green slopes around them were consumed by darkness Rachel felt exhausted, confused, and a little bit afraid.

The old wagon's right front wheel was mired in the mud again, and for the fifth time that morning Catherine and Leopoldina got out, rolled up their sleeves, and applied shoulders to the cart until it rolled free. Their backs ached and their habits were caked with mud, but Catherine told herself this was no less than she deserved. She had owned up to her unforgivable behavior to Rachel, and after a stinging reproof Mother had sent her and Leopoldina in search of the missing girl. All morning it had been like this: they would travel half a mile along Damien Road, the wagon would lurch into the muck, and they would have to get out and push the cart free. On those rare occasions they were actually moving, they scanned the roadside for some trace of Rachel. At one point they were forced to stop a few yards east of the small trail leading to Kauhakō Crater; then, after extricating their wagon wheels, they moved on.

They reached Kalawao by noon and went directly to Pono's house; but before Leopoldina could knock, Catherine heard something like a gasp from inside.

She stayed Leopoldina's hand, nodding toward a window. They approached it and Catherine took a quick peek inside.

Pono was in bed, his arms wrapped around Haleola, who lay moving atop him; both were as naked as the day God brought them into the world. Catherine flushed scarlet, but before she could stop her Leopoldina stepped up for a look — her eyes at once resembling silver dollars.

Pono's color was not good, his gasps not entirely passionate. "I'm sorry," he said between breaths, "just . . . just a —"

Haleola looked worried. "Pono, are you sure —"

"I *want* to," he said, a desperate need in his voice.

Catherine yanked Leopoldina away from the window and back to the wagon.

199

"Well," Leopoldina said.

"I didn't see Rachel inside," Catherine said, "so I see no reason to interrupt them, do you?"

"No no," Leopoldina agreed.

"Maybe Brother Dutton can help us."

They hurried over to the Baldwin Home for Boys, soon to be abandoned in favor of a new one under construction; scattered around the unpainted frame of the new buildings were dozens of eucalyptus saplings Brother Dutton had planted. The tall, bearded lay brother — come to Moloka'i to serve penance for sins he never spoke of, though it was said to involve alcohol and a failed marriage — quickly organized house-to-house search parties. One burly resident, apparently fearing discovery of his home-brewed liquor, refused the brother entrance to his home; Dutton stared him down calmly. "I dug graves for hundreds of men in the Civil War," he told the man, "and I'll likely as not bury you too. In the war I sometimes had to do a hasty job, and I imagine some of those old bones are still being gnawed over by dogs. I'd hate to be that sloppy again, but you never know, do you?" The man rubbed the bones of his wrist and stepped back to admit Dutton.

But there was no trace of Rachel anywhere in Kalawao, and Catherine finally had to relay that disturbing news to Haleola. Pono was too frail to be of any help, but Haleola joined the two sisters as they expanded their search to include the coastline. Catherine would make her way to the edge of bluffs and peer down at sharp lava teeth fringing the maw of the sea. Each time she prayed she would not see Rachel's tiny body impaled on the lava rocks or floating on the raging surf. She didn't, but by evening she was overcome with guilt and fear — the fear that Rachel lay injured somewhere, or dying, was perhaps already dead, and it was all her fault. Leopoldina returned to St. Elizabeth's to inform Mother Marianne, but Catherine remained at Kalawao, spending the night at Baldwin Home, where she prayed fervently for Rachel's safe return and then cried herself asleep.

Moko made a hearty breakfast, frying some eggs from his henhouse and serving them with more ripe papayas. They were out of milk and so he asked Rachel to milk the cow again; when she was finished she asked if they could go to Uncle Pono's now. Moko said soon, soon, but soon somehow never came and she spent the morning on her knees, picking and cleaning sweet potatoes, taro, and carrots from the garden.

By now Rachel was angry, and when Moko told her they would be washing clothes she refused and snapped, "I want to see my

201

Uncle Pono!"

"After we do wash, okay?"

"No!" she shouted. "I want to see him!"

The old man's gnarled hand lashed out and struck her across her face. Not a slap like Sister Catherine's, but a blow that staggered her, sent her tumbling to the ground.

She lay there, blood trickling from her split lip, gazing up with terror at her attacker. "You forget what I said?" he barked at her. "About the lake, about what they do to little girls who don't do what they're told?"

He grabbed her by the scruff of the neck and, with more strength than she had thought he possessed, lifted her three feet into the air. He shook her roughly, pointed her in the direction of the gleaming lake below. "You want me to throw you down there? Would you like that?"

Rachel screamed and cried, begging him not to do it.

"How long you think it'd take for you to fall? Long time, I bet. Let's see, eh?"

He swung her back as if preparing to cast her like a stone into the ocean. *"No! No!"* she shrieked. *"Please!"*

But instead of hurling her to the crater floor he just tossed her aside — to land, messily, in the taro patch.

She cowered as he stood above her. "Ready to do wash?" he asked.

She nodded mutely.

She spent the next hour drowning Moko's dirty old clothes in a tub of soapy water, then rinsing, wringing them out, and laying them down to dry in the sun. When she was done he inspected her work and with a sunny smile declared, "Very good! Nice job! You hungry?" Cheerful again, he gave her more *poi* and let her drain two glasses of milk, and after her midday meal it was time to hoe and weed the garden.

But the exertion of lifting and terrorizing Rachel had taken its toll on Moko; he seemed weak, fatigued. And as he sat in the shade of his house, watching Rachel work the garden, he actually dozed off.

Rachel stared at him, her heart pounding as she contemplated this sudden opportunity. She looked up at the rocky crown of the crater rim, only a hundred feet above her, and then at Moko, slumbering not ten feet away.

She flung down the weeds in her hand and ran.

The snap and crunch of leaves and vines being trod underfoot awakened Moko, who saw his unwilling servant dashing up the slopes of the crater and cried out, "Hey! God-damn it!" He sprang to his feet and started after her.

Rachel scrambled up the slope, Moko no more than a dozen yards behind her. She slipped, fell, and in the few seconds it took her to right herself the gap between them closed even further. Panicky, Rachel grew even clumsier, falling and tumbling back down the slope several feet until she stopped her descent by grabbing hold of a tree root. Moko was now almost upon her, cursing, eyes ablaze. Rachel cast about desperately for some sort of weapon.

She lunged for a moldering tree branch as Moko called her a little shit and pounced at her.

Rachel twisted around and propelled the stick with all her strength into the old man's throat.

Flesh tore; blood spurted. Moko gagged and grabbed at his throat. The stick had not penetrated too deeply, but it had obviously caused him considerable hurt.

Good, she thought, shinnying up the slope as fast as she could. She didn't look back until she reached the summit: Moko was on his knees, moaning, holding his bloodied throat.

Rachel's hands found the crater's lip. She pulled herself up and over, then tumbled down the outside slope.

She quickly got to her feet and ran through the prickly, smelly lantana scrub, finally locating the trail she had ascended two days ago. She glanced back to see if she was being pursued, but there was only sunlight behind her. The trail was no longer so muddy and she covered its length in half the time it had taken during the rainstorm.

When she reached the main road she had no idea which direction to take, and didn't care. She stopped for only a moment to catch her breath, then ran down the road.

When it became apparent Moko was not following her, Rachel slowed to a fast walk. She was thirsty, tired, and achy, but she did not stop.

After what seemed like an hour but was probably only half that, Rachel was startled to hear a sound behind her. She turned, prepared to run again.

It wasn't Moko but a man on a horse, moving at a leisurely gait up the road. When he saw Rachel his eyes widened and he brought the horse to a stop.

Rachel took a step backwards, uncertain what to make of this. The man was a leper, not as old as Moko, and he was smiling puzzledly at her.

"*Aloha,*" he said cheerfully.

Rachel just stared silently at him.

"You lost?" the rider asked.

Rachel nodded hesitantly.

"Where you tryin' to get to?"

Rachel told him, "Kalawao." She added, "I'm looking for my Uncle Pono."

"Kalawao's where I'm headed, too. You want a ride?"

Unsure whether she could trust him, Rachel shook her head. "No thanks."

She turned and started off down the road again, at least confident now she was heading in the right direction. The rider seemed amused and paced her on his horse. "Well, how 'bout I tag along? That okay with you?"

Rachel shrugged. "If you want."

"How'd you get all the way out here, anyway?"

"I walked."

"From where? Kalaupapa?"

She nodded. He made a low whistle. "That's some walk," he said admiringly. "And you still got a ways to go. Sure you don't want that ride?"

After five minutes Rachel finally relented and allowed the man, whose name was Nohi, to lift her up onto the saddle in front of him. She grabbed hold of the saddle horn, and they went galloping up the road — like real cowboys!

By noon they had arrived in Kalawao, where their presence was made known to Brother Dutton. Dutton rounded up Sister Catherine, now searching farther down the coast, and whose joy on seeing the child was considerable. "Rachel!" she cried, running in a most indecorous manner to meet her. Rachel fell into Catherine's arms and wept with exhaustion and relief, her anger at the sister not forgotten but insignificant. Catherine held her, stroked her hair, and thanked God for bringing her back safely.

Brother Dutton rewarded Nohi with a bountiful lunch at Baldwin Home. Catherine replaced the rag on Rachel's leg with a clean bandage, then took her to Pono's house.

When Rachel saw her uncle she knew that despite everything she had been through, she had been right to come to Kalawao. Though his drawn face brightened on seeing her, for once he didn't make a joke upon seeing her; he seemed unable to collect his thoughts to think of one.

Haleola and Catherine watched from the doorway as Pono tried to tickle Rachel in a weak mimicry of his old self. "It's like he wants to be Pono," Haleola said, "but he's forgotten how."

"He hasn't forgotten. He just doesn't have the strength." Catherine added gently, "It's a hard thing, to love someone and not be able to show it."

The tenderness, the womanliness, in the sister's voice surprised and touched Haleola.

Rachel lay with her arms around Pono until, fatigued by the attention, he drifted off to sleep. Rachel wanted to stay there, to keep holding him so he couldn't slip away, but Haleola gently took her in her arms and carried her outside. Feeling more grown-up than she wanted to be, Rachel asked her, "Is Uncle Pono going to die?"

"Yes, Aouli, I think so."

"Can I stay?"

Catherine made a special trip to Kalaupapa and back to ask that very question of Mother, who agreed that she could — for a few days, at least. Over the course of those days Rachel rarely left Pono's side; and in the middle of her third night in Kalawao, as she slept on a pallet between Pono and Haleola, Rachel woke to familiar laughter. Pono was sitting up in bed, awake and alert — and laughing that old cackling laugh Rachel recalled from so many a family feast. Haleola woke now and watched in amazement as Pono reached out and took Rachel in his arms. " 'Ey, there's my favorite niece!" he said in a clear, strong voice, tickling her with all the zest of Pono in his prime. "My special girl!" He held and tickled her for nearly five full minutes, continuing to laugh long after he finally let go of her and leaned back onto the bed, his eyes drooping slowly shut. He even seemed to be chuckling in his sleep.

He never shared the joke with them, but whatever it was, it must have been pretty funny.

Brother Dutton had Pono's grave dug in the little cemetery bordering Siloama Church. Its pastor, Reverend Waiwaiole, officiated at his funeral. Sisters Catherine and Leopoldina attended along with Haleola and Rachel, as did Ambrose Hutchison, who gave a brief eulogy for "President" Pono.

Rachel kept a brave face throughout the funeral, but afterward, alone with Haleola, she allowed herself to cry, mourning not just Pono but everyone she had lost so suddenly. Haleola cradled her in her arms and said, "You still have me, Aouli. Can I be your *hānai* aunt — your adopted auntie?" Strictly speaking, only blood relatives could *hānai* a child, but Rachel nodded gratefully. Yet even as she held onto Haleola's comforting warmth she was afraid it too would be taken from her.

Rachel said hopefully, "Sister Catherine says that when people die, they go to Heaven."

Haleola considered that. "Sister Catherine's Heaven is not mine," she told Rachel, "but certain things are true for both of us. In the old days it was said that the world beyond was made up of two realms: one of eternal sleep and darkness, and another in which the dead were reunited with the spirits of their ancestors — their *'aumākua.* There were forests and streams in this place, and newcomers enjoyed life there as they do here — dancing, playing games, cherishing family. If that is Heaven, then yes, some of us go there."

Disappointed, Rachel asked, "So you have to die before you see your family again?"

"No," Haleola said, "not always. Our *'aumākua* often look after us here on earth. Some take the form of sharks, and if a descendant is drowning in the sea, the shark may offer up its fin to pull them to shore. Other spirits become owls, fish, lizards, whatever permits them to watch over their family.

"There is an old prayer: ''*Aumākua* of the night, watch over your offspring, enfold them in the belt of light.' "

Rachel smiled a little at this; for the moment, at least, her soul seemed lighter. And as the *pali* carried away the afternoon sun, it took with it the remainder of Rachel's time at Kalawao. She got into the wagon beside Catherine, waved goodbye to her new aunt, and was back at Bishop Home by sunset. Emily and the other girls had already heard rumors of Rachel's journeys and they stayed up late listening to Rachel tell her tale again and again, especially the part about the wild pig. Rachel skipped over her time with Moko, but that night it came back to her, unbidden. She dreamt she was back at Kauhakō, washing Moko's clothes, feeling the flat of his hand against her cheek, and she woke sobbing from the nightmare. As she wept she heard someone suddenly ask, *"Who?"* — but when she looked around, saw there was no one else awake in the room. She heard the query again and realized it was coming from outside. She went to the window, peered into the darkness . . . and saw, sitting on the branch of a small sapling, an owl. There was a momentary flash of moonlight in its great round eyes — then swiftly, silently, it took to the air, and Rachel watched its noiseless flight over the building and out of sight. Rachel smiled, somehow no longer afraid, and went back to bed: surrounded by darkness yet enfolded in light.

CHAPTER 9

It was now painfully evident that Sister Victor's "moods" seemed to have an almost gravitational pull on Catherine, who felt the currents of her own thoughts drawn in a dark tide toward Victor's depression and instability. Hers was a soul in torment and Catherine could not abandon her — but the next time she sought a drinking companion Catherine declined, urging her friend to join her in prayer instead. On that occasion and a few others they knelt together in the chapel, in private or shared devotions; but as far as Catherine could see, to no visible effect.

Catherine's first confession after her late-night swim brought a stunned silence from Father Wendelin, followed by a soft chuckle. "Ah, Sister," he said, "it's the sweet wines one has to be wary of." He recommended zinfandel: "It has a bit of an edge to it." Father Wendelin shared Catherine's concern for Sister Victor, but as often as he extended a hand to the troubled sister it was rejected.

And there was only so far Catherine could go without herself falling into the abyss.

Of more immediate concern to Catherine was the problem now facing Mother Marianne: whether Haleola, not a blood relative and a living embodiment of Hawai'i's pagan past, should be permitted to continue visiting Rachel at Bishop Home. It deeply disturbed Mother that such a woman should have any influence over one of her charges, but Catherine knew how much Haleola cared for Rachel and argued that her occasional presence might discourage the girl from running away again. "And if we are to bar all remnants of paganism from the Home," she went on, emboldened, "then I assume we shall not be putting up a Christmas tree this year."

"Christmas trees," Mother replied evenly, "do not spout heathen nonsense." She was adamant: Haleola Nua was not to be allowed back onto the convent grounds.

Catherine could not disobey her Mother Superior, and Haleola was henceforth barred from Bishop Home.

But the Reverend Mother had said nothing about Rachel meeting Haleola *outside* convent grounds, and thereafter, by an odd coincidence, whenever Catherine took a group of girls to the beach, or to the *pali,* or exploring tide pools, Haleola just happened to be there, doing those very things.

On one such excursion — to a spooky sea

cave along the shore — Rachel told her friends about the giant eel, Keko'ona, and his battle with brave Ku'ula. She quickly became a rollicking success as a teller of tales on black stormy nights. For Rachel, Haleola's tales of the goddess Pele and the demigod Māui spoke of another world — a large, exciting, colorful world both far away and all around them. The bright pagodas of Japan, the Great Barrier Reef, China and San Francisco, all seemed impossibly remote now — *kapu,* forbidden. But these giants of Hawai'i's past, straddling mountains and snaring the sun with rope, took the place of the *kapu* lands in Rachel's imagination.

Josephina, the little girl who slept all day, confounded all expectations by making a complete recovery and was back playing tops and marbles with the other girls by spring; while another girl, Mary, who had seemed the picture of health, suddenly came down with pleurisy and was gone within a week. A rumor spread that her ghost was haunting the dispensary, and for a week and a half the younger girls scuttled past the building amid a flurry of whispers and a tingle of chicken skin. Then, having held on to Mary for just a little while longer, the girls quietly put the rumor to rest, and Mary with it.

Summer brought the arrival of Rachel's old crony from Kalihi, Francine, who smuggled in candy and chewing gum the like of which could not be found at the Kalaupapa Store. With summer also came more and longer trips to the beach and a lassitude that seemed to infect everyone when it came to chores, even the sisters. On one such lazy day Mother Marianne personally led an expedition into one of the lush little valleys tucked into the *pali,* where the girls cooled off in the spray of a waterfall and picked newly ripened breadfruit, which the convent's cook made into a fine *poi.*

Not long after, Rachel received a parcel mailed all the way from Buenos Aires, inside which was a beautiful sienna-skinned doll in a bright yellow flamenco costume. The accompanying letter from Papa was short but welcome; he would always recite a new chantey he'd heard, or describe a port he had just visited, and a month did not go by without at least a postcard from some exotic corner of the earth.

But letters from Mama were becoming far less frequent. At first Rachel got something from home nearly every week, and that same day Rachel would sit down to compose a reply:

Dear Mama,
Today we went to the beach and I swam and saw lots of fish and the biggest turtle ever. I swallowed a lot of water and got sick. Sister Catherine says it's O.K. to

throw up if you really have to. Do you think so?

But gradually Mama's letters went from once a week to one every two weeks to once a month, and then . . . once in a while. When two months went by without any letter from Mama, Rachel dropped her a note on the pretext of telling her about the girls' trip to the sea cave; but no reply came on the next steamer, or the one after that. Rachel wrote again, a bit more plaintively this time.

A week later, Rachel's neatly lettered envelope came back to her with a red, rubber-stamped frown across its face: MOVED, NO FORWARDING ADDRESS.

Rachel must have stared at it for ten whole minutes. She convinced herself it was just a mistake and prepared a new envelope, making absolutely sure she had copied the address correctly, then re-mailed the letter.

A week later, it too bounced back like a boomerang, an ink smudge obliterating Rachel's old address in Honolulu.

Was it true? Had her family moved out of their little house two blocks from Queen Emma Street? She waited for a letter from Mama that would explain everything, give her their new address, tell her about their new home.

It never came. Rachel breathed in its absence and felt increasingly anxious, restless, afraid. Week after week her only letters came from Papa; but where once she thrilled to see the colorful stamps of Argentina or New Zealand or Hong Kong, now she wanted nothing so desperately as a Honolulu postmark and one of the familiar brown portraits of King Kalākaua, or the violet likeness of Queen Liliu'oklani (now branded with the words PROVISIONAL GOVT).

But the only such stamps she saw were on letters received by other girls, and when yet another Steamer Day passed with nothing for Rachel — and she noticed, on Hazel's bed, an envelope with a return address on O'ahu — Rachel waited until no one was looking, and stole it. She read it over twice, pretending it had been written to her, then hid it under the mattress of her bed.

She was found out quickly enough and sent to bed without supper. Soon she was stealing other things: one of Emily's dolls, a family photograph from another girl's bedstead. Each time the theft was discovered and the culprit obvious; Rachel regularly felt the sting of Sister Albina's ruler across her knuckles.

She and Francine resumed their truant ways, playing hooky to body-surf at Papaloa as they had once cooled off in Kalihi Bay. After three or four whacks of the ruler, Francine was deterred from further truancy, but not Rachel.

Sister Catherine was baffled by her behavior. "Rachel, what on earth has gotten into you?" she asked, but Rachel would just shrug and say, "Nothing" — or angrily declare it was none of her business, and to leave her alone!

Concerned, Catherine wrote to Rachel's mother, asking if there had been any bad news from home that might have disturbed Rachel. It went out on Thursday's steamer, and Catherine was startled to see it come right back the following week, stamped with lettering as red as leprous sores: MOVED, NO FORWARDING ADDRESS.

The words cut Catherine nearly as deeply as they had Rachel.

While Rachel was in school she peeked inside the old cigar box of Pono's in which Rachel kept her letters from home. The peek sadly confirmed Catherine's suspicions.

The next day, during chores, Catherine took Rachel aside and led her, quite to Rachel's astonishment, to a back door at St. Elizabeth's Convent. Rachel hesitated on the threshold. "I — I'm not supposed to go in there."

"I know," Catherine said, and opened the door for her.

Ushering Rachel into her spartan quarters, Catherine confided, "I'm quite sure Mother would punish me for this." A smile passed between them at this flaunted *kapu*. Catherine sat on her bed, motioning Rachel to join her.

"It's good sometimes, isn't it," Catherine said, "being punished? When you think you've done something wrong. Maybe when you don't know *what* you've done wrong."

Rachel stared at her blankly. Catherine reached into the pocket of her robe and pulled out the envelope she had mailed to Dorothy Kalama, now defaced by mocking words, and let it drop like a leaf onto the bed.

Rachel saw what it was. Tears blinded her. All at once her shoulders hunched, her body quaked with grief. Catherine took her in her arms and held her close, a shudder of loss and shame passing from Rachel's body into Catherine's, becoming Catherine's loss too, Catherine's shame. She stroked Rachel's hair and told her it was all right, told her it wasn't her fault. Rachel buried her face in the sister's robe, breathed in the laundered scent of the wool, felt the beating of their shared heart, and wanted never to let go.

On a gloomy, windy morning in October, Rachel, woolgathering as she gazed out the schoolhouse window, was startled and chagrined to hear her name called aloud. With not the faintest idea what was being discussed, she straightened in her seat, hoping to make up for in posture what she lacked in particulars. Sister Leopoldina stood in the rectangle of the doorway. "Rachel, you're excused for the day," the teacher announced. "Please go with the sister and mind her as you would me." Confused, Rachel followed Leopoldina out of the schoolroom. Was she being punished? For what? She hadn't stolen anything lately — well, nothing important, just a pencil, from . . .

Oh *no,* she remembered. A week ago, when Mother had scolded her for truancy, Rachel had snatched a pencil, a nice red one, off the nun's desk when her back was turned. Had Mother discovered it missing? Had she known all along?

"It's a lovely day for a walk, don't you think?" Leopoldina asked, leading Rachel off the convent grounds. They strolled past the Protestant church and the Kalaupapa Store toward the wharf where a small crowd had gathered to meet rowboats off the steamer *Lehua,* and now Rachel realized what was happening. She was being sent away again! As punishment, like at Kalihi. But to where? It wasn't fair, she had friends here, and an aunt — she wouldn't go! She thought suddenly of her dolls, and was about to run back to Bishop Home to get them — they couldn't begrudge her that, could they? — when she saw a stocky figure walking toward her, a broad grin on his tanned face, and all of Rachel's fears dissolved in an instant, like salt in water.

"Papa!" she cried at the top of her voice, racing frantically down the wharf to Leopoldina's great amusement.

" 'Ey, little girl. Catch!" He feigned throwing his duffel bag to her, she laughed, and then she was in his arms, feeling the comforting bulk of him for the first time in two years. And if this was in violation of settlement regulations, Ambrose Hutchison, standing nearby, was perhaps too distracted by his duties to raise an objection.

They laughed and cried and held one another, and finally Henry found his voice again. "I missed you so much, baby girl," he said softly.

"I missed you, too, Papa. I saved all your letters." She looked around, looked back at the launch bobbing near the pier. "Where's Mama? Is she still on the boat?"

Henry's smiled dimmed a little. "Mama couldn't make it, baby. But she sends all her love."

Rachel's disappointment was outweighed by her joy at seeing Papa. Leopoldina stepped up to introduce herself and to show him to the visitors' quarters, where he stopped only long enough to drop off his duffel bag.

As they walked, Leopoldina explained settlement rules. Rachel was not allowed inside the visitor's cottage, but she could talk to her father through the fence enclosing it; all other visits would take place on the convent grounds at the discretion of the sisters. At Bishop Home Leopoldina had lunch brought for them, then left Henry and Rachel on the convent's lawn to eat their rice and *poi* from separate calabashes, and to talk.

"Papa, when did you get back from South America?"

"Couple weeks ago. Did you get the doll?"

"She's beautiful, Papa! All the other girls wanted to play with her."

"Did you let them?"

"Uh huh."

"Good girl." He looked around at the cozy little bungalows and the neatly trimmed lawn and said, "You like it here, baby? They treat you all right?"

Henry was shocked when Rachel blurted out, "No. I hate it here! Take me with you!" She burst into tears and desperately wrapped her arms around him.

Henry held her and told her would like nothing better than to take her with him, but . . . he couldn't. Between sobs, Rachel told him about the returned letter to Mama. Henry looked pained and embarrassed.

"Oh, baby, I didn't want to tell you till you were older," he said softly. He was forced to admit that on his return to Honolulu he stayed at the Seamen's Home in Kalihi and not with Dorothy — who, he said, had taken Ben, Kimo, and Sarah to live with Dorothy's sister on windward O'ahu.

"She couldn't stand the shame," Henry explained. "The way people looked at her — the way they treated the *keiki*. She loves you, baby, but she loves your sister and brothers, too — in a new place, she thinks, where nobody knows about Kalaupapa, maybe they'll be better off."

Rachel said nothing. She'd heard about this happening to other girls, here and at Kalihi, but . . . when it happened to you, it was different. It was a stab in the heart.

Just then an explosion of girls out of the schoolhouse signaled the end of class. Rachel put aside her hurt and called out, "Francine! Emily! This is my papa!"

Emily said, "You lie."

Henry laughed. "No lie."

"You come all the way from Honolulu?" Emily looked skeptical. Henry nodded.

Francine said wistfully, "Must be nice."

After a few minutes the girls left for the dining hall and Sister Catherine came up and introduced herself. "You have a wonderful daughter," she told Henry, adding with a smile, "though a bit more resourceful than we'd like."

Henry chuckled. "Takes after her mama."

"I'm very sorry about your brother," Catherine said soberly. "If you'd like to pay your respects, Mother has authorized me to take you and Rachel to Kalawao."

Henry thanked her and said he would like that.

"Can we see Auntie Haleola, too?" Rachel said.

Henry looked at her blankly. "Who?"

"Your brother's . . . friend," Catherine said delicately. It took Henry a moment, but then he laughed and said, "Pono, he was a very friendly fellow."

Catherine drove the wagon across the peninsula to Kalawao, where Rachel was soon racing down the main street, Henry in tow, to Haleola's house. "Auntie, Auntie!" Rachel cried when the door opened. "This is my Papa, he's come to visit me!"

Haleola was a bit startled to find herself face to face with her lover's brother; and because Henry was not permitted to accept the hospitality of Haleola's home, the four of them walked to Siloama Church and the small cemetery that stood in its lee. At Pono's grave — a crude wooden cross bearing his name, date of birth, and date of death — Henry knelt down and wept freely for his brother.

Haleola was pleased to see that Henry was as fine a father as Rachel had led her to believe. They spent the afternoon wandering along the shore, Catherine nominally chaperoning the visit but trying not to intrude; at one point she helped Rachel look for the glass balls, used by Japanese fishermen, which often washed ashore here, allowing Henry and Haleola a few moments alone.

"Your brother always spoke of you with love," she told him. "And he cherished Rachel as if she were his own."

Henry glanced at Rachel as she plucked a glass ball weighted with seaweed from the water. She tossed away the bulbous kelp and held the globe aloft triumphantly; it looked like a marble from a land of giants.

"I'd give anything to stay," Henry said softly.

"It's not like the old days, when they welcomed *kōkuas*. Today they make it more difficult."

"They take our country, and our families, from us," Henry said. "What next? The sun? The stars?"

Haleola had no answer for that. "I cherish her, too," she said simply, and Henry smiled to know it.

By mid-afternoon the long shadow of the *pali* had brought its early twilight to Kalawao, and Sister Catherine reluctantly announced they would have to start back to Kalaupapa. Rachel hugged Haleola. Henry simply told her, *"He mai iā ka 'ohana"* — welcome to the family.

That night, since he couldn't enter the girls' quarters, Henry stood outside the window nearest Rachel's bed and sang her "Fire Down Below," one of the more genteel sea

225

chanteys; then blew her a kiss and returned to the visitors' house. The next day he played croquet with the girls and laughed when told of his brother's prowess at the game. Rachel found herself wishing that the week would never end — that her father could stay here forever — but knew he couldn't. If there was one thing she had learned in her brief time at Kalaupapa, it was that all things end.

Sister Catherine liked Henry Kalama from the start: liked his warmth, his humor, the gentle way he had with Rachel. She was pleased to be able to take them to Kalawao, but in the course of the trip she began to feel something quite unexpected and unwelcome. Watching Henry with his daughter she felt a twitch of sorrow at the thought that she would never have a child like this of her own. She thought she had reconciled herself to this before she'd taken her vows, but there it was — a nugget of envy and regret, impossible to deny, difficult to ignore.

She had not planned to intrude on their time together and now made certain she did not. She concentrated on her chores — cleaning, dressing sores, washing soiled bandages in boiling water. She was in the midst of this latter, particularly onerous task when Sister Victor appeared in the laundry. She took in the tub full of bloody, soapy bandages and declared, "That looks utterly revolting."

Catherine lifted a handful of bloody suds and smiled with mock brightness: "Oh no, it's quite the gay time. Join me?"

Sister Victor blanched. "Almost as bad — Leopoldina's talked me into chaperoning one of these bloody beach trips. Please say you'll come, if I have to go with her I'll surely go mad."

"Chaperoning? This is very out of character for you, Sister."

"A moment of weakness," Victor said. "I don't plan on making a career of it."

"Which girls are you taking?"

"Molly, Bertha, Emily, Noelani, Priscilla . . ."

"Not Rachel?" When Victor shook her head, Catherine asked, "What time?"

Catherine still enjoyed these trips to Papaloa, and even Sister Victor seemed to be having a good time: she chatted away as Catherine kept one eye on Bertha, Molly, and Noelani. The three girls were treading water, waiting for another set of waves to roll in; but they'd chosen a spot too close to shore and instead of the wave lifting them up it broke right on top of them. They disappeared in a spray of foam, to the laughter of their peers.

"I hear Dutton may get some Sacred Hearts brothers from Belgium to help out at Baldwin Home," Victor was saying. "Bishop Gulstan is going to Louvain to ask for —"

Catherine stopped listening. Molly and

Noelani had surfaced again, but Bertha was still underwater. She'll pop up in a moment, Catherine told herself.

But she didn't. Catherine's eyes tracked up and down the surf, searching for Bertha's crop of black curly hair above the whitecaps, but saw nothing.

Catherine got to her feet.

"What is it?" Sister Victor now stood as well.

"Bertha," Catherine said, hurrying toward the ocean, turning it into a cry, "Bertha! *Bertha!*" Now the girls in the water also began to look around for their friend.

Catherine caught a glimpse of something pale under the surface of a wave as it shrugged to shore.

"There!" Catherine yelled, pointing. Emily and Noelani immediately began swimming to the spot. Catherine threw off her veil, dove into the sea, and swam toward the pale shape in the water. The sodden habit weighed her down just as she'd always feared it would, but she swam as hard and as fast as she could. Emily and Noelani reached Bertha first, pulling her head — bleeding where it had apparently struck a rock — out of the water in which she had been submerged. Bertha didn't respond in any way; they kept her afloat until Catherine arrived and hooked an arm around the child's torso. With Emily's help Catherine began pulling Bertha shoreward, but the girl's underclothes were ballooned with water, the extra ballast slowing them down; Catherine tore off the underclothes and dragged the naked, unconscious girl through the surf and up onto the beach.

Catherine laid Bertha on her back as Sister Victor ran up. The girl was in an advanced stage of leprosy, her whole body covered with suppurating sores, and the few unblemished parts of her skin were now a pallid blue. Catherine had no experience with drowning victims and what little she recalled from her nurse's training seemed impractical. "Aren't we supposed to — rub her body with salt — ?"

Victor shook her head dismissively, shouldered Catherine aside. She turned Bertha over onto her stomach, then straddled her. The girl's back was a mass of ulcerated tissue, and seeing this Sister Victor hesitated a moment; but only a moment. Placing her hands firmly on Bertha's back she pushed down as hard as she could, but nothing happened. She tried again, even harder, and Catherine thought she heard a bone crack. On the third try water suddenly spurted from Bertha's mouth and Sister Victor zealously began pushing again and again, pumping as much water from the girl's lungs as she could.

On the last push Bertha started coughing, started breathing again. Sister Victor flipped her over again, began furiously massaging the ulcerated skin of her left arm. "Take the other arm," she directed Catherine, "get the blood flowing!" They rubbed Bertha's arms and legs until the bluish cast of her skin began to fade and Dr. Oliver — summoned by a frantic Emily — appeared on the scene.

Oliver examined the child's head wound; listened to her heart; opened one eye and looked into it. "Possible concussion, but respiration's normal. She'll need some stitches, but that's the worst of it, I think. Fine work, Sisters." Catherine felt an immense rush of relief as Oliver lifted the girl up in his arms. "I'll get her into a hot bath straight away. Follow me to the infirmary and we'll get you two cleaned up as well."

The two sisters became aware for the first time that their hands were sticky with fluid — pus and blood from Bertha's sores. Catherine looked from her hands to her companion's face. Sister Victor was kneeling on the sand, staring at the blood and yellowish discharge covering her hands with a look not of horror but of surprise — as though she were waking from a dream to find herself soiled.

Catherine stood. Sister Victor did too, more slowly. "You saved her," Catherine said softly.

Victor was silent; she just kept staring, glassy-eyed, at her hands. Catherine repeated, "You *saved* her, Sister."

Victor nodded, as though merely affirming a fact.

Leopoldina, who had followed in Dr. Oliver's wake, took charge of the girls as Catherine and Victor stumbled up the beach and into town, to the hospital. There they stripped off their habits and scoured their skin with carbolic acid, then washed them again with soap.

Sister Victor scrubbed her hands until they bled.

In hospital gowns they stopped to see Bertha, now conscious, who thanked them weakly but sincerely. Their habits were taken to be washed in boiling water; on their return to the convent they took baths which seemed nearly as hot, then changed into fresh clothes.

Catherine and Victor received a hero's ovation from children and sisters alike. Mother commended them for their quick thinking and their courage. "Sister Victor is the real hero," Catherine told them, but Victor seemed almost not to hear, her mind's eye turning inward again.

At dinner Victor ate a little sweet potato and part of a biscuit, then excused herself, retreating to the privacy of her room. Catherine considered following but decided to give her the time to herself; only after dinner did she go to her friend's room, to find her sitting alone in the dark, rubbing incessantly at her hands.

Catherine squatted, taking Victor's hands in hers.

"It's all right, Sister," she said, stilling Victor's hands. "I get soiled all the time when I dress their sores. You wash up afterward, that's all."

Victor nodded dully. Her hands twitched between Catherine's.

"You showed great courage," Catherine told her. "You didn't hesitate. Mother was proud of you — just like the old days, at St. Joseph's."

Sister Victor glanced up at that, a ghost of a smile lighting her face.

"Yes," she said, a dim pleasure in her voice. "She *was* proud . . . wasn't she?"

Catherine nodded and let go of her hands.

Sister Victor's smile became less ghostly — more alive. Her whole face began to seem more alive, more vibrant.

She said, "I just need a good night's sleep."

Catherine started to leave, stopping at the door long enough to say, "You were very brave today, Sister."

Sister Victor smiled. It was a proud, radiant smile. Catherine would never forget it.

She went to her room, said her nightly devotions, and as exhaustion overtook her she slid gratefully into bed.

At three A.M., Catherine was awakened by a scream.

At first she thought it was an animal being

232

butchered in the village slaughterhouse. But as she sat up she heard a very human agony in the shrill cry and knew at once from whose strangled heart it came.

She rushed out and down the corridor to Sister Victor's room. The scream was long and ceaseless, changing only in pitch and tone — terrified one moment, mournful the next. Catherine flung open the door and in the darkness saw Victor sitting up in bed, backed up against the wall as though facing down some demonic intruder, body convulsing as if from St. Vitus's dance.

Catherine ran to her, held her, trying to quell her spasms. "It's all right, Sister, it's all right!" But the convulsions were so fierce that Catherine lost her grip and was actually thrown backwards onto the floor.

Now the others rushed in, Albina and Crescentia and Leopoldina, clumping together in the doorway in mute, uncomprehending horror. Then, as Catherine got to her feet, Mother herself appeared — and all the sisters stepped aside to give her a path into the room.

Mother Marianne listened to the agonized cries of her colleague of old, and for the first time her sisters saw something other than serenity or mild annoyance on Mother's face. They saw the face of true anguish. Mother Marianne went to Sister Victor, sat down on the edge of the bed, gazing with inexpressible sadness at the torment she saw in her old friend's eyes. Mother leaned forward, enfolded her in her arms, and Sister Victor's convulsions ceased. Her screams dissolved into sobs. Mother held her tight and wept with her; wept for the woman she once was, and the woman she had been again today, briefly but bravely.

The sea was particularly rough this afternoon, the launches from the *Lehua* often swamped as they ferried passengers to and from the Kalaupapa Landing. Henry held Rachel to him as fiercely and tenderly as Rachel hugged her dolls at night. Over her shoulder he saw the last boat bobbing precariously by the landing. He watched as Sister Leopoldina and Sister Catherine, supporting between them the unsteady figure of Sister Victor, helped their friend to the ladder, where a sailor was poised to assist.

As she stepped down onto the first rung, Sister Victor stopped suddenly, turned. "No. Wait," she said, losing her balance, Catherine catching her. Victor straightened, steadied herself with a hand on Catherine's shoulder . . . then leaned in and grazed Catherine's cheek with a kiss.

"God bless you, Sister," she said. With the ghost of her old smile, she added, "Remember me to the cannibal's pot."

Catherine kissed her cheek and bade her

Godspeed, and the sailors gently gathered her into the boat.

Rachel wept, certain that she would die if she had to let go of her father. "Papa, don't leave me," she begged him. "I need you all the time!"

The words both touched and grieved him. Henry's eyes filled with tears. He kissed his daughter and told her, "I love you, little girl. No matter where I am, no matter how far away, I'll never stop loving you."

Henry hugged Rachel one last time — then handed her to Haleola, who held her as tightly and tenderly as he had, stroking Rachel's hair with her clawed hand. As he descended the ladder, he called out, "I'll be back!" — and then the boat bearing Henry and Sister Victor pushed off and began its bumpy journey to the *Lehua*. Henry waved to Rachel all the way to the steamer. He didn't stop until the ship had pulled anchor and turned about. And as she watched the *Lehua* climb the steep incline of the ocean and gain the summit of the horizon, Rachel was filled with grief, loss, anger — and the wordless resolve that someday, somehow, she would follow her father over that horizon and down the other side, where the world lay hidden.

■ ■ ■ ■

Part Three: Kapu!

■ ■ ■ ■

CHAPTER 10

1903

Haleola could feel it inside her, the leprosy germ, stirring restlessly after a long sleep. She'd taken to calling it "the bug," sometimes addressing it as she might an old acquaintance she didn't particularly like. *Hello bug,* she'd say; *so there you are again, eh? Don't make yourself too comfortable, sorry you can't stay longer, aloha.*

But of course the bug stayed as long as it wished, weeks or months during which joints ached and nerve sheaths became raw and inflamed. On days like today she lay in bed all morning, barely able to move, husbanding her energy for tasks that afternoon. It was close to noon, to judge by the light, and Haleola had promised to meet Rachel at the beach. She propped herself up on one elbow, wincing, then took a deep breath and sat up. She was still a little disoriented by her surroundings: her new house, twice the size of the old one in Kalawao, still smelling of fresh

239

lumber and paint. It had been not quite a year since the last residents of Kalawao — all but Brother Dutton and his boys — had at last fled for the warmer shores of Kalaupapa; and at sixty-seven, Haleola had to admit she didn't miss the chill and the damp.

I'm getting up now, bug. Don't try to stop me. She got out of bed, the bug kicking and griping inside her, and was on her way. She ate a little *poi* and boiled water for tea. She wrapped some Hawaiian salt — the color of pink coral — in ti leaves, then took it and the teapot with her as she left the little cottage near Damien Road.

Obligation, not affection, made her stop at the home of George Wakina, not the best of company even on his good days. He met her at the door with his customary scowl. " 'Bout time you showed up," he grumbled as he let Haleola in. "Everything hurts like hell."

"Good morning to you too, George."

"It's afternoon," Wakina corrected her.

These days more residents chose to consult the settlement physician, Dr. Goodhue, rather than a *kahuna;* Haleola wished George were one of them. But he didn't trust *haole* doctors. "I brought something for your rheumatism," she said, and proceeded to heat the wrapped salt on Wakina's stove. When it had cooled a little she poured the salt into a flour bag and applied it to George's joints.

"Ahh," he sighed, "feels good." His smile

quickly darkened to a frown. "Could've used you in that goddamned jail." Arrested last year for brewing "swipe" alcohol, Wakina, while in the Kalaupapa jail, had suffered a severe recurrence of rheumatoid arthritis — but superintendent C. W. Reynolds, who had replaced the late R. W. Meyer, refused to permit him any medical aid. Around the same time another prisoner, Philip Miguel, came down with fever, was also denied medical attention, and ultimately died. The Board of Health investigated and fired Reynolds for negligence — along with the probably blameless Dr. Oliver, who had tried and failed to get the prisoner sent to Bay View Home.

"I also brought you some herb tea," Haleola said, pouring from the teapot, "for general debility."

Wakina took a sip, blanched. "This tastes like shit."

"What do you think it's made of?" Haleola replied sweetly.

Wakina regarded her uncertainly, not sure if she was serious; then broke into an uncharacteristic guffaw.

"Long as it's not dogshit, 'ey?" he said with a laugh, and drank down the tea without further complaint.

Walking through the center of town, Haleola passed the superintendent's office, a small house encompassed by one of the white picket fences these *haoles* seemed to love and which looked to Haleola like a string of shark's teeth erupting from the earth. The new superintendent, J. D. McVeigh, was tying up his horse in front; he was an easygoing *haole* who sported a drooping mustache and a cowboy hat, and in less than a year at Kalaupapa had shown himself to be a fair and decent *luna.* He was forever raising funds to build recreational facilities which R. W. Meyer would have dismissed as unnecessary and frivolous, considering that the residents were here to die, not to live. McVeigh tipped his hat and wished her good morning. Haleola nodded and returned the greeting; she liked McVeigh well enough.

But she hated what flew from a staff above him. At the top of a tall flagpole a banner of stars and stripes snapped in the wind with a sound like gunshots. Its colors flew higher than anything else in Kalaupapa, its stars supplanting the stars in the sky, reminding Haleola and all Hawaiians in the settlement of everything they'd lost.

In 1898, while at war with Spain in the Pacific, the United States Congress decided Hawai'i would be a strategic asset and issued a joint resolution annexing the islands, which President McKinley signed into law. Hawai'i became only the second sovereign nation to join the United States. But unlike the Republic of Texas, where a public referendum was held, no one asked the thirty-one thousand native Hawaiians whether they wished to give up their country. Twenty-nine thousand of them signed a petition of protest, which was submitted to Congress and politely ignored.

When a group of American commissioners arrived on an inspection tour of Kalaupapa in September, the Sisters of Charity sewed miniature American flags for patients who wished to wear them. Few did, and Haleola was not the only resident to grind the hated symbols into the mud.

If there was one thing that *haoles* were good at, though, it was spending money, and when the settlement was taken over by the U.S. Public Health Service, Kalaupapa became the beneficiary of Federal largesse. The first years of the century would see construction of a home for elderly men unable to care for themselves, and another for women; improved visitors' quarters; McVeigh's many new recreational facilities; and an assortment of patient-owned businesses including a bakery, a dry goods store, and a fish market.

Haleola, for one, would have traded every scrap of lumber to see her kingdom's flag flying again from this staff.

In minutes she found herself at Papaloa Beach, no longer the exclusive preserve of the Bishop Home girls. Some were here, to be sure, but now there were adults from the village as well — swimming, fishing, surfing.

243

One surfer stood tall and steady on a crudely fashioned board, poised on the surging crest of a wave.

Haleola was not surprised to see that it was Rachel.

Her *hānai* niece coasted toward shore for another few seconds, then, as the wave slowed, gracefully stepped off the board and into the surf. In one smooth motion she spun the nine-foot board around, bellied onto it, and paddled out to meet the next set of waves.

Haleola watched her with pride. At seventeen Rachel was still lithe and strong; if not for a few small sores on her legs no one would have suspected she had leprosy. She was taller than her parents but her body nevertheless owed something to her father's: shoulders broader than most girls, a boyish build with small breasts and slim hips. Her face was no longer chubby but neither was it delicate; even from here Haleola could see the wide smile on Rachel's broad face as the next wave rolled beneath her surfboard and she stood up on it, the board skimming the surface of the sea like a flat stone skipped across a pond.

Haleola noted that some surfers seemed to crouch on their boards, arms outstretched, constantly striving for the proper balance; others stood straight as a statue, arms at their sides, gliding serenely on the surf as if untroubled by balance or gravity. Rachel fell in between: poised but fluid, her knees bending and hips twisting as she shifted her weight to change the board's direction. Not serene, perhaps, but graceful and self-assured.

Haleola carefully descended the sand dunes (no mean feat with the fire burning in her nerves) to join Sister Catherine standing watch over her flock. Of Rachel's contemporaries when she first came to Bishop Home, Noelani, Hazel, Bertha, and Josephina were gone; only Emily and Francine survived to swim alongside Rachel in the surf.

"Is that Nahoa's board?" Haleola asked, her gaze going from Rachel to a young leper sitting idly ashore.

Sister Catherine, her face slightly weathered by years in the tropic sun, nodded. "He's being rather generous; she's been out there at least an hour. And I do worry," she added with a frown, "that eventually he'll expect some sort of . . . compensation . . . for the use of his board."

"Ah, you nuns, you have nothing but sex on your minds," Haleola sighed. "This problem could be easily solved, you know, if Rachel were allowed her own board."

Catherine laughed and said, "I'll let *you* have that discussion with Mother."

Within minutes Rachel emerged from the water carrying the board under her arm. Haleola and Catherine watched as Rachel returned it to Nahoa and thanked him; and

245

though the young man did seem a bit smitten with Rachel he just smiled good-naturedly, took the board, and headed into the surf.

Haleola said, "That was a near thing, eh? Did you see that wild, crazed look in his eyes?"

Catherine shot her a sidelong glance, but this was old sport for both of them.

Rachel came running up the beach to them. "Auntie!" She gave Haleola a hug. Catherine said, "We'll be heading back in ten minutes, all right?" Rachel nodded, and as the sister moved down the beach to corral the younger girls, Rachel and Haleola sat down on the sand together.

"Today I rode a wave all the way from the Indian Ocean," Rachel declared. Haleola smiled. Years before, Rachel had read in a magazine how an ocean wave might begin as a small ripple in the aftermath of an earthquake in China, then roll across the breadth of the Pacific, gathering force and momentum until it reached Hawai'i's halo of coral reefs, which slowed it and pushed it to the surface. So each time she rode a wave, she decided, she was riding a piece of China or Japan or Samoa. It would cement Rachel's love of surfing, and give her a touchstone to those faraway lands she still longed to see.

"Oh, I heard from Papa! He's in Australia." She hesitated, then added, "He says Sarah's getting married." Her tone was wistful, quickly covered by an impish smile: "Do you suppose she'll ask me to be a bridesmaid?"

Rachel's smile poorly masked the hurt she felt at the way her mother and siblings had vanished from her life, and she from theirs. In Kalaupapa they had a word for it: *ho'okai,* to reject, be rejected. Henry Kalama, on a later visit to the settlement, admitted to Rachel that he too rarely saw Ben and Kimo and Sarah; Dorothy had ended the marriage and did not encourage visits from Henry. As painful a wound as it was for Rachel, she felt worse for Papa: one child in exile, and he himself exiled from the others. Small wonder that he always returned to the sea — the only place, she imagined, he felt at home any more.

Soon Sister Catherine appeared again, trailing a ragged line of wet, exhausted girls. "Rachel. Time to go."

"Let me just say *mahalo* to Nahoa." She started back down the beach.

Catherine shook her head. "You already thanked him."

"Well, I want to do it again!"

"Once was sufficient," Catherine said. "Come along."

Rachel glared, kissed Haleola on the cheek, and fell in step behind Catherine with ill-concealed resentment.

Haleola started back the way she had come,

climbing over a low dune — when she somehow lost her footing, slipped, and went sprawling onto the sand.

Feeling like a fool, she quickly righted herself. Luckily Rachel hadn't seen, and neither had anyone else.

Very funny, bug, she told the leprosy germ. *But don't try that again.* Gathering her dignity about her like a slightly tattered shawl, she walked slowly away from the beach, doing her best to ignore the protests of her body.

That afternoon Dr. William Goodhue, a cheerful, bespectacled Canadian who'd replaced Dr. Oliver as resident physician, made one of his frequent visits to Bishop Home. He examined the girls for cuts or scrapes that might fester into gangrene — frequently such cuts went unnoticed due to anesthesia of the skin — and offered other treatment as well. This included the intravenous injection of chaulmoogra oil, derived from an East Indian tree and used in Asia for centuries to treat leprosy. Many girls shied from the hypodermic needle, but not Rachel. She was determined that someday, despite all odds, she would get well and leave Moloka'i — return to Honolulu, see her family, see the world. Every year a handful of patients were discharged from Kalaupapa; most had been incorrectly diagnosed and never had leprosy in the first place, but a few were those in whom the disease had "burnt out," as sometimes happened to no one's understanding. Rachel, however, was resolved to *make* it happen. So she agreed to have the brownish-yellow oil injected directly into her bloodstream. The result was nausea, indigestion, loss of appetite — all too common side effects that were not lessened by the eventual development of an oral form of chaulmoogra. It was a far from pleasant course of treatment, but she submitted to it uncomplainingly. And to keep her immune system strong she followed Dr. Goodhue's advice to abstain from alcohol, get plenty of fresh air and exercise, and consume a nourishing diet, low in salt.

But Bishop Home was currently in the grip of an epidemic even Dr. Goodhue couldn't treat, one that periodically afflicted all Bishop girls. It was an outbreak of restlessness and rebellion which the nuns called "spring fever" — as though it were spread by pollen — but which even they knew was the girls' natural enough desire for greater freedom in leading their lives. The latest flare-up had been ignited by the sisters' strict rules regarding courtship. A girl and a boy were permitted only supervised visits on convent grounds, each lasting no more than an hour. After a chaste courtship, if the couple chose to marry they did so with the nuns' blessing.

But before that first chaperoned visit prospective suitors had to be approved. A sixteen-year-old girl, Louisa, wished to see a young man named Theo, but Mother Marianne considered him a troublemaker — reprimanded by Brother Dutton several times for insolence and truancy — and refused to grant him the privilege of courting Louisa.

That night the older girls — Rachel, Emily, Francine, Louisa, a Filipino girl named Cecelia, and the recently arrived Hina from East Moloka‘i — swapped grievances after lights-out.

"They treat us like little *keiki*," Louisa griped, to somber nods all around.

"No," Emily corrected her, "they treat us like prisoners!"

"We *are* prisoners," Cecelia said.

Rachel told how she'd tried to give a simple thank-you to Nahoa and been thwarted; the girls groaned in unison.

Doing her best impression of Sister Leopoldina, Francine said airily, " 'Why girls there's so much for you to do here, if you desire social companionship there's church, and the funeral societies —' "

Hoots and hollers drowned out the remainder of Francine's impersonation.

"Oh, yes," Rachel said, "the funeral society! Just the place to meet men — if you don't mind them a little cold and moldy!"

" 'You know, girls' " — Francine glowered — " 'when you abandon chastity, you open

250

the doors to Hell!' "

"Can't be worse than Kalaupapa," Emily noted, and everyone dissolved into laughter again.

Hina, who had quietly taken all this in, suddenly announced, "Hey, who wants to go to a party Friday night?"

"Not another church social," moaned Louisa.

"No no no," Hina said. "Friend of mine's throwing one. In Kaunakakai."

There was a long startled silence.

"Kaunakakai?" said Rachel. "But that's topside."

"Yeah, so?"

"We can't go topside," Louisa protested.

Impatiently Hina snapped, "Hey! Wake up! It's alla same island! Kaunakakai's only twelve miles from here." She rolled her eyes. "Look. Simple. Right after sunset we go up the *pali,* my friend Luka meets us at the top with a wagon, we go party, be back here by dawn! If we're lucky, sisters don't even know we were gone."

It was a bold, audacious idea. All of them had occasionally fantasized about escaping, but no one had ever suggested escaping *temporarily.*

A suddenly less militant Emily said, "That's crazy. How do we get up the *pali*?"

Excitedly, Rachel pointed out, "I climbed a quarter of the way up once with the sisters!

251

It's not so hard."

"Don't they have guards up there?" Louisa asked. "With guns and dogs?"

Francine shook her head. "No more dogs. McVeigh got rid of 'em."

"What if they find out at the party that we got leprosy?" Cecelia wanted to know.

Hina shrugged. "Nobody care."

"I don't know 'bout this," Louisa said, hesitant.

"Oh, I forgot," Hina said acidly, "we're *prisoners.*"

Silence all around. Emily thought a moment, then said emphatically, "Hell we are."

By late afternoon on Friday, as soon as it was judged dark enough, Hina led the half-dozen conspirators off the convent grounds and along the curving black sand beach that lay between Kalaupapa and the *pali.* At the base of the cliffs a thick stand of pandanus trees hid the girls from sight as they started up the narrow trail. Rachel, right behind Hina in the lead, craned her neck to take in the towering face of the *pali:* from down here it looked alarmingly sheer, relentlessly vertical. But she reminded herself that mail carriers made their way down each week, that even cattle were driven down the trail. How hard could it be?

Each girl wore her wine-colored uniform and carried a change of clothes in a knapsack slung across her back: the white gowns with pink or blue sashes that Bishop girls were supposed to wear only on special occasions. Well, Rachel thought, this sure qualifies! They joked and laughed as they made their way along the switchbacks that zigzagged up the *pali,* and the mood was jolly for the first half hour or so. But then the constant to-and-fro of the turns became tiresome, and the trail itself, crumbling a bit with each step, sent loose gravel tumbling onto the girls taking up the rear. Cawing gulls dropped other presents on their heads. Laughter fell into short supply.

Sometimes the trail was canopied with vegetation; sometimes it clung rather precipitously to the *pali.* Rachel made the mistake of looking down and felt a jab of vertigo as she realized she was virtually suspended hundreds of feet in the air — and the only thing that kept her from plummeting down was a frangible ledge of earth barely a foot wide in spots.

Wild goats clung to even narrower ledges above them, and as the goats scuttled back and forth their hooves dislodged more dirt and gravel onto the girls. Soon, the path narrowed even more, and was now decorated by the occasional bleached bones of a cow that had been unsuccessfully herded down. Looking at the carcasses, buzzing with flies, Rachel had a sudden unwanted vision of her body lying pulped at the foot of the *pali*.

As they ascended into clouds floating a thousand feet above Kalaupapa, visibility decreased to zero and sprinkles of rain added to their misery. The trail grew muddy and slippery and Emily lost her footing; Rachel grabbed her by the wrist, saving her from joining the cattle.

Emily got shakily to her feet, nodded gratefully at Rachel. "Thanks." Then she said to Hina, "Alla same island, huh?"

Hina just shrugged.

It was among the longest two hours of Rachel's life, and except for her journey to Kauhakō, the filthiest — by the end of the climb their faces and dresses were caked with mud. But at last they reached the summit and stood on solid rock overlooking the peninsula. And as they gazed down and saw the white and green bungalows of Bishop Home shrunk to the size of pebbles, it occurred to all of them at the same time: *they were out.* The hold the sisters had over them was gone, left behind like the clouds they had pierced. They could go anywhere, do anything they wanted.

And what they wanted was to go to a party.

A padlocked gate was easily surmounted. They climbed over it and hiked through an arbor of trees, emerging into a green meadow grazed by cattle, when they heard a voice.

"S—Stop!"

They turned, unsurprised, and saw a young guard in his twenties, startled by this procession of young women with muddy faces. He was holding a shotgun in his right hand but it was pointed at the ground; the thought of aiming it at them seemed not to have occurred to him.

Hina smiled. *"Aloha,"* she said cheerfully. The other girls added their greetings as well.

The guard just stared at them. Occasionally girls from Bishop Home climbed the *pali* for sport, but not this late in the day and certainly not unescorted by nuns. "What — what are you doing up here?" he stammered.

"Oh, just goin' to a social," Hina said casually. She turned to the others and announced, "We better change."

As one, the Bishop girls dropped their knapsacks onto the grass, and began stripping off their purple uniforms.

Blouses and skirts fell to the ground in heaps. None of the girls was wearing any underclothes, and the young man found himself staring at six unabashedly naked women.

"No worry," Hina said as opened her knapsack, "we gonna be back by dawn."

Emily passed around a canteen so that each of them could wash up with a little water. "Girl's gotta look good if she's goin' to a social," Emily winked to the guard. They all took slightly longer than necessary to remove

255

clean clothes from their knapsacks.

The guard was blushing, but no one saw him turn away either. The girls stepped into clean dresses, adjusted straps, slipped on fresh sandals.

"Hina," Rachel asked as she stuffed her dirty uniform into her knapsack, "we change again on the way down?"

"Sure, sure. Can't go down in these." Hina hiked up her skirt, asked the guard, "You be here when we get back?"

He made no response at first, then slowly nodded.

"We'll see you later then, 'ey?" Hina signaled the girls to follow, blowing the guard a kiss as they passed; he watched, nonplussed, as the girls sauntered up the trail to Kala'e. As they rounded a bend Rachel looked back and saw that the guard was still staring. She waved at him. After a moment he waved back.

They ran laughing through pastures scattered with guava trees, finally reaching the government road where Hina's friend Luka (alerted by a clandestine telephone call) waited in a rickety old wagon. And then they were off, the wagon bouncing over roads rougher than anything Rachel had known on O'ahu. She watched the landscape roll past, green hills and deep valleys, endless acres of arable land. Most of this, Hina told them, had once belonged to High Chief Kapuāiwa, who became Kamehameha V; now it was the property of the American Sugar Company. "Some day *haoles* gonna own everything except the nose on your face," Hina predicted.

In the vastness of these open spaces, even the air tasted different to Rachel. It tasted of freedom.

On the outskirts of Kaunakakai, houses began springing up along the road, everything from tumbledown shanties to fine whitewashed cottages on stilts. Even the most ramshackle of them seemed to sit regally amid acres of taro, pineapple, or coffee. The wagon slowed to allow a man on horseback to cross its path; the handsome rider smiled and tipped his hat at the wagonload of pretty, giggling girls. Then a gust of wind blew Rachel's hair back into her face, and with the wind came — something else.

It was a voice raised in song — a beautiful voice. A man's voice, not low and deep but high and sweet, singing in some unfamiliar language:

"E lucevan le stelle
ed olezzava la terra . . ."

No; not totally unfamiliar. Rachel had heard something like it at the docks once, spoken by a sailor, or a stevedore, a man from . . .

Italy! That was it!

257

The wagon started moving again but Rachel cried out, "Wait!" and jumped out of the cart. Who on earth could be singing so sweetly in Italian, here in the wilds of Moloka'i?

"O! dolci baci, o languide carezze —"

She probed the darkness for the owner of the beautiful voice, but saw no one. Now she noticed, too, that the singer was accompanied by a piano, equally invisible. And there was something else about it, some unique quality of sound Rachel couldn't quite identify.

Emily jumped out of the wagon to join Rachel. "Who's that singing?"

"I don't know, but it sounds like it's coming from over there." She started toward a small clapboard house standing about fifty feet in from the road.

"Rachel, come on, come back!" Hina called out. To her dismay the other girls, out of curiosity, got out and followed Rachel down the path to the house. "Aw, hell!" Hina swore, and went after them.

A *haole* man sat in a rocking chair on the *lānai* — the porch — his eyes closed, a blissful smile on his face. There was still no sign of the singer himself, but as Rachel drew nearer she noticed an unusual device on a wicker table beside the man. It looked like a fancy shoebox made of dark polished wood, with a crank on the side. Atop the shoebox was a mechanical apparatus of some kind, inside which a grooved cylinder was rotating. But most strikingly, rising up out of the box was an enormous metal funnel — black with golden highlights, twice the size of the box itself — which resembled nothing so much as the trumpet-shaped flowers of a morning glory.

With a start Rachel realized that the voice, the music, was coming out of that enormous metal flower!

As Rachel and the others approached, the man on the porch opened his eyes, gave them a friendly smile, motioned them closer as the song concluded.

"E muoio disperato!
E non ho amato —"

The voice soared to impossible heights, at once tremulous and strong, finishing with a flourish:

"— mai tanto la vita!"

The cylinder stopped rotating and the *haole* — amiable looking, bald but with a fringe of white beard — turned to greet his guests. *"Aloha."*

"Aloha," Rachel said. Then, with a wondering glance at the machine: "What is that?"

259

"A gramophone," he replied, with a slight Irish accent. "You've never seen one?"

"I have," Hina said, bored. "Victrola?"

"Columbia, actually. The horn's a beauty, isn't she?"

"How'd that voice get inside the box?" Francine asked.

"Ah, well," the man said, pleased for the opportunity to show off, "it's not in the box, it's on this cylinder. It's called a recording. Different sounds become different grooves on the disc, you see, and this stylus" — he pointed to a kind of needle — "turns them back into sound."

Francine eyed him dubiously.

"Who was singing?" Rachel asked.

"Ah, that was Caruso! The greatest tenor in the world."

Rachel eyed the wax cylinder on the gramophone. "Was this . . . 'recording' . . . made in Italy?"

The man nodded. "Milan, I believe." He cranked the phonograph, and in moments the same voice, with precisely the same inflections, again floated out of the horn.

Rachel marveled at it. Here she was in Hawai'i, listening to a voice that had first stirred the air of Milan, Italy, on the other side of the world. Part of that distant place had been engraved onto the cylinder spinning in front of her, to be conjured up again anywhere, anytime. And not just a place to be conjured, but etchings of a past time brought to life again, at will. When this man Caruso died this recording would live on, the sound of his voice continuing to stir the air long after.

"Who cares, a gramophone!" Hina shouted. "We got a party to go to!"

Hina prodded the girls back to their wagon, Caruso's *canto di addio* bidding them sweet farewell.

Downtown Kaunakakai was a single street no more than three blocks long; it looked more like a plantation camp than a town. All of its businesses — including the biggest, Chang Tung's general store — were closed, with the exception of a saloon owned, Hina said, by Rudolph Meyer's son Otto. That was boisterously open, but Luka drove past it and down a side street to a little cottage. Inside and out there were people laughing, talking, drinking. Guitar music drifted out through the open door.

Thrilled to be topside, pleased with their own daring and wickedness, the Bishop girls mingled with the other guests. Soon Emily was asked to dance and Hina was laughing with old friends. Rachel accepted her first beer ever; she took a swallow, started to blanch but turned it into a smile. Louisa seemed not to share Rachel's distaste, downing three Schlitzes in rapid succession. Cecelia disappeared with a boy early on.

Only the usually gregarious Francine shied from joining in the fun. Rachel noticed that she was hiding her disfigured left hand; nearly fingerless now, it never came out of her dress pocket. Rachel joined her and they listened to the guitarist singing and playing Hawaiian tunes. She was surprised to see that he strummed the strings not with his fingers but with a kind of steel bar; the result was music unlike anything Rachel had ever heard, the chords sounding almost crystalline. Someone passed a calabash of *poi* around the room and Rachel was about to dip into it when she stopped, realizing the risk to which she would be exposing the other guests. She passed the calabash on; a minute later she was disturbed to see tipsy Louisa scoop some *poi* from the bowl with two fingers, eat it, then take some more. Rachel tried to get Louisa's attention but it was no use — her mind seemed to be somewhere between Moloka'i and the moon.

A tall, good-looking young man came up and invited Rachel to dance. She knew how — the nuns had taught her — but she had never danced with a boy before and she felt her cheeks growing hot with embarrassment as he led her onto the makeshift dance floor.

He took Rachel's left hand in his and slipped his other hand around her waist. "I'm Tom Akamu," he said.

"Rachel Kalama." Her skin tingled where he was touching it; she found it difficult to

262

look at him without blushing.

"I don't see you here before," he said. "You local?"

She shook her head. "From Honolulu. I'm . . . visiting." Technically it was true.

"You pretty tall for a *wahine.* I like that. Not many girls I can almost look in the eye, you know?"

They danced and talked about nothing in particular — how Tom was born in Hālawa Valley and now worked for the Moloka'i Ranch — and Rachel spoke about her family as though she had just left them for a pleasure trip and would be seeing them in only a week's time, as though the last nine years in Kalaupapa had never happened. She liked the pretense; she liked the comforting sensation of normality she felt in this boy's arms. Ever so gently he drew her closer, leaving no air between them. With more ease than she had expected she leaned her head against his shoulder, liking the feel of his chest rising and falling as they danced to the sweet strains of "Hali'alaulani."

"I am your new love to be kissed
My flower, my lei, my love for you
Is unforgettable . . ."

Tom leaned in to her, his breath grazing her cheek. Rachel tipped her face up to meet his and his lips brushed hers. What began as the lightest of touches quickly became more urgent. Rachel's whole body thrilled at the sudden, unexpected intimacy: a man she barely knew was kissing her, wanted her, and she found to her delight that she wanted him as well. She thought neither of her past nor her future; for a moment she was gloriously normal, a girl like any other in the arms of a boy who desired her.

But as she reveled in the normalcy of her passion a voice within reminded her why she found it so exciting.

you dirty leper

She broke away from him, a reflex. Tom looked at her with confusion. "Something wrong?" he asked.

He stepped toward her and she shrank back.

"I — I'm sorry," she said. "I . . . can't."

She couldn't bear the hurt and disappointment in his eyes. She turned and ran away, away from the sweet music and sweeter temptation — and past a knowing Francine.

Rachel bolted out of the house, into the balmy night. She ran through the front yard and onto the dusty path on which Luka's wagon sat, the horse chewing its cud. Tears blurred her vision as rain had that long-ago day at Bishop Home; after a few blocks she saw the backs of the buildings along Main Street, and rounded the corner.

She hurried past the raucous laughter and

264

loud music of the saloon, only slowing when she was safely past it. She paused in front of Chang Tung's closed store and found herself peering into its window. Much of what she saw in it was familiar, but it was the unfamiliar which drew her attention: a cherry-red sign showing a regal woman in an ivory gown, carrying a feathered fan, promoting something called *Coca-Cola (Delicious · Refreshing · At Soda Fountains · 5¢).* A bottle whose yellow label identified it tersely and mysteriously as *Bayer Aspirin.* A hand-lettered sign announcing, *Now taking orders for new "Gillette Safety Razor."* A handful of magazines stood propped up, covers fading in the sun: one showed a young couple riding in a shiny new carriage gliding horseless down a country road, giving Rachel her first glimpse of an "automobile." Another magazine had fallen over and its back cover, upside down in the window, entreated Rachel to *Take a KODAK with you* — a "folding" camera a fraction of the size of the bulky tripod cameras she had seen in Honolulu as a child.

It was like gazing into the future, except the future had already happened.

"Rachel. You okay?"

Rachel turned to find Francine at her side.

"Yeah," Rachel lied, "sure."

They were silent a moment as they took in the contents of the store window, and then

Francine said, "This maybe wasn't such a good idea."

Rachel took Francine's gnarled hand in hers, cupped her fingers around it, and nodded.

The party looked to go on all night but Hina began gathering the girls together around one A.M. This was still cutting it a little close. The wagon ride to Kalaʻe would take a couple of hours, the descent down the *pali* another two; they'd be lucky to get back before dawn.

Cecelia very nearly had to be pried, like a flapjack off the griddle, from the arms of a deliciously naked young man behind the house; and Louisa, having passed out long ago, was mercifully pliant as Rachel and Emily poured her into the wagon, though halfway across the island she woke with a start and began vomiting over the side.

When Luka stopped the wagon on the outskirts of Kalaʻe and the Meyer estate, the girls got out and all stood there silently a moment, the same thought passing through all their minds. Emily was the one to vocalize it: "Why the hell we going back?"

Rachel's heart was racing, out of excitement or fear, she wasn't sure which.

"Yeah," Cecelia said thoughtfully, "good question."

Hina pointed out that there were parts of East Molokaʻi so remote a person could live there for years without being found.

"Same thing on Ni'ihau or Kaua'i," Cecelia said. "We could hide there forever before anyone finds us!"

Rachel breathed in the air sweet with freedom and adventure. She wanted to keep breathing it, wanted it more than anything else on earth. But now the unease she'd felt in Kaunakakai assumed a shape she could recognize.

"You're not free," she found herself saying, "if you're in hiding."

Hina sneered. "Says who?"

Rachel said, "I won't spend my life running and hiding like some criminal."

Hina laughed shortly. "We're already criminals."

Rachel replied with a vehemence that startled even herself.

"No, we're not!" she snapped. "They can arrest us. They can send us here, make us prisoners. But they can't make us criminals!

"I want to leave Kalaupapa as much as anybody," she told them. "But when I do it'll be because I'm cured — discharged! That's the only way *I'll* ever be free."

Before she could think twice about it, she turned and started walking down the road to Kala'e.

Francine fell in step behind her. One by one the other girls followed.

The guard was still there at the summit —

seemed to be waiting rather eagerly, in fact — and once again they disrobed and changed back into their burgundy uniforms, waving a cheery goodbye to him as they headed toward the trail. He waved and called out, "Come back anytime!"

Descending the *pali* was a hundred times worse than climbing it. The dark of the trail beneath their feet blended with the darkness of the sky and the ground far below — every time Rachel took a step she worried that she was stepping into space. Francine stumbled once and Louisa needed to be supported for part of the way, but at long last they could glimpse the black sickle of 'Awahua Beach in the moonlight; in minutes they were back on solid ground. They hurried to Bishop Home, stealing across the convent's back lawn, tiptoeing toward their dormitory.

And as they rounded a corner, they suddenly found themselves facing Mother Marianne — older but no less intimidating — holding a lantern and equally surprised to see them there, in their dirt-encrusted uniforms, at five in the morning.

Louisa threw up again.

Hina grasped at something, anything, to say. "Ah . . . we were just . . . just —"

She stopped, not having the vaguest idea what they were "just" doing. Mother stared, clearly amazed and relieved to see them . . .

and after a long moment, she let out a weary sigh.

"I don't want to know," she said, much to the girls' astonishment. "I really don't." She took in their dirty faces and filthy uniforms. "For heaven's sake get yourselves cleaned up. Go wash your clothes in the stream, no one's going to do it for you. And we won't speak of this again. Is that understood?"

The girls nodded. Louisa still looked queasy. "Child," Mother said, "if you're going to retch, by all means do so. The bushes are right over there."

Louisa headed for the shrubbery and did as she was told. The others gratefully ran for the dormitory, but as Rachel passed her Mother called out, "Rachel?"

Rachel stopped. Looked nervously at her. But all Mother said was, "Why did you come back?"

Rachel hesitated . . . then broke into a mischievous grin. She shrugged nonchalantly. "We just went to a party."

She turned and ran off, and Mother just stood there, quite at a loss for words.

CHAPTER 11

1904

There is nothing sadder, Catherine thought, than a child's grave. On a visit topside a few years back she had attended services at Our Lady of Sorrows Church on the island's south shore. Built thirty years before by Father Damien, it was a charming white-washed chapel with a red steeple and roof, tucked in the lee of green mountains — a scene as still and peaceful as the waters of the ancient fishpond across the road. It was one of the most serenely beautiful spots Catherine had ever seen, and after the service she spent over an hour — thinking, praying, meditating — on the grassy apron of land that surrounded the church and in the shady tangle of trees that bordered the property. She wandered amid gravestones scattered like runes between trees and church, the saddest burned into her memory even as names were burned into plain wooden markers: *Beloved Son, James K. Hua, March 2, 1892–August 12,*

1894. She tried to imagine what had happened in that short span of time. Had he spoken his first word, could he name his mother or father before he was taken from them? *William Makana, January 1, 1882–January 4, 1882. Christine Mililani, August 4, 1893–August 4, 1893.* These were the most heart-rending: had they ever been cradled in their mother's arms? Had their eyes even opened to see the parents who birthed them? She would never know, and would never stop wondering.

Here in the Catholic section of Kalaupapa's own cemetery there was no wondering. Catherine had known almost every young soul committed to this earth. *Lucille Wong, November 12, 1888–January 19, 1899. Marianna Kalakini, February 14, 1891–February 16, 1891. Hazel Naa, May 2, 1880–October 12, 1898. Noelani Kapaka, June 5, 1882–July 22, 1899. Josephina Consuela Marcos, March 18, 1887–September 7, 1901.* She knew the sound of their voices, the things that had made them laugh; had seen too vividly the scars their illness left behind in its cruel march through their bodies. She came here once a week to remember those she feared might otherwise be forgotten and to meditate on the question she had asked Sister Victor a decade before. Why does God give children leprosy? She still had no answer for it, but

271

smiled at least to think of Sister Victor, living in quiet, happy retirement in Syracuse.

Catherine said a prayer for her sleeping girls, crossed herself, and left the cemetery for an occasion far from tragic but nevertheless sad, at least for her.

Normally the dining hall would have been closed this late in the morning but today it bustled with activity and chatter. Sister Leopoldina was cutting and serving slices of chocolate cake as the girls of Bishop Home said goodbye to one of their own: Rachel Kalama.

A week ago Rachel's adopted aunt had failed to appear for a planned rendezvous at the beach and a worried Rachel insisted they check on her. They found Haleola abed, her nerves so inflamed that she had been effectively paralyzed for two days. After a week in the infirmary she was greatly improved, but clearly she was no longer able to live on her own. Dr. Goodhue suggested, to Haleola's horror, the Bay View Home for Elderly and Helpless Women; but before Haleola could cry "No!" Rachel declared she would take care of her auntie. She was two months shy of her eighteenth birthday, at which point she would be free to leave Bishop Home; and Mother, perhaps suspecting that Rachel would do so with or without permission, gave her dispensation for an early discharge.

The girls at the farewell party were so

distraught one would have thought Rachel was moving to Australia and not merely half a mile away. They hugged her and cried with her, and Catherine wondered how many of them would be here a year from now. Despite occasional "spring fever," many girls stayed in the Home until they married, and a few even chose to remain all their lives . . . however long that might turn out to be.

Catherine waited for a lull in the well-wishing, then stepped up to Rachel and joked, "Promise me you'll write!"

Rachel laughed. "Sure. I'll even deliver the letter, too." She hugged Catherine, who found it a bit harder to speak than she had expected and was touched to see that Rachel was trying hard not to cry.

"Thank you for taking my papa and me to Kalawao," Rachel said, "and for about a million other things too."

Emily rapped a spoon on her cake plate, calling for quiet. "Okay, finish stuffing your mouths and listen up!

"Bunch of us were trying to figure out how to say good luck to Rachel, out there in the big bad world" — she rolled her eyes — *"three blocks away."* Everyone laughed at that, even the nuns. "So Rachel — you want to come with us?"

A puzzled Rachel was led out of the dining hall, onto the front lawn, and instructed to keep her back turned until told otherwise.

Catherine smiled at the look of confused anticipation on Rachel's face and when Emily announced, "Okay, you can turn," Rachel fairly spun around.

Francine, Emily, Louisa, and Cecelia were standing next to — were in fact dwarfed by — a nine-foot surfboard, crudely fashioned but no less beautiful for that.

Rachel gasped in amazement and delight. She hugged each girl in turn before she allowed herself to touch the sleek board. "It's beautiful! It looks just like Nahoa's!"

" 'Cause it *is* Nahoa's," Emily laughed. "We didn't have time to have one made, so Nahoa sold us his. He wanted to make a new one anyways."

"But where'd you get the money?"

Emily shrugged. "Around." She didn't elaborate and Catherine hoped Rachel wouldn't inquire further, or notice the brief flick of Emily's gaze toward the sister.

Rachel was too enamored of her new board to ask questions, though one did now occur to her. *What if Mother sees it?* She turned to suggest that they might discreetly move the board before the Reverend Mother got wind of it . . . only to see, standing on the front steps of St. Elizabeth's Convent, the frail figure of Mother Marianne herself, a bemused if not entirely approving smile on her face. And more than anything else could, that smile told Rachel that she was on her own now.

Later, she discovered how difficult it was to squeeze the past seventeen years inside her old steamer trunk. When she had turned ten, with a growing thirst for reading barely quenched by the Bible and religious story-books on hand in Bishop Home, Rachel had asked her father if from now on he wouldn't mind sending her books instead of dolls. A month later came the first volume of her library: an illustrated edition of Verne's *Around the World in Eighty Days.* The next decade would see added *Alice's Adventures in Wonderland, The Adventures of Tom Sawyer, Treasure Island, Twenty Thousand Leagues Under the Sea, Captains Courageous,* and *The Call of the Wild.* Only one book was ever confiscated by the Sisters: Henry James's *The Turn of the Screw,* which they feared might be too horrible for her sensibilities. Clearly they had never heard a good old Bishop Home ghost story in all its glory.

So it was a heavy trunk that the convent's handyman helped Rachel carry to Haleola's small cottage off Damien Road. She didn't have the fine bed she had in Bishop Home, just a simple straw pallet, but that didn't matter; she had Haleola, who despite protestations that she could take care of herself was immensely pleased to have Rachel here.

In Bishop Home all of Rachel's needs —
food, lodging, clothing — had been met by
the sisters. This was technically true outside
the convent as well: the territorial government provided each resident of Kalaupapa
with a weekly allotment of taro, beef, sometimes rice or fish, as well as "ration tickets"
good for clothes and other incidentals. But
the diet was limited and the clothing allowance inadequate. Residents could supplement
their diet by fishing, hunting, growing their
own vegetables, or by purchasing other items
at the Kalaupapa Store. Some patients came
to Moloka'i with adequate funds; many did
not. If they needed or wanted more money
they could work — at the infirmary, the
dormitories, or other settlement offices —
and be paid a modest government salary.
Even in Kalaupapa there was some distinc-
tion between rich and poor: *haole* patients
generally had more money, and the government even provided them better food, justify-
ing it on the grounds that non-Hawaiians
could not be expected to subsist on a "native
diet."

Rachel received a little cash each month
from Papa, and Haleola had some small savings as well. Rachel was able to enjoy a few
small luxuries in addition to the basic government supplies. In the days that followed her
release from Bishop Home, she took unexpected pleasure in some of these: getting up

early to buy fresh bread from Galaspo's Bakery (as Mama once had at Love's), or drinking a cup of hot tea at Will Notley's coffee shop. It was the freedom to do whatever she wished that excited her most, a freedom she hadn't known since her childhood in Honolulu.

But freedom could be scary too, as she discovered on the beach one day when her surfing pal Nahoa suddenly kissed her — and though part of her wanted to return his friendly ardor, another part made her pull back.

"You're so pretty, Rachel," Nahoa said, so sweetly Rachel felt guilty for pulling away.

Flustered, all she could think to do was to say *"mahalo"* for the compliment, kiss him on the cheek, and run back into the surf. It seemed to work — Nahoa accepted the mild rebuff gracefully enough — but how much longer it would work, how much longer she *wanted* it to work, she didn't know. The sudden license she had to make love with him if she wished was overwhelming, and more than a little frightening. Sisters Catherine and Albina and Leopoldina were no longer there to stand sentinel over Rachel's virtue . . . and she was actually beginning to miss them!

The latest of Dr. Goodhue's therapies, and the most popular, was the eucalyptus bath. Similar to Dr. Goto's old treatment, now abandoned, it was essentially a pleasant immersion in hot water infused with eucalyptus oils. The baths didn't cure leprosy, but did alleviate many discomforts associated with it; and the eucalyptus scent kept away mosquitoes bearing other diseases. One day, while helping Haleola as she stubbornly continued to make her rounds of patients, Rachel made the mistake of suggesting to George Wakina that the eucalyptus bath might relieve some of his aches and pains. He exploded at her.

"Hah! Last time I went to a *haole* doctor was to get a vaccination — so I don't get sick with measles or smallpox! Instead I get leprosy! You think that was an accident?"

"It wasn't?" Rachel asked innocently.

"Hell no, no accident! *Haoles* wanted our land, right from the start. They give us shots, we get leprosy and die, they take our land! Big coincidence, eh?" He snorted contemptuously. "No *haole* doctors for me!"

Rachel had to admit, she flinched a little at the hypodermic needle the next time she saw Dr. Goodhue for her weekly dose of chaulmoogra oil. But this time Goodhue surprised her by saying, "Rachel, it's become apparent the chaulmoogra hasn't yielded much in the way of results for you. I'd like to try something else."

"You mean like Solol treatment?"

Goodhue chuckled. "You know the lingo almost as well as I do, don't you? No, this is a new approach — my own, for better or worse. I want to try treating leprosy as a surgical disease."

"Surgical?" Rachel asked nervously. She could only imagine what Mr. Wakina would say to this!

"Yes. You see, leprosy is a fairly localized disease; it isn't present in a person's blood, just their tissues. I believe that by excising the tumors where they grow, it might discourage the growth of new tumors, might even eliminate the disease entirely from your body, eventually.

"Now I must admit, some of my colleagues disagree with me rather vociferously about this. But I can't help thinking that they oppose it out of fear I may be right — fear of performing surgery on infected patients."

"And you're not afraid?"

Goodhue shrugged. "I'm hardly fearless, but I suspect leprosy isn't nearly as contagious as is generally assumed. Father Damien contracted it, but he welcomed patients into his home and would even eat from the same calabash as his flock. Yet look at the Franciscan sisters: in fifteen years, not a single nun has come down with the disease. Why? Because they take commonsense precautions."

Rachel frowned. "If it isn't contagious, what are we all doing here?"

"It *is* contagious, to an extent. And your people are more susceptible to it for the same reason you're susceptible to measles or smallpox. You simply had no resistance to it, or any of the other foreign plagues we've brought you.

"Some of you have more resistance than others, though, and I think you're one of them, Rachel. I think I can help you. I'd like to try."

Though a little apprehensive at the thought of someone actually cutting into her body, Rachel agreed to the surgery.

Her apprehension wasn't mitigated any when, on the day of the operation, Goodhue wrapped her in Esmarch bandages so tight she had difficulty breathing — or perhaps that was just her anxiety. "What are these for?" she gasped out.

"To reduce bleeding. To arrest your circulation."

"Well, boy, it's sure working then," she said breathlessly.

"Just try to take a deep breath and relax." He started to describe the procedure. "This first operation, I'm only going to excise this sore on your left leg. I'll do what's called a radical dissection of all the leprous tissues, then irrigate it with zinc chloride —"

Rachel said queasily, "Can you put me to sleep now?"

Goodhue complied and administered the anesthetic. Rachel took a deep breath of it and the world went away.

When she awoke, hours later, the doctor was at her bedside, assuring her that all had come off without a hitch. The tumor was completely gone, and in its place Rachel bore a bandage which would remain on for some weeks.

Rachel looked down at the bandage and thought: goodbye, sore. Goodbye, leprosy. Someday I'm sending you into exile, like you sent me.

She leaned back in the bed and smiled, feeling excited at the prospect; feeling hope.

The recuperation from surgery necessitated a brief sabbatical from surfing, but she was able to participate in most other activities — the including the weekly ritual of Steamer Day. If she couldn't actually be ocean, at least she could get close to it by greeting the newest ship on the Moloka'i run, the SS *Likelike.*

The assistant superintendent, J. K. Waiamau, met each new arrival much as the now-retired Ambrose Hutchison once had — taking down names and ages, arranging for lodging. As the passengers in the last rowboat came ashore, Rachel couldn't help noticing a tall, slim, strikingly attractive young woman, a little older perhaps than Rachel, climbing up the ladder and onto the concrete breakwater. Her skin was honey-brown, her features delicate; her black hair was piled beneath a straw hat adorned with plumeria blossoms;

she wore a tailored blouse, colorful scarf, and long dark skirt, belt cinching a tiny waist. Why, she looks like the Gibson girl! Rachel thought, recalling the fashionable lady whose picture she'd seen in magazines. The newcomer smiled a dazzling smile at the man who'd given her a hand up, then with a confident stride that belied any need for help, she approached Mr. Waiamau, who seemed to take extra pleasure in his job today as he inquired what her name might be.

"Leilani Napana," she answered, seeming to enjoy his barely concealed admiration.

"Age?"

"Let's just say, somewhere between fifteen and fifty."

Waiamau laughed. "It's not me asking. It's Mr. Roosevelt."

"Well, if he wants to know that badly, Teddy can come ask me himself," Leilani said with a wink.

Waiamau sighed. "Place of residence?"

"Here, I would think."

"Pardon me. *Former* residence?"

"Honolulu."

"Do you have friends or relatives with whom to stay in Kalaupapa?" Waiamau asked.

"I'm afraid not."

"In that case you need to talk with the sisters at Bishop Home. They provide lodging for many unattached women in the settlement."

Leilani frowned. "Um, I don't think so. I'd prefer to live on my own."

"Unless you can tell me for a fact that you're over eighteen," Waiamau said with a twinkle of mischief, "regulations require that you go talk to the sisters."

She thought about that, then muttered, "Well, it never hurts to talk," and started for Bishop Home, her retreat keenly observed by every man within a hundred yards.

Later that day, Rachel was startled to see the same woman moving into a vacant cottage. A boy from Baldwin Home, strangely, carried her suitcases inside; she rewarded him with a dime, then removed her hat and hairpins, allowing her long black hair to tumble down her back.

Rachel thought this very odd. There was usually great pressure on newly arrived single men and women to live in one of the large group homes; if they wouldn't, they either had to share houses with roommates or pay to construct their own homes, as Haleola had. But here was this woman, this Leilani Napana, settling into a house all her own!

Her stares brought the young woman out onto her *lānai,* where she smiled and greeted Rachel. "Hello."

Embarrassed, Rachel shyly returned the greeting.

The woman came down the porch steps and extended a hand; she seemed so poised and worldly that Rachel felt like a country bumpkin beside her. But her smile was warm and open. "I'm Leilani."

"I know," Rachel said.

"You do?"

"I was at the dock when you came in. I'm Rachel." She peered into the roomy cottage and said, "I, uh, guess you must be at least eighteen after all or Mother Marianne wouldn't have let you get away."

"Oh, let's just say . . . somewhere between —"

"Eighteen and eighty?" Rachel smiled and Leilani laughed, a rich warm laugh: "I'm becoming predictable. I apologize." As if to show she wasn't really as vain as she let on, she added, "I'm twenty-two." She was as tall as Rachel, but where Rachel's face was round Leilani's was long and narrow, her features more refined. "You have beautiful hair," Rachel said with a trace of envy.

"Oh, thank you. But it takes so long to dry I'm thinking of cutting it — maybe to here." She held two long tapered fingers halfway up her chest. "Yours is lovely too. Have you ever thought of braiding it?"

"I wouldn't know how."

"Oh, I can show you!" Rachel was swept inside, where Leilani — after emptying one bag of a dizzying assortment of combs, pins, and brushes — began skillfully braiding Rachel's hair as Rachel watched what she was doing in a small hand mirror. "So how long have you been here?" Leilani asked. "In Kalaupapa?"

"Ten years. And a year before that in Kalihi."

"I was in Kalihi for two years, off and on." When Rachel looked puzzled, Leilani explained, "I tried not to let incarceration interfere with my social life."

Rachel laughed and quizzed her about what Honolulu was like these days; and after Rachel's hair was twirled and teased into a series of long braided locks they both decided it looked better before, then spent another hour undoing what they'd just created. Rachel learned that Leilani had grown up in a small town on the north shore of Oʻahu, but moved to Honolulu when she was seventeen. When Rachel asked how she made a living Leilani mentioned something about having male "sponsors," and a flustered Rachel decided against further exploration of that subject.

"So how did they catch you?" she asked instead. The question brought a hard glint of pain to Leilani's eyes.

"One of my . . . benefactors . . . became jealous," she said quietly, "and demanded I see him and him alone. When I refused, he told the authorities I had the *maʻi pākē.*"

"That's awful," Rachel said, realizing as she spoke them how inadequate the words sounded.

285

"I have terrible taste in men," Lani admitted. "But how do you make yourself want vanilla or strawberry when you really don't have a taste for anything but chocolate?"

Rachel helped her unpack the rest of her bags and was staggered by the sheer volume of dresses Leilani owned — at least twenty, everything from bright floral *mu'umu'us* to the latest French fashions, all of which she claimed to have made herself. She offered to do the same for Rachel. "I enjoy it. I like starting with nothing, just a piece of cloth, and making something smart and saucy."

Within a month she had fashioned Rachel a colorful frock from a bolt of fabric ordered from Honolulu. And because Rachel and Leilani shared similarly slim, boyish figures, they discovered they could also share clothes.

Leilani introduced her to other new things as well. Whereas before a beach trip meant one thing — surfing — now she and Lani would sit on the sand, sizing up the male surfers and the contours of their wet bathing suits. "That one there," Lani would point out, "has a huge *ule.*"

"Oh, that's Nahoa. He's kind of sweet on me."

"He's very handsome."

Rachel shrugged. "I guess."

"Has he asked you out?"

"I don't have time," Rachel replied without

286

really replying. "I have to take care of my aunt."

Leilani studied her, then said, "You're still — ?" She didn't need to finish; Rachel blushed her affirmation.

"Sometimes I wonder," Rachel admitted after a moment, "if I'm waiting too long."

"And what is it you're waiting for?"

Rachel considered that.

"I want someone to look at me like my Papa used to look at my Mama," she said at last. "The way they used to love each other, that's what I want."

Lani said, "Then it's worth waiting for, isn't it?" and the subject never came up again.

Leilani herself was in great demand among Kalaupapa's bachelors, who considerably outnumbered females. And though she spent many evenings with Rachel, Lani spent many another dancing with handsome young men at the weekly socials. She enjoyed another kind of dancing too, the *hula,* as Rachel discovered the first time she had Leilani over for dinner.

Haleola watched with fascination as Lani scooped up some small stones from the back yard, cupped them in her hands and artfully shook music from them, performing a traditional Hawaiian "pebble dance." Haleola was impressed that anyone of Leilani's age knew the *hula;* the missionaries' prohibition had driven it underground for many years. Leilani had learned it, she said, at one such secret school, run by her aunt. Haleola nodded slowly, as though something were falling into place in her mind. "You do the dances proud," she said, and Leilani bowed her head in happy acknowledgment of the compliment.

That weekend Leilani succeeded in dragging a reluctant Rachel to a party at the home of a young man Lani had just met, but only after Haleola insisted, "Am I going to break into a thousand little pieces while you're gone? Go!" Rachel went, though not happily. The man's house, on the outskirts of town, was a slightly run-down cottage filled partly with couples dancing and kissing, and partly with men getting very drunk on "swipe" beer. People had been drinking at the Kaunakakai party too, but this was different. It seemed these people were drinking not to celebrate, but to forget. There was a sullen desperation in their faces that made Rachel nervous, even more so when, after Leilani's first dance, she was whisked away by a handsome young man with the stocky frame of a fireplug. When another nice-looking boy asked Rachel to dance she accepted, and tried to lose herself in the sweet sound of the ukelele.

Halfway through the dance she heard a sudden, piercing cry — coming, it seemed, from outside.

She asked her dance partner, "Did you hear that?"

He hadn't, and now Rachel noted — faintly, over the sounds of music and chit-chat — another, definitely feminine, cry.

Rachel ran outside, into the back yard. There Leilani's stocky suitor was savagely battering her in the face — blood pouring from her nose as she kneeled on the ground, as if in violent prayer. Each time she struggled to stand up his fist drove itself into her face as he shouted curses at her. In the dark the blood spotting her dress looked black, like ink stains from a careless pen.

Rachel ran up and grabbed the man from behind, clawing at his cheeks. "Leave her alone!"

He threw her off easily, onto the stony stubble of the ground. Rachel cried out as a rock tore at her bandage and gouged the already-tender tissues of her surgical incision.

The fireplug of a man returned his attentions to Leilani, who had had time to scoop up a handful of pebbles, and now hurled them with surprising force into his face.

He screamed, clawing at the dirt and stones, trying to clear his eyes. Leilani got shakily to her feet.

Rachel got to her knees, ignoring the pain in her leg as she searched the ground for a suitable weapon. She lifted up a heavy rock, and just as Leilani's attacker was able to see again Rachel sent the stone crashing down onto his head with a loud, disturbing crack, his legs folding under him.

Incredibly enough, he was still conscious. As he attempted to rise, Rachel rushed to Leilani's side. "Can you walk?"

Leilani's lovely face was bruised and bleeding. "Hell, I can *run*," she said, voice husky with pain.

They hurried through an open meadow and across Waihānu Stream, glancing behind them constantly, at last reaching the hoped-for sanctuary of Haleola's house. Rachel's auntie took one look at them and sprang to her feet. "Some sonofabitch beat the hell out of her," Rachel explained breathlessly. Leilani's knees buckled and Rachel caught her. "Bring her to my bed," Haleola directed, and between the two of them they were able to get her into Haleola's bedroom and onto her straw pallet.

Haleola examined the bruises on Leilani's face, then, noting a patch of blood soaking through Leilani's dress, said, "I'll have to take this off." Leilani looked terror-stricken but Haleola had already lifted up the torn skirt.

Leilani had a nasty gash along her ribcage that was bleeding copiously, and livid bruises to match the leprous sores on her legs, but Rachel saw none of these; all she could see was what dangled between Leilani's legs.

In a shocked whisper Rachel said, "You got an *ule!*"

Lani winced, half in pain and half in embarrassment.

"Yes," she sighed, "I'm afraid I do."

Rachel was so stupefied she couldn't speak. Then she noticed that Haleola, who was pressing a clean cloth against the gash on Leilani's side, did not seem in the least surprised.

"You knew?" Rachel accused her.

Haleola shrugged. "The role of *māhūs* in preserving the *hula* is well known."

"Why didn't you tell me!"

Haleola said simply, "It was not mine to tell."

Rachel's face was flush with anger, betrayal. "You're a lie," she accused Leilani, "a big fat lie!"

Leilani seemed in greater pain than when she was attacked. "No," she said softly, "that thing down there is the lie."

Good God, Rachel thought; am I so naive or stupid, not to have realized? She felt furious, ashamed. "Some joke," she said coldly. "Just a big joke on me!"

"Rachel . . ." But Rachel was already storming out of the bedroom and the house. Lani tried to rise, but Haleola pushed her down: "Don't."

"She hates me," Leilani said miserably.

"Can you blame her?"

Leilani allowed as she could not.

Rachel drifted aimlessly through Kalaupapa's quiet streets, many of them named for thoroughfares in Honolulu — Beretania, Kapiʻolani, School Streets, all of which seemed to mock her as Leilani had mocked her, not a damn one of them what they pretended to be. She couldn't believe the extent of her own gullibility. Had she really lived so cloistered a life that she couldn't have seen the truth? *You grew up in a convent, you blockhead, how much more cloistered does it get?* And yet all those men who ogled Leilani — they'd been fooled, too. No, wait, they'd slept with her — him — so they *had* to know. Maybe they just didn't care. She was shocked at the idea, and shocked that she was shocked! Stupid naive little convent girl!

But the man who'd assaulted her had been fooled, and he sure as hell cared. So maybe Rachel could give herself the benefit of the doubt.

She wound up sitting on Papaloa Beach, watching the tide come in, and when her concern for Leilani's injuries had finally eclipsed her anger, she returned home, where Haleola was dusting Leilani's cuts with powdered herbs.

Rachel stood in the doorway a moment and asked her aunt, "Is she all right?"

My God, Rachel wondered, why do I still

think of her as a *she?*

Haleola nodded. Leilani smiled gratefully. "Your aunt is a talented healer."

Rachel took a step inside. "So I guess this is why Bishop Home didn't take you."

"Brother Dutton at Baldwin Home wasn't too thrilled to meet me either," Leilani admitted with a bruised smile. "Poor man was rather tongue-tied. Mr. McVeigh was called in, and he thought it best I had my own quarters."

Haleola dressed the last cut and Leilani gingerly slipped her dress back on. She thanked Haleola, offered to pay, but Haleola wouldn't hear of it. After an awkward pause, Leilani said, "Well . . . I'd better get on home."

Rachel said, "I'll walk you." Leilani looked surprised. "In case your friend comes back."

"If he comes back you call for the constables," Haleola cautioned.

Rachel promised that she would, but the streets she and Leilani traveled were nearly empty, with not a sign of Leilani's angry suitor. Maybe they'd killed him, but she doubted it. He looked too mean to die.

They walked in silence until Rachel said, "I never heard that word before. *Māhū.*"

"You mean there are some things a Catholic education still doesn't teach you?" Leilani smiled. "They say that in the old days in Hawai'i, *māhūs* were accepted as part of everyday life here — like a third sex."

Rachel walked another step or two, then asked timidly, "How do you . . . I mean, two . . . men, how do you —"

She didn't finish. Leilani told her, and despite herself Rachel looked a little queasy.

"That doesn't sound very sanitary," she observed.

Leilani laughed.

"We can't all be lucky enough to have a *kohe,* like you. So we make do with what we have." Lani paused, then added quietly, "Since as long as I can remember, I knew I was meant to be a girl. I played dolls with my sister and wanted desperately to wear the pretty *mu'umu'us* she did. A few years later, I got into a fight with a boy in my neighborhood, we were wrestling on the ground — and, my goodness, my *ule* suddenly stood up and took notice!" She laughed. "He was quite taken aback by it! Though eventually we did become, um, better friends.

"Every night of my life 'til I was sixteen I'd pray to God, asking Him to please make me a *wahine.*" She shrugged. "He made me a leper instead."

Now, as they neared her house, Leilani said, "I'm sorry, Rachel. I should have told you. But it was so . . . nice . . . being accepted *as* a woman, *by* a woman."

As they stood for a moment in front of Leilani's cottage, Rachel suggested, "Maybe I

294

should stay a while. You think he'll come back for you?"

"That kind is usually too embarrassed to admit they were taken in by someone like me. I wouldn't worry."

Rachel nodded. "So, you . . . want to go to the beach tomorrow?"

Leilani looked pleased. "Yes. Sure."

Rachel turned and started back the way they'd come; then suddenly turned, walking backwards as she called out, "If that sonofabitch comes back, we'll show him he can't get away with hitting *wahines*!"

Leilani smiled as Rachel turned and headed for home.

On November Emily celebrated her eighteenth birthday by moving out of Bishop Home, and readily accepted Leilani's invitation to share her cottage. Six months later, when Francine also abandoned the sanctuary of the convent, Leilani and Emily decided the house was really more than big enough for three. And as they and Rachel enjoyed the first thrilling flower of their adulthood, the settlement too came of age, in a different way.

CHAPTER 12

1908–09

The horses thundered down the track to the rising cheers of the crowd. There were three ponies, black, brown, and calico, with riders just as distinctive. On the black mare was a Portuguese boy of fifteen, a mere cavity where his nose had once been; on the brown mare was a twenty-year-old Hawaiian lad, a bright red kerchief around his neck masking the tracheotomy incision through which he breathed; and on the calico was a determined *wahine* with the reins looped around the vestigial stump of her left hand, her good right hand wielding a whip. The *wahine* was Francine, and she was in the lead. In the grandstand Rachel, Emily, Hina, and Leilani shouted themselves hoarse as Haleola, quiet but no less excited, watched along with her "girls."

Francine's mount easily cornered the next curve, but the black pony was closing on her. "Go! Go!" Hina yelled. "You can do it!" Rachel cried. But as the ponies rounded the bend the black one inched into the lead and the brown mare came up hard behind Francine — who did not, it must be said, look at all disturbed. By the time they rounded the next bend and began the second lap the brown mare was running neck and neck with Francine and the black pony had pulled ahead by half a length.

Francine suddenly snapped her whip, the air cracking next to the calico's face, and as Francine knew it would the animal tapped into a wellspring of strength and speed. In less than ten seconds Francine made up half the distance between herself and the lead pony. Rachel and her friends whooped with joy. As the ponies came out of the turn and into the last stretch, Francine and the Portuguese rider were almost on top of each other, barely a foot of air separating them, and the Hawaiian boy fell back by a length and a half. The crowd was now on its feet, cheering. As the riders swung into the final turn, Francine, who seemed most confident in her cornering, squeezed the calico's sides with her knobby little knees and pulled into the lead, by a nose — which is exactly how she finished the race.

"She did it again!" Rachel cried in delight.

"Damn," Emily laughed, "I bet on the Portagee!"

Rachel gaped at her. "You *what*?"

297

"Hey, six in a row, I figured she was due! Nobody's lucky streak lasts *that* long!"

Leilani laughed. "You traitorous little bitch," she said cheerfully.

Emily shrugged.

A triumphant Francine rode her calico to the reviewing stand and collected her purse of ten dollars: big money at Kalaupapa. Haleola smiled, bemused at the thought of where she was and what she was watching: a horse race, one of many that would be run this week. And on the inside of the track lay the baffling geometries of a baseball diamond, those games held even more frequently than the races. There were also athletic clubs, two brass bands, a rifle club, glee clubs — a far cry from the somber funeral societies Damien had founded. Kalaupapa had evolved from a "given grave" where the afflicted could only wait for death to a place where people lived as well as died.

Physically, too, the settlement had changed; Kamiano would hardly have recognized it, but would surely have approved. Mature foliage now covered much of the peninsula, providing breaks against the endless rake of the wind and shade for homes that once sat roasting in the sun. There were newly built stables; a new hospital; a new landing to replace the decrepit old dock; a dozen new patient cottages; a steam laundry; a bandstand; and most popular of all, a factory in

298

which fresh *poi* could be steamed without dependency on the arrival of often-rancid blocks of taro from Honolulu.

Less pleasant to contemplate were the faces of Haleola's girls. Emily's eyebrows were long gone, her eyes heavy-lidded under the weight of leprous flesh; Leilani's once-fine features were becoming puffy and bloated; and Hina's hair mercifully obscured long distended earlobes. Only Haleola's sweet Aouli was relatively unblemished, the result of half a dozen operations by Dr. Goodhue to remove sores. She bore faint scars where surgeries had removed the tumors — as did many residents, since Goodhue's surgical approach to leprosy had proved both successful and popular. The pleasing cosmetic results not only lifted the patients' spirits, but the excision of the tumors also seemed to slow the progress of the disease.

After the race Francine treated everyone to coffee and cake from the bakery; it had been a while since they had all been together like this. Emily and Francine had boyfriends in whose houses they spent as much time as the one they shared with Leilani (who put the privacy to good use). Hina lived with a boy from Hilo; only Rachel was still unattached, and taking her time to rectify the condition. "When the hell you getting a boyfriend?" Emily would ask, to which Rachel would snap, "When you getting a new mouth to replace that big one you got now?"

Afterward they all wandered down to the dock where the *James Makee,* the second steamer to arrive at Kalaupapa this week, was anchored offshore. Kalaupapa Landing was busier than anyone had ever seen it, men and material arriving constantly to service two major construction projects. The first, a multimillion-dollar Federal Leprosy Investigation Station to do research into a cure, was being built at Kalawao. The second was the new lighthouse being erected at the tip of the peninsula. A temporary light had stood there for at least a year, but it was little more than a keeper's house and a tall mast crowned with a red lantern; this new structure would be more permanent and far grander. The steamers *Makee, Likelike,* and *Iwalani* regularly deposited onto the shore tons of powdered concrete, iron, and lumber, which were then hauled a mile up the coast on the backs of men and mules. The base of the lighthouse had already been poured, an eight-sided foundation thirty feet in diameter, each side some five feet thick.

Over the months residents watched the structure take form, its iron bones flexing higher and higher into the sky as men on scaffolding slowly gave the skeleton skin and shape. The lighthouse tender *Kukui* soon joined the other steamers on the Moloka'i run — and for the first time since the Board of Health had forced the original residents of the peninsula to leave, the people of Kalaupapa, pleasantly enough, knew again what it was like to have neighbors.

Emily's jibes about Rachel's virginal state left a greater impression than Rachel was ready to admit. She was twenty-two years old, and as she looked at her friends, happily settled with their various lovers, she worried that Uncle Pono's joking prediction would come true and she *would* be an old maid. What if, while she waited for the right man to come along, her leprosy worsened and she became ugly and deformed? Would any man want her then?

Anxious and afraid she might die without ever knowing love, she made her decision. Surfing by moonlight with Nahoa, their boards balanced on the phosphorescent crest of the same wave, Rachel waited until a break between wave sets. As they lay on the beach together Rachel turned to Nahoa, took his face in her hands and kissed him. Surprised at first, Nahoa eagerly returned her ardor; as Rachel pressed closer to him she felt him growing hard, his *ule* swelling against her belly. In moments they had shed their swimsuits, Nahoa's gorged penis found its way inside her, and she gasped upon this shocking but exciting penetration of her body's most private space. His thrusts were clumsy though no less pleasurable for that, but too soon she felt his orgasm inside her and he withdrew, leaving her empty and unsatisfied. They made love again, and this time she came closer to reaching her own climax, but still fell short; after which Nahoa seemed to lose interest.

They tried once more, days later, but the results were no more rewarding and they soon fell back, with some relief, into their accustomed roles of surfing pals.

Leilani assured Rachel that hers was not an atypical first time, and urged her not to give up on the notion. But the only positive thing Rachel could see coming out of the whole experience was that the next time Emily harped on her about getting a boyfriend, Rachel could say, "Had one, thanks," and bask in Emily's stunned silence.

"Ouch!"

"Sorry." Goodhue's scalpel had just nicked the calf of Rachel's left leg. "But pain is a good sign. It means your tissues are healthy — no new nerve damage." He turned his attention to Rachel's right foot, from which only recently he had excised a leprous mass.

"Four years, six surgeries, and the tumors haven't grown back," he noted as he scraped a skin sample from Rachel's heel. "You've made excellent progress, Rachel."

Rachel beamed with pride. She was keenly

aware that the Board of Health had just "paroled" a patient who, like Rachel, had been among the first to have his tumors surgically removed. After six skin snips failed to show any trace of the Hansen's bacillus, his leprosy had officially been declared "bacteriologically inactive."

"If this one's negative," she said hopefully, "that makes two in a row, doesn't it? Only four more to go?"

"Let's not get ahead of ourselves, now. This could take another nine or ten months," Goodhue cautioned. "But I think we have every reason to be optimistic. Be patient."

The words made her spirits soar. Ten months! In less than a year, she might be cured — paroled — free!

The next day the *Makee* brought a parcel from Papa, postmarked in San Francisco; the possibility that she might someday go to what locals now called the "mainland" no longer seemed so remote. The package contained a book Rachel had requested, *The Sea Wolf.* Its author, Jack London, had visited Kalaupapa a year and a half ago; Rachel had liked *The Call of the Wild,* and worked up the nerve to tell him so. He seemed surprised to find a fan here, but was very friendly and gracious. Shortly after, he published an even-handed, sympathetic account of his stay at Kalaupapa.

Papa was still shipping out ten months of every year, but it was clear from his letters

303

that at fifty-five he was tiring of the work and the travel:

If I had one wish that God could grant to me it would be to come to Moloka'i to live out the rest of my days with my little girl, but since that won't happen I might as well sail the globe as I always have, thinking of you every day and wishing I were with you, or you with me.

By now the memory of Rachel's ugly adventure with the late and unlamented Moko was far enough distant that she could return to Kauhakō without fear of reawakening old nightmares. Haleola enjoyed the occasional picnic there, and together astride a brown stallion Rachel had recently purchased they would ride up Damien Road and onto the narrow trail Rachel had discovered fifteen years before.

At the summit they sat and looked out at the emerald bowl of the crater, abandoned now by human habitation but still very much populated: not far away a spotted deer rooted about in the underbrush; above them a flock of birds wheeled in a cloudless sky; far below, deer drank from the brackish water of the lake on the crater floor. "It *is* beautiful here," Rachel admitted.

"This crater, you know," Haleola said, "was said to be the first one dug by Pele on

Moloka'i."

"I, um, thought Pele lived inside the volcano on the Big Island."

"This was before. You see, Pele was the offspring of two gods. Her mother was Haumea, and one legend says Pele and her siblings were 'born from the brain,' that is, they sprang from their mother's head, not her loins. They lived far across the ocean in the land known today as Tahiti.

"Now Pele, like someone else I know, dreamed always of faraway places. So she set off in a canoe with two of her brothers, who controlled the tides and the currents; and after a while they found our islands, our Hawai'i Nei. Because her elemental form is fire, Pele sought an island in which to dig a deep volcanic home for herself.

"But her older sister Namakaokaha'i — a goddess of the sea, who delighted in tormenting Pele — followed her to Hawai'i. On the first island where Pele tried to dig a crater for her fire — Ni'ihau — her sister sent ground water surging into the hole, quenching Pele's flames, and Pele had to move on to Kaua'i. There she dug even deeper holes, but once again her sister flooded them, wiping out what would have been Pele's homes.

"On O'ahu she dug at Koko Head and other places, but Pele's wicked sister destroyed them too. Pele came here to Moloka'i and you see the result below us. Finally, on

305

Maui, Pele and her sister waged a fearsome battle. Pele shot streams of angry lava into the sea as her sister pounded the coastline with hundred-foot waves, trying to collapse the crater Pele had made — what we know today as Haleakalā. After days of war Pele's sister finally extinguished the fire inside Haleakalā and her pounding surf broke apart the lava bones of Pele's body. Namakaokaha'i rejoiced because she believed that she'd succeeded in killing her sister.

"But the bones were only *part* of Pele's body, and while her sister was lulled into believing she'd won, Pele traveled to the Big Island, going far inland — far out of the sea's reach — and digging a hole so deep that her sister could not breach it. The sea goddess raged in defeat and returned to Tahiti. Pele and her family have lived ever since in Kīlauea."

Rachel gave a low whistle. "I guess I'm lucky my sister only got me sent to a leper colony," she said with a smile, then worked up the nerve to ask something she had long wondered. "Auntie? Do you . . . still believe in the old gods? Are they still real to you?"

Haleola seemed surprised, even amused, by the question. "Aouli," she said, "is a daughter 'born from the brain' of her mother any less believable than a virgin who gives birth to the Son of God?"

"That wasn't what I asked."

"I know." Haleola stood, a bit shakily, and sighed. "I wish that I had been born fifty years before I was," she said. "Before the *kapus* were overthrown. When things were more certain. All my life I've lived in two worlds — the world my mother raised me to believe in, and the world around me. As a healer I was taught that sickness came from the soul, from a person's past actions and state of mind. Yet I've seen with my own eyes the tiny creatures that live in our blood, the 'microbes' that supposedly make us sick. Which do I believe? Maybe both."

She looked around her, at the lush green slopes of the crater, teeming with life; at the ocean pounding the lava coast as if Namakaokaha'i were still futilely battering her sister's bones; and up at the towering face of the *pali.* She smiled.

"I'll tell you what I believe in," she said. "I believe in the *'āina* — the land and the sea and the air around us. When our ancestors first saw the fury of the surf or the angry fire spitting from volcanoes, they saw that there was a power to these things that they could not explain. They knew they had *mana* — power. And they do. Can you look at the beauty around us, Aouli, and doubt that there is *mana* in this crater, and in the land and sea and sky that surround it?"

"No," Rachel allowed.

"No land is more beautiful," Haleola said,

"and therefore more powerful. That is what I believe in, Aouli. I believe in Hawai'i. I believe in the land."

Sister Catherine dropped into the confessional's seat and said in a trembling voice, "Bless me, Father, for I have sinned. My last confession was on Friday last."

Father Maxime André clearly noted the distress in the sister's voice and waited to hear of its cause.

"I have questioned God's will. I have felt anger toward Him. I have doubted His wisdom. And I still do."

"Sister, what has caused you to doubt?" he asked.

"I don't know where to begin." And she didn't know Father Maxime half as well as Father Wendelin, who'd left Kalaupapa after friction with superiors in Honolulu. "My . . . father committed suicide. When I was seventeen."

"I'm sorry."

"He hadn't seemed depressed or anxious," Catherine went on. "He wasn't in any financial trouble, or having an affair. One day he just took out his pistol and shot himself. Left a note saying he was sorry, but no more.

"My mother came to blame herself. She thought, when the man you've loved all these years is so troubled that he's driven to kill himself, shouldn't you know? Shouldn't you be able to see it coming? And then it's a small step to wondering, Maybe it's my fault. Maybe I failed him as a wife. What did I do? What did I fail to do?

"Well, ever since, Mama would have trouble sleeping. She'd spend half the night awake sometimes; I used to hear the floorboards groan as she paced the house. Her physician, Dr. Almont, prescribed laudanum to help her sleep."

"Laudanum. That's tincture of opium, isn't it?"

"Yes. And it did help. We all knew she'd become addicted to it, but . . . the alternative seemed somehow worse. And now my brother telephoned today to tell me" — her voice caught — "last night Mother took a fatal overdose of laudanum and died in her sleep."

"Catherine. Dear God," Maxime said softly. "I'm so sorry." He added hopefully, "Was it an accident?"

Catherine shook her head, though he couldn't see. "No. Quite deliberate. She left a note." She added quietly, "There's no way I can get back to Ithaca in time for her funeral. I'm going to miss my mother's funeral." She began to weep.

"Sister," Father Maxime said, "you've nothing to confess to. You've had an awful shock, of course you'll experience some doubt, some —"

"Listen, Father, please listen." She wiped

309

away tears, tried to order her thoughts. "When my father killed himself, our parish priest took the view . . . the charitable view . . . that my father had not been in full possession of himself. He'd had a drink that night, and Father Bernds took that into consideration and concluded that my father's suicide was not a mortal sin; and that therefore he could be given a church burial.

"I don't know if Father Bernds was right. I don't know what sort of reckoning my father had with God. But —"

Maxime said, "Your mother was under the influence of an opiate. This wasn't a rational decision —"

"It was *very* rational! She'd planned it for weeks, hoarding enough medication to do the job. She put her legal affairs in perfect order, to lessen the burden on her children. And she left a long note apologizing to us, saying she was simply tired of living with the guilt and the grief, and all she wanted was for the pain to end.

"But now I'm frightened, Father . . . so frightened . . . that far from being over, her pain is just *beginning.*"

She wept inconsolably now, and Father Maxime left his side of the confessional and came over to Catherine's; he squatted beside her, took her trembling hands in his. "She was not in her right mind when she did this," he insisted.

310

"What about my father? Was *he* not in his right mind?"

The priest hesitated. Catherine asked, "Is it a mortal sin to love someone as much as my mother did? To feel such guilt for his death that you can't bear it another day? Is that a sin punishable by damnation?

"Tell me, Father, that my mother is in Heaven. Tell me she's with my papa, and God has forgiven them both."

Father Maxime looked helplessly at her. She broke down again, and wordlessly — for he had no words — he took her in his arms and cradled her; offering her not God's comfort but his own, merely human, consolation.

On a stormy winter's day in January, as Haleola felt the rain in her bones and listened to its comforting percussion on the roof, she received her first portent. As she sat sewing, her house — closed tight against the damp cold — was suddenly suffused with a familiar fragrance: that of the sweet purple flowers of the silversword plant, which Haleola had once witnessed in rare bloom on the Haela'au trail. The silversword didn't grow on Moloka'i — even on Maui it could only be found on the slopes of Halcakalā and in the West Maui mountains, and it bloomed only in summer. But its scent now seemed to fill the room as vividly as if she were sitting on the terraced slopes above Lahaina!

"Aouli?" Rachel glanced up from *The Sea Wolf* and looked at Haleola. "Do you smell that?"

Rachel's nose twitched. "Smell what?"

"Oh . . . nothing. Never mind." Haleola, still breathing in the fragrance, wondered whether this was perhaps a trick of memory. She decided to enjoy the remembrance, if that was what it was, for as long as it lasted . . . about five minutes, after which it dissipated as though she were descending a trail into a valley, leaving the silversword high on the slopes above.

But Maui came to her in other ways as well. That night she dreamt she was floating on the surface of the sea, drifting with the current and gazing down at brilliant yellow, white, and purple coral reefs passing below her. Even in dream she recognized where she was: Olowalu, just below Lahaina, a favorite swimming spot of her youth. She was delighted to be back, pleased that everything she saw was familiar as an old friend: a great blue bush of branching coral, schools of striped and yellow fishes fluttering around it like butterflies; pink brain coral looking as if plucked from some inhuman skull; spidery little crabs skittering through a crevice in a mountain of bright green lobe coral. She smiled and floated toward a bulbous mass of white coral, another friend of days gone by....

And then one of the white coral heads opened a pair of eyes and looked at her.

Its black irises expanded in the gloom, the eyes slowly tracking her as she floated past, and Haleola panicked; she shut her eyes, as if by doing so she could shut these others too.

When she opened them again, she was no longer in the water but on the beach with Keo and the children and their old dog, the one they had found as a puppy with its jaw broken. Haleola had mended the pup, and they named it Papa Ku'i, "jawbone."

They were sitting on the sand at Kā'anapali, a pig roasting in a pit. Keo asked her to take some pork from the pit, but she was somehow afraid. The flames seared the pig's skin, blistering it black, but no matter how much Keo begged her to go to the pit she wouldn't do it.

Papa Ku'i began to howl.

Haleola woke.

She knew at once what she had just experienced: a "revelation of the night." The opening eyes, the pit, the howling dog — all of these were portents of death.

In her dream she had been afraid; here in the cool quiet night a great calm surrounded her. All this was as it should be; she'd been granted a glimpse into the future that would allow her to make the most of the present.

It was four in the morning but Haleola rose immediately, unwilling to waste even a moment. By candlelight she wrote letters to her sons and had them sealed before Rachel stirred at seven. The rain's persistent monotone on the roof became more inconstant, then ceased entirely, though a wet wind still ruffled the palm trees. Haleola was outside frying eggs on the griddle of the stone oven when Rachel came out, stifling a yawn. "Auntie, I'd have done that."

"You were sleeping." Haleola handed her a calabash and smiled. "I wanted to cook today. Have some *poi.*"

After breakfast she staggered Rachel by announcing that she would like very much to climb the *pali.*

"What! With your foot the way it is?"

"Not all the way up, just part. Would you believe in all these years I've never so much as set foot on the trail?"

"You're not missing anything, believe me."

"I want to. I'm going to." Haleola was adamant, and a worried Rachel was forced to acquiesce.

At the *pali* they threaded through thick undergrowth and onto the trail, widened again several years ago after a mail carrier's mule lost its footing and plunged to earth, nearly taking the mailman with it. Rachel kept one hand firmly gripped around her aunt's arm as they made their way up the zigzag path, first one direction, then the other, then back again. Haleola's bad foot gave her some trouble and she slipped twice, Rachel always there to support her; finally she made it without too much difficulty some fifty feet up the cliff. From here on the trail was more precarious and Haleola motioned her niece to stop.

"This will do," she said, trying to catch her breath.

"I'm so glad," Rachel sighed, still holding on to her.

Haleola saw the whole of the peninsula spread out below her: saw both eastern and western shores at once, the green bowl of Kauhakō in the middle. Foaming surf hammered the craggy shoreline, her old friends 'Ōkala and Mōkapu standing watch over Kalawao. The scaffolded tower of the lighthouse looked from here like a child's sandcastle; farther down the coast the U.S. Leprosy Investigation Station was nearing completion. And Kalaupapa with its whitewashed cottages looked deceptively normal, like any small village in the islands. Haleola smiled with satisfaction.

"I wanted to see it, once," she said, "without seeing the *pali*. Without the walls. As though I were free."

Haleola seemed uncommonly happy the rest of the day; after supper she sewed and sang a chant Rachel had heard before, one

315

that celebrated a place on her beloved Maui, then began another. Rachel, reading, only slowly became conscious of what her aunt was singing in Hawaiian:

"Hot fire here within
The act of love
Overpowers my body
Throbbing last night.
Two of us
Have felt the power
Calm after passion
Making love within my body . . ."

Rachel's eyes were wide, her cheeks hot. "Auntie!"

Haleola turned to her niece. "Yes, Aouli?"

Rachel was momentarily speechless — then burst into embarrassed laughter. "You've never sung that one before."

"Not to you," Haleola said with a grin. Rachel laughed again, went to Haleola and put an arm around her.

"Who were you singing it to? Keo or Pono?"

"Both. I loved them both, so I sang it to both." She paused, then shrugged a little apology. "I never learned a song for a daughter," she said, "because I had none."

She reached up with her good hand and touched Rachel's cheek. "You have been a gift of the land to me," she said softly. "It took me from my sons, but gave me a daughter."

Rachel took Haleola's frail body in her arms and said, "I love you, *makuahine*," a word that meant both aunt and mother; and Haleola enjoyed the warmth of her Aouli's touch for what she knew could be the last time.

She slept well that night, and the night after, and dreamt no more troubling dreams; but on the third night she was awakened by a familiar sound. Her eyes fluttered open and she saw, in a brilliant shaft of moonlight, an owl perched on the branch of the eucalyptus tree outside her window. The owl hooted again, and now she heard, as from a distance, the sound of drums and a chant. She blinked in surprise, and the owl was gone. The chant grew louder, familiar words and a familiar voice, and when she turned away from the window, there was Keo sitting at the foot of her bed. *The act of love overpowers my body,* he sang to her, *throbbing last night. Two of us have felt the power. . . .* He smiled, and beckoned her with his eyes.

She went with him.

CHAPTER 13

Catherine grieved for her mother's soul and raged against the God she was supposed to love. After confession she and Father Maxime had knelt together in prayer at the altar of St. Francis's Church, Catherine focusing on the priest's voice with its melodious accent, allowing no words but his to enter her thoughts. But on her return to the convent, kneeling in the sisters' own chapel, she had no such anchor; the supplication in her whispered prayers became edged in anger and her humility before God was transfigured into contempt. She watched wax drip down the length of a candle, its flame writhing as if in torment, and only then realized the breadth of her anger, far worse than what she'd felt on the long-ago day she'd struck Rachel. It was a deep, black, bottomless rage and as she plumbed its depths it seemed to possess her: she wanted to lash out, to overturn the altar and smash the sepulcher, hurl the holy relics to the floor and watch the candles ignite the fine white linen. She wanted to destroy it as God had destroyed everything she held dear. She didn't know which was worse, the sacrilege of the thought or the black exhilaration it brought her to think of it. With a shout of sudden contrition she leapt to her feet and ran from the chapel out of fear for what she might do.

She took refuge in her room, seeking the oblivion of sleep, but this time the angry darkness would not lift with first light. Quite uncharacteristically she stayed in bed the whole of the next day, leaving the room only to void herself or to drink from a bathroom faucet. When one of her sisters would meekly knock and inquire if she was all right, she feigned illness but doubted any of them believed it. Still, no one violated her privacy by opening the lockless door, for which she was grateful; she didn't trust herself to contain her rage and knew that none of the others would truly understand it. More than anything she wished that Sister Victor were still here; then with an unhappy laugh realized that in a way she was.

She slept a great deal and remembered little of her dreams but for sensations of sorrow and jolting movement, and long silences that were somehow loud and frightening. By the end of the second day she tried again to pray, *Our Father who art in Heaven,* but the words made her weep and not adore, and what began as devotion turned quickly to confrontation. *Why?* she demanded of God. *Why do you make us fallible and then condemn us when we fail? Why do you punish us for being human?*

The morning of her third day of seclusion she was awakened by an insistent knocking and Leopoldina's urgent tone. "Sister? Sister, do you hear me?"

To Catherine's surprise the doorknob turned, the door swung open. Leopoldina stood hesitantly in the doorway.

"I'm sorry," she told Catherine. "But I have a message for you. From Rachel Kalama."

Catherine sat up, suddenly attentive.

Leopoldina said, "Her aunt passed away last night," and Catherine was up and out of bed before she could think about it.

Rachel woke at seven A.M., saw Haleola still in bed, and knew at once something was wrong: rarely if ever did Haleola sleep longer than she. At first Rachel thought she was sick, a recurrence of the "bug," but when she called to her and there was not the slightest movement, Rachel knew. She rushed to her aunt's bedside and saw her once-puffy features now strangely clear, fluids drained from diseased flesh: death's mocking gift to the leper, an illusion of life and health when both had long fled.

Dr. Hollman, the assistant physician, concluded after a brief examination that Haleola had succumbed to a heart attack in her sleep. "A gentle death," he consoled Rachel, who nodded mechanically, too stunned yet to weep. He asked her what kind of funeral arrangements she wanted to make, but Rachel just looked at him blankly. "I don't know."

"Was your aunt Catholic? Protestant?"

Rachel said softly, "She believed in the land," and Dr. Hollman, hardly enlightened, told her he'd make arrangements for the body to be transferred to one of the settlement's funeral societies.

"I'll wait here for them," she said.

"Are you certain you want to do that?"

"Yes, I am. Thank you. Would you mind telephoning the convent and telling Sister Catherine what's happened?"

He said that he would, and reluctantly left. Rachel dragged a chair to Haleola's bedside and contemplated the woman who had been aunt and mother to her these past fifteen years; only now did she begin to comprehend the enormity of her loss. Haleola had been Pono's lover and Pono had embodied everything good in Rachel's childhood. Whenever Rachel had looked at her aunt, she had seen the comforting face of family, of 'ohana. Soon she would see that face no longer and one of the last links to her life's happiest moments would be gone. Tears filled her eyes. She touched her aunt's arm and was surprised at how disturbing the absence of warmth could be. She leaned over her aunt's face, draped in sleep, Rachel's tears trickling down Haleola's cheek as if she too were weeping, and kissed her one last time. And as she sat there watching over her, Rachel understood what she owed her, and what remained to be done for her.

So when the men from the funeral society arrived, Rachel thanked them for coming but told them that although she would welcome their help in acquiring a casket, "I'll be preparing my aunt's body for burial myself."

"You mean you — want to pick out the clothes to bury her in?"

"No, I mean I intend to prepare her body for burial myself. In the traditional manner."

They stared at her in disbelief.

"What about the grave?" asked the first man.

"What about it?"

"Which cemetery do you want her buried in?" the second asked in exasperation.

"I have a spot picked out," was all Rachel would say, and once they'd agreed to deliver the casket to her, she quickly ushered them out of the house.

Once alone she took a deep breath and hoped she was equal to the task she was setting for herself. She went to her aunt's bed, pulled back the blankets. Haleola's arms and legs were a disturbing shade of blue; rigor mortis had set in, but fortunately the body was in the extended position and not flexed to any degree. She had once watched Haleola do this, but that was long ago; she hoped her aunt would forgive her if she neglected anything.

At the Kalaupapa Store she picked out several bolts of *kapa* cloth of two different thicknesses. "Do you have any string *kapa*?" she asked. "Or, um, *hau* rope?"

The shopkeeper shook his head. "Just hemp."

"All right, I'll take a dozen yards of that."

Cloth and rope slung over her shoulder, she carried her purchases back home, dropped them off, then headed for the house shared by Leilani, Emily, and Francine, who immediately offered their help. "We'll need shovels," Rachel told them, and Emily set about borrowing some while Leilani and Francine disseminated the sad news.

Rachel returned home and stood in the bedroom doorway a moment, overwhelmed with grief and loss and more than a little apprehension; and then she began. She unwrapped the thinnest bolt of *kapa* and slid it under Haleola's legs; the body's rigidity made this easier than she had expected, but she paled when she saw that the underside of her aunt's body was covered with a purple mottling where her blood had settled in the hours after death. When Rachel touched one of these spots the pressure of her fingers dispersed the blood, causing the skin to turn white. Her hands trembled as she wrapped Haleola's legs in one bolt of cloth, her torso in another, and her head in a third, until the entire body was bundled head to toe in a thin layer of *kapa.*

She took the heavier cloth and repeated the process, draping it over and under the body, then did it again. Uncoiling the rope, she tied a length of it around Haleola's bundled ankles, cut it with a knife and knotted it. Soaked in sweat, Rachel wiped both tears and perspiration from her eyes, then cut several more lengths of rope. She saw to it each bundle of *kapa* was securely tied, until Haleola's rigid body was tightly cocooned.

The casket arrived within the hour; Rachel and Leilani placed Haleola's body inside it, and with Francine's and Emily's help carried it out to Haleola's rickety old wagon. At this point Sister Catherine arrived expecting to lend comfort to a grieving Rachel — only to find her wrestling with a coffin and tossing shovels into a wagon, as if she were both mourner and mortician, griever and gravedigger.

"You can't be serious," Catherine said, stunned.

Rachel explained her reasons and assured her, "Don't worry. You don't have to do anything more than show up."

Catherine thought about that a moment, then picked up one of the shovels and climbed into the wagon.

"Sister," Rachel warned, "you do realize this won't be a Christian service?"

"At the moment," Catherine admitted, "I'm not sure I care."

Everyone climbed into the wagon as Rachel took the reins. But instead of turning left toward the coast road and the grim necklace of cemeteries garlanding the shoreline, Rachel turned right. Catherine had assumed Haleola would be laid to rest in the graveyard reserved for Hawaiian and Buddhist burials; but as soon as Rachel turned onto Damien Road the sister knew where they were heading.

When they reached the eastern shore, Rachel brought them to a certain abandoned cottage whose disrepair brought tears to her eyes. She tied up the wagon, watered the horse from an old cistern, then began distributing shovels in a businesslike manner. Catherine took hers a little queasily but would not shirk the task. A week ago she might have quailed at it, but just now she was not nearly as concerned with propriety.

They followed Rachel into a back yard overrun with *pili* grass and lantana; Rachel hacked away at the scrub with her shovel until she was able to see the small wooden marker at the rear of the property. Rachel weeded Keo's grave as the others cleared another plot beside it. By the time they'd finished they were soaked with perspiration — all before they'd even turned an ounce of soil.

As her shovel bit into the yielding earth Catherine's mind began circling Death again, gazing into a black sun which seemed to pull her ever closer. She fought off its terrible gravity by concentrating on her obligation to Haleola, but even that led to thoughts better left untouched: here she was, digging a heathen grave for a woman who had been a kind of priest of a pagan religion, and yet she did not hesitate; in fact she rather relished it. Was this the act of a true bride of Christ?

Halfway through the dig a confused Brother Dutton appeared just beyond the broken stone fence bordering the property. He saw a sweaty quartet of girls and one grimy nun digging a hole six feet deep by three feet wide. With trepidation, he called out, "Sister?"

Catherine winced to herself but replied cheerily, "Mr. Dutton. Hello," not pausing in her toil.

"And, ah, what exactly would you all be up to here?" he asked nervously.

"Isn't it obvious?" Catherine asked. "We're digging our way to China."

The girls chuckled. Brother Dutton smiled wanly. No fool, he said, "This is hardly consecrated ground, Sister."

Sister Catherine stopped digging, straightened, and looked at him. The words emerged from her mouth without any prior consultation with her brain:

"It seems to me, Mr. Dutton, that in its own way, this whole peninsula is consecrated ground."

He considered that, and after a moment he nodded.

"I take your point, Sister." He gave them a little salute with the fingers of one hand, then walked away.

When the grave was at last dug they stripped off their clothing — only Catherine retained her underclothes — and washed away the dirt and sweat in the ocean. But Catherine found that the sea was nowhere near as cleansing as it had been on that distant night with Sister Victor, failing utterly to purge her doubt and anger.

Shortly the mourners began arriving on horseback and in wagons. There were fewer than Rachel would have liked, a reflection not on the esteem in which Haleola had been held but on the transience of life in Kalaupapa. Haleola had outlived most of her friends and patients. They, Rachel hoped, had already gathered on the other side of life to welcome the healer who had tended them through illness, alleviated their pain, delivered their babies.

But Ambrose Hutchison was here, and a subdued and respectful George Wakina, and a dozen others who now gathered with Rachel on this side of life. Rachel, standing beside Haleola's coffin, felt a flutter of stage fright, but in her mind's eye she saw the words she needed to speak, like lessons on a chalkboard.

"Lawa, Pualani, 'eia mai kou kaikamahine, Haleola," she intoned somberly. (Lawa, Pualani, here is your daughter, Haleola!)

Ambrose, a Catholic, was dismayed, but others recognized the ancient words and picked up the call to ancestors. *Lawa, Pualani, here is your daughter, Haleola!*

"Keo, here is your beloved wife, Haleola. Pono, here is your lover. Grief for our home without our friend!"

The ritual reply echoed in the gathering dusk. *Grief for our home without our friend!*

Rachel, Leilani, Francine, and Emily lifted the casket, one to each corner, and gently lowered it into the grave, the head of the coffin facing east. Rachel then stood at the foot of the grave and declared in a resonant, confident voice: *"Haleola, 'eia no 'oe ke hele nei!"* (Haleola, here you are departing!)

The words thundered in her chest, filling her with pride and a solemn grace. *"Aloha wale, e Haleola, kaua, auwē!"* (Boundless love, O Haleola, between us, alas!)

Are you here, Auntie? she wondered. *Have you taken the form of a shark in the sea, or a bird in the trees? Was this the farewell you would have wanted?*

Catherine, helping to shovel the soft earth into the grave, was both touched and disturbed that she should be so moved by this pagan rite. After the grave was rounded with earth the mourners embraced Rachel and shared their love and memories of Haleola. Catherine stared down at the freshly turned mound and tried to offer up a prayer, but none would coalesce in her mind. Instead she felt anger, anger that she should be here beside this grave and not at another, more distant one. Rage blossomed again in her breast, hot tears sprang to her eyes. No! No! She couldn't let anyone see her like this. She turned her face away but knew she could not contain the rage with a mere glance; in a panic she hurried away from the grave and the mourners. The crash of the surf against the shoreline sounded a call to her, promising in its fury to drown out the fury in her own heart, drawing her to it.

When the last mourner had headed back to Kalaupapa, Rachel lingered at the graveside saying a private, silent good-bye. It was only when she reached the wagon that she noticed all her friends were gathered there save one.

"Where's Sister Catherine?"

No one seemed to know.

329

Why would the sister leave without saying anything? And where would she go? Something about it struck Rachel as terribly wrong. "Wait here," she told the others. "Maybe she went to see Brother Dutton."

Rachel went to Baldwin Home, but the sister wasn't there. She walked across the road to St. Philomena's Church, but Catherine was neither inside the chapel nor outside paying her respects at the grave of Father Damien. Nor was there was any sign of her farther down the road, at the nascent Federal Leprosy Investigation Station.

She asked a young boy, fishing along the shore, whether he had seen a nun go by within the last half-hour.

He had, and pointed the way down the coast.

Rachel thanked him and quickened her pace, each breaking wave trumpeting her own anxiety and fear, a fear she could not quite put a name to.

And then with a rush of something that wasn't quite relief, she saw her.

Catherine stood on the edge of a low bluff perhaps ten feet high — a bluff that looked down on a lava outcropping vaguely resembling a human hand, its black fingers poking into the turbulent sea. The wind whipped the waves into wild geysers spuming high into the air. With each gust the sister's habit flapped and billowed like a Halloween ghost, and in fact Rachel's first thought was that she looked like a soul ready to leap into the *pō,* the next world.

Rachel's fear found its name and she cried, "Sister!" over the roar of the surf.

In the distance the sister turned, saw Rachel, and smiled cheerlessly.

Rachel started toward her.

Sister Catherine turned away sadly, then stepped off the bluff and into the raging sea.

Rachel screamed, running so fast she could barely take in air. At the edge of the bluff she saw the sister bobbing in the frothing surf between jagged, unforgiving rocks like the teeth of the wicked Namakaokaha'i.

Rachel knew this spot, knew the water was deep enough that the fall, at least, would not kill anyone. She leaped in after her friend, plunging into high winter waves.

Once submerged, she fought against the treacherous current and kicked herself upwards. Her wet clothes slowed her ascent, but finally her head broke the surface — only to be immediately inundated again in the spray of a crashing wave. She could scarcely find enough air to breathe.

Through eyes stinging with salt she saw Catherine, less than ten feet away, but unlike Rachel the sister was making no effort to resist the buffeting waves. Rachel swam toward her, but the swells slapped her back and she lost two feet of headway for every foot she gained. She watched helplessly as Catherine was thrown up against a huge lava rock and lost to sight amid an explosion of surf.

Rachel took in the biggest gulp of air she could and dove underwater. Here below the stormy surface it was a little calmer, but the currents were still perilous.

Up ahead she saw one of the sister's legs jutting at an odd angle into the water, a plume of blood trailing from it. Rachel mustered every bit of strength she had, got halfway there, broke surface briefly to take in more air, then dove under again.

The sister's leg floated in a red haze ahead of her.

When she thought she was close enough Rachel propelled herself to the surface and up to Catherine's side.

The sister appeared to be semiconscious and Rachel grabbed her just as a wave in turn grabbed them, lashing the women against a rock. Rachel twisted her body to take the brunt of the impact; it knocked the breath from her, but somehow she managed to hold on to Catherine. Gathering her strength in the brief pause between waves, Rachel swam for shore with one arm, the other holding tenaciously onto Catherine. The waves battered them, but though aching and bleeding Rachel was able to reach the tip of one of the smaller lava fingers poking into the sea. She waited until the tide ebbed away from them, then pushed Catherine up and onto the tiny promontory. Once she was perched there, however precariously, Rachel pulled herself up as well.

Rachel took in ragged breaths of air as the waves impotently pounded the rocks around them. The scrape of the lava stone on Catherine's face roused her from her stupor, and she looked around her for the first time.

"Oh, God," she whispered.

Rachel cradled her in her arms. "How do you feel?"

With each breath Catherine felt a sharp stabbing pain in her side. "I . . . think I broke some ribs."

"Your leg's banged up pretty good too. Let me take a look." She raised Catherine's sodden skirt and saw that her right leg was swollen, bloody, and projecting at an unnatural angle from her hip. Rachel winced.

Now Catherine noticed, for the first time, Rachel's own injuries: bruised arms and legs; an array of bleeding cuts; a swollen, battered foot.

"Oh, no," she said through sudden tears. "Rachel, I'm sorry. I'm so sorry!"

Rachel held her as she wept, stroking her wet hair as Catherine had once stroked the young Rachel's.

Within a few minutes they heard the clatter of wagon wheels above them and Rachel shouted for help. She was rewarded, moments later, by the appearance of Emily on the precipice, a look of pallid shock on her face.

"Jesus Christ! What happened!"

Before Catherine could speak Rachel called up, "I slipped and fell into the water! The sister jumped in after me. Her leg's broken!"

Leilani, similarly horrified, appeared next to Emily. "Hold on, stay there. We'll carry you out!"

As Emily and the others scrambled down the bluff, Catherine started to say something but Rachel pegged her with a look that said *Don't.* Catherine's eyes reflected gratitude and guilt. Rachel's foot throbbed. She took a deep breath and sighed.

"If you don't mind my saying, Sister," she said wearily, "this has been a *hell* of a bad day."

Dr. Goodhue confirmed that Catherine had indeed broken a pair of ribs, one of which had come uncomfortably close to puncturing a lung; and that her right leg was fractured in four places, including an especially messy impacted fracture of the tibia where the ends of the broken bones had been repeatedly driven into one another. He set the bones and applied a cast up to her hip, but since he'd had to remove some of the splintered bone he told her there was a good chance her right leg would always be slightly shorter than her left. Catherine assured him she was just happy to be alive. Which, oddly enough, she was.

Rachel had fractured only the metatarsus in her left foot but her lacerations, abrasions, and contusions had to be carefully cleansed of bits of rock and coral, then disinfected with carbolic acid. Goodhue insisted she stay overnight in the infirmary, and that night, as she and Catherine lay in adjoining beds, Catherine told her everything: her father's death, her mother's suicide, her anger at God leading to a moment of dark impulse. "I honestly don't know how it happened. One moment I was just thinking about jumping, and the next I was doing it." She hesitated. "Do you know what I was thinking when I jumped?"

Rachel shook her head.

"I thought, 'I'm coming, Mama. I'm coming, Papa. Wherever you are, your Ruthie's coming to join you.' " Her eyes filled with tears again. She looked away and for a minute the only sound in the ward was the sister's weeping.

Then Rachel said, "Mama used to tell me that God saw everything — knew everything — even what was in our hearts."

"Yes," Catherine agreed, "especially there."

"So He'd know, wouldn't He, what kind of pain was in your mama's heart when she took that medicine?" She didn't wait for a reply. "So why can't you trust that God knows enough not to blame her for what she did?"

Catherine thought about that. "Well, whether He does or not . . . even attempting suicide is a sin, so perhaps my salvation is as uncertain as my parents'. That should shame me, but . . . I find it oddly comforting."

Rachel smiled. "You're not disappointed I saved you?"

"Oh, Lord, no! I can never thank you enough, Rachel. I'm just sorry that I endangered you. You pulled me from the abyss . . . and an awfully soggy one at that," she added with a laugh.

After a moment, Rachel said with faintly disguised amusement, "Your real name is Ruthie?"

Now Catherine smiled. "Ruth. Only my father ever called me Ruthie."

"So why aren't you Sister Ruth?"

"It doesn't work that way. The church gives us our religious names. Actually priests can choose their own but nuns take what they're given."

They fell into a companionable silence and Rachel's thoughts drifted back to how this day began, to Haleola lying so still in her bed, and to the empty house that awaited her tomorrow.

Now Rachel said softly, "I miss my *makuahine,*" and Catherine heard again the voice of the little girl she first met fifteen years before. The cast on her leg prevented her from reaching all the way over to Rachel, but she held out her bruised right hand and Rachel reached the rest of the way with hers, their fingers knitting together.

"I miss mine and yours," Catherine said, and they stayed like that, holding each other's hands, until sleep claimed their battered bodies and exhausted souls.

When her cast came off eight weeks later Sister Catherine's right leg was, as Dr. Goodhue had feared, slightly shorter than the left; she would have some small difficulty walking for the rest of her life. She didn't mind. It was a minor disability compared to that which most residents of Kalaupapa had to bear, and if anything it helped her feel their pain more acutely; she no longer felt at such a great remove from them, as in her own small way she came to understand the tyrannies of weakened flesh.

"And perhaps," Father Maxime said, "it comforts you that your body now reflects the damage you feel in your soul." She allowed as he might be right.

Rachel's injuries healed more quickly, and even the pain of going home to an empty house subsided after a while, though a day did not go by that she did not feel her aunt's absence. Word that her third skin snip was negative buoyed her spirits, as did the news, relayed by Goodhue, that the Board of Health had asked the legislature to pass a statute legally recognizing the parole of patients whose leprosy had gone inactive. Rachel's hopes would now have the weight of law behind them.

Then, on a Thursday evening in March, something nearly as remarkable happened for the people of Kalaupapa.

That night, virtually the entire population of the settlement — a thousand residents from both Kalaupapa and Kalawao — gathered out under the stars for a purpose none of them knew. When they arrived at the grandstand overlooking the baseball diamond, they saw two visitors setting up what looked like a large sheet of white canvas near home base. Rachel took a seat in the second row and thought she had an idea of what it might be: the canvas, the odd mechanical contraption some distance away, reminded her of the magic lantern shows she had seen as a child in Honolulu. Was that what this was?

Once the grandstand was filled, Superintendent McVeigh settled the crowd and handed the proceedings over to a dapper *haole* in his forties, who stood in front of the canvas sheet.

"Good evening. *Aloha.*" He smiled without self-consciousness at the maimed, misshapen audience gazing at him with such curiosity.

338

"My name is R. K. Bonine. I've been asked by the Board of Health to introduce something new to Kalaupapa — something many of you have probably never seen, but which we hope will soon become commonplace here.

"I'm a photographer, from a family of photographers. My father documented the tragedy of the Johnstown Flood, while my brother Elias has recorded, in stereographic photographs, the scenic glory of the American West. But my work differs a little from theirs: I take *moving* pictures." He smiled at the blank looks he saw in the crowd. "Some of you, the more recent arrivals, may know what I mean by that. As for the rest — well, why don't I just show you?"

He activated the apparatus and two large metal wheels began to revolve, reminding Rachel of a gramophone cylinder. The machine whirred and clicked as if chattering away to itself, then a cone of light erupted from a lens in front.

The lantern threw words onto the screen, white letters on a black background declaring *Edison Kinetoscope,* then fading and followed by more words: *Beginning of a Skyscraper.*

This title faded as well, replaced by a photograph — in shades of black, white, and gray — of a city all steel and concrete, asphalt roads, windowed buildings tall as a *pali.*

Astonishingly, the photograph *moved.*

Rachel gaped as burly workmen swung picks and shovels at a construction site, dirt flying around them — and a cart drawn by two horses emerged from a gray cloud of smoke!

The audience, gasping and muttering their amazement, barely had time to take this in before the scene faded and another title appeared: *Horse Loading for Klondike, No. 9.*

All at once they were transported to a busy seaport as dock workers marched a parade of horses onto a huge steamer, the SS *Willamette* — which in the next shot then steamed out of port, crowds waving goodbye as the mighty ship backed out of its berth and toward open sea.

The gasps from the audience had given way to delighted laughter and enthusiastic applause.

Now they were on a train racing through the Yukon, the railroad track whizzing beneath them like the blurred spokes of a bicycle in motion. There was a moment's darkness as they were swallowed up into a long tunnel, and when they burst again into sunlight they found themselves looking down from the dizzying vantage of a railroad trestle high above a vast canyon. Cries of astonishment and even a little fear rose up from the audience as the train seemed to float hundreds of feet above snowy ground.

In the next several minutes the audience was shown the very length and breadth of the world. They saw San Francisco before and after the earthquake of 1906 — the gilded ruins of mansions along Nob Hill, the tumbled shanties of Chinatown. They saw the skyline of Manhattan at night, its constellations of electric lights, the glamorous marquees of Broadway. They saw the splendor of the Pan-American Exposition of 1901 and the tragedy of same, President McKinley's funeral cortege.

And then, changing pace with a change of reels, the delighted audience found themselves laughing at a feature called "The Whole Dam Family and the Dam Dog," which asked "Do You Know This Family?" then presented short looks at the sneezy Mr. J. B. Dam, his jabbering wife, their daughter U. B. Dam and nicotine-fiend son Jimmy Dam. Rachel would never have imagined that watching someone sneeze or smoke a cigarette could be so entertaining, but along with everyone else she was enthralled. They roared at this and other comedy shorts; and at the conclusion of the presentation the crowd gave Mr. Bonine a long and heartfelt ovation. For he had done something, brought something, which most of them had never dreamed they would ever see again. Tonight, miraculously, the world had come to Kalaupapa; but these gray shadows moving on the screen only whetted, not quenched, Rachel's thirst to see it all for herself.

CHAPTER 14

1909–10

On September 1, 1909, just before sunset, the Moloka'i Light's oil vapor lamp was lit for the first time — an incandescent beam blazing from the lantern room like the light of a miniature star. Two hundred feet below an informal delegation of Kalaupapa residents, gathered in a respectful hush outside the fenced square surrounding the tower, burst into cheers; Rachel was among them. The beacon swept across rooftops, grazed the rocky floor of the peninsula, briefly illuminating a slice of the nearly invisible *pali* before sweeping out to sea again — a complete revolution once every twenty seconds. And in its measured, steady arc, Rachel felt an odd and unexpected reassurance.

Within weeks there would be three keepers and their families, all native Hawaiians, living in houses perched on the high ground of Ka-hi'u Point. Their food supplies were shipped in double-packed containers separate from

343

those of the settlement; in theory the only thing they would share with the leprosarium was its water supply. Interaction with residents of Kalaupapa was strictly *kapu*.

But the keepers understood *aloha* in a way the United States Lighthouse Board never could, and even with the keepers' families here, Kalaupapa could be a lonely place. The residents knew this and like good neighbors walked or rode over to say hello, to talk story, and to take in the spectacular view from the Point. From here one could see all the way to the Federal Leprosy Station at Kalawao, scheduled to open in a few months. (Dr. Hollmann, soon to be working there, was asking for volunteers from Kalaupapa to be treated and studied at the station.)

Quickly enough keepers and patients came to share other recreational activities as well. One of these, despite official prohibitions on gambling, was the occasional midnight poker or crap game; another, more sanctioned, activity was baseball.

America's pastime was also Kalaupapa's, as keepers enthusiastically joined the settlement's men on the baseball diamond tucked inside the racetrack. Residents crowded into the grandstand to watch, as on a cloudy Sunday when Rachel sat in the stands: third inning, three out of four bases loaded, head keeper James Keanu at bat. Rachel barely noticed as the ball, lobbed by a pitcher with only four of the regulation five fingers on his pitching hand, eluded Keanu's first swing. Rachel's attention was on the third baseman, a young assistant keeper named Jake Puehu: a wide smile in a round face, his cap shading bright attentive eyes. Like many players he was wearing only an undershirt with his blue Lighthouse Service trousers, revealing nicely muscled arms and broad tanned shoulders; sweat formed a kind of map on his cotton undershirt, continents Rachel was eager to explore.

She had first noticed Puehu the day he arrived at Kalaupapa (alone, unlike other keepers who came towing wives and children), his radiant smile drawing her attention like a planet to the sun. Her first instinct had been to hurry away, afraid of the feelings that smile ignited in her: Puehu was a keeper, not a patient, just like that boy in Kaunakakai. He was *kapu,* forget him! But as she meditated on the young man's smile the reservations she had felt about Tom Akamu seemed remote. Was it because Francine had just gotten married and Emily was now living with her boyfriend? Or had she just never encountered a man who stirred her as Jake Puehu did?

Besides — she was almost cured, wasn't she? One more negative snip and she would be free to marry or make love with anyone she wished. There would be no more *kapus.*

345

Keeper Keanu's second swing connected solidly with the ball, now arcing like a comet toward left field where it fell to earth with a bounce. Keanu headed for first, the runner on third went for home, the one on second ran to third. An outfielder snapped up the ball, threw it to Puehu, who tagged out the man running for third and smoothly tossed the ball to first base. But all Rachel cared about was the way the muscles in Puehu's arm tensed when he caught the ball and the flex of his shoulder as he threw it.

The next day, on the beach with Leilani, Rachel suddenly asked, "How do you get a man to notice you?"

Lani was a bit nonplussed. "Who's the lucky boy?"

Rachel squirmed in embarrassment. "Jake Puehu."

Leilani cocked a neatly arched eyebrow at her. "The keeper? You're full of surprises, aren't you?" Rachel blushed. Lani asked, "You're sure about this?"

"No."

"Bully for you! The uncertain affairs are usually the most fun. Well, first: he'll notice you, he'd be blind not to. The real question is, what kind of man is he? If he's like most, he thinks with his *ule* and he may try seducing you almost as a reflex. If he's more of a gentleman, or shy, then you'll need to give him a sign that you wouldn't mind if he approached you. A smile usually does it. Nothing tarty, mind you, not one of these . . ." She illustrated with a sidelong, teasing smile. ". . . but like this." She smiled shyly, then demurely looked away.

Rachel could only stare in unabashed admiration.

"You can also try using a prop," Leilani added, "to use the theatrical term. A book, a magazine, your surfboard, anything he can comment on to break the ice."

"And then what?"

"You talk. You flirt."

"I don't know how to flirt," Rachel said, panicky.

"Eye contact is crucial. Look at him as though he's the only thing in the world. Smile, to let him know you're enjoying talking to him. If he says something funny, laugh and put your fingertips lightly to his arm, like this. No, wait, against the rules, isn't it? Well, sit as close as you can and let *him* break the rules." She looked into Rachel's eyes and said, "You're terrified, aren't you?"

"Yes," Rachel said, terrified.

"Fear is good. In the right degree it prevents us from making fools of ourselves. But in the wrong measure it prevents us from fully living. Fear is our boon companion but never our master."

At home Rachel practiced her smile in front of a mirror for two withering hours before deciding to go with a prop — the book she was reading, Jack London's new novel, *Martin Eden*. Early the next morning she slipped into the colorful frock Leilani had made for her, then strolled down to Kahiʻu Point. She'd been here before, of course, so she knew that the head keeper's shift ended at six A.M. and that Jake's began right after. She sat atop a lava rock close to the Light, just outside the fenced square, and pretended to read. On schedule Jake left his cottage, heading toward Rachel. Her timing was impeccable: when he was just a few steps away she turned the page she wasn't reading and her eyes just "happened" to drift upwards at his approach. He stood silhouetted against bright sunlight from the east; he saw her; she started to smile, a shy demure little smile that would steal his heart.

She sneezed instead.

It was out before she could even raise a finger to her nose. No! No!

"Gesundheit," he said, and walked right past her.

The damn sunlight had made her sneeze! It wasn't fair! She watched disconsolately as Jake vanished into the lighthouse tower. It was all ruined now. His first look, his first impression of her, would forever be the view up her nostrils. She would never be the girl of his dreams, only "the sneezer." Mortified, she wanted to flee, but she worried that an abrupt exit might seem odd and cause her even greater embarrassment (if that was possible). She decided to do what she'd only been pretending to — read her book. She would skim it for a few minutes and then leave, forget this whole silly business, and go surfing.

But as those minutes passed she became so absorbed in the novel that she forgot to leave — until half an hour later someone asked her, "Good book?"

Annoyed at the interruption, she looked up and saw Jake Puehu on the other side of the fence smiling at her.

Oh my Lord, she thought; what did he say? Was he talking to *me*?

"Excuse me?" she said, in something of a squeak.

"I said, is it a good book?" That smile of his could heat the earth with its warmth. "I've read Jack London, but not that one yet."

Rachel somehow managed to form an intelligible thought. "It — it's all right," she said, forcing the squeak from her voice. "I like his Alaska stories better though."

"They're fine reads," he agreed. "So who's your favorite — Buck or White Fang?"

Rachel considered that. "Buck, I think. White Fang didn't know any other life but the wild, but poor Buck had a safe, comfortable life on the farm and then he's stolen away to the Klondike and has to struggle to survive."

"Yes," Jake said quietly, "I see."

"I met him. Jack London. When he was at Kalaupapa."

"You did? What was he like?"

"Friendly. Went to the horse races, talked story with people. He signed one of my books." She held up *Martin Eden*. "Would you like to read this when I'm finished?"

He hesitated. "I . . . don't know if that's allowed."

"Oh. Right."

"Then again," Jake said with a grin, "I've won a few dollar bills in crap games and they weren't allowed either. Let me know when you're done with it, okay?"

Rachel beamed. "Okay."

"Well. I've got chores to do, and you've got a book to finish." He tipped his cap to her, turned away.

"My name is Rachel," she blurted to his back. He turned and looked at her with what seemed like amusement.

"Jake Puehu," he said. "Nice meeting you, Rachel." He gave her a nod and a smile, then headed into the tower. Later Rachel would have no memory of how exactly she got back to Kalaupapa and to Leilani's house. Perhaps she levitated there, Jake's smile lifting her aloft on the air currents; at the very least she ran.

350

■ ■ ■ ■

She took to reading on the rocks off the Point several times a week and the conversations with Jake continued. Sometimes it was just a few words as he headed into the tower; sometimes he would come out and eat his lunch on the rocks beside her and they would talk about books or baseball or the weather. Once she rode up on her horse and Jake seemed delighted, stroking the stallion's mane and feeding it sugar that would have gone into his coffee, as he told her about the pony he'd had as a boy growing up on the Big Island. His family had grown taro but he hated farming, left it to his brothers while he worked on the docks of Kona as a stevedore, then applied to the Lighthouse Service. He'd been stationed at one other lighthouse, Nāwiliwili on Kaua'i. He was twenty-six.

Sometimes Rachel just sat on the rocks watching him up on the catwalk outside the lantern room, cleaning the salt spray and bird droppings from the windows. His duties were the usual duties of an assistant keeper: polishing the second-order Fresnel lens, dusting the machinery, cleaning the lamp and keeping it filled with kerosene, trimming or replacing the wicks. "Polishing all the brass is Keanu's bailiwick," he told her with evident relief.

Eventually he grew bold enough to borrow a mount and go riding with her across the peninsula or into one of the narrow valleys cut into the *pali*. Another day, on the otherwise empty diamond, he taught her to play baseball. With each visit his smile seemed to grow warmer, his laugh easier. She saw unmistakable attraction in his eyes. One day he even touched her: as they straddled a stream, Rachel slipped on a wet rock and nearly fell but for Jake quickly grasping her arm. He let go once she'd regained her balance, but even through the pain of a bruised ankle, Rachel's skin tingled deliciously where he had touched her.

At home later, rubbing away the ache in her ankle, she noticed what appeared to be a pink patch of skin just above it. She told herself it was just a scrape, an abrasion, from her near-fall. She started to probe the spot with her index finger just to be sure . . . but before her nail touched the skin she drew back, and instead went to the refrigeration plant for some ice to lay against her swelling ankle.

In November head keeper Keanu left on a trip to Honolulu and Jake assumed his duties as well as his shift between sunset and midnight. One evening as dusk fell Rachel was surprised and pleased when Jake asked her if she'd like to see the inside of the lighthouse. "Yes, very much," she answered

352

without hesitation, and as she crossed the threshold of the tower door she felt as though she were entering a world apart and remote from Kalaupapa. He showed her the watch-room, appropriately named since it looked like the inside of a giant pocket watch: a huge metal clockwork mechanism whose weights and pulleys caused the lens above them to revolve. He led her up the winding staircase, its wrought iron steps clanging with each footfall, and into the lantern room. Rachel gasped on seeing the lens for the first time: it looked like an enormous jewel, tapered like a candle's flame, with thousands of glittering facets. It was a crystalline teardrop revolving smoothly in a vat of liquid mercury. Jake showed her the lamp at the jewel's heart, the wick which he would soon ignite. He explained how the light from the oil vapor lamp would be refracted and amplified to a candle-power of 620,000, where its brilliance could be seen twenty-one miles out to sea.

"It's beautiful," Rachel said, thinking of how lights like this had guided her father's ships, perhaps even saved his life. Then, her attention moving from one breathtaking sight to another, she noticed the blue expanse of sky outside the 360-degree windows. Jake took her out and onto the catwalk surrounding the lantern room. The wind tugged at her hair as she went to the railing and held on with both hands. Two hundred feet below Kalaupapa fanned out to her right, Kalawao to her left; rising up between them was the green-mantled cinder cone of Kauhakō. Delightedly she made her way around the catwalk to the opposite side overlooking the sea. In the deepening twilight she could just make out the line separating sea and sky, the slate gray ocean choppy with whitecaps, the familiar profile of Oʻahu in the distance. She breathed in the salt spray and repeated softly, "It's beautiful."

"So are you," Jake said, as softly. He was standing so close that the hairs on her arm felt the brush of static electricity, a promise held in the air between them.

Her face tipped up to meet his; his arm moved to her waist. She could feel his breath on her lips, on her cheeks. She waited for the brush of his lips against hers.

It didn't come.

She looked into his eyes and saw desire; longing. But she saw something else too. She saw fear.

He stood there, paralyzed it seemed, the want in his eyes at war with the fear. Then, like a man who had found himself about to step on a poisonous snake, he cautiously took a step back.

The relief in his eyes brought tears to Rachel's.

"I . . . I'm sorry," he stammered. "I just . . ."

He stopped, at a loss for what to say. Rachel stared at him, hoping that her eyes would pull him back toward her, that this moment of apprehension would pass.

It didn't. In a gentle, almost loving tone he said, "You're a very beautiful girl, Rachel," and it hurt worse than if he had called her an ugly hag.

Wordlessly he led her back down the corkscrew staircase, but before he could say anything else Rachel was out the door and over that threshold which only minutes before had seemed to promise so much. She jumped on her stallion and rode away as fast as the animal would take her.

She galloped down the rugged eastern shore, away from Kalaupapa and her humiliation, finally stopping at an isolated spot just outside Kalawao. Sitting alone by the sea, she wept angry tears; anger less at Jake than at herself. How stupid could she be to think a clean person would love her — would risk death and decay and banishment for love! A blossom of self-hatred flowered inside her and she jabbed her fingernail into the rosy patch of skin on her leg. She poked and jabbed until it bled, but felt no pain; it might as well have been someone else's flesh, someone else's body. She looked up at the *pali,* at the trail she had ascended years before, and cursed herself for a fool. She could have stayed topside, traveled, loved, married, lived! But she *came back,* damn it.

355

She thought of all she'd given up in that moment, places she couldn't imagine and would never know, and she wept.

Night fell on her sorrows. Riding into Kalawao to water her horse, she noticed a large crowd gathered down the road from St. Philomena's Church.

There were women there as well as men, which meant they had come all the way from Kalaupapa; but for what? Rachel tied up her horse and joined the crowd congregating outside a fence posted with signs warning: UNITED STATES LEPROSY INVESTIGATION STATION–KEEP OUT! Though it was too dim, even in the glow of oil lamps, to make out much of the station's buildings, the grounds were clearly bustling with activity. Laborers were hanging lamps on poles throughout the compound, and stringing wire from pole to pole. They were the same sort of lamps, Rachel realized, as those that lit Honolulu's streets beginning in the early 1890s.

"Are those electric lights?" she asked an old man standing next to her.

He nodded. "First on Moloka'i!" he declared proudly.

Rachel watched in fascination with the rest of the crowd. The air was charged with anticipation, but when the moment finally came it took everyone by surprise. Somewhere an electrician merely flipped a switch and dozens of incandescent bulbs outside blazed into life along with others inside the buildings — and with more candlepower than a thousand oil lamps, night turned brilliantly into day.

Now Rachel could see that the station's buildings, moments ago hidden in gloom, were painted a soothing yellow, the windows and doors trimmed in white, and were crowned by green shingled roofs. She saw too the green of the lawn covering the sprawling compound and the blossoms — changed from yellow to red with the fall of night — of the *hau* trees decorating the grounds. Copper screens on the buildings' *lānais* gleamed like pennies. The lamps also threw light on the *pali* behind the station and on a tiny waterfall trickling down a narrow crevice. Even the ocean was illuminated; where seconds ago only the luminescent crests of the waves could be glimpsed, now Rachel saw the shoulders of the waves as they crashed ashore.

The crowd cheered almost as thunderously.

All this, the old man said, from one thirty-horsepower gasoline engine and dynamo. And the station's refrigeration plant was capable of making a thousand pounds of ice each day! Rachel was as captivated as he was by this marvel of engineering, and like many present there that night she wondered what other miracles these scientists might be able to accomplish once they put their minds to it. It hardly seemed as though anything were beyond their reach.

She stayed there for a while, thinking and wondering, before heading home to Kalaupapa. She went to bed but couldn't sleep, the flash of another light — once every twenty seconds — streaming through open windows. Even after she shuttered them the light seeped in around the edges, mocking her with its brilliance, reminding her of things best forgotten. Beyond the light was that distant line of horizon she had glimpsed from on high — a line like a solitary prison bar, needing no intersection with other bars to keep her jailed. And she decided then and there that she would not stay here and be mocked; she would *not.*

Dr. Goodhue took a scraping from the rose-colored spot on Rachel's leg, and a microscopic examination confirmed what she already knew: she was bacteriologically active again. "Leprosy can go dormant for a long time, then flare up all at once," he told her sadly. "But that doesn't mean it won't go into remission again." When this patch of skin became a tumor, he assured her, he would remove it too.

"Don't bother," Rachel said, and immediately went to Dr. Hollmann and informed him she wanted to volunteer to be a patient at the Federal Leprosy Investigation Station.

He asked her why, and she answered,

"Because I'm sick of being a damn leper." He warned her that no one could guarantee the station's work would result in a cure for leprosy, much less a cure for her, specifically. She understood, but was willing to take that chance. He told her she would have to leave Kalaupapa — would have to move to, live at, the station in Kalawao. "Good," she replied.

There were examinations to be done and papers to be signed; it would be weeks before the station was even ready to open. Rachel gave up her house, Haleola's house, allowing the settlement to reassign it to new residents; entrusted most of her belongings to Leilani for safekeeping; and left her horse in the care of Francine and her husband, Luis. She took with her only her clothes, pen and writing paper, and a few books. And two days before Christmas, when the station opened with the flourish of a formal ceremony, Rachel was among the first patients to be admitted for purposes of treatment and research.

When she was shown the station for the first time, she was even more impressed than she had been as a spectator outside the gate. The neatly landscaped grounds were divided into three compounds — Hospital, Administrative, and Residence — circumscribed by not one but two picket fences, four feet high and ten feet apart, creating a "safe zone" for station and staff. There was a hospital building, a laboratory, surgery, executive offices, stables, storage building, refrigeration plant, powerhouse, staff residences, laundry facilities, and (discreetly not pointed out on Rachel's initial tour) a morgue. Populating this was a staff of about thirty: doctors and administrators, a nurse, a pharmacist, an engineer, and others.

The hospital was clean and bright with twelve-foot ceilings and *lānais* that wrapped around both first and second stories. The patients' rooms were comfortable if institutional with windows that opened to admit fresh sea breezes, thought to be therapeutic. And like all the buildings it boasted the miracle of indoor plumbing.

Although Rachel was one of only nine patients admitted that day, the administrators expected many more in the months to come. The nine of them were gathered together on the hospital's main ward, gleaming with shiny metal instruments and linen so white it almost made you squint; the only touch of warmth was provided by a small Christmas tree in the corner, dripping with tinsel. They were welcomed by the staff: Dr. Donald Currie, the director of the station, a handsome man with a military bearing; Mr. Frank Gibson, pharmacist and general administrator, a kind-looking gentleman with a mustache; and of course Dr. Harry Hollmann, the only familiar face among them. All wore crisp white uniforms. "I have labored against

360

many blights in my time," Dr. Currie told them, "from bubonic plague in San Francisco to yellow fever in New Orleans. Like them, leprosy at present eludes our understanding. But by volunteering at this station you are all helping to provide us with the tools and the knowledge necessary to someday, God willing, obliterate this scourge."

The patients applauded and settled into their rooms, and talked among themselves in the common areas. They were men and women, young and old, some with few traces of the disease and others with faces bloated and red. But they were all enthused at the prospect of turning their curse into a cure, of it lending some higher purpose to their lives. That evening Rachel stacked her books in neat piles on her nightstand and went to bed excited and hopeful.

The next day, Christmas Eve, Rachel and the others had breakfast in the hospital dining room before being transferred to examining rooms. There doctors wearing surgical masks, gowns, and gloves asked questions about the beginnings and the duration of the patients' leprosy, filling medical charts with column after column of notations. After disrobing Rachel was examined as thoroughly and as dispassionately as she had been at Kalihi — every square inch of her poked and probed and scraped for tissue samples which were then placed on glass slides and labeled.

The one area not yet breached was her private parts; now the doctor rectified that, asking her to please open her legs. "Have you ever had syphilis or gonorrhea?" he asked, and Rachel shook her head. A small mirror was inserted into her vagina, the doctor rooting about inside as if spelunking; Rachel's whole body felt flush with embarrassment. She consoled herself with fond memories of the doctor at Kalihi whose testicles she had squeezed like lemons.

Plumbing new depths of mortification, an assistant then opened the window shutters, bright sunlight streaming over Rachel's naked body, and used a camera to photographically document each leprous symptom on Rachel's body.

Later she compared notes with the other patients, all of whom were as offended by their examinations as she was. "Just like bloody Kalihi," one man summed it up nicely.

Christmas dawned the next morning but there was little to distinguish it from any other day. A Christmas tree, yes, but no presents under it as the nuns had provided for their charges. Of course they were all adults here, not children to be gifted with toys; but even Christmas spirit was in short supply, with the assistants on duty seeming none too happy about it. The only nod to the holiday came with dinner: a Christmas ham, potatoes, applesauce, and freshly baked bread. Even so it was a gloomier Christmas dinner than most, until halfway through the meal when they suddenly heard, from somewhere outside:

"Hark! the herald angels sing
Glory to the newborn King —"

To the dismay of the kitchen staff everyone jumped to their feet and poured out of the dining hall, onto the grounds of the hospital compound. When they reached the first of the double fences surrounding the station they saw — just beyond the second, outermost fence — a choir made up of boys from Baldwin Home and familiar faces from Kalaupapa, friends and neighbors come all the way across the peninsula, Francine and Luis among them. Like all the volunteers Rachel was overjoyed; she listened happily to the carolers as they sang, their voices somewhat off-key but no less sweet for that.

Doctors Currie and Hollmann appeared out of their residences as the carol ended. The patients and visitors began calling to each other, laughing, waving, exchanging season's greetings. One of the patients asked Hollmann, "Can we invite them inside for some Christmas supper?"

The doctor shook his head. "I'm afraid not."

"Why not?" Rachel asked.

Currie said brusquely, "As you were told when you agreed to come here, we have to keep the station under strict quarantine. No contact with other lepers."

"Why don't we go out, then, and bring some supper to them?" Rachel suggested.

"That's not permitted either," Currie said with some impatience. "If we're to properly study the course of your disease, we *must* keep you isolated or the results simply won't be reliable."

The crushed looks on the patients' faces prompted Gibson to add gently to the visitors, "But perhaps you'd do us the pleasure of singing another carol?"

After some brief consultation among themselves the carolers began singing "Silent Night." Their friends on the other side of the double fence listened with tears in their eyes; and when the carol was over, the visit was too. Francine blew a kiss to Rachel, wished her a merry Christmas, and joined the other disappointed carolers starting back to Kalaupapa, as the nine men and women standing behind the double fence were left alone to celebrate this least festive of yuletides.

Occasionally in the weeks that followed Rachel would see an experimental animal — a rabbit or a dog or a guinea pig — being taken from one laboratory building to another, and she almost came to envy them. The animals were merely injected with contaminated fluids, then watched to see if they contracted leprosy. (They didn't.) Human guinea pigs had to contend with more disconcerting procedures. Blood was drawn from their veins; tissue scrapings taken from every part of their bodies; the full weight of modern medical science brought to bear on them. One old man whose crippled feet were to be fluoroscoped was scared out of his wits by the metal bulk of the X-ray machine; when they tried to allay his fears by showing him a developed plate of another patient's hand he pronounced it sorcery and declared he would have nothing to do with it. Those who didn't believe in sorcery still found the instruments of *haole* medicine forbidding, to say the least.

Dr. Goodhue's soothing eucalyptus baths were tried here as well, but the principal treatment was chaulmoogra oil, injected into the skin and muscles a little at a time; the idea, Rachel was told, was that the oil would force the leprosy bacilli from the infected tissues, bit by bit, injection by injection. The treatment was painful and measured in months, and since the injections were methodically administered in a grid pattern the skin of Rachel's leg and back began to resemble a checkerboard. Some patients' faces, Rachel noted, looked as though they had fallen asleep on a waffle iron.

None of the patients could say that the

experiments didn't yield some benefits. It was the way the experiments were conducted that grated: with cold, clinical detachment. Masks, gloves, and carbolic acid were the order of the day for all staff, and while this may have been prudent it only made isolated people feel even more isolated. As though the double fences and strict quarantine weren't sufficient reminder that they were pariahs. Few staff attempted to make any personal contact at all. It slowly dawned on the volunteers that they were not patients but subjects; separated from their friends and community in Kalaupapa, they felt like outcasts among outcasts. In the settlement they could swim, fish, hunt, visit with friends, make love, enjoy life as best they could. Here they could go no farther than the fence separating the hospital compound from the administrative buildings; and all they could do was sit, sleep, eat, and be reminded day after day, night after night, of their disease and eventual death.

One by one the subjects tired of the boredom, loneliness, and dehumanization of life at the station. One by one they left, returning to their lives, and their dignity, in Kalaupapa.

Rachel was the last to go, the last to give up the dream of a cure and a normal life; the impetus being, quite literally, a sign from the heavens. On a cool evening in April she joined the hospital staff as they stood on the second-floor *lānai* admiring the bright streak of Halley's Comet, which had just fully appeared above the distant horizon like a luminous bullet fired out of the depths of the sea. It hung in the sky, a brilliant tail flaring out behind it, motionless and yet somehow imbued with motion — like a blurry photograph of something too fast to be captured clearly on film. In the weeks to come it would arc up and over the *pali* like one of the sorcerous fireballs said to originate from the black heart of Moloka'i, but for now it merely rode the horizon. Rachel shared the staff's wonder at its brilliance and its beauty. "Take a good look," Mr. Gibson advised; "none of us will see this again in our lifetimes."

When Rachel looked at him in puzzlement he explained that though the comet circled the sun as the planets did, its long orbit carried it far from the earth and it would not be close enough to be seen here for another seventy-six years. By the time it returned they would all be long dead.

The thought sobered her: her eyes sought out the bright bullet with its burning tail. It was eternal, ageless; while she and those around her were ephemeral. For a moment she saw her life from the comet's perspective: a blink and it was over.

That night she had a dream, what Haleola would have called a revelation of the night. She dreamt that she and Jake Puehu were observing Halley's Comet from the top of the lighthouse, standing close as they watched it hovering above the horizon. Jake slipped an arm around her waist; she looked up at him expectantly; and this time he did not turn away but kissed her, her heart taking flight. And then he was making love to her, Rachel feeling him inside her — and somehow with every thrust of his flesh into hers, one of her sores disappeared as if by magic. As the last of them healed and vanished Rachel climaxed, waking to find herself wet. And she felt ashamed, not for the dream but for what it told her about her passion for Jake. She wasn't just aroused by his strength and his health, she wanted them for herself; as if by making this clean man love her she could make herself clean as well, and deny what she was.

Enough, she thought. Enough.

She left the next morning — packing her books into a suitcase, signing out and going home. Though she'd given up her house in Kalaupapa, she knew she could always move in with Leilani. As she left the bright sterile rooms of the station she felt an immense relief; and as she rode into Kalaupapa on a wagon borrowed from Brother Dutton, she felt a surge of joy. Friends called out to her; the surf beckoned to her; her horse, on seeing her, happily nuzzled her neck. This was life, and if some things were *kapu,* others weren't; she had to stop regretting the ones that were and start enjoying the ones that were not.

CHAPTER 15

1911–12

Baby girl,
It was so good to get your last letter, reading them is almost like having you here. I'm so sorry about your friend Emily. I know you cared for her very much. It's hard to lose things and hardest of all to lose people. But she is with God now.

A few months ago I started having some pain in my joints, it started in my big toe but went away so I never mentioned it to you. Then I started getting the pain in my knees and elbows, and my skin got red and hot and tender to touch, and I was so happy, I thought — maybe I'm getting leprosy! Maybe they'll send me to Kalaupapa to be with my little girl! So right away I turned myself in to the doctors at Kalihi and stayed overnight while they did some tests, but the next morning Dr. Wayson came in with a big smile on his face and tells me, real loud — he's kind of deaf — Good news, Mr. Kalama, you don't have leprosy, you only have the gout! And I broke into tears right then and there — he thought I was pupule — crazy! I wanted so bad to be a leper and hold my little girl in my arms again!

So now they're giving me medicine and the gout is getting better but hasn't gone away. Sometimes my ankles and knees hurt so bad I can hardly walk. No more sailing for papa — I'm living in the Seamens Home and I work a little at the docks when my arms and legs don't hurt. When the medicine works better maybe I can get back to Kalaupapa. Meantime write soon, O.K.? I love you little girl,

Papa

Papa was not alone in his medical problems. Emily's health worsened throughout most of 1911, and as her face became more deformed her boyfriend grew disgusted, leaving her for a prettier girl in an earlier stage of the *ma'i pākē*. Rachel had never thought much of the boyfriend but was sad to have her opinion so vividly confirmed. Emily stubbornly refused to check herself into the infirmary. "Dying stinks enough without doing it in a strange bed." But since she was hardly able to take care of herself, Rachel temporarily moved in with her. She cooked for her, dressed her

371

sores, took her out to sit in the sun or to the movies that now played regularly at the settlement. Emily was never too sick not to laugh at comedies like *Happy Jack,* or to shudder at Edison's horrific *Frankenstein.* She particularly liked the films featuring the lovely "Biograph Girl" and the dimpled "Girl With the Golden Hair," beautiful young women with faces but no names, who lived lives filled with glamour and adventure. She spoke often of the Bishop girls' daring journey topside. "Remember when I slipped and almost went *splat*?" She grasped Rachel's hand, her weak grip turning firm: "You saved me, Rachel. You been the best friend I've ever had." A few weeks later she contracted what the doctors here called "swollen-head fever," an adenitis of the lymph nodes, and died soon after. She was laid to rest in the Catholic cemetery with Father Maxime officiating and Sister Catherine attending alongside Rachel, Leilani, and Francine. Emily had lived seventeen years in the settlement — a relatively long life by Kalaupapa standards, but Rachel still wept for the years she might have had.

When, after six weeks, Rachel returned to the cottage she shared with Leilani, her housemate seemed a bit jittery to have her back. For half a day Lani fluttered nervously around the house, prattling on at great length about nothing in particular. And though they'd seen each other often enough while

Rachel had cared for Emily, only now, at close and sustained proximity, did Rachel notice that Lani seemed somehow . . . different. She'd gained weight, that much Rachel could tell, but . . . had her voice always been that high-pitched? Something was different, and Rachel's suspicions were confirmed at dinner when Leilani put down her fork, leaned forward and announced breathlessly, "Rachel, I have something to show you. Something wonderful!"

She stood, grinning as she contemplated whatever delicious secret she was bursting to reveal. "Wait here," she instructed, "until I tell you to come in." She hurried into her bedroom, shut the door. Rachel heard the faint strike of a match as a kerosene lamp was lit; then after a minute, Leilani's muffled voice: "You can come in now!"

Rachel went to the door and opened it.

Leilani stood by her bed, her body bronzed by the lamplight. On first glance the only thing Rachel noticed was her state of complete undress, but there was nothing unusual in that; Lani could be quite casual about nudity.

But on second glance Rachel could hardly believe what she was seeing. Leilani's body bore the familiar marks of her disease, her skin mottled with sores — but it had changed dramatically in other ways as well.

Leilani had breasts.

Not male pectorals. Not the muscled contours of a man's chest. Breasts! Tapered and firm, each the size and shape of a large papaya, hanging ripely from her chest. Rachel was dumbfounded. The more she stared the more Leilani laughed, the odd protuberances jiggling as she did.

"Aren't they *wonderful?*" Leilani giggled.

Rachel said, "Where in hell did you *get* them?"

"And look!" Lani hurried over, and reflexively Rachel recoiled a bit, as though caught in the headlights of an oncoming train. Lani cupped a hand beneath her left breast, holding it out for Rachel to inspect. "Areolae!" she said in a tone of hushed wonder. It was true: each nipple was ringed by a pink halo of flesh, distinctly female flesh.

"I know it sounds incredible," Lani said, "but a few weeks ago I noticed that my chest seemed a little swollen. I thought, well, it's the disease, that's what leprosy does, isn't it? But the swelling kept getting bigger and bigger, rounder and rounder, until —" She thrust her chest forward and raised her hands, as if to say, *Ta-da!*

"Your voice is different, too," Rachel said, trying to make some sense of all this.

"Yes, I've gone from a tenor to a soprano! But oh, Rachel, that's not all! As my breasts got larger, these" — Leilani pointed south — "got smaller." Rachel looked down and saw that her friend still had an *ule,* but her testicles had shrunk to the size of marbles.

"Now, I'd be worried about that," Rachel said.

"Why? Good riddance!"

"But can you still get a — uh —"

Leilani glanced down at her flaccid *ule* and admitted she could not. "I don't care! I'm more than happy to trade it for the feel of a bouncing bosom." She admired her new curves in the dressing mirror, but Rachel viewed them with a bit more concern:

"Did you . . . see Dr. Goodhue about this?"

"No. Why should I?"

Rachel said, exasperated, "Because you up and sprouted a pair of titties! If I suddenly grew an *ule* you can bet I'd be down at the infirmary before I had time to pee!"

But Leilani just laughed, happily taking Rachel's hands in hers. "Rachel, don't you understand what's happened? Don't you see? God finally answered my prayers! He's made me a woman!" She laughed again, a joyous laugh. "I go to church now every Sunday and I thank God for His gift and His goodness, and I beg His forgiveness for ever doubting Him!"

Rachel harbored enough doubts for both of them. "Lani — what if it's not God, but like you said, the disease? What if they aren't breasts but — tumors?" Leilani pursed her lips in a sulk. "It can't hurt to let Dr.

Goodhue take a look."

"No! He'll try to cure me!"

Rachel sighed. "Lani . . . when have *haole* doctors ever been able to cure anybody of anything?"

Try as she might Leilani couldn't rebut that, so she reluctantly accompanied Rachel to the new infirmary with its green gabled roof and wide verandah. Dr. Goodhue was in surgery and Rachel and Lani had to wait to see him; as they did a young Japanese man entered pressing a cold compress against his mouth, and took a seat across from them. At least Rachel thought he was Japanese; it was hard to tell. A gash on his forehead trickled blood into his swollen right eye, his cheeks looked as if they'd been sandpapered, and his lip had been split open like an overripe guava.

When he noticed her staring at him, Rachel quickly asked, "Are you all right?"

"Relatively," the man said in perfect, unaccented English: probably a *Nisei,* a second-generation Japanese.

"What on earth happened to you?" Lani asked.

The man shrugged lightly. "Got into a scrape."

"Looks more like the scrape got into you," Rachel said. He smiled, but his split lip seemed to protest the movement; wincing, he pressed the ice pack harder against his mouth. "I hope you won, at least," she added.

376

He sighed. "Only in the most figurative sense."

"Can I ask you a question?" Lani said. Even before the young man could answer: "Do I look healthy to you?"

Rachel rolled her eyes. Puzzled, the *Nisei* looked her over. "As healthy as any of us in this place," he allowed.

Leilani turned to Rachel and said, "See? See?" She turned back to the young man, proudly puffed up her chest and blurted out, "Do you like my breasts?"

His cheeks reddening, the *Nisei* seemed too flustered to vocalize an answer. Luckily a nurse entered just then to escort him to an exam room; he smiled nervously at Leilani, nodded to Rachel, then fled.

"I hope you're satisfied," Rachel said. "You scared that poor man half to death."

When Dr. Goodhue came to examine Leilani he was, to say the least, bemused. "Well," he said as she slipped out of her dress, "what have we here, hm?" He proceeded to study the recent additions to Lani's chassis, clinically hefting one breast and then the other in his hand; palpating the tissues of the breasts; peering over his glasses as he examined the areolae. He looked down her throat, palpated the larynx, had her sing the musical scale: *"Do, re, me, fa, sol, la, ti, do."* He told her she had a lovely voice, then moved his attentions lower, frowning as he examined her shriveled

377

testicles. When he was finished, he took a step back as if contemplating the entirety of the problem and nodded soberly.

"Well," he said finally, "this is quite remarkable. I've read about such things in the case literature, but never seen one myself, till now."

"Are they tumors, Doctor?" Rachel asked, fearful.

"Oh, no," Goodhue said cheerfully. "They're breasts."

Leilani glared triumphantly at Rachel.

Rachel said, "But how is that possible?"

"Ah, that's what's so remarkable. Leprosy bacilli, you see, have a preference for cooler parts of the body. The larynx, for instance, is a cooler organ, relative to others, and when an aggressive colony of *M. Leprae* invade it, it can cause the sort of change in vocal quality you've noticed in your friend.

"The testicles are cooler as well, and in this case they've been pretty well infiltrated and, I'm sorry to say, destroyed." To Leilani he explained, "Your body is in the throes of a hormonal imbalance; it's producing more estrogen than testosterone. The result is gynocomastia — enlargement of the breasts — and gynocotilia, development of female nipples. You understand?"

"Yes." Leilani was beaming. "I'm a woman."

"Well," Goodhue said lightly, "let's just say you're more of a woman than I am. Now,

378

I'm afraid we can't reverse the damage to your testicles; you won't ever, I regret to say, be able to . . . function as a man again. But I might be able to surgically remove your breasts."

Leilani stared daggers at him. "Don't you dare!"

Unsurprised, Goodhue nodded. "They are," he admitted, "rather well-formed."

Tears were welling again in Leilani's eyes. "I was right," she said softly. "God answered my prayers."

"Lani," Rachel said, "it's the leprosy that did this."

"I know that." Lani was unfazed. Her eyes shone, her smile was almost beatific. "It all makes sense now. I prayed to God to make me a woman and He gave me leprosy — so it could make a woman of me! Don't they say He works in mysterious ways?" She closed her eyes and recited, "Be thankful unto Him, and bless His name. For the Lord is good; his mercy is everlasting; and his truth endureth to all generations."

It was hard to contest her logic, and really, what was the point? Dr. Goodhue assured them this posed no threat to Leilani's health, so Rachel saw no reason to dampen her friend's newfound piety. She even agreed to accompany her to services that Sunday — at the Church of Latter Day Saints, chosen primarily because of their enthusiasm for dancing — and Rachel had to admit she had never seen Lani quite so happy. In all the rest of her days at Kalaupapa Lani would never miss a service, always singing loudly and joyfully along with the choir. And when one Sunday the pastor told the congregation, "Miracles are all around us, we have but to look," Leilani smiled to herself, knowing even more surely than he that this was so.

Not long afterward, Rachel was returning from a day of surfing at Papaloa when, nearing the baseball diamond, she heard the sounds of a game in progress. Not a serious match-up hosting a large crowd, but a friendly practice game between two of the town's rival teams. The grandstand was empty and Rachel, having nothing better to do, took a seat in the front row. She was relieved to see that Jake Puehu was not among the players, but at least one of them was familiar to her: the young *Nisei* from the infirmary sat in the dugout, awaiting his turn at bat. His injuries had healed nicely and Rachel idly noted that with his swellings gone he was rather handsome. Yet for someone engaged in what was supposed to be a relaxing activity he seemed extraordinarily serious: unsmiling, eyes downcast, almost brooding.

When it was his turn at bat he swung and missed the first pitch but connected solidly with the second. As the ball arced over left field, he ran and took first base. The next batter bunted and was tagged out on his way to first, but the *Nisei* made it safely to second. Then a big stocky Hawaiian hit a line drive and all bets were off. He lumbered to first, the *Nisei* made it to third — and unwisely decided to steal home. The ball was quickly thrown from an infielder to the catcher, who stepped onto home plate at pretty much the same moment the *Nisei* slid into it.

There followed a spirited disagreement over whether he was safe or out. The umpire called him out; the *Nisei* disagreed. Refusing to leave the field, he yelled an obscenity at the umpire, then gave him a rude shove. The imposing-looking catcher shoved the *Nisei*.

This, Rachel decided, would have been a good time for him to storm off the field in a huff. Instead he dove at the catcher, knocking him to the ground; the umpire lunged at the *Nisei;* and something of a free-for-all erupted. Rachel was startled by this violent outburst from such an otherwise unassuming fellow; but then she reminded herself what had brought him to the infirmary in the first place.

Calmer heads converged on home plate and pulled the combatants apart. The umpire was bleeding from the head and the catcher, with a nasty cut on his leg, was helped to the bench. The game was called off and the players dispersed. Rachel watched the *Nisei,* sporting fresh bruises, as he limped off the field alone. She considered going down to see if he was all right, but she held back; it had been his belligerence, after all, that had started the whole donnybrook, and there was something in the way he kept himself apart from his fellows that suggested he wasn't interested in anyone's sympathy. She left, but found herself thinking about him despite herself.

A few weeks later, straddling her surfboard off Papaloa Beach as she waited for the next set of waves to roll in, she noticed a swimmer heading in her general direction. It was the *Nisei* again. He was a good swimmer, capable of powerful strokes, and he was experienced enough in the ocean to know to dive into the base of the larger waves as they approached. Rachel thought at first he was swimming out to meet the incoming waves for bodysurfing . . . but then he passed her and kept right on going.

Rachel was curious enough to forego the next ride and let the wave pass under her. Bobbing on the swell she watched the young man swim well past the wavebreak . . . and a distressing thought occurred to her.

She bellied onto her board and paddled after him.

He was only a short distance ahead; it wouldn't take her long to overtake him. She hoped he'd be turning around any moment now, but he kept on swimming. Rachel paddled like mad to close the gap between them.

"Hey," she called, now only a few feet behind him. "You gotta watch yourself, there's a bad undertow out here."

Over his shoulder the *Nisei* called, "Thanks," but didn't pause in his stroke.

Rachel paddled up alongside him now; it took some effort to keep pace. "No, really, it's dangerous. You get tired, get a cramp, doesn't take a lot to suck you under."

He didn't reply at all this time, just continued swimming. But although his stroke was still strong, his breathing was becoming a bit more labored. She glanced behind them and saw the white, red, and green buildings of Kalaupapa growing ever more distant.

"Hey," she called again. "C'mon. I know what you're thinking, but it's crazy."

He didn't answer. Rachel said, "O'ahu is twenty-two miles away! That's a lot farther than it looks."

For the first time the *Nisei* stopped swimming — turning round in the water to face her.

"Go away!" he told her, the exertion beginning to show in his face. "For your own sake!"

He turned and started swimming again.

Rachel continued to paddle.

He swam north/northwest for another ten

383

minutes, the *pali* shrinking to the size of a sandbar, the surf growing heavier in stiff winds. Rachel stubbornly followed.

"Remember what the boat trip here was like?" she said, hoping to taunt him into turning back. "That nice smooth ride — how many times did *you* throw up? You think you're gonna swim the Kaiwi Channel like it's somebody's bathtub?"

"I'm going to try!" he snapped back, but Rachel could hear the mounting exhaustion in his voice.

"And if you don't drown, some hungry shark's gonna bite off your leg — right there, right under the knee!"

"Let him! What the hell difference does it make!"

He was slowing, and now by paddling furiously Rachel was able to overtake him — she guided her board directly in front of him, forcing him to a stop. She sat up, straddling the board with her feet in the water, and shouted, "*Hey!* You're a leper! Get used to it!"

Her words struck him like the slap of a wave. He floated there, momentarily at a loss, as Rachel's tone softened. "You can swim to China," she said sadly, "and it's not going to change anything."

Was that resignation in his eyes or just fatigue? He treaded water for long moments, looking away from Rachel and across the whitecapped waters to the distant shores of O'ahu on the horizon. When he looked back Rachel was startled to see tears welling in the corners of his eyes.

"All right," he said, his voice thick with emotion. "All right."

He turned and started swimming back toward Moloka'i.

When he grew too tired to swim, Rachel convinced him to join her. Together they straddled her board — the *Nisei* sitting forward, Rachel behind, their legs brushing against one another — riding the swells toward shore and paddling between waves. Rachel found herself staring at his broad shoulders, the sharp ridge of his shoulder blades, the way his muscles tensed as he leaned forward to paddle.

"You're good in the water," she said, no small compliment for her.

He sensed that and thanked her. "So are you."

"You surf?"

"Not really. Just a little body-surfing at Wai-kiki."

"Honolulu boy, 'ey?"

He nodded.

His name was Charles Kenji Utagawa, the second son — literally, *kenji* — of a planta-tion worker who had emigrated to Hawai'i in 1885 aboard the steamship *City of Tokio*. As a contract field laborer Haru Utagawa earned

385

all of nine dollars a month, and like many *Issei* wasted little time in fulfilling his obligations and leaving the plantation for higher paying work. Eventually he opened a shop in one of the Japanese neighborhoods, or "camps," in Honolulu.

And he prospered, enough that Kenji could pursue an education beyond the reach of many immigrants' children. "Although, in Japanese families," he explained, "it's also the responsibility of the first-born son to help finance the education for the latter-born sons."

Rachel had not seen his face in five minutes, had heard only the sound of his voice, a pleasant baritone. His polite speech and quiet tone were quite at odds with the violence which she had seen him capable of. "So your brother helped pay for your schooling?"

"Yes. Jataro apprenticed with a Japanese boat builder. Between his job and my father's shop they were able to send me to St. Louis College in Honolulu."

"You're Catholic?"

For the first time she heard amusement in his voice. He chuckled. "Actually my family's Shintō and Buddhist. But thinking to improve my chances of getting accepted at St. Louis, my father converted. Down came our little Buddhist shrine, up went a picture of the Virgin Mary. At his first confession he asked the priest, 'What do I confess?' 'Confess your

386

sin,' the priest told him. 'It doesn't have to be something you did, it can be something you just thought about.' Well, my father wanted desperately to please him, so he thought a moment and said, 'I kill a man, back in Japan. I feel very bad for it.' "

Kenji laughed warmly. "He concocted this tall tale about a man who'd made unwanted advances on my mother and challenged my father to a duel with ceremonial swords. Had the priest spellbound. After that we called my father 'Saint *Samurai.*' "

Rachel was actually disappointed to see Papaloa Beach drawing nearer; she wanted to hear him laugh some more, wanted to see what his face looked like when he did.

"Well," Kenji said as they skimmed over the shallows. "This looks like my stop."

Was that disappointment in his voice, too? They got off the board and waded to shore. They were both a little wobbly and dehydrated; Rachel found a bottle of water she had half-buried in the sand and handed it to Kenji. He took a gulp, then another, then handed it back to her and thanked her. She took a swallow — was she imagining the taste of his lips on the bottle?

They stood there on the beach looking at each other as if for the first time. He was very handsome, even with his hair wet and knotted by salt; there was still an intensity in his face but now it was leavened by a certain diffidence. In fact he seemed downright embarrassed.

"I must apologize," he said slowly, "for the trouble I've caused you."

"Forget it. I've thought myself about what it would be like to ride a wave to Maui or Lāna'i."

He nodded once, a faint intimation of a smile on his lips . . . bowed slightly . . . then turned and walked away.

Rachel realized that she was sad to see him go.

He was waiting for her on the beach when she came out of the water the next day. There was a real, not merely hinted, smile on his face as he watched her carry her board from the surf, and Rachel found herself smiling back. He wore denim pants and a loose fitting cotton shirt, no shoes, and he looked both relaxed and friendly. Hard to believe this was the man who only yesterday had either tried to swim to Honolulu or to lose himself in the cold embrace of the ocean.

They bought doughnuts and coffee at Will Notley's shop and walked down the coast to 'Awahua Bay, where their feet left the only marks of any kind on the black sand, and they talked for hours. Like her, he was a child of Old Honolulu. They each knew that a Tahiti lemonade tasted more of lime than lemon; knew the sound of Ah Leong cursing in

Chinese at *keiki* pilfering candy from his store. More importantly, they were both readers. Rachel was humbled to find that Kenji had read books by writers of whom she hadn't even heard: Lafcadio Hearn, August Strindberg, G. K. Chesterton, Herman Hesse. But they both enjoyed Conan Doyle's stories, especially *The Hound of the Baskervilles;* both found Theodore Dreiser a crashing bore; both loved O. Henry and Jack London and H. G. Wells.

Kenji had studied business at St. Louis College, and a month after graduation he was offered a job at a Honolulu stock brokerage, Halstead & Company. "I might not have been the most brilliant student in school, but I was a hard worker, and I was going to work just as hard in my new job. I had dreams of buying my family a new house, maybe someday working on the mainland."

He looked down at his cooling coffee. "The bounty hunter came for me my first week at work. Right there in Halstead's office on Fort Street, with my boss looking on, he said, 'Charles Utagawa, you must come with me to Kalihi Hospital on suspicion of being a leper.' Everything just . . . stopped around me. I could feel my life, my future, end in that one moment. Even if the tests had been negative I knew I would never have gotten my job back."

"You lost a lot," Rachel realized. "No

wonder you get angry."

"It's what I deserve," he said, much to her surprise. His voice was low. "I shamed my family; my ancestors. When a Japanese gets leprosy, it disgraces the entire lineage for all time. It's written into the *Yakuba,* a neighborhood archive for family histories — a black mark that can never be erased. The family with leprosy is shunned, no one wants to marry into it."

His eyes looked away from her and out to sea. "And all the money my father and brother put into my education, that's all wasted. I'd hoped to repay them if I became a successful broker. Now I never can."

Without thinking about it Rachel took his hand in hers and they sat there wordlessly, sharing more than silence.

The next day they went riding together, and the tenor of it was entirely different from her rides with Jake Puehu. With Jake she had been the resident showing the sights to a welcome guest — for that's all he was, really, no matter how long he might stay. But she and Kenji took in the same landscape with the eyes of those for whom this green triangle, these six square miles of shore, rock, and *pali,* were all the world they were ever likely to see. They knew that within these boundaries — the implacable geometry of their confinement — they would have to make a life for themselves. And they began to suspect it was

390

a life they would share.

Kenji was unlike either of the men Rachel had truly loved in her life: her father, easy-going and affable; Uncle Pono, boisterous and funny. But Kenji did have a sense of humor, a dry one, and the fact that he was unlike any man she'd ever known only made him more appealing. She waited for the angry outbursts of the sort she had witnessed on the baseball field, but they never came; perhaps the anger had burned itself out, as leprosy sometimes did, that day on the sea. Or was it, like leprosy, merely lying dormant?

The first time they made love Kenji kissed her in places no one had ever touched before (certainly not Nahoa). If Rachel became at all hesitant or self-conscious he would hold her until she was ready to go on. And when Kenji entered her, that was different, too — having the privacy of her body breached but rejoicing in it, giving it up for an intimacy both frightening and wonderful.

No one was more thrilled for Rachel than Leilani, who often shared breakfast with the new couple and only occasionally forgot to drape her lovely breasts in front of Rachel's beau. Once or twice Rachel thought Kenji would literally die of embarrassment right before her eyes, but not only did his reserve remain intact, he even warmed to Leilani in time. And since Rachel hadn't revealed Lani's true gender to him, Kenji would listen to

Leilani's opinions on men, women, and love and find himself marveling, "That girl really understands men," and Rachel would agree that yes, Leilani was uncommonly perceptive.

But in February Lani caught what she believed to be a cold; within a matter of days it was apparent she had contracted influenza. Dr. Goodhue admitted her to the infirmary at once and placed her in isolation. He treated her with salol, quinine, and aspirin for the fever that soon spiked to a hundred and three degrees. The same disease that had given Leilani her womanly body now sapped her resistance to the virus, her condition rapidly deteriorating. And for someone as hungry for touch as Lani, being placed in isolation was the most terrible of ends.

Rachel was allowed to visit for very brief periods and only while wearing a mask and gloves, which would be burned afterward — as much because of Rachel's disease as Leilani's. She held her friend's hand, called for the nurse when Lani collapsed into a coughing fit, even held the bedpan when Lani needed it. Still grieving for Emily, Rachel was terrified for what tomorrow might bring, but Leilani claimed to be at peace. "I would happily live a hundred years as a leper," she said, "for one day as a woman." She thought about that, then smiled wanly. "And I believe I have." On the next visit she amended that: "I've changed my mind. I'd like *two* days."

There was no next visit.

She was buried on a clear, cold morning in the Mormon cemetery, the pastor believing that his late parishioner had been nothing more remarkable than a devout young woman. Rachel stood at the graveside with Kenji, pleased that he was here to share her grief; but aware too that no one could ever quite share another's grief, that no one would miss Leilani in the same way as Rachel would. Before the casket was closed she took one last look at her friend. In death the outward signs of leprosy had vanished and Lani's face was as clear and finely featured as the day she had stepped off the SS *Likelike*. Laid out in her favorite floral dress she looked, Rachel thought, like Sleeping Beauty awaiting a prince's kiss. Because she was, she truly was, the most beautiful woman Rachel had ever known.

CHAPTER 16

1913–16

Henry Kalama stood on the rolling deck of the steamer *Claudine,* tossed on the perpetually angry waters of the Kaiwi Channel. Foaming surf broke over the bow as the ship plunged down the steep face of a wave, water streaming up the tilting deck to soak Henry's shoes. His knees, already inflamed by gout, were jolted with every spasm of the ship; his hands, stiff with arthritis, gripped the railing like pincers. The blustery wind chilled him under his wet clothes, the salt spray stung his eyes, and the roar of the engines conspired with the wind to deafen him.

He hadn't been so happy in years.

He hadn't been to sea in years, and hadn't realized how much he missed it. He missed its moods, one moment becalmed and the next stormy, the exciting inconstancy of it. He had seen some of that in Dorothy, so fiery and unpredictable, and had loved her for it; and after he lost her the sea had been both balm and bitter reminder. And then he lost the sea as well, and his life these past two years had been one of landlocked stability, the ground dull and steady beneath his feet.

But now he felt alive again. Not to say he didn't feel some nasty pain in his joints, and his doctor would harangue him about making this voyage — but no way could he have missed it, whatever the cost in aches and pains.

Now land crept up from below the horizon: the green towering *pali* brooding above the low plain. It had been a while since Henry had made this trip and he was surprised to see how lush the peninsula looked, how tall the trees had grown: eucalyptus, algarobas, and ironwoods shouldering one another on a plain once flat as a griddle, and just as hot. His heart rose as the steamer neared shore and the crowd clustered at the landing. Rachel was not, as best he could see, among them, but he did spy a tall figure robed in black, a cowl of white framing her face, and he smiled.

The *Claudine* anchored and put out its boats, and soon Henry was climbing stiffly up the ladder at Kalaupapa Landing. From above a woman's hand was offered in assistance: it was, like his, a hand worn and callused by hard work, and as he took it he looked up into the smiling eyes of Sister Mary Catherine Voorhies.

"Welcome back, Henry," she said, knowing better than to try and call him "Mr. Kalama" after all these years. *"Aloha."*

"Aloha, Sister!" In one hand he hefted a pair of duffel bags, filled with two weeks' worth of sea rations and clean linen, as he stepped off the last rung. He squeezed the nun's hand affectionately. "Good to see you."

His gaze as it swept across the crowd revealed his puzzlement at what he didn't see. Catherine explained, "Rachel asked me to come and take you to the visitor's compound. She'll meet us there."

"Ah, good, good." Henry took in the sleepy town, somewhat energized by the arrival of the steamer, and smiled as if he were a traveler coming home after a long absence. "Kalaupapa," he said in a tone of affection few in the islands would have echoed.

He followed her off the breakwater and onto the well-trod shoreline path, and now he noticed for the first time the stutter in the sister's step, the way one leg hit the ground with a slight roll of her hip. "Sister, what's the matter with your leg?"

"Oh, I just took a wrong step, a while back." She changed the subject. "Rachel wanted to meet you today —"

"I know, she's gotta be busy. I remember when Dorothy and me got married — so much running around that day I thought I was gonna die."

"My brother Jack very nearly did, or so he claims. Before the ceremony he was standing in front of a mirror, clipping his *nose hairs* — I swear this is true" — she stifled a laugh — "and he was so nervous he cut his nostril with the clippers, a deep cut. He was so mortified he was afraid to leave the bathroom" — Catherine did laugh now, and Henry with her — "but luckily the family doctor was among the guests and stitched him up with a little catgut, so he didn't bleed to death on his wedding day."

"You saw this?"

"Would that I had! But by that time I was already here in Hawai'i."

"You go back, ever, to see him?"

Catherine said wistfully, "No. We write letters — talk on the telephone, sometimes — but I haven't actually seen either him or my sister in . . . twenty-one years."

Henry nodded, understanding all too well how the healthy also suffered from "the separating sickness."

They walked in silence a moment, then Henry said with studied casualness, "This Kenji sounds like a nice boy."

Catherine heard the nervous question in his voice and nodded. "He is. He's a very nice young man." Henry looked visibly relieved by her endorsement, but before he could say anything more Catherine stopped and announced, "Here we are. The visitor's compound."

They were standing before a two-story plantation-style building with a number of individual *lānais* on each floor. Fronting it was a well-kept yard with lawn and garden seats, encircled by not one but two corral-style fences, one an interior fence.

"Big," Henry said, impressed. He looked around at the other buildings, many of them still sporting their first coat of paint. "Things've changed a lot."

"Yes," Catherine said, a bit softly, "they have."

She escorted Henry into the house and into a dormitory-like room with six beds; there were six on the other side of the house, she said, for women.

Henry quickly gleaned that he was the only occupant of the men's dormitory. "Guess I got my choice of bunks, 'ey?" he laughed, tossing his duffel bag onto the nearest. "So, when can I see Rachel?"

Catherine looked and felt acutely uncomfortable. "As I said, things have . . . changed. The rules against . . . fraternization . . . are more strictly enforced these days."

Puzzled, Henry followed the sister out of the dormitory, down a long hall, and into what Catherine called the "reception room" — a comfortable sitting room with chairs, tables, and curtained windows through which sunlight sifted brightly. So comfortable, so pleasant, that it took Henry a moment to apprehend its most salient feature.

Bisecting the room — from wall to wall and from nearly ceiling to floor — was an enormous pane of plate glass.

And on the other side of this transparent barrier stood Rachel.

Her father stared, dumbstruck. Catherine was chagrined. "I'm sorry, Henry. I think it's ridiculous myself; if one could contract leprosy from casual contact I'd have come down with it years ago."

"Then why?"

"Alas, I don't make the rules. Bureaucrats in Honolulu and Washington make them, and they're still very much afraid of leprosy. And even more afraid that they'll be accused of endangering the public welfare. If you wish," she added sheepishly, "you can go outside and sit on opposite sides of the inside fence, if you find that more . . . sociable." Embarrassed, she slipped quietly away to leave father and daughter alone, if not quite together.

"Hello, Papa," Rachel said, her voice slightly muffled by the glass. Henry slowly approached and touched the pane with the tips of his fingers. Rachel did the same, their fingers separated by less than a quarter of an inch — only light slipping through the barrier, no warmth.

"At least at Kalihi," Rachel said, reading

399

the thought in his face, "you could feel something through the mesh."

"Bastards!" Henry's astonishment gave way to anger. "I come alla way to Moloka'i for my daughter's wedding, and I'm gonna see it from behind some damn window?"

"No, not for that. Sister Catherine talked to Mr. McVeigh, they've made an exception for the wedding." She looked at him, his hair speckled with gray, his face deeply lined, and said softly, "I've missed you so much, Papa."

"I missed you, too, baby." Henry looked at her — at *her,* and not the glass wall — for the first time. "My God, baby . . . you're so beautiful. Such a beautiful woman!"

Rachel felt herself blushing. "Thank you, Papa."

They sat down, pulling their chairs closer so that only a few feet — and the glass — separated them. They chatted about his steamer trip for a while, then Rachel asked him, "Do you ever see Ben and Kimo and Sarah?"

Henry seemed flustered by the question. "Oh sure. Now they're all grown up, they invite me over alla time. Mama's not so much a problem like before."

"How are they?" she asked.

"Well . . . Kimo's a salesman. At McInerny's Shoe Store."

Rachel whooped. "He hated shoes worse than Sarah!"

400

Henry chuckled. "Yeah, well, not now! He sells five, six, seven pair a day, makes a good commission too. You know Kimo, he could talk a fish right out of the water!"

"Is he married? Am I an auntie?"

"Yeah, sure. Two boys."

"And Ben?"

"Oh, Ben's building fishing boats in Kaka'ako. Says that's as close to the sea as he wants to get — he builds 'em, somebody else goes out on 'em. I told him that was okay by me. Still not married yet."

"Sarah? She's got *keiki,* right?"

"Yeah, sure." Rachel looked at him expectantly and he elaborated, "There's Charlie, he's the oldest, Miriam, and Gertrude, everybody calls her Gertie."

"And how's Mama?" Rachel felt a sudden weight in her heart.

"I . . . don't know," Henry admitted. "I don't see her."

Rachel decided to let it go at that.

"Papa," she said, "would you like to meet Kenji now?"

His face brightened and he said that he would.

Outside there was more distance between visitor and patient, but the picket fence was somehow a more decorous barrier. Out here, at least, patient and visitor shared the same air. Rachel joined Kenji on their side of the interior fence. Kenji seemed to Henry a fine

401

handsome young man, if a little more serious than he had expected; but the moment Rachel's hand slipped into Kenji's Henry saw the faint flush of color in his daughter's cheeks, saw the happiness in her eyes and an answering gladness in Kenji's.

"I'm pleased to meet you at last, Mr. Kalama," Kenji said. "I only wish I could shake your hand."

"Me, too." They all settled into lawn chairs, and but for the fence between them it might have been a meeting between any anxious father and prospective son-in-law.

"How was your trip over?" Kenji asked.

Henry shrugged. "The usual."

There was a moment of nervous silence and Rachel filled it with, "Papa, did I tell you we're holding the ceremony in Kana'ana Church?"

"The little church down near the landing?"

"Yes. And you remember Francine? She's my bridesmaid."

Henry smiled, nodded. Another awkward silence as father and groom sized each other up; then Kenji cleared his throat and said, "Yes, there's only one detail we haven't decided, and that's where to go on our honeymoon."

His tone was so dry it even took Rachel a moment to realize it was a joke; but Henry got it a moment after her, and burst into laughter.

"Maybe you try Kalaupapa, eh?" Henry suggested with a smile.

Rachel joined in. "Or maybe, I don't know, Kalaupapa?"

"Then again," Kenji said, straight-faced, "I understand Kalaupapa is quite lovely this time of year."

They all laughed with equal measures of mirth and rue, and conversation came more easily after that. Kenji spoke of his family back on Oʻahu and it turned out that Henry had even been in Haru Utagawa's shop more than once. Henry shared the latest news from Honolulu, principally the pride and excitement generated by native son Duke Kahanamoku, now world-famous. A Waikiki beachboy of no special ambition, Duke was cajoled into entering his first swimming meet in the summer of 1911; and to the astonishment of the judges he casually broke the world record in 100-yard freestyle. The following year he did it again at the Olympic Games in Stockholm, earning a gold medal. Six foot one, 190 pounds, he was a godlike bronzed figure, cleaving the waters with his massive hands, feet kicking up almost as much chop as a propeller. Even more exciting to Rachel was Duke's prowess at surfing. She was delighted to hear that the sport was enjoying a renaissance in Waikiki, no longer the "godless" activity reviled by missionaries. Hawaiʻi was beginning to reclaim its past, and in Duke

Kahanamoku — handsome, unassuming, whose accomplishments could not be denied — Hawaiians found again the royalty they had lost, and which this time could not be taken from them.

Henry, Rachel, and Kenji talked well into the evening, skipping the supper they could not share, feasting on one another's company instead; and Henry went to bed content. Walking home with Rachel, Kenji said, "Your father obviously loves you very much to come here."

"I'm sure yours would have, too."

Kenji shook his head. "It would have been a great shame for him or my mother to come. Even just inviting them would have put them in an embarrassing position."

"So you'd never see your family again, just to let them save face?"

"You don't understand what it's like for the *Issei,*" he said sharply. Rachel didn't press the point. He took her hand in his, squeezed it, and they walked on. Tomorrow at this time, they would be married. And despite whatever differences there were between them, it was still a thought that warmed her in a way nothing ever had before.

Henry, along with Rachel's bridesmaid Francine, waited nervously in the rear of Kana'ana Church, a tiny, tin-roofed Protestant chapel dating back to Damien's time. He was ner-

404

vous not just for the usual fatherly reasons but because he found it difficult to look at Francine's ravaged face — and impossible not to, since she kept jabbering away at him. The energetic little jockey he'd once known had been spirited off and replaced, as if by sorcery, with a crippled old woman of thirty-one. The fingers of both hands had been resorbed into fleshy stumps; her flower bouquet had to be tied to her wrist with twine. Her once-lively eyes now seemed drowsy, occluded by pouchy eyelids; her cheeks were rosy with swollen tubercles; her nose and mouth, subsumed by her disease, were the smiling cavities of a jack-o'-lantern. And yet she did, in fact, smile.

"Mr. Kalama! Look," she cried, turning. "She's so beautiful!"

Rachel walked up the path to the church wearing one of the long white gowns which had been reserved for special occasions at Bishop Home, carrying a bouquet of plumeria in her hands and smiling nervously.

"Oh," Francine said, a wistful sigh, "isn't she? Isn't she beautiful?"

Henry looked at Francine and told himself his daughter would never look like this — that her bright smiling face would never be so blemished or the fingers stolen from her hands — and as Rachel approached he tried to think only of the happy event about to take place.

"Baby girl," he said softly, "you look so pretty."

"Thank you, Papa."

They were barely a foot apart, no longer separated by glass or fences, and Henry wanted so badly to reach out and hold her. But he knew the rules and knew the only exception that had been granted. He crooked an arm and held it out to her: "My little girl ready?"

She nodded and looped an arm through his, each happy for the other's touch, such as it was.

Francine started up the aisle to where Kenji, in the dark suit he'd worn his first and only week at Halstead & Company, was waiting. Once the bridesmaid was in position a proud Henry Kalama escorted Rachel to the altar. Walking as if in a dream, Rachel saw a pleased, smiling Sister Catherine, beside her an aging Ambrose Hutchison. She saw Kenji standing so handsomely at the altar and though she wanted to give herself to him, she also wished she could have held onto Papa, like this, forever; but that wasn't possible, even in a world without leprosy. When Pastor Kaai ultimately pronounced the couple man and wife, Rachel first kissed Kenji, then spontaneously turned to her father and gave him a long, loving hug. No one reported them.

After the ceremony the wedding party

repaired to the visitors' compound, with Henry and Sister Catherine on one side of the picket fence and Rachel, Kenji, Francine, Ambrose, and other patients on the other. The wedding cake, baked by the Franciscans' cook, had already been apportioned on each side; punch and coffee was prepared in similar fashion. There was laughter and talk well into the night. And though they never said as much to one another it reminded both Rachel and Henry of the old Kalama family feasts that now existed only in the distant kingdom of the past.

Henry stayed at Kalaupapa the remainder of the week, and when the *Claudine* arrived the following Tuesday, it was harder than ever for him to board it. He feared that his health might never permit a trip like this again, that this would be the last chance he would have to see his daughter, and as usual he waited at the landing until the very last launch returned for the departing passengers. Rachel and Kenji were here to see him off; and the sight of them together, hands entwined, faces bright and happy in a way Henry remembered from the first years of his own marriage, made easier the prospect of leaving.

"You'll take good care of my little girl," he told his son-in-law. "I won't worry." Touched, Kenji nodded.

"I love you, Papa," Rachel said, tears appearing in her eyes. "Write me. Every day if you want."

"Yeah, I will. Yeah." Not caring what he did or who saw, he stumbled forward and took her in his big arms; Rachel pressed her face against his chest like she did when she was small, breathing in the familiar papa-smell of his sweater. "Baby girl," Henry said softly. "My baby girl." He kissed her on the cheek, told her he loved her more than anything on earth, then let her go and descended the ladder into the rowboat. As the oarsmen maneuvered the launch toward the *Claudine* Henry waved and, as ever, didn't stop waving until the steamer had turned and put out to sea. He was right: it would be his last visit to Kalaupapa.

Kenji moved into the house Rachel had inherited from Leilani and their lives settled into a comfortable routine. Kenji was a fine cook and a fair fisherman. In the afternoon he would often take a tiny boat out and net a fat tuna or *mahi-mahi;* sometimes they ate the fish raw, marinated with *kukui* seed paste in the Hawaiian style. And with the purchase of a rice cooker from the general store, Kenji was able to whip up great heaping servings of *ozaku* — rice cooked with fresh shrimp or dried sardines.

Rachel enjoyed married life but Kenji — though passionate in bed and generally companionable — had a tendency to brood, and frequently seemed restless. Finally one evening, as they sat on the porch watching the daylight fade, Kenji suddenly announced, "I need to do something."

"What?" Rachel asked.

"No, I mean — I need to *do* something. I'm still young, still healthy — I can't just sit here on the *lānai* for the rest of my life."

"All right," Rachel said, and waited.

"Yesterday," Kenji went on, "I got to talking with the manager of the Kalaupapa Store. I mentioned my business degree and what a waste of time it had been, and to my surprise he said, 'Well, hell, come to work for me. You can keep the books — learn the ropes of ordering.' He said he couldn't pay much — believe it or not the Board of Health pays *him* less than seventy dollars a month — but he said, 'I can start you at twenty dollars a month.'

"I know it doesn't sound like much, but at least I could put my skills to use. And maybe I could send some of the money back to my family. To try and reimburse them for the costs of my education. What do you think?"

He was trying to sound casual, but Rachel could tell how important this was to him.

"I think it's a fine idea," she said.

Seeing Kenji's spirits rise with something to engage his mind, Rachel too began to itch for something more than surfing and reading to occupy her time . . . something that might also bring in a few extra dollars for Kenji's family. But what? She hadn't a clue, at first. Then one morning as she rode a five-foot wave in to shore, Rachel looked up at a familiar cluster of green and white buildings in the distance, and the answer was suddenly obvious.

The next day Rachel went to work at Bishop Home as a housekeeping aide — cleaning the dormitories, laundering sheets and blankets, scrubbing floors and washing windows. All tasks she had performed as a resident here years ago, and comforting in their familiarity. She also enjoyed being a big sister, of sorts, to a new generation of Bishop girls, helping new arrivals who were as scared and lonely and angry as young Rachel had been. Arrivals like ten-year-old Myrtle, who wouldn't leave her bed her first day here. Rachel sat down beside her and Myrtle admitted, "At Kalihi they said that everybody who goes to Kalaupapa dies." Rachel squeezed her hand and said, "I've been here almost twenty years. Do I look dead to you?"

She crossed her eyes and fell backwards onto the bed. Myrtle giggled, then laughed, and was soon out playing kickball with the other girls.

But there were fewer Bishop girls these days, even as the population of Kalaupapa had dwindled to roughly eight hundred souls. However badly conceived and cruelly enforced the quarantine had been over the years, the number of leprosy victims in the islands was indisputably on the decline. The government took this as confirmation that its policy of segregation was working.

Sister Catherine was only too happy to have Rachel around and sometimes they would sit together on the lawn, eating separate lunches, gazing out to sea. On one such occasion Catherine looked at her friend and said, "Rachel?"

"Uh huh?"

"What's it like?" Catherine asked, a bit shyly. "Being married?"

"Cold feet," Rachel answered flippantly. "Middle of the night you're sleeping, suddenly, wham, you've got icy cold feet warming themselves on the back of your legs." She made a *brrrr!* sound and rubbed her arms.

Catherine laughed. "No, I'm serious, what's it like?"

Rachel was surprised at the genuine curiosity in the sister's face.

"It's . . . nice," she said. "It's nice, even if I'm home alone, seeing Kenji's things around . . . feeling his presence even when he's not there."

Catherine nodded to herself. "I wish I felt God's presence as often," she said quietly.

Rachel's response was cut short by what sounded like an automobile motor — but although there were a handful of motor cars

411

in operation at the settlement, a quick glance around revealed not a single Model T in sight.

The cough of the motor grew louder, and Rachel suddenly realized the sound was *above* them. She looked up.

Swooping down from the green heights of the *pali* was an aeroplane — the first either of them had ever seen. Its double tier of stiff wooden wings tilted as the aircraft banked away from the cliffs, a lattice of wires strung between the double wings like a spider's web. Rachel and Catherine got to their feet, gawking as the plane dove toward them. They could see its propeller spinning in a fuzzy radius around the nose; could hear the staccato of its engines; and when it was only a hundred feet or so above their heads they could see its pilot, capped and goggled, as he genially waved to them.

Awed into silence, they waved back.

The biplane banked again, gliding like a hawk above Kalaupapa town. Residents stopped in their tracks, gazing up in wonder and delight at the aeroplane, which tipped its wings back and forth by way of saying "hello."

"I think they call them 'barnstormers,' " Catherine said. "Could it be that fellow who was in Honolulu recently? Tom Gunn?"

In a rousing display the pilot, whoever he was, opened his throttle and sent the plane climbing up and into a loop, the vehicle briefly upside-down before leveling out again.

412

People in the street cheered. Rachel applauded.

"Bravo!" she cried. "Bravo!"

The speeding plane was already past Kalaupapa and buzzing over the Pelekunu Valley. Soon it had scaled the heights of the *pali* and was lost from view. The pilot surely had known that he couldn't land at the settlement, but perhaps he had just been curious to see the infamous leper colony close up.

Rachel thought of how quickly the plane had traversed the peninsula and she marveled at how swiftly one could travel now, how close the farthest lands could be. She would gladly have given a year of her life for just one ride in that amazing flying machine.

But Sister Catherine had seen something else in it. "How can one doubt the presence of God," she said wonderingly, "in the sight of men whom He has given wings?"

The year 1915 saw the construction of the settlement's first social hall, with both a dance floor and a stage for amateur theatricals and movies. It quickly became the fulcrum of Kalaupapa's social life, even for the *kōkuas* (the word now referred chiefly to the medical and administrative staff). Not that patients and *kōkuas* were permitted to actually socialize in the social hall: there were separate entrances for each, and the *kōkuas'* portion of the dance floor was demarcated by a row of potted plants. Here Rachel and Kenji learned the latest dances, like the foxtrot and the tango. At the movies they laughed at this new character of the Little Tramp, gasped at *The Golem,* and watched the actress once known only as "The Girl With the Golden Hair" — now "America's Sweetheart," Mary Pickford — in *Cinderella.*

It was while walking home from a screening of *The Tramp* that Francine stepped unknowingly — for she had no feeling left in her feet — on a rusty nail that penetrated her shoe. By the time she realized she'd been injured the foot had turned quite gangrenous. Dr. Goodhue was forced to amputate it, but the infection had already become systemic and Francine soon lapsed into a coma. Rachel and Kenji joined Francine's husband, Luis, at her bedside, but in the early morning hours of June 30, 1915, Francine died without awakening. Luis was devastated; Rachel felt the loss almost as keenly.

Francine had been the last of the Bishop Home girls she had grown up with, and Rachel felt suddenly bereft. Emily, Francine, Leilani, Josephina, Hazel, Hina, Louisa, Cecelia, Bertha, Mary, Noelani, Violet . . . all gone now but for Rachel, alone on the shore. Kalaupapa seemed to thunder with the silence of their voices, their absence becoming a constant presence. For the first time in all her years on Moloka'i, Rachel slipped into

414

depression. She steered clear of Bishop Home, corridors of memory that now evoked only pain, and feigned illness to Sister Catherine; illness that shortly seemed to become real. She began to experience fatigue, body aches, nausea and vomiting. Kenji, fearing influenza, rushed her to the infirmary and waited nervously in the waiting room as Rachel, in a cloth gown, was examined by Dr. Goodhue.

He took her temperature — only slightly elevated — and listened as Rachel recounted her symptoms, including "a little pain in my side" — she ran her hand up and down the right side of her abdomen — "like a pulled muscle."

"Any surfing mishaps?"

She shook her head. "I haven't been surfing lately."

"Because you've been feeling depressed?"

Rachel nodded. "Since Francine." Tears welled in her eyes. "Why are they all dead," she said softly, "and I'm not?"

Goodhue sat down beside her. "The disease takes different forms in different people, Rachel. The stronger a person's resistance, the milder the symptoms, the more slowly it progresses. Look at old Ambrose, he's had it going on fifty years and I don't count him out yet. You could easily live as long."

"What if I don't want to?"

Goodhue ignored that and said, "Let's take

a look at you." He had her remove her cloth gown; his examination was brief but thorough. When he finished he had her put the gown back on, then asked, "Did you have your regular menstrual cycle this month?"

She was startled to realize that she hadn't.

"Are you urinating more frequently these days?"

"Yes."

"That's due to enlargement of the uterus as it presses on your bladder. Also your vaginal tissues have a bluish tinge to them, as they retain more fluids . . . am I embarrassing you?"

Rachel felt numb, number than any leprous anesthesia of her flesh. "Are you sure?"

"There are no laboratory tests we can do at this stage, but I know the signs pretty well — my wife just had a boy. I'd say you're about nine weeks along."

Without a word or a thought for the doctor's presence Rachel shrugged off the hospital gown, retrieving her dress from the hook on which she'd hung it.

"It's not like it used to be, Rachel," Goodhue said gently. "We keep them at Kalaupapa for up to a year, to see if they show any signs of the disease. With the proper permits you can visit them . . . ."

Rachel stepped into her dress, slipped on her sandals, said, "Thank you," and walked out into the waiting room. Kenji looked up, and knew at once something was wrong. "Rachel? What is it?"

Softly she said, "I'm pregnant," and ran weeping from the hospital.

At home Kenji held her in his arms and comforted her. The birth of a child was a happy occasion anywhere but in Kalaupapa, and for any parents other than those afflicted with leprosy. Babies were never actually born with the disease, but only contracted it after sustained, intimate contact with an infected person. For thirty years now the policy at Kalaupapa had been to immediately remove infants from the custody of their parents, lest the child become infected as well.

Now Rachel had to ask herself, where was the joy in bearing a child she would never see grow up? A babe who would never remember her mother's laugh, as Rachel remembered Mama's? What was the point in bringing life into this world if it could never be part of *her* life?

Rachel wrapped her arms around Kenji and asked, "Do you want it?"

"I don't think we have any choice in the matter."

Rachel hesitated, then said quietly, "There are ways." In the hush of his silence, she elaborated: "In the old days women ate the leaves of the *noni* bush three times a day. Or took hot infusions of *'awa . . .*"

Kenji just stared at her. Rachel shrugged.

"Haleola thought I should know."

"Is — that what you want to do?"

"I don't know," she said. "I don't know."

He held her more tightly to him.

"Then wait until you do know," he told her. "I almost did something in haste, once. I'm glad I didn't; it would have been a terrible mistake."

In the weeks that followed Rachel wondered every waking moment whether it was fair to bring a child into the world only to see it immediately orphaned. She wished she could find some faint wisp of happiness or excitement at being pregnant, and ached to talk about this with another woman; but all her closest friends were gone, and of course Sister Catherine was out of the question. Finally one night, in desperation, she closed her eyes and appealed to her 'aumākua for help, Pono or Haleola or whatever family gods might be hovering near; but when neither owls nor sharks appeared to counsel her, she sought refuge in sleep.

She opened her eyes in her dream and discovered to her surprise that she was no longer Rachel Kalama Utagawa. She was, in fact, no longer human. Her body was made not of blood and bone but of earth and stone: she was a colossus, towering thousands of feet above the ground. The bedrock was her spine, the rich earth was her flesh, and her face was fringed in green life: a living *pali* who felt every rivulet of water trickling down her valleyed cheeks, felt the flutter of bird's wings in her tree limbs and the skittering of mice and lizards through her undergrowth. She felt as powerful as her stone heights and as fragile as her tiniest blade of grass. She knew all at once who she was: Haumea, mother of Pele, of whom Haleola had told her; "Haumea of four-thousand-fold forms," from whom all the people of Hawai'i were descended.

No sooner had she realized this than another change came over her: a part of her broke off from her head, the earth and stone transmuting into water and salt, a child of the sea born from her brain — Pele's sister, Namakaokaha'i. For a moment Rachel was both Haumea and her offspring, as a woman and her child are for a moment the same; and then she was just the child, a torrent of water cascading into the dry bed of the ocean, filling it with herself. She was Namakaokaha'i, goddess of the sea, angry from the very moment of her birth, strafing the surface of her waters with raging surf. She felt powerful, capricious, violent. She felt her body touching every continent on earth at once, felt the pull of the moon on her tides, felt waves rippling across her vast surface . . .

She woke.

And wide awake, felt the ripple of waves again, but this time within her.

In the quiet darkness Rachel touched her hand to her stomach. She felt as if a stone had been dropped deep inside her and the ripples were radiating outward, through blood and bone and organs up to the surface of her skin.

I am me and not me, she realized. This is no dream.

Only days later, she felt her baby kick for the first time — an extraordinary sensation, and one fiercely independent of her. It was the first willful act, the first assertion of its separate existence by this new life growing inside her. It was as if she were a garden, her flesh the loam from which new sprouts emerged: a medium, a culture, in which something new might flourish.

She told Kenji of her dream and of her belief that Haleola had sent it to her. She told him of being Haumea but more importantly of being Namakaokaha‘i, as different from Haumea as could be imagined. As different, perhaps, as this child inside her would be from Rachel herself.

Her depression had given way to a characteristic determination. "I may never leave Kalaupapa," she told Kenji, "but a *part* of me is damn well getting out of here."

Her husband agreed. Once he'd aspired to make his mark on the world. "This," he admitted, "is the only way I ever will."

"What names are you thinking of?" Catherine and Rachel were sitting on Papaloa Beach, watching stiff autumn winds comb the sea.

"If it's a boy," Rachel said, "Henry, William, James, and Charles Jr. If it's a girl, Mary, Emily, Anna, Jenny, and" — a hint of a smile — "Ruth."

The sister was surprised and touched. "Really?"

"Well, it's a joint decision —"

"Oh, of course. I understand."

Rachel's gaze wandered back to the high surf in the distance. "Those waves," she said wistfully, "must be a good four and a half feet."

Catherine laughed. "Stop torturing yourself. In your condition you might make a good buoy, but that's all."

Rachel sighed and patted her belly, the size and shape of an enormous conch shell. "Papa once sent me a stuffed doll from Australia — a kangaroo with a little joey in its pouch. That's what I feel like right now."

Catherine hesitated. "Rachel? Would you mind if I —"

Rachel nodded her assent and Catherine placed her hand tentatively on Rachel's stomach. She wasn't sure what she was expecting but all at once she felt a faint pulse in her fingertips and exclaimed, "I can feel its heart beating!"

Life — in Kalaupapa! It was enough to make Catherine forget, just for a moment, all the lives that had been lost here. A moment she would always cherish.

Rachel's water broke late on a January morning, but she did not contact Dr. Goodhue. Her contractions began in mid-afternoon, and instead of Rachel going to the infirmary as she'd promised Goodhue she would, Kenji went to fetch the midwife they had secretly agreed to retain in the event Rachel went into labor after sundown. By having the child at home, at night, they would be able to delay its inevitable transfer to the authorities until morning, giving them a few precious hours alone with their baby. Other patients had done the same, and none of their children had ever, to the best of Rachel's knowledge, come down with leprosy after only a few hours' contact with their parents.

The midwife's name was Dolores and she claimed to have delivered hundreds of children before her exile to Moloka'i. But they had to be circumspect. Rachel could not cry out too loudly, so she tried to swallow the pain of the contractions in deep gulps of air, attempting to transmute it, through some alchemy of the mind, into joy.

Alchemy, she soon discovered, was a myth.

By two A.M. the contractions were three

minutes apart, a minute and a half in duration, and Rachel was biting on a towel to keep from screaming. This was far worse even than chaulmoogra oil injections; giving birth from the brain, like Haumea, seemed infinitely preferable. Dolores prepared a tea made of hibiscus bark to ease the pain and Rachel drank it down despite its acrid taste.

Rachel was pleased to find, however, that once she was fully dilated, the pain subsided and she could enjoy the exquisite sensation of seeing her baby's head crowning between her legs. Dolores pressed down on Rachel's abdomen and told her to push. With each push a little bit more of her baby's pink head showed itself, like the sun reappearing after an eclipse; and then suddenly the baby was spurting out of her and into Dolores's hands.

"Eh, it's a *wahine*!" Dolores announced. She swiftly cut the umbilical cord with a knife, tied it up with thread, and handed the infant girl to her mother.

Rachel held her as she remembered holding the very first doll her parents gave her: tenderly, and with wonder that something so beautiful was hers. Kenji gazed into his daughter's blue-gray eyes, the contours of which bore more than a slight resemblance to his own. Gently he dabbed at his daughter's face with a soft towel, wiping away some of the birth fluids, and he smiled.

"You know, she looks like a Ruth to me,"

he said, knowing that was Rachel's favorite of all the girls' names.

Dolores washed little Ruth in warm water as Rachel ejected the placenta; and when she was satisfied that all was well the midwife accepted her payment and sneaked away into the dark morning.

Kenji stroked a finger against his daughter's cheek, soft and pliant. She smelled new, like the earth after a rain. He called her his sweet *akachan,* his baby. For a little while, now, he and Rachel could hold her, feel her softness, let her hear their heartbeats. They could kiss her, and caress her, and cup her tiny hands in theirs. They could see Ruth's eyes on them and know that they were the first things she had seen in this life; and they could hope that some part of her might remember that. And when, too soon, the sun's light slitted through closed shutters, they cradled their Ruthie against them one last time, kissed her and told her they loved her, bundled her in blankets and carried her outside and to the infirmary, where they gave her up; gave her freedom.

Parents surrendering their children could *hānai* them — give the child to relatives to raise — or put them up for adoption through the Kapiʻolani Home in Honolulu. Kenji's family refused to take her — the shame was too great. Rachel asked Papa if one of her siblings might *hānai* her; Papa wrote back offering to raise Ruth himself, but with no mention of whether Ben, Kimo, or Sarah had even responded. Rachel was touched by her father's offer but knew it was too much to ask of an ailing man nearly sixty years of age; and not fair to Ruthie either. Reluctantly she and Kenji decided that adoption was in their daughter's best interest — even though this meant they would surely never see her again after she left Kalaupapa.

Immediately after she was handed over to settlement authorities, Ruth Dorothy Utagawa was transferred to the Kalaupapa nursery. In this pretty little clapboard building near the *pali* she was assigned a crib — the nursery accommodated up to twenty-four children at a time — and cared for by the nursery matron, Lillian Keamalu, and a Japanese couple who served as lay nurses. A handful of cows grazed in a nearby corral, providing milk the infants would never receive from their mothers' breasts.

Rachel and Kenji applied to the superintendent's office for a permit to visit their daughter, which they were allowed to do twice a week. Each Wednesday and Sunday they would go to the visiting room where Ruth would be placed in a crib on the other side of a glass window. They could see her, talk to her, sing to her — do everything but touch her. Over time they watched as her eyes

425

turned from blue-gray to brown and the pigment in her skin darkened. They thrilled when she smiled at them or made a burbling sound that might've been a laugh; and when she was colicky and started to cry Rachel ached to rock her and hold her. Instead Miss Keamalu came in to cradle and comfort her, and Rachel, teary-eyed, had to flee the room.

A year was an excruciatingly long time to be able to watch, but never hold, a child; to see her smile but never feel her breath on you; to watch a tiny hand wrap itself around empty air. But Rachel never wanted to touch her baby so much that she would risk seeing a florid blossom on Ruth's clear skin as a consequence of a year's contact with her mother.

There were perhaps half a dozen other infants being cared for in the nursery at this time, and Rachel and Kenji came to know some of their parents, who sometimes shared the visiting room with them. One couple, Mr. and Mrs. Pua, came often to visit their six-month-old son, a chubby little boy named Chester. The two couples exchanged compliments over their *keiki* and shared their frustration and heartache. Then, over a period of several weeks, Chester began to lose his baby fat at what seemed to Rachel an unnatural rate. At the same time he seemed to cry more, and began sneezing and coughing so much that he was transferred to a crib in another, isolated section of the nursery. Not long after, Rachel and Kenji learned that Chester had whooping cough, and that the other babies were at risk for it as well. And then one grim day Rachel and Kenji arrived at the nursery to find Mrs. Pua raging hysterically at the nursery staff, as her husband wept and restrained her. "You killed him!" she screamed, equal parts rage and anguish. "He was sick, you wouldn't let us take care of him, but then you let him die!" She tried to attack the nursery matron, who looked heartsick, but Mr. Pua held her back. And as the grief-stricken woman collapsed into her husband's arms, Rachel looked anxiously at her daughter on the other side of the glass, and prayed that she might live to see her freedom.

Eleven months and three weeks from the day they gave up their daughter, Rachel and Kenji stood at Kalaupapa Landing and watched as Miss Keamalu handed a tiny bundle to Sister Catherine, bound for Honolulu and the Kapi'olani Home. Catherine carefully took little Ruth and held her close, shielding her from the day's brisk wind. Rachel took considerable comfort in Catherine's presence; she would not have wanted anyone else to do this, nor could she have trusted anyone more.

Catherine looked down at her tiny namesake — at the brown eyes gazing up at her, the unknowing smile on her face — and felt something quite unlike anything she'd ever experienced, a surge of joy and pride she thought she would never know in this life. She gave Ruthie her little finger to play with, then glanced up to see the last launch from the *Claudine* nearing the landing. She ached at the love and heartbreak in Rachel's and Kenji's faces, and before the boat arrived she hurried to them while she still could.

As Rachel gazed into her daughter's eyes she fought an overwhelming impulse to snatch her away — to run with her to some distant place where no one could ever take her away. But she knew that that place, the only place Rachel could take her, was called death, and she would not let her daughter go there before her time.

"Good-bye, *akachan,*" Kenji said softly as Ruthie's eyes focused on his face for the last time. "Papa loves you. He'll always love you, and he'll always be your papa."

Rachel looked at her daughter and thought: Go. Go and be free. Go everywhere I ever dreamed of going, but never did; or stay at home, it doesn't matter, as long as it's your choice. Go!

Then the boat arrived, and Catherine promised Rachel she would keep their Ruthie safe. At the ladder a sailor briefly took the infant in his arms as Catherine made her way down the rungs and into the launch. Then she took back her precious cargo as the boat pushed away from the dock.

And as it made its way toward the steamer in the distance Rachel knew now how her mother must have felt some twenty years before; knew the loss and longing that would nest forever in her heart; and knew that without question this was the worst, the most unbearable *kapu* of all.

■ ■ ■ ■

PART FOUR: 'OHANA

■ ■ ■ ■

CHAPTER 17

She woke early these days, rising before dawn to take the dogs — Hōku and Setsu, brother and sister terrier mixes — for their morning constitutional. When Rachel's neuritis was bothering her, she just walked the dogs around the block, pausing for Hōku to pee on every scrap of vegetation he encountered (his sister, more dignified, merely sniffed). When Rachel was feeling better, as she was today, she took them to the beach, where the dogs played tag with the waves as the sky brightened above Papaloa.

She kicked off her sandals and sat on the sand, keeping one eye on the dogs and one on a surfer paddling out toward the wavebreak. His surfboard was longer than most, a good fifteen feet, and narrower as well; but the real surprise came when he stood up on it. It floated higher on the water than the redwood boards Rachel had ridden, and it was fast, skimming the waves as if shot from

433

a gun. More maneuverable, too — the surfer leaned to the right and the board responded smoothly, sliding up and down the face of the wave — and when the young man emerged from the water Rachel decided to get a closer look.

"Nice board," she told him, as Hōku and Setsu orbited, casting cautious eyes on the stranger.

"Thanks." No more than eighteen, he brushed wet hair from his eyes and regarded her dubiously. "You surf?"

"Not anymore," Rachel said wistfully. "Can I look?"

He handed it to her, flinching a little when he saw her right hand, contracted now into something like a question mark. He was still young and unblemished, but Rachel did not envy him that; she envied him his board!

She didn't try to lift it but just rotated it, its tip pivoting in the sand: "It's so light!"

"Yeah, 'counta it's hollow."

"Hollow! You lie!"

"Friend of mine back in Honolulu, Tom Blake, made it for me. Gonna get a patent, make plenty more."

"You new here?"

He nodded. "Been on Moloka'i a week."

Rachel was bemused to see a small fin at the aft of the board. "Never seen one of these before either."

"Helps you turn. Makes it more stable.

Want to try?"

Rachel would have liked nothing better, but shook her head sadly. "Can't," she said. She lifted one of her bare feet, showing him how her toes were clawing, being resorbed into her body. "Shoots the hell out of your balance."

The young man winced.

Rachel gave him back the board. *"Mahalo."*

"No mention," he said. Hōku and Setsu in tow, Rachel headed back to town, sobered by the queasiness in the surfer's eyes. Most of the time she was barely conscious of her affliction; leprosy, like age, had crept up so stealthily she had scarcely noticed it. Hers was a borderline, or mixed, case of the disease, but tending more toward the neural form: her skin was still largely free from ulcers, the bacillus infiltrating instead her ulnar and peroneal nerves. It had taken the fingers from one hand and most of the toes from her feet, but this seemed a small sacrifice compared to the disfigurement and short life that was the lot of so many here. She was learning to write passably well left-handed, and as for surfing, well, she told herself that, too, was small sacrifice.

At home she left the dogs to play outside as she padded into the house. The small moon of a clock face told her it was half past six; she sat on the edge of the bed and looked fondly at her sleeping husband. Kenji had a

435

mixed case of leprosy as well, but in him it tended more toward the "lepromatous," or skin-related. His eyebrows were long gone, and he'd had scads of tumors excised from his skin, removed these days with powdered blue stone or carbon dioxide "snow." More serious was the damage that couldn't be seen: a year ago the muscle that controlled his right eyelid became paralyzed and he found he could no longer close that eye. Left untreated this could have cost him half his sight, but Dr. McArthur caught it in time and arranged for him to go to Kalihi for corrective surgery. All the surgeons could do, though, was to suture the eyelid into a fixed position — leaving the eye open enough to permit some degree of vision, yet closed sufficiently to keep out irritants which might damage the cornea.

So even as Kenji lay dozing his right eye remained half open: one eye squinting up at the ceiling, the other staring into a dream. Rachel didn't know how he was able to fall asleep that way but Kenji assured her he'd had plenty of practice when the eyelid wouldn't close at all.

Slowly, now, his other eye opened.

"Morning," he yawned, his one eye perpetually drowsy.

"Morning." Rachel lit an oil lamp, there still being no electricity in private homes at Kalaupapa. Kenji glanced at the little wind-up clock. "I should get up."

Rachel slipped back into bed, snuggling close. "Why?"

He smiled. "I don't know; work?"

"Don't worry about being late. Confidentially? I'm sleeping with the manager."

"Ah," Kenji grinned, "so you are," as his mouth found hers and her arms wrapped around him, and the failings of their flesh were of no moment, their bodies sufficient to the need. And the need was as strong as ever.

It was starting to rain when Kenji tardily opened up the Kalaupapa Store, management of which had been his these past five years. He was still being paid far less than a non-patient would have received — pennies for every dollar he should have gotten. But his earnings had helped defray the cost of his "wasted" education, as he insisted on calling it, though not one word of thanks had ever come from his family in Honolulu. When he had gone to Kalihi for eye surgery, and he was back on Oʻahu for the first time in fifteen years, no one had even come to the hospital to visit him. After that he stopped sending money home. "*This* is home," he said simply, and never spoke otherwise again.

Most days Rachel worked as Kenji's assistant manager at the store, but Thursday was her day at Bishop Home, now a part-time position she'd returned to out of loyalty to Sister Catherine. She hurried through the

437

rain to St. Elizabeth's Convent, still haunted by the absence of Mother Marianne, who had died in August of 1918 — just two weeks before Rachel received word that Henry Kalama had passed away at the Seaman's Home in Honolulu.

Inside it was obvious Bishop Home had not aged gracefully. The winter squall pelted the roof, which leaked like a colander: the newer drips wept slowly into shallow porcelain bowls while ones of long standing streamed into buckets. The floorboards were decrepit and dangerous, and drafts blew in around the edges of windows. Dormitories that had been nearly new when Rachel was a girl were now woefully inadequate, but lack of funds prohibited anything more ambitious than a yearly whitewashing. The whole settlement, for that matter, was feeling its age, even before the retirement of Superintendent McVeigh and Dr. Goodhue three years ago.

As Rachel entered Catherine looked up from the bed she was stripping. "I think," she said with trademark wryness, "we have more waterfalls in here today than on the *pali.*"

Rachel glanced up at the ceiling and said, "Why don't we just tile the floor and call this a shower?"

"No money for tile," Catherine quipped.

But though Catherine's spirit remained unbroken, at fifty-six the physical cost Moloka'i had exacted on her was apparent:

with hair more gray than brown, a furrowed brow and weathered hands, hers was a palpable exhaustion born of hard manual labor and the death of children.

Wielding a mop in her good hand, Rachel scrubbed down the already damp floor as Catherine gathered linens. They finished just as the current crop of Bishop girls escaped from school — as rambunctious a crew as Rachel and her friends had been. Thirteen-year-old Alice was the class rebel, who upon arriving at Bishop Home had stubbornly refused to wear the wine-colored uniform. "Yow, those *ugly*," she announced, and no amount of coercion could get her to put them on. Catherine figured to bide her time until Alice grew out of her old clothes; what she didn't know was that Rachel had already conspired to buy Alice new ones, when needed, from the Sears catalog.

— she's thirteen now, too — day after tomorrow —

Rachel pushed the thought away and helped Catherine with the laundry. By late afternoon the storm had largely passed but the voluptuous waterfalls cascading down the *pali* were still gorged with rain — some feeding pools of water so clear Rachel could see every pebble on the bottom. Admiring them from the *lānai,* Rachel was surprised to see Catherine, just minutes ago peppy and joking, now slumped at the far end of the porch, staring

439

at a slip of paper.

"Sister? What's wrong?"

Catherine looked up. A cataract of pain clouded her eyes. "My . . . sister Polly has died," she said.

"Oh, Catherine. I'm so sorry."

Catherine appeared uncomfortable. "Thank you, but . . . truthfully, Polly and I were never close. She could be selfish and bull headed — so could I, I suppose — and we always seemed to clash at the least provocation."

"You don't hold the patent on that," Rachel noted.

Catherine glanced at the cascades spilling down the *pali*. "We used to play in falls like these. In Enfield Park." She smiled at whatever memory Rachel couldn't see and said quietly, "I always thought I'd get back someday, to visit her and Jack, but . . . too late now."

"For your sister, maybe," Rachel said. "But what about your brother?"

"You see how much work there is to do around here. How can I possibly leave?"

Rachel shook her head, bemused. "Catherine, don't you think you deserve a vacation every thirty years or so?"

But the sister didn't take the question in good humor. "We're wasting time," she said shortly. She slipped the letter into the pocket of her robe. "Let's get back to work, shall we?"

Rachel let the subject drop. She'd learned by now that when Catherine got her nose out of joint about something, there was no getting it back in place easily.

At the end of the day she headed for Kenji's store. It was nearly closing time, and as usual several customers dawdled near the cash register, shooting the breeze. Kenji listened patiently from behind the counter as the men held forth today on the subject of aviation, specifically the first nonstop flight from the mainland to Hawai'i — successfully undertaken by Army pilots last year, but overshadowed by the deaths two months later of ten fliers racing in an air derby from Oakland to Honolulu.

Garrulous old Abelardo was of the opinion that commercial air flight between Hawai'i and the mainland would never be feasible. "The Army can afford it, but who else gonna pay dat kine money to sit in a little tin can when Matson Line give 'em a stateroom for half da price?"

"Abe, you fulla shit." Gus's reedy voice was somewhat at odds with his thickset frame. "Them big dirigibles gonna be goin' back 'n forth to San Francisco by '35, '36."

"You're both full of it," said Walter, twenty-two and bespectacled, "I got a copy of *Modern Mechanix* that shows the underwater tunnel they're gonna build between New York and France. They'll do the same here, lay it down

441

right next to the telephone cable." This was met with hoots of derision from pretty much everyone in the room.

"I think it's gonna be blimps," Rachel said. "We got so much hot air right here they'll never run out of fuel." This sparked much laughter but did not, as she'd hoped, end the discussion; they just started debating which of them was the bigger blowhard. Rachel would have kicked them all out long ago, but Kenji, far more patient and accommodating, let the conversation sputter to a natural halt before announcing, "Okay, boys, that's all for today."

"Kenji, I forget, I gotta buy butter."

"Abe, you've been here five hours and you only just remembered what you came for?"

"Eh, dese jackasses make anybody lose track of time."

"You don't need us for that!" Gus taunted.

"Eh, go to hell!"

"Yeah, and he's gonna go in a dirigible!"

The friends left in a fading burst of laughter, Abelardo staying long enough to use part of a ration ticket to pay for a pound of butter, and at last Kenji was able to post the CLOSED sign on the front door. Rachel asked, "They been here all day, or does it just feel that way?"

"Only a few hours. Evelyn Yamada was in before that, showing off pictures of her new granddaughter in Hilo. And Mack and Ehu,

442

of course, arguing politics." He opened the till and counted the day's receipts, consisting primarily of ration tickets. "Father Peter dropped by, buying cigarettes and trying to pretend they were for someone else; he was quite chatty, but with that fractured English of his I'd be hard-pressed to tell you what we discussed."

"Don't they all drive you *pupule* — crazy?"

He shrugged as he closed out the cash register. "What can I do? Back in Honolulu they'd go to a saloon, have a few beers: but here, where else can they go?"

"*I'd* tell them where to go." Rachel switched off the electric lights granted the store but not their home. "But you, you're a good man."

Kenji locked the door behind them. "No, I'm just *pupule*." He slipped an arm around her waist and they began the short walk to their cottage on Kaiulani Street.

The SS *Hawaii* landed the next morning and Kenji was up early to pick up the weekly consignment for the store. Rachel had been a salaried employee for as many years as Kenji had been manager, and took her duties seriously. Even with her crabbed hand and neuritis she insisted on helping stack crates of canned goods and ten-pound bags of rice, flour, and cereal onto a rickety old hand truck, which Kenji then pushed the short distance to the store.

While Kenji was gone, Rachel took inventory of the remainder of the consignment. Nearby, a clerk from the superintendent's office — a bookish, middle-aged bureaucrat named Diedrichson — supervised the unloading of other provisions for the settlement. As always Diedrichson seemed to relish the opportunity to throw his weight around, waspishly snapping orders to workers who then transferred the supplies to either the storehouse or the Provision Issues Room.

After counting all the crates of canned vegetables, Dinty Moore beef stew, and other nonperishables, Rachel glanced at Diedrichson's manifest and couldn't resist a little dig. "Why bother taking inventory? You already know what's there. Same as last week. Same as every week."

Diedrichson seemed a bit ruffled by the question. "And what's wrong with that?" he said. "There are places in this world where people would be damned grateful to know that come hell or high water there'll be food on the table next week."

"What's wrong," Rachel said, not for the first time, "is that the food allowance for patients hasn't changed in *twenty years.* Seven pounds of beef, twenty-one pounds of *poi,* per week, per person. God forbid they send us a few vegetables. I like beef and *poi* as well as anyone, but every week? Fifty-two weeks a year, for twenty years?"

"That's what ration tickets are for. So if somebody doesn't want beef or *poi,* they can get rice or canned fish or whatever they want from your store."

"*If* we have it in stock. My point is, shouldn't somebody at the Board of Health maybe think about what residents here need in 1928, and not what they needed in 1908? I bet you *kōkuas* aren't eating what you ate twenty years ago!"

Diedrichson looked at her a moment as if processing a foreign and generally unwanted thought — then, to her surprise, his frown up-ended itself into a smile.

"No. I suppose we're not." In a oddly confidential tone he added, "Look. If you want a little variety . . . maybe we can do something about that."

Startled by this sudden flexibility, Rachel said, "What do you mean?"

"Maybe if we got to be better friends," Diedrichson suggested, "I could get you some of the *kōkua* rations."

Rachel was too taken aback to respond. And just then Kenji returned from the store and Diedrichson hastily went back to his inventory. "Something wrong?" Kenji asked.

"No," Rachel said, red with embarrassment, "nothing." She loaded more supplies onto the hand truck and studiously avoided making any further eye contact with Diedrichson.

At the store, after she and Kenji finished shelving the new supplies, Rachel sat down to open a package — specifically addressed to her — that had come in on the same steamer. Inside a cardboard box, buried in a nest of newspaper like her long-ago *matryoshka,* lay a smaller box containing a set of combs and hair brushes made of "Pyralin," a new kind of opalescent plastic that gleamed like mother of pearl.

"They're very pretty, aren't they?" Kenji said.

Rachel smiled. "Yes."

"A good choice," he said.

Rachel nodded.

That night she placed the combs and brushes on a bed of tissue paper inside a gift box. She touched the smooth pearly surface of the combs, ran a finger over the brushes' stiff bristles, then carefully swaddled tissue paper around them and closed the lid. She wrapped the box in white gift paper, tied it with pink ribbon and a big pink bow, and admired her handiwork a long moment. Then she opened the bottom drawer of her dresser, placed the gift box inside, shut the drawer and went to bed.

In the middle of the night she woke, looked at the clock, and saw it was past midnight. Thinking of that night now thirteen years ago, Rachel found herself weeping. She tried to stop, tried at least to mute her sobs so

Kenji wouldn't hear, but in moments he was awake and she was being enfolded in his arms, and her pain was his as well.

"I just wonder, sometimes," she said after a while, "what she looks like now. How tall is she? How long is her hair? Does she braid it, or does she wear it long and loose? I'd give anything I own for a picture. Just one picture."

Kenji held her as he had on so many other nights like this, thought a moment, then said, "She's exactly five feet tall but still growing. Her hair is shoulder-length, but sometimes she wears it pulled back with a hair clasp. She'll love those combs you got her. She lives in a small house near Punchbowl with brothers and sisters and parents who love her very much. And she's happy."

Rachel nestled her body against his and chose to believe him.

A week later, Kenji was home sick with a cold and Rachel was minding the store, doing her best to ignore an ongoing debate between Mack and Ehu over the relative merits of Herbert Hoover and Alf Landon. In the midst of their heated discussion the front door opened to admit Diedrichson, who noticed the two men and apparently, wisely, sought to avoid them by roaming the aisles.

Rachel shook off a shudder of anxiety at the clerk's presence, and was actually disappointed when Ehu suddenly lost his temper, called Mack a Fascist bastard, and stalked out, bringing their colloquy to an abrupt end.

As Mack paid for a carton of Chesterfields, Rachel attempted to draw him out. "So you're a Hoover man?" she said, but Mack just snapped, "I'm a Fascist, to hear some tell!" and hurried out with his purchases, leaving Rachel alone in the store with Diedrichson — who, she now noticed, was carrying a small paper bag.

The *kōkua* came up to Rachel and smiled. "Saw your husband at the infirmary," he mentioned off-handedly. "Guess you're holding down the fort today, eh?"

"Yes. Can I help you?"

"Actually, maybe I can help you." He reached into the bag, pulled out a box of imported Belgian chocolates, a tin of crabmeat that boasted of coming all the way from Maine, and a wedge of something called Edam cheese. "You were looking for a little variety in your diet, weren't you?"

Rachel didn't know which repulsed her more, the smug little smile on his face or the inference that she could be had so cheaply.

"I'm afraid you misunderstood me," she replied evenly. "I was speaking about the diet of the community as a whole." She started to turn away. "But thank you anyway."

Unexpectedly, Diedrichson came round the counter to face her. As he did he pulled from his bag an odd, square-sided bottle, labeled GLENLIVET. "Maybe you're on a . . . liquid diet?" He opened the bottle and Rachel caught a strong whiff of alcohol from its contents. "Single-malt scotch whisky. Best in the world. Costs an arm and a leg to smuggle into this dry, enlightened country of ours."

"Please leave," Rachel said flatly.

He put down the bottle.

"Surely I must have something you might want?"

Suddenly he lunged forward, backing Rachel up against a wall, pressing his body against her. To her horror she could feel his erection against her pelvis, and then his mouth was on hers, his tongue breaching her lips.

Rachel planted her hands on his chest and shoved with all her strength, which was still considerable. The clerk went toppling back into the counter, and Rachel ran out of the store as quickly as her crippled feet allowed.

She raced up Beretania, heads turning at her frantic flight up the street. It was four blocks to the superintendent's office and by the time she got there her heart was pounding so hard she thought it might burst. She rushed up the porch steps and, unthinkingly, to the nearest door — the one marked DO NOT ENTER HERE — KAPU! She yanked it open and charged into the offices, where her presence caused immediate consternation among the staff.

"What the hell do you think you're doing!" one man snapped at her. "That's the *kōkua* entrance!"

"I came to see Superintendent Cooke —" Rachel began.

He wouldn't let her finish: "Then you can use the sick door like every other patient! You don't just —"

"A man just tried to assault me! A *kōkua.*"

He seemed more offended by her use of the "clean" entrance than by the charges she leveled, but at last she was taken to a waiting area for patients before being ushered into the office of Superintendent R. L. Cooke. Rachel took a seat on a wooden bench against the wall; a low railing surrounded the superintendent's desk like a brass halo. Rachel told him about Diedrichson, about his proposition on Steamer Day, about his unwanted advances today. Cooke took it in soberly, and by the time she had finished Diedrichson was back at work and Cooke called him into his office. Diedrichson didn't deny coming to the Kalaupapa Store, but he vehemently denied assaulting her. He admitted bringing some food to her, but claimed that Mrs. Utagawa misinterpreted the feelings of pity that inspired his generosity.

Rachel called him a damned liar.

Cooke didn't know who was telling the truth, but in the end, a man who counte-

450

nanced a metal railing between himself and a patient simply could not bring himself to believe that any healthy man would take the risk of kissing a leprous woman, much less having sexual relations with her. He called the incident regrettable, and "doubtless the result of an unfortunate misunderstanding."

Rachel stormed out. Through the "sick door."

When he heard about it, Kenji had to be restrained from seeking out Diedrichson and cold-cocking him. Rachel convinced him it wouldn't solve anything, and the problem wasn't likely to recur. Even so, Kenji would never again leave his wife alone at the store — not even if he was sick and running a 105-degree fever.

Six months later, Diedrichson was caught *en flagrante* in the back of the Provision Issues Room with a sixteen-year-old girl from Bishop Home. He was promptly terminated and sent packing up the *pali,* and the Superintendent learned something of the limits of man's fear when at odds with his lust. But Rachel never did receive an apology.

Around this time there was talk in Honolulu of closing Kalaupapa and transferring its residents to a new facility to be built on Oʻahu. Science was slowly recognizing that the disease which today was called leprosy was not the same as the Biblical scourge of that name, but the Biblical stigma was hard to overcome. It would ultimately prevent the construction of any Oʻahu facility — and while bureaucrats argued over Kalaupapa's future, they allowed its present to sharply deteriorate.

In striking contrast to the old one, the new clerk in charge of provisions for the settlement was never less than professional to Rachel as they worked side by side at the landing. Mostly he went about his business with just a smile and a nod, but sometimes he made small talk, as on one Steamer Day in September when he nodded toward a *haole* visitor climbing out of a rowboat and up the ladder at the landing. "Big shot," he announced, "from Honolulu."

Rachel noted the man wearing a white shirt, dark trousers, and patent leather shoes who walked off the landing carrying a small suitcase. He seemed unassuming, about forty years old, with spectacles and thinning hair; he had the face and mien of an accountant, or a bank manager.

"Who is he?" Rachel asked, but the new clerk didn't know anything more, just that he was a "big shot." And indeed, there was someone from the superintendent's office greeting him at the dock. Cooke's envoy tried to take the man's bag, but the unassuming fellow wouldn't hear of it, and together they made their way toward the guest quarters.

The next morning, on her way to the *poi* shop, Rachel saw the man again, this time as he strolled ahead of her down Baldwin Street. He slowed, staring at an ox-cart taking on a load of trash from somebody's house . . . and on a whim, Rachel walked up to him and said, "Excuse me?"

The man turned, looked at her. "I hear you're somebody important," she declared.

He laughed at that. "What makes you think so?"

"Well for one thing, they wouldn't let you wander around here by yourself if you weren't."

"Ah. True enough, I suppose. Well, I wouldn't take any bets on how important I am, but I am in the territorial senate. My name's Judd — Lawrence McCully Judd." He started to extend his hand, then drew back, no doubt remembering it was against settlement regulations.

Like everyone in Hawai'i, Rachel knew the Judd name. "Ah — missionary boy," she said with a smile.

"Yes, my grandfather. And you are — ?"

"Rachel Aouli Kalama Utagawa."

He laughed again. "Well, that trumps me! A veritable League of Nations of names. May I call you Rachel?"

"Sure."

"Rachel, may I ask you something?" He jerked a thumb at the ox-cart trudging to the next house. "I was looking at our four-footed friend over there. Don't you have a truck for that?"

Rachel laughed. "You're looking at it. We call it the Model P, for *pipi kauō*" — Hawaiian for "dragging beef," oxen. "At least it doesn't have to carry it very far."

"Where does it take the garbage, do you know?"

"Sure. Hard to miss. You want to see?"

"Yes, I would, thank you."

As they walked together down Baldwin Street, Rachel said, "Getting an early start on campaigning, Senator?"

"Actually, I'm not running this year. But is that the only time you're accustomed to seeing politicians? Election time?"

"No offense, Senator, but . . . candidates come here promising the moon, then they get elected and we never hear another word, nothing changes." Casually she added, "Do you know the basic food provisions here haven't changed in twenty years?"

He expressed disbelief at that, and Rachel repeated the shortcomings of diet she had cited to Diedrichson. But Judd seemed sincerely interested; when she'd finished he eyed the houses they were passing and noted, with some dismay, "It's been a few years since my last visit. Many of these buildings are in considerable disrepair."

"Yeah, half of them need new roofs. The

454

other half need new floors. It averages out to about half a town." She was intrigued. "You've been here before?"

He nodded. "I've been interested in Kalaupapa ever since I was a boy. I was down at the waterfront one day, riding my bike, when I saw a group of people being herded onto on an old cattle boat. Men, women, children just like me." His tone still held a hint of the young boy's puzzlement. "I didn't understand. I asked someone what was going on, who the people were, and he said, 'Dey go to Molokai. Dere dey stay. Dere dey die.' "

He lapsed into an awkward silence. "I'm sorry. I shouldn't have said that."

Rachel stopped suddenly and announced, "We're here."

Judd looked up.

The street they'd been walking on had dead-ended. Close by — uncomfortably close — a garbage dump squatted on the grassy plain outside town. Horseflies buzzed the rotting food and stinking sewage. Old automobile tires, abandoned furniture, the rusting hulks of jalopies and wagons — these were the ugly detritus of forty years' habitation at Kalaupapa. The wind shifted and Judd and Rachel got a good whiff off the refuse heap.

Judd looked aghast. "But this is appalling! It's not sanitary, having this so close!"

"How far can you take garbage when you're using broken-down old oxen?" Seizing what

455

she realized was a rare opportunity: "We have running water but no sewer lines, so the waste just dumps onto the ground behind our houses. No indoor toilets, except in the dormitories, and no electricity in private homes. We're still living in the nineteenth century here, Senator."

"But the legislature allocates ample funds for Kalaupapa every year! Where on earth is the money going?"

Rachel let that question hang in the foul air. Judd stared at the trash heap a moment longer, then turned to Rachel. "Thank you," he said, "for showing me this. I'm nearing the end of my term, but in the time I have left I'll try to do something about what you've told me today."

As they started back into town he asked, "How long have you been here, Rachel?"

"Since I was eight. Thirty-four years."

"We're roughly the same age, then. You're from Honolulu?" Rachel nodded. "Did you ever go to the Elite Ice Cream Parlor?"

"Oh, sure. All the time."

"We might've waited in line together for a chocolate cone. Or passed each other, playing at the beach."

"I might've been one of those people," she said matter-of-factly, "you saw getting on that boat."

He didn't say anything to that, keeping his own counsel until they came to the intersection of Beretania and McKinley Streets, where he stopped. "Well," he said, "I'm going in to see Superintendent Cooke, and I'll be sure to bring up that festering sore outside town. Thank you, Rachel. It's been a pleasure meeting you."

And then he *did* extend his hand to her. Rachel stared at it, shook her head. "We'd both get in a hell of a lot of trouble. But thank you." He dropped the hand, smiled again, and headed for the superintendent's office.

"Good luck, missionary boy," she called after him. He laughed at that, then disappeared into the building.

Of course nothing came of it. Months passed; the roof at Bishop Home still leaked and its floorboards still creaked; the air remained rank on the outskirts of town. In November a fire broke out in McVeigh Home; everyone escaped unharmed, but as the population of Kalaupapa looked on helplessly the building was consumed in a spectacular blaze. In no time at all it had burned straight down to the ground — the settlement lacked the firefighting equipment to extinguish much more than a birthday cake. Rachel watched a cloud of embers fall to the ground like dying fireworks, only luck and a lack of wind preventing the sparks from igniting the physician's residence next door. She wondered with a shudder what would happen, some night, if fire *did* spread to the next building — and the next, and the next? If all of Kalaupapa were set ablaze, and then the grasslands surrounding it, where would they go, where could they run? And did anyone even care?

In the summer of 1929 Sister Catherine boarded the SS *Hawaii* to Honolulu for the first time since delivering Rachel's daughter to Kapi'olani Home; and then onto a much grander steamship, the SS *President Jackson,* bound for New York City via the Panama Canal. The voyage was a pleasant one, perhaps too pleasant. After decades of spartan diet, the lavish meals in the ship's dining room seemed excessive, even decadent; and her enforced leisure time was anything but relaxing, Catherine feeling guilty to think of all the work she could be doing back in Kalaupapa.

Manhattan looked strange indeed to her eyes after so many years in Hawai'i, but Catherine didn't linger in the city; at Penn Station she boarded the *Black Diamond Express,* which was soon rattling through the New Jersey countryside and Pennsylvania coal fields. It was one of the few major trains to service the city of Ithaca, New York, whose hilly terrain actively discouraged the laying down of rail — hills carved millennia ago by glaciers, which then thawed to create deep

458

clear lakes.

A familiar succession of towns flashed past: Towanda, Athens, Sayre, Owego, Wilseyville. The hills and valleys had the comforting contours of childhood. Catherine spied the inlet to Cayuga Lake and thought back to the big steamboats that used to come in from the Erie Canal, grand old ships like the *Frontenac* that would tie up at Renwick Pier, where Ruth and her brother would sneak aboard and pretend they were steaming down the Mississippi.

The brakes shrieked and sparked as the *Black Diamond* slowed into the station, where Jack was waiting for her. The last time she'd seen him he'd been a frail fourteen-year-old, toxic with grief over their father's death. But the nearly fifty-year-old man who stood on the platform smiling at her was stocky if not stout, robust, and cheerful. "Sis!" he cried out. (He'd never called her "sis" until after she'd taken her vows.) He hurried to her faster than she could manage with her game leg, then took her in his arms and gave her a bear hug that squeezed the breath from her. "Ruth," he said with surprising softness, considering the vise grip in which he held her. "Oh, Ruth."

"I've missed you, too," Catherine said, and wept.

Outside, driving down State Street in Jack's big Plymouth, Catherine found it odd to

459

think that when she'd left these streets had been filled with horses and buggies. Some familiar names greeted her: Rothschild's Department Store was still here, albeit bigger, as were the Ithaca Hotel and Brooks Pharmacy. She was pleased to see Ithaca was still recognizably Ithaca. Soon Jack was turning onto East Court Street, and there it was: the house in which Catherine had grown up. A modest, two-story Italianate home, fronted by a porch whose supports were simple square posts rather than the Doric columns adorning its gaudier neighbors. Harold Voorhies had reviled the more rococo homes going up around town, with their cupolas and ornate arched windows. "Our home," he told his wife, "will not look as if it floated in from the Piazza San Marco."

They climbed the steps to the porch where the young Ruth had spent many happy hours playing jacks and reading books — and where a somewhat older Ruth had entertained the only young man she had ever fancied, John Van Splinter. They would sit here on the porch on warm summer nights, talking and laughing; and once, only once, they kissed.

They entered the house and were swept up in a tornado of shouted greetings and running children.

"Hi Pop!"

"Daddy, Daddy!"

"Is that her?"

460

"She *is* a nun!"

"Ssshh!"

The photographs Catherine had seen of this brood may have been the only moments they weren't in constant motion. Jack's sturdy blonde wife, Isabel, clapped her hands, imposing order on exuberant chaos: "Settle down, settle down," and Catherine was introduced to her nieces and nephews: Becky, Lacy, Guy, Hal, Beverly. She was happy to meet them, and quietly ashamed that she never had before.

She had been apprehensive about returning to this house, had expected it to be a crucible of memories, of ghosts; but the laughter and shouts of these children seemed to drown out any whispering phantoms. Jack and Isabel's presence here — the comfortable way they filled the space — discouraged Catherine from loitering in the past. After a pot roast dinner and a dessert of Jell-O and whipped cream, the family gathered around the big Majestic console radio to laugh at this new program called *Amos 'n' Andy,* and then an exhausted Catherine was shown to her room: literally the room she had grown up in, now tenanted by sixteen-year-old Beverly, temporarily dispossessed.

As Catherine lay there in the dark she felt the comforting shape of the room around her — the familiar distance of wall from wall, of the ceiling above, an intimacy of space that

461

brought her unexpected pleasure. The street lights outside were electric, not gas, but they cast much the same shadows on the wall as when she was a girl; and the crickets in the yard chirped as they always had. The air she took in, faintly musty and woody, could have been the same air she breathed on her last night here, thirty-six years before. She felt warm, protected, safe.

In the two weeks that followed, Catherine played endlessly with the children and attended Mass at her old church on Geneva Street. Steamboats no longer docked at Renwick Pier, but Cayuga Lake was still a fine place for a picnic; after which the family went for a swim at Enfield Falls. As the children peeled off their outer clothes, they were frankly astonished to see Catherine strip off her habit, revealing a borrowed swimsuit beneath. "Last one in," she announced, "is a rotten egg!" She dove into the water, breaking surface a few moments later. "Seems like we have quite a lot of spoilt eggs out there!" They all jumped in at once, Catherine sputtering and laughing at the geysers suddenly spouting on every side of her.

"Do you think," Beverly asked her hopefully, on the way home, "you might consider staying in New York?"

Catherine said, "I hadn't really thought about that," and hoped God would forgive her the lie.

Back home that evening, after yet another dinner far more sumptuous than any she had ever had on Moloka'i, as she laughed and played with her nieces and nephews, Catherine considered how much of God's work could be done right here in Ithaca, or Syracuse. There were poor people to be fed here too, after all, and souls to be saved. She had spent thirty-six years away from home and family, had sacrificed all her adult life for the people of Kalaupapa; where was the harm in tending to a flock closer to home and being able to share moments like these with her family?

That night she lay in bed in her old room, feeling happy and at peace, the ghosts from whom she had fled to Hawai'i having somehow been put to rest, either by time or by the sheer exuberance of Jack's family.

She loved it here. She loved her home.

She wanted desperately to stay, wanted it more than she had ever imagined she would; and despite that, because of that, she knew she had to go back.

She had never heard God more clearly in her life.

CHAPTER 18

Early in the morning of Tuesday, June 17, 1931, the destroyer USS *Gamble* anchored off Kalaupapa, having left Honolulu just two hours earlier — a considerable improvement on the night-long, stomach-churning crossings of the Kaiwi Channel of decades past. If anyone parted company with his breakfast on the present voyage, it was not noted. The entire population of the settlement turned out to greet the *Gamble*'s passengers as they came ashore; the majority gathered in front of Kenji's store as the manager and his wife watched from the doorway. As the visiting dignitaries, including the territorial governor of Hawai'i, climbed up the ladder and wobbled onto the dock, the Kalaupapa Band greeted them with appropriate fanfare.

After the welcoming airs, the landing party was whisked off for an inspection of recent construction at Kalaupapa. The visitors saw the new laundry pavilion with its electric

464

washers and hot and cold running water. They toured the new hospital, the renovated and expanded McVeigh Home, and the (named without apparent irony) Bay View Home for the Blind and Helpless. At Bishop Home, when asked by the governor what she would do to improve conditions here, Sister Catherine looked up at the leaky roof and down at the ancient floorboards, then suggested with a smile that a lit match might be the most effective course of action.

And the dignitaries stopped at the Kalaupapa Store, squeezing inside as the governor stepped up to the counter behind which Rachel and Kenji stood expectantly.

Rachel said, "Welcome, Governor."

The governor — an unassuming man in spectacles with the mien of an accountant, or bank manager — gave her a look of mock irritation. "Rachel, have you forgotten my name?"

Rachel smiled and amended herself:

"Welcome, Governor Missionary Boy."

The governor of the Territory of Hawai'i, Lawrence McCully Judd, laughed heartily. "*That's* better." He turned to her husband. "Kenji, good to see you again. How have things been coming along here since my last visit?"

"Very well, sir. The new adding machine and typewriter are much appreciated."

"And what about that new accounting

system? Has the Auditors Office been making your life easier or harder?"

"Remarkably for something designed by a government agency, the new system is much simpler and more efficient."

"Don't worry, I'm sure they'll find a way to make it complicated and wasteful. You are both coming to the meeting this afternoon, aren't you?"

Rachel asked, "Who'll mind the store, Governor?"

"Perhaps I could declare this a territorial holiday," Judd suggested, "and require you to shut down for the day."

Rachel whipped out the CLOSED sign and handed it to Judd. "Put this in the window on your way out?" she said, and the governor laughingly did as he was told.

For most Kalaupapa residents it was already a holiday, and they crowded into the social hall for what turned out to be a stupefying number of speeches: politicians, sheriffs, military officers, everyone short of the ship's bosun. Even the president of the much-despised Board of Health was here to reluctantly commemorate passing of control of Kalaupapa to a newly-formed Board of Leper Hospitals and Settlement. After an official study had concluded that Kalaupapa was "far below par with other territorial institutions," the governor had wrested jurisdiction away from the Board of Health — not least because

466

it was discovered that in the six years between 1923 and 1928 the Board had allowed to lapse $136,000 in funds allocated to the settlement by the Legislature. Money that might have bought so much, allowed to simply evaporate because the Board of Health lacked the foresight, vision, or will to use it.

"Today," Judd addressed his audience, "for the first time since this settlement was established in 1866 the government is presenting a united front for improvements at Kalihi and Kalaupapa.

"Your problem is one of my main interests as governor. It was difficult to get the people to realize the need here. But now we are ready to stop blowing bubbles and to do definite things for your welfare."

He enumerated the further improvements that would soon be made: a new water system, sewer lines, fire hydrants, a refrigeration plant, a gas station, and at long last, a real garbage truck (the old ox would be "pensioned"). The announcement that work would soon commence on an airfield at Kalaupapa brought cheers from the crowd. When Judd told his audience they would also be getting equipment to screen *talking* pictures, they cheered even louder.

But the biggest ovation came afterward, when the residents of Kalaupapa followed the governor down to the new power station where Judd threw the switch that electrified every home and building in the settlement.

The governor caught sight of a pleased and proud Rachel, winked at her and said, just audible over the cheers of the crowd, "Welcome to the twentieth century."

The following day Rachel borrowed an old jalopy — a neighbor's 1922 Model T of shabby gentility — and set off across the Damien Road. She was able to steer passably well even with her clawed right hand; the only thing that worried her was her inability to actually feel the clutch under her left foot, which required constant monitoring to make sure she wasn't inadvertently stripping the gears.

The familiar remnants of Kalawao town soon ghosted into view: scattered piles of *pili* grass, heaps of kindling that once were houses. A pig sat on its haunches in the collapsed remains of an old store, eyes nervously tracking the loud machine that stuttered past. Rachel's heart ached as always when she came to the remains of Haleola's home, its termite-ridden posts and beams rotting away in the sun. After six months Haleola's grave was again choked with weeds and Rachel had to hack away the undergrowth with a hoe; she did the same for Keo's. In the stillness of dying Kalawao, disturbed only by the crashing metronome of the surf, she paid her respects to her aunt and then left to do likewise for Uncle Pono.

But as she drove up the road to Siloama Church, closed these past four years, she noticed someone sitting in the middle of the street ahead of her. Perched on a folding chair midway between St. Philomena's Church and the Baldwin Home for Boys, a large man sat facing the church, a paintbrush in hand, dabbing at an easel. Out of curiosity Rachel drove past Siloama cemetery and up another hundred feet to St. Philomena's; beyond it lay the razed ground of the United States Leprosy Investigation Station, in whose abandonment Rachel felt no satisfaction, only sadness.

At the sound of the car's engine the painter looked up, surprised. He was Hawaiian, perhaps eighteen or nineteen years old, and his nose had begun to collapse in on itself as leprosy eroded the nasal cartilage; but his smile on seeing her was bright and whole.

"Aloha," he said happily as Rachel parked the car a respectful distance from Damien's church.

"Aloha." She approached him, but his easel was angled so that she couldn't quite make out what rested on it. "Lucky I didn't run you down," she said with a smile. "Sitting here in the middle of the street with all this traffic."

He chuckled. "Yeah, maybe I get run over by a wild pig." He gestured toward a drowsy-

469

looking swine sunning itself under a pandanus tree.

She nodded to the canvas. "Mind if I take a look?"

"Sure. But it's not finished yet." He turned the easel around so she could get a good look at the half-completed painting. The outlines of St. Philomena's had been lightly brushed in, its sea-green roof floating above half-formed white walls. Behind it the *pali* rose in vibrant green strokes, crowned by a white mist. Rachel was impressed. "It's beautiful," she said, "even unfinished."

She noticed that the painter was gazing at her as intently as she'd been studying his work. He saw her discomfort and laughed sheepishly.

"Sorry for the stink-eye, but we don't see many *wahines* over here, you know?" He nodded toward Baldwin Home across the street, its frame cottages squatting behind a low plastered stone wall. "Brother Dutton used to go through our magazines, and if there was a *wahine* with this much skin showing below the neck" — he pinched two fingers together — "out came the scissors, and out went the paper lady, into the trash!" He laughed with more fondness than resentment. "He was specially vexed by that *National Geographic* magazine — alla those bare bosoms. He'd cut 'em up into tiny pieces, and oh, what work to put 'em back together after you pick 'em outta the trash!"

Rachel laughed too, if a bit nervously. "This, uh, might be a good time to mention I'm a married woman."

"Oh, sure, sure," he said with a wave of his hand, "no worry. I always figure, what *wahine*'s gonna want to kiss a face like this, eh?" He held out a hand. "I'm Hokea."

"Rachel." He had a gentle grip, like ferns brushing against her hand.

"So what's life like," she asked, "without Brother Dutton?" After a lifetime of uncertain penance but undisputed service, the seemingly indestructible Ira Barnes Dutton had passed away just one month shy of his eighty-seventh birthday. And with the passing soon after of seventy-six-year-old Ambrose Hutchison, the last living ties to Damien's time were finally severed.

"Oh, the other brothers ain't nearly as strict. They let us have the *National Geographic* without big holes in it." Hokea sighed. "No more thrill."

Her gaze was drawn again to the half-finished painting of St. Philomena's. "This really is beautiful."

"Ah, not yet. Not as good as others I've done."

"You've done others? Of the church?"

"Yeah, plenty. Like to see?"

She said she would and Hokea was immediately on his way to Baldwin Home. "I go get 'em," he said. "Brother Maternus'd have a stroke if I brought you inside."

Minutes later he returned with a stack of canvasses under one arm. "I only bring the best ones." He spread them out on the surface of the road, unmindful of the dust.

Her neuritis objecting, Rachel bent down to take in the paintings. St. Philomena's was their common subject, but there the similarities ended — each was unique. Some depicted the church's east face, some the west; some showed backdrops of lush green *pali,* some a blue wedge of ocean. Most were rendered in watercolors, a few in oils, one in charcoal. Each captured the church in a different mood as well: radiant under bright skies; storm-tossed, the white cross over its door just visible through sheeting rain; somberly framed by the graveyard in the foreground or joyously reaching toward heaven, its steeple reminding Rachel of the tall spires of Kaumakapili Church.

Hokea said, "I never get tired of looking at it. There's strength to it, but also *maluhia.*"

Serenity. Rachel nodded. "I have a friend who says the same about another of Damien's churches, up topside. Our Lady of Sorrows."

"I'd love to paint that," Hokea said wistfully. "Next, though —" He turned around to face the aging facade of Baldwin Home. "I'm gonna do this. While it's still here. Won't be

472

long 'till they ship all of us over to Kalau-papa."

"You think so?"

"Only thing kept us here was the old man. Cheaper to have us all over in Kalaupapa. Soon as they figure out where to put us, you bet we'll be gone. You bet."

Hokea grew quiet, looking around at Baldwin Home, the church, the ocean, the twin talismans of 'Ōkala and Mōkapu in the distance. "Maybe that's right," he said quietly. "Maybe this place ought to be empty, so we remember better. So we hear better the voices of the dead." He shrugged his massive shoulders. "But I'll miss it."

He stood there silently, and in the emptiness Rachel could hear those voices; some even called her name.

"Hold still, now."

A sound rasped in Rachel's right ear, as if a dull knife were scraping the surface of some thick fabric. At the periphery of her vision there was a gleam of light on metal, and then the new resident physician, Dr. Luckie, drew back the scalpel which Rachel saw bore a thin shaving of her own flesh. He pronounced it "Excellent," and smeared the scraping onto a glass slide. "One more ear — unless you have a third one you're keeping from me," and again the scrape of steel on skin, but no pain at all, not even a sensation of pressure against her ear.

"You don't flinch. That's good. Most patients, even though they can't feel anything, they flinch a little when they see the scalpel coming."

"I've gone through this often enough," Rachel sighed, "with Dr. McArthur and Dr. Goodhue." After the latter's retirement it seemed as though there were a constant rotation of doctors through Kalaupapa, either lacking Goodhue's commitment to the settlement or, frustrated by the old Board of Health, walking away in disgust.

Luckie glanced at her chart. "So I see. This is your . . . fourth snip this year? All negative." He swabbed her earlobe with alcohol, then moved on to her right hand. "Two more after this, you know, and you're eligible for temporary release."

Rachel rolled her eyes. "You know how many time I've gotten my hopes up, only to have the rug pulled out from under? I swear the damn bug is in there laughing at me."

"Speaking as a physician, I can assure you that *bacilli leprae* rarely laugh. They don't have much in the way of a sense of humor."

Rachel said, "Fourteen."

Luckie tapped the shavings onto a slide. "Pardon me?"

"That's how many patients got T.R. last

year. Fourteen out of six hundred! Lousy odds."

"If that's how you feel, why even bother with this?"

"I only do it because my husband wants me to." This was not strictly true but she was feeling obstinate today.

"Yes, he's next. He's had two negatives in a row, I believe." Luckie labeled the last slide. "Well, that's it. I'll have the results in a day or two."

"Take your time," Rachel said lightly, as if she didn't care. She waited as Kenji had his snips taken; then as they walked back home together he asked, "What would you do if we tested negative all six times?"

"Buy a house in Honolulu. With our winnings from the Irish Sweepstakes."

"Seriously, what if we did?"

"It's called *temporary* release," she reminded him. "We'd still have to get tested every two months, and the first time we went positive again —"

"I know. But even just two months of freedom . . . what would you do?"

Rachel conceded, "I . . . guess I'd try to find Mama, if she's alive. And Sarah and my brothers." After a moment she added quietly, "And I'd like to see her. Just once."

Kenji knew that by "her" Rachel did not mean her mother or her sister. He took her hand in his.

The next day, when Dr. Luckie confirmed that both their snips had been negative, Rachel just nodded and thanked him, a bit tersely; and when Kenji expressed excitement at their prospects she dismissed it with a short, "Don't count your chickens before they're snipped," which didn't make much sense but he understood nonetheless.

She said much the same thing two months later, when Kenji's fourth snip and Rachel's fifth again tested negative — but secretly she found herself dreaming of Honolulu, and cursed the bug for doing it again, for getting her hopes up one more time.

With the long-overdue arrival of electricity in their homes, Kalaupapans embraced American domestic engineering with a vengeance. Now Steamer Day became more than just the day the mail arrived and the groceries were delivered. Steamer Day was standing on the shore waiting for the new Frigidaire you'd ordered, the excitement of seeing the big carton with your name on it, the pride of showing it off to your neighbors. It was getting your first Philco so you could listen to the Army-Navy football games on KGU, or music broadcast live from the Royal Hawaiian Hotel, or *Lum 'n' Abner.* It was vacuum cleaners and phonographs and waffle irons and toasters and even cocktail shakers . . . all the little luxuries and indulgences that helped make life at Kalaupapa seem a bit more normal.

(And when, after the repeal of Prohibition, Governor Judd quietly rescinded the settlement's long-standing ban on beer, Steamer Day also meant Schlitz and Pabst and Anheuser and Blatz.)

For Rachel and Kenji, this particular Steamer Day meant the arrival of a brand-new short-wave radio, which promised contact with the far corners of the earth: station XEWW from Mexico City, ZRL of Capetown, South Africa, PLP from Bandoeng in Java, XGOY all the way from Chungking, China — they would even receive a signal from the distant shores of Ankara, Turkey!

There was human cargo aboard the SS *Hawaii* as well, and these new arrivals to Kalaupapa were welcomed with a *lū'au* of splendid proportions. Like everyone who had ever come from Kalihi these exiles arrived believing that banishment to Moloka'i was tantamount to a death sentence, only to find themselves feasting on roast pork and fresh *poi* and *haupia* pudding, surrounded by music and laughter, looking confused but relieved.

One of the newcomers, a young man in his twenties named David Kamakau, soon found a fast friend in Kenji. Both had attended St. Louis College, though twenty years apart. David had gone on to the sort of career which

477

for Kenji had been stillborn, as a loan officer at the Bishop Bank. The first time Kenji and Rachel had him over for dinner he and Kenji talked long into the night, principally about economics and the current downturn:

"It's a normal cyclic decline," David maintained. "Stocks bottom out but open up possibilities for investments and profits; unsound companies are weeded out."

Kenji, who followed world events via several newspaper subscriptions, didn't agree. "Even before the stock market crashed the banking system was a house of cards, it's a wonder it didn't collapse before this . . ."

"There are rumors this man Roosevelt plans to take us off the gold standard —"

"We're already off it, it's just not official!"

Rachel was able to follow, if not contribute much, to the discussion so far, but as terms like *multilateralism* and *hyperinflation* began flying over her head she felt herself taking on more and more the aspect of a floor lamp. Sensing her unease Kenji shifted the subject; but it wasn't just economics that intimidated Rachel. The more they saw of David, the more Rachel realized she didn't know: the philosophy of Santayana, the theories of Spengler, the writings of Jung and Freud. . . . For the first time she realized how inadequate her education at Kalaupapa had been; true, she was a voracious reader, but there was only so much one could teach oneself. Every time

Kenji paused to explain something to her, the more ashamed she felt. Her genuine pleasure that her husband had found someone he could talk to on a certain level was quickly joined by jealousy that she was not that person.

She was careful to keep her feelings of frustration and inferiority from him; she couldn't allow them to ruin his friendship with David. And Kenji certainly wasn't remiss in his attentions to her — they still discussed books they'd just read, the poetry of Frost and Yeats, the novels of Somerset Maugham. But now she had knowledge of her lack of knowledge, and as the date of her next snip approached, a furtive, ugly thought began festering in her: what if she and Kenji *did* get temporary release? And what if, upon reentering the world at large, Kenji discovered that what bound them together had been exile, not love? That here in the smaller world of Kalaupapa they had more in common with each other than they did with anyone else, but once outside it, he would quickly see how little they truly shared?

She would wake in the middle of the night unable to think of anything else, telling herself that maybe she shouldn't get the last test; maybe that way she could stay here, she could keep him. By the time the sun rose on a sleepless night she had talked herself into it, made her decision: she wouldn't go for the sixth test.

Then in the light of dawn she would watch Kenji as he slept, his half-open eye stirring some depth of emotion in her; he would wake, smiling sleepily as he saw her, grazing a finger gently against her cheek as he wished her good morning; and Rachel's plans vanished in a word and a smile. She couldn't do that to him; he had lost so much. She would get tested, and if the result was negative — if Kenji's next two tests were also negative — they would apply for temporary release. And if she found herself released from her marriage as well, then she would bear it as she had borne so much else in her life.

But oh, how much worse it would be than everything else!

It was a slow, rainy day at the store — Mack and Ehu didn't even show up to argue over FDR's latest accomplishments or transgressions — and Kenji was sitting in a wicker chair reading *The New York Times* when Dr. Luckie entered, shaking water from his coat.

"Quite the monsoon out there, eh Kenji?" he said.

Kenji looked up, nodded, but didn't quite smile. It was not lost on him that he and Rachel had had their snips taken just the day before. "I like rainy days. They're quiet. How are you, Doctor?"

"Wet, cold, and embarrassed." Luckie

peeled off his coat, sighed. "It probably won't come as a surprise to you to learn that until recently, the medical department kept little in the way of case files on individual patients."

Kenji stood up. "No, that doesn't surprise me."

"Before the new Board took over each physician was pretty much his own secretary — and most of them, frankly, were better physicians than they were secretaries. Anyway, the upshot is, things got lost. Excluding yesterday's test, I've performed four 'snips' on you in the last year — all negative — but now I find that your last 'snip' under Dr. McArthur was also negative. That makes five."

"Four plus one is five? Are you sure?"

Luckie laughed sheepishly. "Well you might ask. Clearly mathematics is not my strong suit. Well, the long and the short of it is, you and Rachel both had five negative snips going in to yesterday's test."

"And?"

"And," Luckie said, "I'm afraid that Rachel has tested positive again." He paused. "You, on the other hand, tested negative."

Kenji just stared at him.

"What?" he said, uncertain of what he'd heard.

"Your snip was negative, Kenji. Your leprosy is biologically inactive. You're eligible for T.R."

Kenji could not, for the life of him, formulate a response. He was completely unprepared for this. Finally he said, "Temporary release?" — the words seeming to ring in his ears.

"Now, understand," Luckie explained, "you'll be free to leave Kalaupapa, but every two months you'll have to report in for another snip, either here or in Honolulu. If you test positive again at any time you will be considered to have relapsed and will be readmitted to Kalaupapa."

The reality of it was starting to sink in. Kenji asked, "What about Rachel?"

"She'll continue to be tested here. And when she tests negative six times in a row, she'll be eligible for T.R. and can join you."

Kenji's mouth was dry. "What if she doesn't?"

Luckie didn't answer.

Kenji had dreamed of this, had often tried to imagine how he might feel if this moment ever came; but never had he expected to feel merely numb.

"I can't leave my wife," he said.

Luckie spread his hands. "It's not necessarily a permanent separation."

"You don't know that," Kenji said sharply. "She's my family, my *'ohana.* I'm her *'ohana,* the only one she has."

"You can come back anytime, Kenji. See her whenever you want, as often and as long as you want."

"A part-time marriage, you mean?"

"Surely," Luckie said, "you have family back on Oʻahu you'd like to see again?"

Kenji declared flatly, "Rachel is my only family."

Luckie nodded. He may even have expected this.

"Well, we do have several parolees who've chosen to stay here at Kalaupapa," he said. "Apply for T.R., stay here with your wife, and if you ever change your mind —"

"I won't change my mind. I don't need T.R. status. And I'd appreciate it if you didn't mention any of this to Rachel." He picked up his paper again and sat down in his chair, signaling that the discussion was over.

"Yes, of course. Whatever you wish." Luckie shrugged on his wet coat, gave Kenji a little nod of farewell, and hurried out into the rain again.

Kenji returned his attention to *The New York Times.*

At five o'clock he closed up, walked home, and saw Rachel, back from a day at Bishop Home, playing tug-of-war with Hōku and Setsu. He joined in for a while, then suggested they go inside. "I have bad news," he told her as they entered the house. "Dr. Luckie stopped by the store. We tested positive."

He couldn't quite read the emotion in her

483

face. "Oh," she said. Then, quickly, "I told you. The damn bug's laughing at us."

To her surprise, Kenji reached out, touched her cheek, and said, "I love you." A tear welled in his good eye. "I love you so much, Rachel."

He cupped a hand around her neck, drew her to him, and showed her how much.

CHAPTER 19

1941–43

From the beginning there were relatively few *haoles* sent to Kalaupapa: the first, an Englishman named William Williamson, arrived in 1867, having apparently contracted leprosy while working at the Honolulu receiving station. There was no counting the number of Caucasians who became infected but had the wherewithal to buy quick passage out of the islands before, or even after, their condition was discovered; but dozens of Americans and other people of Northern European stock did find their way to Moloka'i, and one of these arrived shortly after New Year's Day, 1941.

Former Seaman First Class Gabriel Tyler Crossen came ashore in a boat with six other bedraggled newcomers: four Hawaiians, one Portuguese, and an elderly Chinese. In his Navy whites — white cap and jumper, black neckerchief, white starched trousers — he was a peacock among sparrows. Waiting at the dock for a produce shipment, Rachel

485

couldn't help but notice the sailor in bright cotton twill, though at first she took him for a visitor mistakenly placed in a launch with patients. It wasn't until he stepped onto the landing that she noticed the angry red welt on his neck only partially hidden by his crisp white collar, and realized that he was, however improbably, one of them.

As he gave his name to settlement officials Rachel detected a slight drawl to his speech, but had no clue what state he hailed from: her familiarity with mainland accents came primarily from movies, and Southern accents from *Gone With the Wind.* Now as the newcomers followed the officials into town, the young sailor looked around for the first time — taking in the maimed faces of those he would be living among for the rest of his life — and Rachel clearly read the dismay and horror in his face. She could hardly begrudge him that — they'd all felt it at first. But there was something else, noticeable in the way his shoulders began to sag and his proud bearing seemed to wilt. She remembered seeing some of it in Kenji when he first came to Kalaupapa: the shame not merely of having leprosy but of having lost one's station in life.

Then the first cargo boat landed, and Rachel thought nothing more about the sailor until she and Kenji — and aging Hōku, sisterless since the death of Setsu — came home that evening to discover that Seaman First

486

Class Crossen had been settled, alone, in the cottage next door. It was unusual as ever for a single person to be assigned their own home; but given that he was *haole* she supposed she shouldn't have been surprised. The administration of the settlement was quick to make allowances for the lifestyle of what used to be called "white foreigners."

Crossen, no longer in uniform but wearing denim pants and a short-sleeved shirt, stood on his *lānai*, his back to Rachel and Kenji as he gazed down Kaiulani Street. As they approached Rachel called out, *"Aloha."*

The man jumped as if someone had cried "Boo!" He pivoted around, seeing his neighbors for the first time; gave them a tight smile and a perfunctory nod; then quickly turned away and hurried into his house.

"Good meeting you, too," Kenji said to empty air.

"It's his first day. You remember what it was like."

"As I recall," Kenji said dryly, "I was friendly, gregarious, and generally of sunny disposition."

Rachel poked him in the ribs.

"Give him a couple days to get settled," she said.

But though they would eventually exchange brief pleasantries with their new neighbor, that was as far as it went. He came into the store often enough, to buy Wrigley's gum or

487

Lucky Strikes, but was always coolly unapproachable: he paid promptly for his purchases and departed quickly, never engaging in small talk with Kenji or his regular customers. Only once did he contribute even a single sentence: during a heated discussion about the settlement authorities' recent attempts to convince patients to be voluntarily sterilized. Some patients, told they couldn't go to Honolulu on T.R. unless they underwent the procedure, acquiesced under pressure; others flatly refused. Crossen listened in disbelief, then disgust, then snapped out, "Anyone tries that on me, I'll return the favor. *Without* surgery." The regulars laughed, but Crossen just turned on his heel and left the store.

He declined invitations to parties and dances, never going near the social hall but for the occasional movie. When the shades of his house were raised Rachel and Kenji could see him downing one bottle of Pabst Blue Ribbon after another, only to pass out afterward, sitting stewed in his chair like a hermit crab tucked in the cleft of a rock. Sometimes they heard those bottles shatter and caught glimpses of amber shards lying in acrid pools on the floor.

Crossen's sole apparent friend was the only other mainland American patient, an affable Californian named Brady; and on one of Brady's visits to the store Rachel asked him pointblank whether or not their new neighbor was *pupule.*

"Oh, he ain't batty," Brady told her, "just angry. He drinks to forget where the hell he is — or not care."

"I was angry too at first," Kenji admitted. "Maybe if I talked to him . . ."

Brady shook his head. "I wouldn't. Gabe's got no use for Orientals — thinks he got the *ma'i pākē* from a Chinese whore in Honolulu. He was stationed on the USS *Nevada,* and when the ship's medico told him he had leprosy, he went on a bender — went AWOL, beat the crap out of that poor whore. The brass had him march up and down the deck carrying a full pack for six hours."

"But I'm not Chinese," Kenji pointed out.

"You're close enough for him."

"I'm surprised he's even here," Rachel said. "Isn't there a leprosarium on the mainland?"

Brady nodded. "Carville, Louisiana. But it's kinda close to his family in Baton Rouge. Didn't want to go back and shame them. Sounds silly, I know, but there it is."

Kenji just nodded.

It wasn't until the annual Fourth of July celebration that Crossen allowed himself to be coaxed from his house by the gregarious Brady. The Fourth was traditionally festive at Kalaupapa, memories of those tiny flags ground into the dust in '98 having been long forgotten. Food was abundant; there were canoe races, a baseball game, pony races, and

489

most colorfully, *pā'u* riders — a Hawaiian princess and her six attendants astride horses, ginger wreaths around their necks, their long sweeping skirts grazing the ground as they rode. Crossen didn't participate in any events, but he did watch them, particularly the baseball game between patients and staff physicians (the doctors lost nine-four). After this there was a motion picture in the social hall, followed by ice cream, cakes, and other desserts. For the first time since the young seaman arrived here he seemed to enjoy himself — seemed to realize that it was possible to enjoy himself here — and by the end of the evening he was even dancing with a pretty young Portuguese girl named Felicia. Kenji and Rachel joined them on the dance floor, as a blind eighteen-year-old named Sammy Kuahine — something of a musical prodigy, despite his handicap — strummed his ukulele and sang a song of his own composition.

"The Sunset of Kalaupapa
Smiles through the evening rain;
The tradewinds of Kalaupapa
Sing like an old refrain
There's music of romancing,
Moonlight and stars above;
Your magic charms, your dancing
Fill every night with love . . ."

Rachel's cheek brushed against Kenji's as they danced, as out of the corner of her eye she saw Gabe Crossen cradling Felicia in his arms, swaying to the music with a smile that somehow changed his whole face; and for these moments at least, Moloka'i truly seemed the place of romance and beauty of which Sammy sang so sweetly.

That first Sunday morning in December was as drowsy and quiet in Kalaupapa, but for the crowing of settlement roosters, as it was on O'ahu. As Kenji slept in, Rachel took Hōku to Papaloa Beach. The swells were moderately high and well-shaped, perfect for surfing. There was only one other person on the beach, a man in his thirties whose face and legs were riddled with sores, his right foot amputated at the ankle; he sat on the sand, gazing out at the big waves rolling in. He turned at her approach, and Rachel nodded a hello to the surfer she'd first met here thirteen years before, the one with the hollow surfboard. The eyes in his ulcerated face reflected the same longing and frustration he must have seen in hers back in '28. She gave him a consoling smile and walked on, playing catch with Hōku a while before heading back to town.

At 8:30 A.M. half of Kalaupapa was still asleep as the other half readied for church. As Rachel skirted the stony garland of cem-

eteries north of town she heard from somewhere up ahead — the Church of Latter-Day
Saints was the closest structure — the tinny
music of a radio broadcast, a chorus of
angelic voices raised in song.

"Gird up your loins; fresh courage take;
Our God will never us forsake,
And soon we'll have this tale to tell,
All is well! All is well!"

The voices, she would later learn, were
those of the Mormon Tabernacle Choir,
recorded in Salt Lake City and now being
broadcast on KGMB in Honolulu. But even
as she passed the church — its parishioners
gathering in anticipation of the 9:00 service
— the chorus was suddenly choked off,
silenced by a burst of static, followed by the
urgent voice of an announcer.

*"This is Webley Edwards in Honolulu. A
sporadic air attack has been made on Oʻahu.
Enemy planes have been shot down, and the
Rising Sun sighted on the wingtips!"*

All conversation among the parishioners
ceased.

"This is no maneuver!" the announcer barked
out. Rachel had never before heard such
emotion in a voice coming over the airwaves.
"This is the real McCoy!"

The congregation, joined now by Rachel
and Hōku, clustered around the radio in

disbelief. A church deacon, perhaps fearing he was being taken in by some sort of dramatic program, flipped the dial over to Honolulu's other radio station, KGU, but there too he heard, *"Repeat, we are under attack! Do not use the phone, stay off the streets! Keep calm, the situation is under control!"*

Even more disturbing than the rush of words from the none-too-calm announcer were the muffled echoes of what sounded like explosions in the background.

"My God," someone said. "My God."

Rachel hurried home with Hōku, woke Kenji, and turned on their own radio set in time to hear, *"All Army, Navy, and Marine personnel report to duty!"* All over Kalaupapa the rasp of distant men urged calm and discouraged panic, but the anxiety in their voices belied their message.

"Get off the roads and stay off!"

"Don't block traffic!"

"Stay at home!"

David Kamakau hurried to the house, breathless from more than just exertion. "Jesus Christ," he said, rushing up the porch steps and through their open door. "What the hell is it? Are we being invaded?"

"Either that," Rachel said, "or Orson Welles is at it again." Within minutes other friends and neighbors — Hokea, Ehu, even Gabe Crossen and Felicia — had joined them, listening in stunned silence to the news from Honolulu.

"Here is a warning to all people through the Territory of Hawai'i and especially on the island of O'ahu. In the event of an air raid, stay under cover. Many of the wounded have been hurt by falling shrapnel from anti-aircraft guns. If an air raid should begin, do not go out of doors. Stay under cover. You may be seriously injured or instantly killed by shrapnel falling from anti-aircraft shells!"

Felicia asked, "But who's attacking? Whose planes?"

Crossen spat out, "Who else? The goddamn Japs."

Kenji kept his gaze fixed on the radio as he switched back and forth between channels.

"Anyone owning a truck or a motorcycle is asked to drive it at once to your local first aid station!"

"All Army, Navy, and Marine personnel report to duty!"

"United States Army intelligence has ordered that all civilians stay off the streets. Get your car off the street. Drive it onto the lawn if neces-sary, but get it off the street! Do not use your telephone —"

"All doctors, nurses, and volunteer personnel report at once to Queens Hospital!"

"Fill all buckets and tubs with water, to be ready for a possible fire. Attach your garden

494

hoses. Keep your radio turned on for further news. . . ."

What became apparent was this: Japanese bombers were laying siege to Pearl Harbor, Kāneʻohe Naval Air Station, Hickam Field, and ʼEwa Marine Air Corps Station. In addition, it seemed that Honolulu itself was taking some direct hits, though it wasn't clear how much of that was the result of enemy bombs and how much due to the anti-aircraft shrapnel the stations were so urgently warning of.

Hokea said, "This is crazy. Since when we been at war with Japan?"

Most of the listeners' faces were drained of color, but Gabe Crossen's was flush with rage.

"It's a sneak attack," he said coldly. "Goddamn Jap cowards didn't even bother to declare war!"

No one was inclined to dispute the point.

For the next hour and a half they listened to the sporadic reports coming out of Honolulu; in between announcements church music played, as in the background could be heard a rumble that was not thunder and the frantic shuffling of furniture as radio staff presumably secured windows and doors.

At 11:15 A.M., Governor Joseph Poindexter came on the air on KGU to declare a state of emergency.

His voice trembling, the seventy-two-year-old governor repeated admonitions to stay calm, to stay home, to not use the telephone. As he was finishing up he stopped in mid-sentence, then said, *"I've just been handed a message . . . General Short is ordering Hawaii's radio stations to shut down immediately, for fear the Japanese will home in on our broadcast."*

To the astonishment of all listening the governor began to weep. *"We are going off the air for the first time,"* he said, clearly a man under great strain. *"We have been under attack and the sign of the Rising Sun has been plainly seen on the underside of the planes."*

The governor was hurried off the air and at exactly 11:41 A.M. the radio fell silent.

That silence was more frightening than the panicky voices and muted explosions. "Try the police channels," David suggested, but as Kenji adjusted the short-wave set the flashes that came in were hardly reassuring:

"Investigate Japanese at 781 Sunset Avenue"

"Proceed to St. Louis Heights, parachutists supposed to have landed"

"Arrest that man! Bring him down here — he's an impostor"

Also faintly heard through static and space were even more alarming, and confusing, bursts from military radios:

"Enemy transports reported four miles off Barber's Point"

"Parachute troops landing on North Shore"

496

"Enemy sampan about to land at Naval ammunition depot"

"Enemy landing party offshore Nānākuli — friendly planes firing on them"

None of these reports turned out to have merit, but the people of Kalaupapa had no way of knowing that just now. Fed up with the conflicting, chaotic broadcasts, Rachel announced, "Damn it! I'm gonna see for myself," and to general bafflement hurried out of the house.

"Where in the hell are you going?" David asked.

"Kauhakō," she called back. Everyone understood at once — those who couldn't squeeze into Kenji and Rachel's Packard found other transportation, and followed her up Damien Road.

Leaving their autos at the foot of the Kauhakō trail, they followed her along the barely-visible path now completely overgrown with lantana scrub. Despite their various handicaps they all managed to climb up onto the crater lip, standing at the summit of this highest point on the peninsula — and looked out across the sea, looked north.

Rachel's breath caught in her chest.

Only twenty-six miles away, the island of Oʻahu lay on the horizon; but none of them had ever seen it like this before. Enormous columns of smoke rose from the tip of the island that was Honolulu, obscuring the

497

harbor and most of the city. Much of the smoke was blacker than a stormcloud, but there also were pillars of gray, brown, yellow, and white straddling the horizon. Licks of flame danced on the water as though the ocean itself were afire — which they later discovered was the case, oil from the shattered naval vessels having spilled and ignited. It was impossible to tell, through the clouds of smoke eclipsing the city, how much of Honolulu survived; for all they knew it could be in ruins, broken to bits by Japanese bombs.

Rachel, Kenji, David, Hokea, Crossen, all of them stood in stunned, horrified silence, unable to take their eyes off the catastrophe written in the clouds. Rachel's eyes welled with tears as she wondered if her family was there, dead or alive, behind the evil-looking smoke. And then an even more horrifying thought: *Ruth.* Was their daughter there on O'ahu, was she hearing the shrill of bombs falling to earth? Had one found and shattered the shelter of her home? As if reading her mind Kenji reached out and took her hand, and from his tight grip and the tears in his eyes Rachel knew that they shared the same fear, the same uncertain dread.

And then — strangely — they were startled to hear the silence broken not by a cry or a curse or a sob, but by the sound of a voice raised in song. Rachel turned, even more surprised to discover it was Crossen. He stood gazing into the distance with eyes shadowed by grief and impotence, something like a dirge spilling out of him, his voice so soft he might have been singing it to himself.

"Day is done, gone the sun
From the lakes, from the hills,
From the skies —"

Rachel recognized the melody, if not the words; they all did. All eyes went to the young sailor singing "Taps."

"All is well, safely rest
God is nigh . . ."

In the distance the water burned, as black fingers of smoke groped helplessly at the sky.

At 4:25 that afternoon, the commercial radio stations went briefly back on the air to announce that martial law had been declared throughout the Territory of Hawai'i; the self-styled military governor was Major General Walter C. Short. Almost everyone expected an imminent invasion, or at least further bombing, and defensive measures were immediately put into effect. Nightly blackouts, a curfew, the issuing of ID cards and gas masks to everyone in the territory, all these actions were seen as prudent and necessary. Less applauded was the suspension of civil law — the U.S. justice system replaced by military justice, civil judges by military provosts — and of elections.

That first night saw people throughout the territory eating dinner in the dark, forbidden to light so much as a candle to guide forks to their mouths. In Kalaupapa this could be downright dangerous, as a stubbed toe or an unnoticed cut could lead to gangrene. Those residents who possessed flashlights and a little blue cellophane could at least see their hands in front of them, as illumination in the blue spectrum was permitted. When it became clear that blackouts were here for the duration, residents and staff lined the inside of their windows with tar paper or painted the glass black on the outside. Cantankerous Abelardo was appointed "blackout warden," mainly because no one else wanted the job, and delighted in descending upon residents whose keyholes were emitting even a flicker of visible light and levying stiff fines. For the first time at Kalaupapa, the sound of a plane passing overhead was no longer a cause for celebration.

Yet the war brought unexpected joy to the settlement as well. In recent years the number of children in Kalaupapa had steadily declined as the Board of Hospitals and Settlement chose to keep more young leprosy patients at Kalihi, closer to friends and family. But now, fearing further attacks on

Honolulu, the Board decided the children might be safer at Kalaupapa. In March of 1942, twelve girls and twenty boys shipped out at the furtive hour of four in morning aboard the SS *Hawai'i,* bound for Moloka'i.

When the children arrived they found themselves the puzzled recipients of more love and attention than they had ever dreamed of. Kalaupapans, delighted to hear the laughter of *keiki* again, spoiled them mercilessly, buying them candy and ice cream, treats and toys. There were birthday parties and *lū'aus* and trips to the beach; the children went fishing, explored sea caves, played softball and volleyball, learned to ride horses.

Rachel found herself spending more time helping Sister Catherine — at seventy the eldest sister at the convent, stubbornly resisting retirement as she helped train a new generation of Franciscans — at Bishop Home. Given her infirmities Rachel couldn't do much manual labor, but she had no lack of energy or strength to play croquet with the girls on the convent lawn, or to read aloud from L. Frank Baum and Jack London. At one such reading, which took place on the beach with children from both Bishop and McVeigh Homes, a ten-year-old boy named Freddie asked Rachel hopefully, "Do you have any comic books?"

Rachel blinked. " 'Comic' books? What are they?"

"They're like the funny pages in the Sunday paper," another boy explained, "except in a magazine."

"I can show you!" Freddie announced, racing back to McVeigh Home and returning a few minutes later with an impressive stack of magazines under his arm, which he handed to Rachel. Every title was an exclamation promising adventure and excitement: *Whiz Comics, Thrilling Comics, Smash Comics, More Fun Comics, Amazing Mystery Funnies, Crackajack Funnies, Slam-Bang Comics, Wow Comics, Sensation Comics, Pep* and *Prize* and *Jackpot* and *Top-Notch.* The glossy covers were populated by a wondrous cast of characters: hawk-winged birdmen swooping out of the sky, muscled strongmen lifting cars, men made of fire, men made of rubber, spectral figures cowled in green, turbaned swamis with magic wands. In gaudy costumes they squared off against leering gargoyles, evil doctors, murderous cavemen, Grim Reapers, rampaging mummies, fiery rockets, Nazi tanks and Japanese Zeros.

"Ah," Rachel said, "I see. Heroes and magic. I know some stories like that." She asked the children, "Have you ever heard of a hero named Māui?"

A boy objected, "Maui's an island, not a hero!"

"Oh? Where do you think they got the *name* for the island?"

"Māui was a real person?" a girl asked.

"He was more than a person. He was the son of a goddess, Hina, and a mortal man, so he was half-human and half something more than human."

"Like the Sub-Mariner," Freddie observed sagely.

"Māui was what they call a 'trickster' because he used his wits as well as his *mana,* his power. And because he was a little mischievous. Like the time he turned his brother into a dog."

"My brother's already a dog," a girl said, and everyone laughed.

"According to legend, when the world was new the sky and the clouds rested on top of the earth. They pressed down so heavily that when the first plants began to grow, their leaves were flat."

A boy nodded soberly. "That makes sense."

"When trees started to grow they pushed the sky up farther — enough that the human race could now walk upright. But the skies were still much lower than they are now. One of Māui's first great deeds was to lift up the sky. He braced himself against the top of the clouds and *pushed,* pushed the heavens up to where they are today.

"Also back then, the nights were longer than the days; the sun moved too quickly through the skies. There was hardly time to dry *kapa* cloth — it had to be taken up at night and put out the next day again. So Māui fashioned ropes of green flax and used them to snare the sun, forcing it to move more slowly across the sky."

A girl looked skeptical. "Why didn't the ropes burn?"

"The greener a plant, the harder it is to burn." The girl seemed placated by this cunning use of science.

"Did Māui ever fight anybody like Hitler?" Freddie asked, impatient to get to the action. "Or the Red Skull?"

"Oh, he had many great battles," Rachel assured him. "For instance against Peʻapeʻa, the Eight-Eyed Bat." This quickly captured their attention. "Māui had been fishing along the shore of Oʻahu when he looked up and saw his wife Kumulama in the grip of a horrible creature — a huge bat with eight terrible eyes, which had seized his wife in teeth like razors and carried her aloft. Māui dove into the sea after it, but the creature was too fast and Māui had to turn back, weeping, as the eight-eyed bat carried Kumulama to a distant island.

"Heartsick, Māui went to a wise old *kahuna,* who told him to gather tree limbs, thick vines, and the feathers of many birds. Māui did this, and from the tree limbs the *kahuna* fashioned the hollow skeleton of a giant bird, then covered it in feathers. The vines were attached to the bird's wings, and when Māui climbed inside and pulled on the vines, the wings flapped — and with Māui's great strength as a motor, the bird took flight!

"Māui piloted the flying machine — the first in the whole world! — to the island of the bat. It was a beautiful island, but Pe'ape'a was its ruler — its dictator, like Hirohito —" The *keiki* booed and hissed. "— and when Māui landed he was captured by the bat's people. They imprisoned him in a cage and took him to their ruler, who rejoiced that he had captured such a mighty warrior.

"Māui waited until the bat became drowsy, watching as first one eye, then another, and another, closed in sleep. When the eighth eye drooped shut, Māui quietly freed himself from the box and, wielding a huge blade, he cut off the bat's head with one swipe!" Rachel swung her hand in a wide arc and made a whooshing sound. Her listeners cheered, but the best was yet to come.

"Now very angry at what was done to his wife, Māui gouged out the bat's eight eyes and had its people make them into 'awa — a kind of bathtub gin usually made from kava root. And do you know how 'awa used to be made?" They all shook their heads. "People used to chew the kava root, then spit it out and strain it. So the Pe'ape'a's people *chewed his eyes and spit them out,* and then Māui *drank* the 'awa made from the bat's eight eyes!"

This was greeted by a chorus of cheers, gasps, *Wow*s and *Yeah*s, from boys and girls alike.

"And then," Rachel finished triumphantly, "Māui flew back to O'ahu with his wife at his side." She turned to the boy who'd expressed doubt about the trickster hero. "And *that's* why they named the island of Maui after him."

There was silence a long moment.

"Tell us again about the eyes," someone said, and so she did.

If most spirits were lighter these days at Kalaupapa, Gabriel Crossen's were not. Reports of his courageous shipmates aboard the *Nevada* — weathering a hail of enemy fire as they struggled to get their ship clear of the harbor — plunged him into a foul depression. War was raging outside, friends were dying, becoming heroes, and he was denied the chance to take his place alongside them. His death, when it came, would be far from the scene of battle: a sickly, anonymous end of no great moment or valor.

Though all liquor in the territory had been banned by the military government, Crossen

506

had no trouble finding enough of it to try and deaden his reignited pain and anger. Once more Rachel and Kenji heard the sounds of shattering glass from next door, or as on one summer night had their sleep broken by a guttural curse, followed by a soft wet sound and a woman's cry.

Kenji immediately went for the police, and in minutes constables were rapping on Crossen's door. "Open up!" a burly officer ordered, Kenji and Rachel a few paces behind. When no one answered he bellowed, "Nice door. Gonna be firewood in a minute if you don't open it!"

Finally the door opened to reveal a disheveled, obviously pie-eyed, Crossen. "What is it!" he snapped, his indignation compromised by the slur in his voice.

The constable shouldered him aside and entered to find empty whisky bottles strewn about and a subdued Felicia wrapped in a towel, her left eye swollen and a cut above it bleeding. "What happened, Miss? Are you all right?"

Felicia nodded and told them, none too convincingly, that she'd fallen and hit her head. "I'm just clumsy, 'ey?" She laughed, but her attempted gaiety made Rachel sick.

Despite pleas from Rachel and the police, Felicia would not change her story. Crossen looked smug, right up until the moment the constable announced he was citing the *haole* for possession of alcohol, drunkenness, and "disturbing the quiet of the night." Crossen was grabbed none too gently and propelled out of the house; he glared at Kenji and Rachel, then was squeezed into a car and escorted to the Kalaupapa jail, where the sheriff showed him to a tiny cell in which he ignominiously spent the night.

Thereafter he was more circumspect about his drinking, but the drinking didn't stop, nor the occasional cry from Felicia — quickly stifled and later denied. Rachel and Kenji never failed to call the police, but Felicia continued to protect her lover; though on more than one occasion enough evidence of drunkenness was found to incarcerate Crossen. After several such incidents the military provost from Kaunakakai sentenced Crossen to a week in jail, which sobered him up for nearly an entire month; after which he again fell off the wagon, and the cycle repeated itself.

More than once Rachel sought Felicia out, begging her to leave Crossen. But the *ma'i pākē* was flowering in the girl's system and her lovely features were becoming its misshapen petals; she was afraid no one else would ever want her. "When he's hitting you he's lashing out at the disease he hates," Rachel told her. "He won't keep you around much longer."

"He loves me." Felicia seemed to cling to

508

the words. "He says he's sorry, and he loves me."

"It won't stop, Felicia, until you leave him."

"He loves me," she said, and left Rachel instead.

Finally, on a warm still night in January, Rachel and Kenji awoke to a curse.

"Stupid Portagee bitch!"

Next came the sound of harrowed flesh. And like a man going to war, Kenji calmly got out of bed, pulled on his trousers, and slipped on his shoes. "That's it," he said, and something in his tone chilled Rachel.

"I'll call the police," she said.

"Yes, that's worked so well in the past." Kenji zipped his pants; shook his head. "Men like Crossen," he said coldly, "understand only one thing."

Rachel got out of bed. "Kenji, please, don't do this."

"Then what *do* I do? Just lie here and listen to her whimper? Hope to God that he doesn't kill her one of these days? Do we just sit here and listen as he murders her?"

In her uncertain silence they heard the crack of Crossen's hand and a wail of pain from Felicia, and then Kenji was out of the house and down the front steps and onto Crossen's porch, Rachel close behind. He didn't knock, just pushed open the door and barged inside.

Over Kenji's shoulder Rachel saw Felicia

lying on the floor, face-down in a pool of her own blood. Crossen was standing above her, kicking her in the side with his foot. Her body convulsed, turning half over with the force of his kick. "Get up!" he was screaming at her. *"Get —"*

Kenji moved faster than Rachel had ever seen him — he was at Crossen's side in three quick steps. With his left hand he grabbed the *haole*'s shirt, yanked him around, and drove the fist of his right into Crossen's startled face. Rachel heard the crack of snapping bone and saw blood spout from Crossen's nose. Crossen staggered back into a wall; Rachel ran to Felicia and helped her to her feet.

Crossen quickly regained his footing, staring at Kenji with cold fury. "You Japs are good at sneak attacks."

"And you're pretty good at beating up women."

Crossen lunged at him, his whole body — younger and less ravaged than Kenji's — driving into his opponent like a truck. Kenji lost his breath, felt a rib crack, burning in his side as he fell backwards onto a table. Crossen was suddenly on top of him, hammering him with blows to the head; it was all Kenji could do to raise his arms in a futile attempt to block the punches. Through blood and sweat he looked up and saw Crossen's face, transcendent with rage, ecstatic with hate.

He's going to kill me, Kenji thought, almost outside of himself. He had no doubt of it.

Then Rachel was grabbing Crossen from behind, the fingers of her good hand digging into the *haole*'s left eye, popping it like a grape. Her wet fingers found the hard bone of his eye socket.

Crossen screamed and lashed out. The flat of his hand dropped Rachel like a stone. As she fell she saw Felicia rush past her and out of the house. *Please bring help* was all she could think as she struggled to remain conscious.

As he saw his wife fall, Kenji's pain seemed to fall away, too; he got to his feet and delivered a hard right cross to Crossen's jaw. Blood was pouring from Crossen's gouged eye, but he still gave as good as he got, driving his fist into Kenji's bruised and battered face.

Rachel looked up to see Kenji falling not two feet away, his body turning as it dropped, head canted to one side, forehead slamming into the doorjamb.

She would never forget the sound.

She would never forget the blood, spurting from the wound in a torrent.

She would never forget.

She crawled to her husband's side even as constables took the porch steps two at a time and rushed inside. An officer grabbed Crossen roughly but all Rachel saw, all she cared

511

about, was the face looking up at her, the head she now cradled in her lap. Kenji was unconscious but she spoke to him anyway, whispering over and over, "I love you, I love you, don't go . . ." She stroked his cheek with her hand, imploring him to stay, telling him how much she needed him; but by the time Dr. Fennel arrived in a mad rush, Kenji was no longer breathing. Her husband's sutured eye looked up at her, open in death as it had been in sleep, as Rachel's tears fell on his face and commingled with his blood: the last thing they would ever share.

CHAPTER 20

The bright red lacquered *torii* gate — Kenji used to joke that it always looked to him like a garish monument to the value of π — welcomed mourners through its ceremonial arch and into the tiny one-room temple. Erected in 1910 as a social hall for the settlement's Japanese population, the building soon took on a religious function as well, as a site of weddings and worship for Kalaupapa's Buddhists. The number of guests now crowding inside strained its modest capacity. There wasn't a person in town who had not known and liked the manager of the Kalaupapa Store, with one grim exception; and many were gathering to pay tribute to him.

Rachel greeted each visitor warmly but the weight of the past few days was apparent on her. Yet despite the strain, she was glad she'd decided on a traditional Buddhist wake. Kenji's body — resting in an open casket surrounded by white lilies — had lain in the

513

spare bedroom once occupied by Leilani, a glum Hōku lying nearby the coffin, standing a last watch over his master. Rachel had gone in now and then to bring an offering of food or drink, to touch his face or say some private words to him. The presence of her husband's body in the home they'd shared made it somehow easier to accept his death, much as her preparation of Haleola's body had done years before.

But her grief was still vast, and her anger so fierce and raw it frightened her. Had she owned a gun she would have long since marched into the Kalaupapa jail and shot Crossen dead with neither a moment's hesitation nor a single regret. She'd been prepared to lose Kenji to leprosy, but not to this. Not to anger and hatred — a hatred which had infected her in turn, for she was possessed by an incendiary fury which she could not imagine would ever be extinguished.

Now Kenji lay here in the temple — behind a candled altar bearing his *kaimyo,* his death name, in Japanese characters — as mourners made offerings of incense and a priest chanted a *sūtra* over the body, and one person after another stood to offer heartfelt eulogies. David Kamakau spoke of finding and losing a brother in Kalaupapa; Mack and Ehu and Abelardo called the store more of a home than the ones they lived in; other customers simply told of Kenji's generosity with his time, his efforts to find and order certain items for them, favorite foods or little luxuries which obviously meant a great deal to them. One young woman told of how as a child she had returned a cloth doll, chewed and shredded by her dog, that she'd purchased at the store. Kenji saw it was beyond repair and ordered her a new one, then told her how the Japanese believed that dolls had souls, and when they were no longer able to be loved they needed to be given proper burials, so their doll-souls could be put to rest. He placed it in an old shoe box, making sure its head faced north, as was proper; lit some incense; chanted a brief *sūtra;* and then he and the girl buried it beneath a pandanus tree.

Rachel had never heard this story before; Kenji, typically, had not thought to tell her. And when it was her turn to speak Rachel rose and said simply, "My husband thought he'd given up his career when he came to Kalaupapa. But listening to all of you today, I see how wrong he was. He had a career, a valuable one. A noble one."

She went to the casket and touched her fingers to Kenji's cold lips, then walked through a mist of tears back to her seat beside Sister Catherine, where her strength finally failed and her legs buckled. Catherine caught her and held tight to her hand as the ceremony concluded; and soon the funeral

515

procession was on its way to the Japanese/
Hawaiian cemetery along the windswept
coast.

As Kenji's casket descended into the grave
the awful finality of it engulfed Rachel like a
wave, and with an intensity of pain far
exceeding any she had ever felt from leprosy.
She wanted to jump into the open grave, to
let the earth swallowing Kenji swallow her as
well; she already felt dead in everything but
name. What remained to be taken from her?
She longed to be enfolded, welcomed, into
the earth — to breathe no more, love no
more, hurt no more.

She thanked everyone for coming, accepted
their condolences, but her heart longed for
Kenji and her thoughts were about nothing
but being with him. When the mourners
returned to their automobiles to form a daisy-
chain winding back toward town, Rachel
stayed behind to watch the last shovel of
earth patted into a freshly-turned mound.
And when she finally turned and walked
away, it was not toward town, but north, to
Papaola Beach.

There she sat and contemplated the con-
stancy of the surf: waves crashing onto the
sand, then receding with a sigh, the alternat-
ing roar and hush a kind of *sūtra* she found
comforting. Deep in her grief the ocean spoke
to her, consoled her, reminded her of the
covenant they'd entered into years before,

one Papa had explained to his little girl the first time she'd ventured into the ocean. The sea, he told her, was always in command, humanity an invited guest; those who did not respect that did not return. Rachel had ridden the waves — had lived or died — at the sea's pleasure. She had accepted its primacy, had given herself over to it time and again — so why not now?

Without quite realizing it, Rachel slipped off one shoe, then the other. She started to rise . . .

But before she could, she heard someone say, "Hi, mind if I join you?" and turned in annoyance to see Sister Catherine lowering herself onto the sand. How long had she been there, watching?

"Actually," Rachel said, "I'd prefer to be alone just now, if you don't mind."

Uncharacteristically, Catherine did not oblige.

"Ah. Too late," she said with a sigh. "Once these old bones are down I'm afraid it takes a while to get them up again." She settled in on the sand, smiling the pleasant smile reserved for those occasions when she was being particularly stubborn. Rachel frowned.

"In that case maybe you should start getting up now," she suggested, just as stubbornly.

"Oh, I have plenty of time. Don't you?" Catherine looked out at the crashing surf, the tide lapping up the beach like a beckoning friend. "The ocean is at its most seductive, don't you think, when it's most dangerous?"

Rachel sighed. "Catherine, what are you doing here?"

She shrugged. "I don't know. Returning a favor?" The elderly sister studied her a moment, then asked gently, "So how are you feeling?"

"I'm just grand. Why do you ask?"

Catherine nodded, understanding the bitterness. "After my father died a friend of mine tried to comfort me, and I made the mistake of telling her, 'You have no idea what I'm going through.' She took great offense at this — an acquaintance of hers, someone she'd worked with, had died in a shooting accident. 'Death is death,' she said."

"Spoken," Rachel said, "like someone who's never lost anyone they loved."

"And yet there's some truth in it too. All the girls I've watched die, over the years — I barely knew some of them, but still they haunt me. Their deaths diminish me — perhaps not as much as my father's, but they do diminish me.

"I don't presume to know what it's like, Rachel, losing a husband. But I knew Kenji and I grieve for him, and for you, even if I can only imagine what you're feeling."

Rachel looked away a moment, then heard herself say, "I want to kill him."

"Crossen?"

Rachel nodded. "I'd do it in a minute if I could. Does that shock you?"

"No. Grief and anger doesn't shock me." Catherine paused. "Rachel, do you remember that day at the convent when we saw the old biplane? Remember what I said?"

Rachel laughed without amusement. "I don't even remember what *I* said."

" 'Who can doubt the presence of God in the sight of men whom He has given wings.' I recall that so precisely because I've had time to consider my error." She smiled. "God didn't give man wings; He gave him the brain and the spirit to give *himself* wings. Just as He gave us the capacity to laugh when we hurt, or to struggle on when we feel like giving up.

"I've come to believe that how we choose to live with pain, or injustice, or death . . . is the true measure of the Divine within us. Some, like Crossen, choose to do harm to themselves and others. Others, like Kenji, bear up under their pain and help others to bear it.

"I used to wonder, why did God give children leprosy? Now I believe: God doesn't give anyone leprosy. He gives us, if we choose to use it, the spirit to live with leprosy, and with the imminence of death. Because it is in our own mortality that we are most Divine."

The foaming waves retreated down the

beach as tears welled in Rachel's eyes.

"I don't want to be strong," she said softly. "I want to be weak and be with Kenji."

"If you're weak, you *won't* be with him."

"Yes? Who will I be with, then? You? Your parents?" The words, out in a rush, were instantly regretted.

Catherine was unfazed. "Possibly," she admitted, adding with a sly smile, "So do you really want to risk purgatory with me there harping at you about it for all eternity? Is that your idea of a good time?"

Rachel laughed — ruefully, but she laughed. "When you put it that way," she said, "hell, no."

Catherine smiled; stood. "Well put. Hell, no."

As she gave Rachel a ride home in the convent's old jalopy she asked, "Are you going to stay on at the store? I'm sure you could have the manager's job, if you asked."

"No, I don't want to be there without Kenji. Maybe I could work more hours at Bishop Home?"

"We'd be happy to have you."

When they reached Kaiulani Street Catherine offered to stay, but Rachel shook her head. "I'll be all right." Catherine hugged her, promised she'd come see her tomorrow, then drove off. Rachel walked up the path to her home and tried not to see the empty house, Crossen's house, next door.

Hōku, dozing on the porch, barked a welcome and jumped up on her, his paws muddying her mourning dress; she'd never been happier to see him. "Hey, *keiki,*" scratching his gray head, "you hungry?" He followed her in and she opened a can of dog food, but within minutes she regretted having sent Catherine away. Everywhere she turned there were reminders of Kenji: his reading glasses half-open on an end table; a store ledger he'd been writing in that night; the pipe he would occasionally smoke, its bowl upturned, a slight fragrance of cherry tobacco clinging to the air. In these small things she felt his absence, not his presence, and it was suddenly too much to bear. She sank onto the couch, an aching vacuum inside her sucking the air from her lungs. She hung her head and wept fiercely, the emptiness inside her growing larger, not smaller; she felt as though it would grow so large it would suffocate her just as surely as the sea would have. And when she began to wish that she'd given herself to the ocean after all, she felt a familiar tickle on her face, and looked up to find Hōku beside her, licking first her cheek, then her hand. She was certain his brown eyes reflected grief — as when Setsu had died and he had lain by the door for weeks, waiting for his sister to come home — and she wrapped her arms around his neck and hugged him gratefully.

They weren't alone for long. Within half an hour David and his girlfriend Helen were at her door, inviting her to supper; she gratefully turned the offer around and insisted on making dinner for them, losing herself in the busy routine of cooking. Hokea showed up not long after and Rachel welcomed him too; soon she found herself eating among friends, grateful for their concern and their *aloha*. But there was still a bottomless hole inside her, and she began to think that there always would be.

That night she fell asleep only after much difficulty, with Hōku draped across her legs like a comforter.

At two in the morning she suddenly woke, a shaft of moonlight lighting her bedroom like a beacon. She got up; went to the window; looked out at the house next door, its rolled shades exposing empty rooms that filled her with sudden rage. On impulse she pulled on a bathrobe, hurried out of the house and up the steps to Crossen's. She pushed open the unlocked door. The living room smelled of stale beer and cigarettes; broken glass littered the floor. Among the glass splinters were red-brown spatters from Felicia's injuries, but as Rachel turned she saw what she feared most, a dark red bloodstain on the doorjamb. Her husband's blood. The blood of his life, of her life, dried and wasted. She felt her jaws clench and suddenly she was hurrying back to her cottage, turning on an outside faucet, dragging a quickly uncoiling garden hose back to Crossen's house in time for the rush of water out the nozzle. She aimed the hard spray at the door, at the jamb, at the floor, blasting away at Kenji's blood, a stream of water running red through the crack between door and *lānai;* and when that ugly stain had been erased from the doorjamb she turned the hose on the living room floor, washing away Felicia's blood, the splintered glass, purging all traces of hate and madness from this house. When the water finally ran clear and the wounds on the wood had disappeared, she calmly shut the front door, took the hose back to her yard, turned off the faucet, and went back to bed; and slept soundly, if not peacefully, the rest of the night.

Under martial law, justice in Hawai'i was swift if not always sure. Crimes for which the punishment did not exceed five years in prison were tried in military provost courts by a single judge advocate, often decided within five minutes — and that decision was usually "guilty." More serious felonies were tried by military commissions, and the members of one such commission arrived in Kalaupapa within days of Crossen's arrest and imprisonment. Major Ballard, the trial judge advocate (TJA) prosecuting the case, interviewed Rachel promptly and thoroughly; he was sympathetic to Rachel's loss and kept her abreast of the case's progress. Crossen was arraigned on, among other charges, two counts of assault with intent to commit bodily harm, against Felicia and Rachel, and one count of manslaughter in Kenji's death. Already Rachel was worried: she had assumed Crossen would be charged with murder. She didn't like the way this was starting.

The procedure of a trial before a military commission followed that of a special court-martial, and under those rules Rachel, as a witness, could hear neither the opening statement nor the testimony of other witnesses, at least not until her own testimony was concluded. She could only watch as the five commission members — a colonel, a major, and three lieutenant colonels — entered Kalaupapa's tiny courthouse alongside Major Ballard and Crossen's defense advocate. She waited outside closed doors as Ballard gave his opening statement, and when the courtroom doors opened an MP ushered in the constable who had arrested Crossen. His testimony was short. Felicia was next, and she was inside for close to an hour. Rachel knew what she must have been testifying to — Crossen's many assaults on her, the broken ribs and bruised kidney she suffered in the last attack and how Dr. Sloan told her that any further trauma might have resulted in uncontrolled hemorrhaging and death. It frustrated Rachel that she couldn't be in the courtroom observing the fate of the man who killed her husband, but soon enough it was her turn to enter.

A subdued Crossen sat at the defendant's table with his TJA, a white patch over his blind eye and the other scrupulously avoiding Rachel's gaze as she headed toward the bench. If she was hoping to see him looking nervous and afraid, she was disappointed: he seemed calm, even confident. And as Rachel looked around at the room filled with Army and Navy uniforms, her stomach churned with the realization that Crossen, though discharged, was still among friends here. How eager, she wondered, would they be to convict one of their own?

She put her fears aside as Major Ballard smoothly led her into her testimony. She recounted the many instances she and Kenji had called the police over Crossen's disturbances, then how they'd been awakened last Thursday night by Crossen's cursing and Felicia's cries, which sent them to the house next door. "And when your husband intervened in the defendant's assault on Miss Hernandez," Ballard asked, "what did you hear the defendant say?"

"He said, 'You Japs are good at sneak attacks.' "

"And had you heard other racial epithets

from him previous to that?"

"Yes. Many times."

"So even before this night you suspected that the accused harbored hostility toward your husband?"

Crossen's TJA objected. "Colonel, we're at war with Imperial Japan. You'd be hard-pressed to find someone who *hasn't* spoken such epithets."

"Sustained," said the colonel serving as president of the commission. Rachel was shocked, and silently indignant. Sustained? This man's bigotry and hate is *sustained*? She tried not to show her anger as they went through the rest of her direct testimony; then Ballard thanked her, reserved the right to redirect, and handed her over to the defense.

Crossen's TJA began, "So it's your testimony, Mrs. Utagawa, that you and your husband entered the accused's home without permission?"

"We were responding," Rachel said evenly, "to a woman's screams."

"Couldn't you have called the police?"

"We'd tried that."

"So when legal remedies failed you, you entered his home illegally, and your husband provoked Mr. Crossen with a physical attack?"

"It looked as if Mr. Crossen was already provoked when we got there."

"Please answer yes or no, Mrs. Utagawa.

Did your husband initiate the conflict with the defendant?"

Fuming, Rachel replied, "Yes."

"And then you yourself assaulted Mr. Crossen, didn't you — deliberately gouging out his left eye?"

"I certainly did! He was trying to kill my husband."

The TJA objected to this speculation on his client's intent and the colonel sustained it. "Please limit yourself to what you know, Mrs. Utagawa," he directed Rachel.

"You deliberately gouged the defendant's eye, hoping to inflict serious injury on him, did you not?"

"Hell yes."

"And when your husband fell and struck the doorjamb — wasn't that just an accident?"

"He didn't just stumble into it," Rachel said, raising her voice. "Mr. Crossen hit him and he fell."

"But the defendant could hardly have foreseen that, could he? Mr. Utagawa struck the door accidentally?"

Rachel snapped, "Accidentally while the defendant was trying to beat him to death!" This brought another, sterner admonition from the colonel.

Both cross-examination and redirect were long and wearying, and as Rachel left the stand she began to see where this was going.

It was Kenji who was being painted as the criminal, not the man who had killed him. She was blindingly angry, but what else could she have expected?

At Ballard's request Rachel was permitted to stay for the remainder of the proceeding, with the stipulation that she would not be called back for rebuttal testimony that could be tainted by her observation. Ballard didn't think they'd need her anymore anyway — or did he just not care?

The defense entered into evidence several affidavits by Crossen's superiors on the *Nevada,* all testifying to his generally fine service record, but called only one witness: Crossen himself. The colonel advised him that he was under no obligation to testify, and Crossen nodded. "Yes sir, I know. But I want to."

Quietly chagrined on the stand, Crossen admitted that he'd been drinking that night. "I had one too many, I admit that. And something Felicia said got me going. It was wrong, and I'm not proud of what I did to her; but it wasn't really me, it was the liquor. I don't hold my liquor well. If that's a crime then I'm guilty of it."

Rachel seethed at his politeness, his sobriety.

His TJA said, "And when Mr. Utagawa broke into your house and struck you —"

"I defended myself."

"And when *Mrs.* Utagawa attacked you?"

528

"I saw red. Last thing I ever did see out of that eye."

"Mr. Crossen, did you intend to kill Mr. Utagawa?"

Crossen shook his head emphatically. "No sir, I did not. He broke into my home, threw a punch at me — I fought back. I guess one of my punches sent Mr. Utagawa into the doorjamb, but I didn't see it — his wife half-blinded me, I couldn't hardly see what I was doing."

"So you didn't plan it that way?"

"No sir; it was an accident. I regret that it happened, but I did *not* intend to kill Mr. Utagawa."

When it was his turn to cross-examine, Major Ballard asked, "Mr. Crossen, do you hate the Chinese?"

Crossen's TJA immediately objected, but Ballard pointed out that this question concerned not the Japanese, as was previously ruled on, but another Asiatic race with which America was *not* at war. The colonel overruled the objection and instructed Crossen to answer the question.

"No sir," Crossen replied. "I don't hate nobody."

"Then why did you assault a Chinese prostitute in Honolulu on June 7th of 1940?"

Crossen flushed red. "That was a personal matter. And again, I'd had a little too much to drink."

"The assault wasn't racially motivated?"

"No."

"You just like to beat up women."

Predictably Crossen's TJA cried, *"Objection."*

The colonel sighed and sustained it.

"You seem to be an angry man, Mr. Crossen," Ballard noted.

Crossen shook his head. "That's not true."

"You're not angry because of what's happened to you?"

"No," Crossen said.

"Didn't you once tell Mr. Brady that you — quote — should've been on the deck of the *Nevada* instead of in this goddamn shithole settlement — unquote?"

Crossen looked at him a long moment, and when he finally spoke his tone lost its polite affectation; for the first time a bitter melancholy seeped through.

"Yes sir," he said quietly. "I should've died on the *Nevada* when the Japs bombed her. It would've been a mercy."

For an instant Rachel glimpsed the young sailor who'd sat with her on the heights of Kauhakō, and she found it harder to hate him. For an instant.

"Nothing further," Ballard said.

In his closing argument Crossen's TJA argued that the considerable amount of alcohol his client had consumed that night had compromised his judgment, and that

Kenji's provocation had precipitated "a sudden heat of passion" that led to "the terrible accident that claimed Mr. Utagawa's life." He stressed again Private Crossen's exemplary service record, omitting mention of the attack on the Chinese prostitute.

Ballard delivered a clear and concise argument against Crossen, but Rachel was only half-listening; all the talk about Crossen's service record had convinced her that this was going to be a whitewash, that the United States armed forces were not going to come down hard on one of their own, much less one who had had the tragic luck to be infected with this disease of savages and sent here. The court adjourned for the five members of the commission to consider the verdict, and Rachel was not surprised when they returned after less than an hour's deliberation.

The president of the commission asked Major Ballard, "Have you any evidence of previous convictions?"

Ballard presented the court with the record concerning the attack on the Chinese prostitute: Crossen had not been tried and convicted for the assault, merely disciplined. Then to Rachel's puzzlement the commission promptly adjourned again and closed the courtroom.

On their way out Ballard threw her a small smile.

Not long afterward the courtroom was opened again and it was announced that "all the members present concurring," Gabriel Tyler Crossen was hereby found guilty on one count of unlawful possession of alcohol; one count of disturbing the quiet of the night; two counts of assault with intent to commit bodily harm; and one count of manslaughter.

Rachel's heart leaped at the pronouncement, even more so when the colonel went on to specify the sentences: six months apiece for alcohol possession and disturbance of the peace, ten years' imprisonment in the assault on Felicia, five years in the assault on Rachel, and twenty years in the death of Kenji Utagawa.

Crossen sat there like a bird shot out of the sky.

It was a grand total of thirty-five years imprisonment for Crossen — but imprisonment where? No prison on Oʻahu would have, could have, taken him; and so Gabriel Crossen was sentenced to serve his term in Kalaupapa. Rachel would have preferred hard labor on a chain gang but the humiliation she saw in Crossen's face when the commission rendered its verdict — he was now a leper *and* a felon — gave her some sweet, if scant, satisfaction.

Unfortunately the Kalaupapa jail was not built or provisioned for long-term incarceration, and to Rachel's dismay it was decided that the prisoner could serve his sentence in a room in the Bay View Home in what was already, after all, forcible confinement. Rachel was appalled. It was almost as though nothing had happened — as if this man had murdered her husband and as punishment they had merely given him another room — with an oceanfront view!

But as she returned to the emptiness of her home she came to realize that the simple fact was this: Kenji was dead, and no degree of justice, no manner of incarceration, could bring him back.

In the end Rachel merely avoided the intersection of Puani Street and Damien Road, where Bay View Home perched on a bluff overlooking the shoreline. And even as she had to suffer the presence of her hated enemy, Crossen, in her midst, the enemy inside her launched a surprise attack.

Wartime life in Kalaupapa was not too removed from its peacetime existence. Many residents already grew vegetables for their own consumption and now these tiny plots of land were proudly declared "victory gardens." Poultry and hog raising increased to supplement occasional shortages of meat from Honolulu. Fresh milk was a memory — only powdered was available — and gasoline was rationed here as it was throughout Hawai'i. The only real hardship was the suspension of steamer service: *sampans* now carried all supplies and mail to Kalaupapa, but rough seas often forced the small Chinese skiffs to anchor at Kaunakakai instead. From there the cargo had to be sent down the *pali* trail, arriving days later. Mail and newspapers took much longer to reach the settlement's residents, isolating them more than they had been in many years.

By the end of 1943, as the world outside was sundered by war, Rachel found her body ravaged by a newly resurgent *ma'i pākē* — Haleola would have said "emboldened." After years of feasting merely on nerves, *bacillus leprae* now began making a meal of her flesh as well. Skin that had been blemish-free but for a few florid patches of skin now erupted in ugly purple bruises. Dr. Sloan explained that these were a result of the bacillus tearing down the walls of tiny blood vessels in her skin; as the tissues broke down, blood congested in purple welts. And because the blood was poorly circulated, the ulcers wouldn't heal. "I thought the bug only liked to eat my nerves," Rachel said.

"I'm afraid its appetites have changed. Perhaps your resistance has been lowered by stress, or perhaps this is simply the course the disease would have taken in any event, but . . . it's clearly becoming more lepromatous in nature. I'm sorry to say it does happen."

Over the next twelve months Rachel's body began to resemble, more and more, those of the friends and family she had lost over the years. Her skin became lax, losing much of its collagen substrate; hair follicles were destroyed in the process and her eyebrows fell out. Leilani in similar straits had simply sketched in a new pair with an eyebrow pencil, so now Rachel did the same, giving herself Carole Lombard's brows one day and Katharine Hepburn's the next. When her eyelashes were the next to go, she ordered false ones from a beauty supply store in Honolulu, but never had the nerve to wear them.

The bacillus, summering in the cooler regions of her body, settled in the air-cooled tissues of her nasal passages, which swelled as if from a bad cold — a cold that never went away. Rachel found it increasingly difficult and painful to breathe through her nose, but when she breathed through her mouth the increased intake of air cooled her throat, and the bug prospered there as well. Her voice became chronically hoarse; ulcers on her tonsils had to be removed.

She buried Hōku in the spring of '45, as she had so many other souls she had loved, even as the ulcers spread from her arms and legs to her chest and face. Sister Catherine insisted on dressing Rachel's sores herself. Both women had seen hundreds of cases like

535

this, but now it was happening to Rachel and in a way it was harder on Catherine than it was on her patient. Rachel had been the beautiful little girl who had grown up and never stopped being beautiful: in a garden of misery she was the rare bud that flowered, bloomed. Catherine now spent hours cleaning Rachel's sores, applying fresh bandages, chatting away as she'd done with so many others over the years — and then upon returning to her convent room she would collapse into tears, as she hadn't since her earliest days at Kalaupapa.

Rachel's joints ached and polyneuritis lit a match to new nerves, but she accepted the new parameters of her disease without complaint. She was hardly alone: Hokea's hands, his artist's hands, were slowly turning inward on themselves to the extent he was barely able to pick up a paintbrush any longer; David was fighting what the doctors called "leprous fever" and his skin, too, was ulcerating. Rachel felt her resistance to the bacillus being slowly worn down, as the surf wore away the volcanic shore, and it seemed to her just as natural a process: in the rock's erosion, after all, the sand of the beach was born. Without Kenji she found it hard to summon the reserves of strength she needed to fight the disease; found it harder to care whether she lived or died.

As the war in the Pacific finally ended amid

a conflagration of atoms, the war within Rachel grew no less heated. Her limbs became swollen with edema, so painfully she could barely walk. Catherine brought her back, after all these years, to Bishop Home, to tend to her; but as Rachel's body exploded into full-blown lepromatous leprosy it became necessary to transfer her to the hospital, where Dr. Sloan could more adequately care for her.

Her memories sustained and comforted her through fever and pain: she thought of Mama and Papa, their little house near Queen Emma Street, the happy years before Inspector Wyckoff took them all away from her. Uncle Pono lived again in fitful dreams, sometimes as himself, sometimes as an owl telling a bawdy joke. Haleola was at her bedside in the moments before dawn, assuring her everything would be all right, that she loved her, would always love her. And at night as Rachel struggled to breathe, she took in gasps of air tasting of Kenji, the scent of his skin, the breath they'd shared in their kisses.

And sometimes — as on the morning of April 1, 1946 — she would dream again of being Namakaokaha'i, her waves rolling across burled coral beds, scattering moonlight, cresting higher and higher the farther she traveled over the reef. She was a colossus of water and motion soaring toward the black crescent of 'Awahua Bay, her soul perched on the curling lip of the wave, riding it in the only way she could now; she felt the *mana,* the power in her waves, felt the rumble in her ocean depths. . . .

She woke, but continued to feel it: a roar in her bones, a vibration coming not from within but without. It was 6:45 A.M., and though the ward seemed quietly normal, some inner sense of dread propelled Rachel painfully to her feet, out of bed, and to the nearest window.

She gasped at what she saw. Out at sea, a wave at least twenty feet high was rolling shoreward — a wall of water pushing up from the ocean floor, as unexpected as lava spilling from a dead caldera, its great rumbling mass resonating inside her.

The rumble turned explosive as the wave crashed into the Kalaupapa coastline, completely engulfing it; even the tall spire of the lighthouse was nearly swamped. Rachel feared that the wave's reach would extend inland to Kalaupapa itself, but it stopped just short of that.

Cries rose up from the startled town; in the hospital, patients and doctors alike flocked to the windows.

The lights in the ward winked out.

Rachel watched in awe as the massive wave receded back into the sea . . . peeling back the ocean over the reef, where fish now flopped and flailed helplessly on the exposed seabed . . . dragging out to sea great handfuls of uprooted trees and broken timber.

Moments later, the next wave arrived.

A series of six huge waves came and went in pulsating surges, shattering whatever remained of the structures unluckily situated at the shore. By now the streets of Kalaupapa were filled with people racing for high ground — sick people crying *"Tsunami!"* as nature played yet another mean trick on them, God's last best joke at their expense. It was, after all, April Fool's Day.

When the waters at last subsided Rachel was amazed to see the lighthouse still standing, but little else along the shore: no trees, certainly no houses. Massive boulders torn from the seabed lay scattered along a beach denuded of sand.

There was no running water in the settlement, the pipes from the reservoir having been smashed to pieces; likewise no electricity. The administration building had been spun around on its foundation, as if someone had played spin-the-bottle with it. Headstones in the cemeteries were strewn about like dice in a crap game. But the only homes destroyed were beach houses owned by patients whose primary residences were in the main town. No one was killed or injured. It soon became apparent that Moloka'i had been remarkably fortunate, despite heavy damage to the island's East End; on Maui the village of Hāna had been nearly obliterated, and Hilo on the Big Island was largely underwater. All told, one hundred and fifty nine people died throughout Hawai'i in the *tsunami.*

Rachel was helpless to do more than watch from her window as work crews cleaned up what was left of the shoreline. Staggering back to bed she felt useless, and reconciled to the idea that her time on earth was nearly over; in fact she welcomed it. She knew she had been luckier than most, luckier than Emily or Leilani or Violet; she had grown up, grown old, fallen in love and been loved. And not just by Kenji — she knew how blessed she had been to have an *'ohana* here to take her in, Pono and Haleola and Catherine and Francine and so many more. Her Kalaupapa family. She lay in bed at night listening for the sound of drums and marchers, content to die.

A month or so after the *tsunami,* as Dr. Sloan examined Rachel with grim purpose, he told her, "Rachel, I'd like to put you on a new medicine, they've had some success with it at Carville. It's called Promin — one of the new sulfa drugs, an antibiotic."

Rachel managed a faint derisive noise. "They tried penicillin, it didn't work."

"Yes, but these sulfa derivatives are quite effective against tuberculosis, which is similar to the Hansen's bacillus." More and more the doctors were calling it "Hansen's disease," the result of fervent editorializing by the patient-run newspaper *The Carville Star,* arguing that the Biblical connotations of the words "leprosy" and "leper" unfairly stigmatized Hansen's patients.

"But it is an experimental drug," Sloan advised her, "and though of low toxicity it is, to some degree, toxic."

"Good," Rachel said, closing her eyes. "Maybe it'll finish me off quicker."

That afternoon she received the first of her daily intravenous injections of Promin: six times a week, two weeks out of three. For most of that time there was no noticeable change in her condition other than a slight allergic reaction, which subsided after a week.

Then, in the third month of Promin injections, Rachel noticed that an open sore on her arm was scabbing over.

Over the next few weeks, to Rachel's amazement, her ulcers began to heal, one by one — the purple bruises vanishing, fluids draining, skin clearing.

After three months' treatment with Promin Dr. Sloan replaced it with another medication called Diasone . . . and within another month her swollen, distended face began to take on its old shape, its aging beauty.

It was a miracle. A *haole* medicine that actually worked! No thunderclaps, no proclamations from heaven; God spoke not from on high, but out of a test tube.

After six months' treatment with sulfa drugs, fifty-five out of seventy-two patients at Kalaupapa showed marked improvement; only eight appeared not to have benefited. David Kamakau saw his fever cool and his ulcers disappear. The clawing of Hokea's hands and the erosion of his nasal cartilage was arrested: the sulfones couldn't reverse tissue damage, but they could prevent further deformation. Astonishingly, a scourge that had plagued humankind for generations was seemingly vanquished — virtually overnight!

"The drugs don't kill the bacillus," Sloan explained to Rachel, "they weaken it enough that your immune system can destroy it." The Hansen's bacilli were not completely wiped out, but Sloan and his colleagues were cautiously optimistic that their numbers would be greatly reduced.

Sister Catherine watched with a kind of stunned joy as hope took root at Kalaupapa for the first time in her fifty-two years at the settlement, and morale soared. Patients who had not been able to respirate without a tracheotomy tube in their throats were soon able to breathe unassisted. Failing vision was arrested; the nearly blind would now be able to see the future, however dimly. And as the cruel distortions of their bodies were halted, patients could consider surgery to repair their disfigurements, without fear that more would inevitably follow. They might yet live out lives measured in decades, not merely years or months.

Catherine was profoundly grateful to have lived to see this day. There would not be too many more for her, she suspected, but the triumph of this moment would light her path to heaven — *or wherever I'm headed,* she thought wryly. She was even able to foresee a time, not so distant surely, when this shore of exile was no more; when no one else would be brought here against their will. She went to the Franciscans' little chapel, knelt before the altar, and with joyful tears thanked God for His mercy — for the spirit that had given men wings and now this miraculous cure, for the many lives that cure would save — and most of all, she had to confess, for Rachel's life.

Long discharged from the hospital and living on her own again, Rachel was at the airport that day in June of '47 when the little twin-engine plane bearing the settlement's new superintendent touched down on the landing strip. A reception committee of staff and patients swarmed around the aircraft as the superintendent and his wife disembarked, Rachel among the first to greet him.

"Just can't stay away, can you, Missionary Boy?" she said, and Lawrence Judd laughed heartily and said, "Apparently not." Like her, he was in his early sixties now; his pleasure at seeing her was apparent and genuine. "You look wonderful, Rachel," he said, extending a hand, and this time she took it.

It was a much different Kalaupapa that Judd was returning to oversee at the close of an enviable career in public service. Dr. Sloan had been right about Promin and Diasone: *bacilli leprae* were dying as leprosy victims once died, by the thousands. The sulfa drugs did not strictly "cure" Hansen's disease, but it so dramatically reduced the number of bacilli in a patient's system that in most cases the disease was arrested within a matter of months, and the patient was rendered non-contagious. The first wave of test subjects were now receiving one negative snip after another; the prospects of parole were no longer so remote.

In the light of the medical community's growing realization that Hansen's disease was even less contagious than tuberculosis, Superintendent Judd immediately set about making changes in the way things were done at Kalaupapa. He started with his own office, throwing out the ridiculous railing between superintendent and patient. He tore down the high wire fence around the visitors' quarters as well as the mesh fence that separated patient and visitor inside the cottage. All unnecessary barriers between residents and staff came down — even the guard at the top of the *pali* trail was eliminated.

Judd was determined that residents feel more like patients than prisoners. And he was doing it all quickly, as he confided to Rachel, "before they toss me out of here on my ear."

"So if leprosy's not so easy to catch as everybody thought," Rachel asked him, "did we all get sent here for nothing? For no good reason?"

Judd sighed and considered that. "I don't know, Rachel," he said finally. "Hawaiians had no immunity to this disease. Did something need to be done to stop it? Yes. Was isolation far from your families and friends the only answer? I don't think so. Was it all for nothing? No . . . but the price you and others paid was far too high."

In December, Dr. Sloan informed Rachel that her sixth and final snip was negative, and she was now eligible for parole. Rachel heard the words, but couldn't quite comprehend them. "Parole?" she said, as if she were slightly tipsy.

"Six negatives in a row, Rachel. You'll need regular check-ups, of course, but once your application's approved, you'll be free to leave Kalaupapa whenever you wish."

It was the moment she had dreamed of since she was seven, and now that it had come she didn't know what to do.

She was sixty-one years old. Her youth was gone and all her friends were here in Kalaupapa. What promise did the outside world hold for her? Unlike some patients, she was not so disfigured that she feared living top-side, but her right hand was definitely and noticeably crippled; how could she even make a living?

Catherine suggested, "Go for a visit, at least. A week or two. Don't you want to see your brothers and sister?"

Now that this was a real possibility, Rachel wasn't so sure. "Why should I go looking for them? I haven't heard a word from them in fifty years!"

"They're still your family."

"You're my family. You and everyone here."

"You have other family too," Catherine reminded her. "What about her?"

That gave Rachel some pause. "I . . . have no idea where she is."

"There are ways of finding people."

Rachel said, "What if she doesn't want to be found?"

Catherine had no answer for that.

Leaving Bishop Home, Rachel drove up Damien Road to the Kauhakō trail and parked her car. Even with her clawed and missing toes she made it easily to the summit — it was amazing how much more energy she had now! She gazed out across the stone leaf of the peninsula and into the misty distance, the south flank of O'ahu peeking out from beneath wisps of cloud like strokes of Hokea's brush. Beyond lay the world her father had brought back to her in pieces over the years — the lands of *sakura-ningyö* and *matryoshka* and Chinese Mission dolls, lands no longer *kapu.*

And somewhere out there, a little girl, grown into a woman, who had never known the mother who birthed her.

She wished Kenji were here. She wished she could be leaving with him. But she knew what he would have done.

She filled out the parole application. She had some money saved from twenty years of her and Kenji's combined salaries at the store, in addition to the small government pension she received for those years of service. Added to the few dollars that Papa had left her, she would be solvent for a while even if she couldn't find a job right away. And she was told she could keep her house in Kalaupapa, in case she decided to come back.

David and Helen threw her a "parole party," and Rachel was touched by the number of people who came. Amid food and laughter and music they celebrated not just Rachel's imminent release but potentially their own. David and Helen were each only one snip away from freedom.

The day before Rachel's flight to O'ahu, there remained only one more person to bid farewell to.

She walked down Damien Road to Puani

Street — to Bay View Home perched on its low bluff overlooking the sea. Inside its blandly institutional hallways she walked past men — aged, blind, crippled — for whom the sulfa drugs came too late. She walked down corridors of despair and loneliness, glancing into rooms on either side, until she found the one she was looking for and she stopped.

She strode into Gabriel Crossen's room, and when he turned and saw her his face went dust-white — almost as white as the patch over his gouged eye.

After a long moment she said, "I'm leaving."

He stared at her, dumbfounded.

"You took the best part of my life," she told him, "but not all of it. I'm going to go look for the rest of it. I'm leaving."

She allowed herself a cold smile. "But you never will," she added with satisfaction.

She could see the pupil of Crossen's remaining eye dilate, as from a sudden light.

"Even if the sulfa drugs cure you," Rachel said, "you'll either be put in prison on O'ahu or just left here, in Kalaupapa . . . for the rest of your life."

Crossen began to look a little sick.

"All this time," she said softly, "and not a word of remorse from you. Of apology. 'Regret,' you said. You regretted the 'accident.' Well, now you can regret the fact that if you hadn't killed Kenji . . . maybe you'd be leaving here someday."

She didn't wait for a reply. She turned, walked out of the room, and never looked back.

The next day Superintendent Judd was at the airport to drape a *lei* around her neck and give her a kiss.

Tearfully, Sister Catherine hugged her. "I love you, Rachel," she said. "Godspeed."

Rachel kissed her on the cheek. "I love you, too, Catherine. Thank you for being part of my life." Before she could start crying, Rachel hefted her suitcase and walked up the short flight of steps onto the plane.

She sat in one of the six seats, fastened her seat belt as the pilot instructed, and was startled and exhilarated when the little Cessna began its fast taxi down the short runway. Then it leapt into the air, Rachel's stomach turning over as the land dropped away from them. She stared out the window in wide-eyed wonder as the plane banked over the settlement and climbed up the green face of the *pali,* once so forbidding, now so easily vaulted; and then it was below them, falling away as from a bird in flight, as she left it behind.

Nine days later the body of former Seaman First Class Gabriel Crossen was found floating in the waters off 'Awahua Bay. Some

549

residents suggested suicide; others thought he'd simply had too much to drink. He was put to rest in the Protestant cemetery along the coast, a small American flag marking his grave. The only mourners were the minister from Kana'ana Hou Church and a single member of the Kalaupapa band, who indifferently blew "Taps."

CHAPTER 21

Flying, Rachel discovered, wondrously distorted space and time. From up here the turbulent whitecaps of the Kaiwi Channel were reduced to tranquil combers, and half a day's steamer travel was miraculously compressed into a mere thirty minutes. It had even transformed her: no longer a sixty-one-year-old woman, she was a girl again, looking out the window with a child's eyes and a child's wonder. For fifty years the distant line of the horizon had been an implacable barrier — the unbreachable ramparts of the sky. And now in a matter of minutes they were breached after all, and so easily at that — not just the air travel but the suddenness of her cure (if it was a cure and not merely a remission, as the doctors were quick to caution). Did everything in the outside world move so fast? Had the nature and pace of time changed in the half century she had been trapped like a fly in the amber of Kalaupapa? The plane banked as it approached Oʻahu,

551

the arc of its flight opening first a wedge, then a quarter, of land in the window — like a second hand sweeping across the face of a clock, revealing more moment by moment. The green crown of Diamond Head greeted her like an old friend, but it was a friend quickly lost amid strangers.

The city of Honolulu, once a sprinkling of low buildings dwarfed by groves of coconut palms, had erupted far above the treeline and expanded in every direction — even *makai,* seaward. It seemed to Rachel that the lush garden of her childhood had been pruned of much of its foliage, the greenery now merely garlanding block after block of concrete and asphalt. The marshes and duck ponds of Waikiki had apparently been drained. There seemed to be a new canal where once three streams fed rice paddies and taro farms on their drowsy way to the sea. Hotels dotted the familiar crescent of Waikiki Beach, including one behemoth, a gigantic, shocking-pink palace in the shape of an H. The sprawl of buildings stretched from Kalihi in the west to Koko Head in the east, and had begun penetrating the Manoa and Nu'uanu Valleys, houses blighting the face of the mountains like leprosy tubercles. Even the shoreline had been added to — a new yacht basin fringed the harbor with the masts of expensive boats.

And then they were landing, and as Rachel walked off the plane and crossed the tarmac she could scarcely believe that the ground beneath her was the land of her birth. Outside the interisland terminal she breathed in as many gas fumes as she did the scent of plumeria *leis* being offered to tourists at curbside. Rachel looked around in bewilderment at the welter of signs offering directions and instructions; taxicabs and buses rolled by every few seconds. Then she saw a bus approach with the word WAIKIKI emblazoned on its steel forehead, and when it stopped, she stepped through its sighing metal doors and boarded it.

She dropped the required coins in a fare box and sat up front on a bench behind the driver. She gazed out the windows with fascination as the bus left the airport and cleaved toward a sign reading NIMITZ HIGHWAY EAST, then onto a roadway bigger than any Rachel had ever traveled and into a flow of traffic faster than any she had ever imagined. Eventually the bus weaved through Kalihi, coming within two thousand feet of the old receiving station, and Rachel was surprised to find her heart beating just a little faster as they passed the road that once led to it.

Across the aisle from her a little boy was staring at Rachel's clawed right hand and she quickly covered it with her other one, ignoring his puzzled gaze and whispered questions to his mother, who shushed him.

When she saw a sign announcing WAIKIKI → she got off at the next stop; but after walking three or four blocks, searching in vain for something resembling a beach, she realized that she must have gotten off the bus too soon. The next to come along was a strange beast: it had the body of a bus but ran like a trolley on tracks, connected by wires to power lines running overhead. She boarded it, but was so fascinated with the "trolley bus" that it wasn't until it was well underway that she noticed it was heading *mauka,* toward the mountains, not *makai.* She yanked the brake cord as she had seen other passengers do, and disembarked this one as well.

This time she asked for directions from passersby and caught a gas-powered bus heading east on a street named after King Kalākaua. After five minutes she yanked the cord as the bus approached the intersection of Kalākaua Avenue and Kapiʻolani Boulevard. She got off at something called "Kau Kau Corner," where a sign proclaiming itself CROSSROADS OF THE PACIFIC pointed the way to NEW YORK → ← SYDNEY, and RIO DE JANIERO, among other far-flung spots. And indeed taxis, cars, and buses seemed busily en route to these very destinations, their wheels jostling over unused trolley tracks still cut into the road.

Suitcase dangling from her left hand, she made her way down this street honoring the king whose funeral procession she still remembered, and thought that there was little royal about Kalākaua Avenue. But it was a wide, pleasant enough thoroughfare, ornamented with tall coconut palms. She passed hotels, gift shops, bars and night clubs, travel agencies, thatched-roof restaurants, street vendors selling *leis,* even a bowling alley. The pace was breakneck compared to the sleepy Waikiki of her youth, but Rachel rather enjoyed the sight of tourists and off-duty servicemen, the cars whizzing by, the conversation and commerce on every corner. She had drowsed enough in Kalaupapa. She was relieved to find that Honolulu was much more attractive at ground level than it had appeared from the air. The difference between Old Honolulu and New, she would come to decide, was the difference between a beautiful woman who was simply being herself and a beautiful woman calling attention to herself: a little vain perhaps, but you couldn't say she wasn't attractive.

She slowed as she came to what looked like a vast estate tucked away behind a tall screen of coconut palms. It was the behemoth hotel she had seen from the air, but like most of Waikiki it seemed more graceful and approachable up close. From the street it looked like a Moorish castle in pink stucco, its Spanish design and colors at once incongruous and felicitous, as if the coral reefs of Waikiki had spontaneously fabricated themselves into this pink palace. Eager for a closer look, Rachel wandered down the entry drive and onto the lushly landscaped grounds of the Royal Hawaiian Hotel. The rustle of the swaying palm trees was not so different from those amid the rice paddies and fishponds of Old Waikiki. Bamboo awnings shaded the hundreds of windows gazing down on guests strolling toward the Coconut Grove restaurant or up to the shops and sights of Kalākaua Avenue. Fancy cars and taxis navigated a circular driveway to the main entrance, fronted by a pink portico; doormen helped passengers from their cars and through the colonnade to the hotel lobby.

Rachel loitered a few feet from the portico, taking in this magnificent structure, so much bigger than anything at Kalaupapa. Without even realizing he had approached, Rachel was startled by a doorman who asked gently if a bit condescendingly, "Ma'am? May I help you?"

His smile was a tad condescending as well, and Rachel's response was sheer reflex.

"Why, yes," she said. "You can take my bag."

She held out her suitcase and the startled doorman took it with a little bow of his head. "Yes, of course. I'll have the bellman bring it to your room." He pointed to the lobby. "The front desk is right through there."

Betraying not a trace of uncertainty Rachel smiled, thanked him, turned, and sashayed into the hotel. She didn't dare do anything else!

The main lobby was tastefully appointed with Spanish tile floors, wicker chairs, and potted ferns; a succession of arched doorways echoed the colonnade outside. Rachel walked up to the registration desk, and with a straight face announced, "I'd like a room, please." Some pragmatic inner voice inside made her ask, "How much are they?"

The desk clerk answered pleasantly, "For single occupancy we have a range of rooms from sixteen dollars to twenty-six dollars a night, on the American plan."

Rachel tried not to look too stunned by that. In for a penny, in for a pound. "I take it the twenty-six-dollar rooms," she said, smiling, "are made of fourteen-karat gold? With diamond doorknobs?"

The clerk laughed. "Yes, absolutely. But our sixteen dollar rooms are quite comfortable too."

Well, why not? She had to stay somewhere until she found an apartment. And if she couldn't celebrate her freedom with a little luxury, what was the point in being here and not in Kalaupapa?

"Yes," she found herself saying, "that would be fine."

A bellboy took her up by elevator — her

first! — to the fifth floor, where she was ushered into a small pleasant room painted sea-green, with two beds, a vase of fresh flowers on a bamboo dresser, and a serene view of palm-shaded paths. The bellboy placed her suitcase on a luggage rack at the foot of one of the beds, opened the windows, and pointed out the amenities. Now Rachel became a little flustered: she knew she was supposed to tip him, but how much? Tentatively she handed him a quarter but by the incipient frown on his face she could tell it wasn't enough; she handed him another, and that seemed to satisfy him. He tipped his cap and wished her a good day.

Rachel sank into one of the comfortable wicker chairs by the window and lifted her face to the cool breeze. She looked about at her surroundings and couldn't help giggling. The Royal Hawaiian Hotel, good God! If her friends in Kalaupapa could only see her. If *Mama* could see her! "Sixteen dollars for a hotel room? Why not toss money in the street, use it to wipe the trolley horse's behind?"

The thought of Mama spurred her to locate a telephone book, but a flip to the "K"s revealed no Dorothy Kalama, nor for that matter a Ben, Kimo, or Sarah Kalama. Rachel hadn't expected to find Sarah; Papa had said she'd gotten married but he'd never mentioned her husband's last name. For that matter even Ben and Kimo might not still be

558

named Kalama. It wasn't uncommon for Hawaiians to take an entirely different surname than their father's, and it was even more likely if one of the family was known to have had the *ma'i pākē*. She sighed and put the telephone book back in its drawer; she knew it couldn't be that easy.

Suddenly tired, Rachel stretched out on one of the comfortable beds and the next thing she knew it was close to six o'clock. She'd napped the afternoon away. Waking to waning sunlight gilding the walls, Rachel for a moment could believe the room was indeed fourteen-karat.

She washed up and went downstairs to the main dining room, getting a little lost on the way. When she finally entered the Monarch Room, she gaped at the high ceiling supported by massive pillars, the glittering chandeliers, the sparkling silverware on crisp white linen. She had never eaten in a restaurant before, but suspected she had started at the top of the heap. When the maître d' asked her if she had a reservation she admitted she did not; but he merely asked for her room number and escorted her to a small table.

The menu he gave her was a window into another world: she wondered what on earth a "Consommé Royal" was, or for that matter "Borscht a la Russe" or "Navarin of Spring Lamb aux Primeurs." Fortunately there were other options in both English and Hawaiian

559

— a few too many in fact. Imagining each item would be a little sample, as at a *lū'au,* she inadvertently ordered two entrees — Filet of Opakapaka and Young Suckling Pig — and three vegetables.

When it arrived she ate all of it as though it had been her precise intention from the start, and was happy at least that the menu bore no prices, so the contemplation of the cost couldn't spoil what was unquestionably the best meal she had ever had.

She listened to the orchestra perform a handful of tunes, then went for a walk on the beach. At last out of the long shadow of the *pali,* she saw the sunset for the first time in fifty years, a blaze of gold on the horizon; it was every bit as beautiful as she'd remembered it. She wished Kenji could have lived to see this, the two of them enjoying this new world together. She looked into the distance of the Kaiwi Channel, toward the island that had been both home and prison to her for most of her life, and Kenji left behind there.

"You would have known not to order two entrees," she said with a smile, and blew him a kiss before returning to her room.

She knew she couldn't afford to stay in a hotel, any hotel, for long, so her first order of business had to be finding an apartment. After *Star-Bulletin* and the *Advertiser;* her breakfast she bought copies of both the search of the classifieds yielded half a dozen prospects, which she then took the bus to inspect. The first was too expensive, the second too down at the heels, but the third, a furnished room on Beretania Street, was clean and affordable at $40 a month. When the landlord asked for references and her last address, unthinkingly she wrote down Kaiulani Street in Kalaupapa and the man's pleasant demeanor chilled. His eyes went to her crippled right hand, then they clouded with fear; he snatched the application from her hands and promptly tore it up. "This no good," he announced, "we got no rooms for you!"

Stunned, Rachel said, "You just showed me a room."

"It's rented. I make mistake. You go!"

She would soon discover that this landlord was more polite than most. The next, a woman renting out a one-bedroom apartment on King Street, didn't even bother to make excuses. "What the hell you doing here? You unclean, don't belong inna city with clean people!"

Rachel tried to tell her, "I'm cured, I'm no danger to anybody," but the woman didn't believe a word and flailed her arms at her. "Get outta here, get outta my house! I call police, they send you back to Moloka'i!"

Rachel stumbled onto the street, trudging wearily to the bus stop and the next faint prospect.

She wasn't about to tell the truth anymore about her previous residence, but with no references she was shown the door almost as quickly. Some landlords deduced her origins on their own, on the evidence of her crabbed hand. One woman became hysterical, screaming for Rachel to get out, she had a child in the house; and an elderly man repeated the threat to report her as an escaped leper.

Rachel said, "I didn't escape, I was released," and took a step forward, hands spread peaceably, trying to make some human connection with him.

In panic the old man snapped up a crystal ashtray and hurled it at her. It grazed the side of her head, dropping her like a fallen deer; and as she lay stunned on the man's filthy rug he screamed, "Get out! Dirty leper! Get out!" and ran for the phone.

Blood trickling down the side of her face, Rachel fled the apartment. She didn't stop running until she was at least three blocks away. She pressed a handkerchief to her temple, and in the reflection of a store window she could see that it was just a tiny cut, nothing serious. But enough to make her want to cry.

Finally, at the end of the day, she found a rooming house whose landlord didn't care that she had no references as long as she paid three months' rent in advance. It was a dreary, one-room furnished flat on South King Street, with a Murphy bed and a greasy little kitchenette, overpriced at seventy dollars a month.

She leapt at it, signing the lease immediately, happy to have found it.

She spent a last night at the Royal Hawaiian but could no longer enjoy its dreamy fantasy. She knew what freedom really looked like now. She rose early to move into her new home, such as it was. Her neighbors ranged from salesmen and seamen to mothers with children but no husbands, and women who might have been prostitutes. But they all smiled and welcomed her, and one fatherless *keiki* even showed up on her doorstep with a batch of cookies his mother had baked. Rachel insisted he eat some of them himself, which — solely to please her, of course — he did.

She bought cleaning supplies and groceries at the Piggly Wiggly supermarket, itself a revelation to her: so many kinds of food, so many different brands! Rachel wandered up and down the aisles, frozen with indecision, overwhelmed with choices. Should she buy a can of Coral Tuna or Mid-Pacific Tuna Flakes? Star-Kist or Chicken of the Sea? Which was the better coffee: Schillings, Chase & Sanborn, Chock Full O' Nuts, Maxwell House? For breakfast cereal there was an array of brightly colored boxes with inscrutable names: Kix, Pep, Cheerios, Post Toasties, Rice Krispies. Did she want to feast tonight on Eastern Grain-Fed Pork or California Stewing Chicken? How about Utah Yearling Leg-O-Lamb? What about her wash — should she use Oxydol or Clorox or Rinso? What on earth was Nucoa Sandwich Spread? Did the phrase "Boston Butt" on the meat package mean what she thought it meant? Why would anyone want to drink sauerkraut juice?

She bought fresh pineapple and papaya, deviled ham and bottles of big Greek olives, freshly ground chopped meat and plump lamp chops. She had to stop herself from buying more; it all looked so good! She also took home an armful of detergents and soaps, where she scoured a layer of grime from the windows and wiped rancid grease from the ancient stove. And as she mopped and dusted and scrubbed, her new home began to look . . . well, not as bad.

She slept soundly that night and the next morning went out intending to see more of Honolulu. She got more than she bargained for. There was an unusually festive atmosphere on the streets, with everyone she saw in bright *aloha* shirts or dresses; women wore fragrant plumeria blossoms in their hair, men wore red carnation *leis* banded around their hats or draped around their necks. There was an air of celebration as hundreds of pedestrians swarmed *makai* for some reason, and Rachel amiably fell in step with the crowd heading toward the harbor. "What's all this about?" she asked one man, who looked at her as if she'd been living underwater and said, "It's Lurline Day," then moved on, leaving Rachel no more enlightened. No matter; she found the mere presence of so many people around her exciting. Being in a real city again, amid a crowd of faces she didn't know, was strangely thrilling. She happily followed the crowd to its mysterious, irrelevant destination.

Suddenly a roar split the air above and Rachel looked up to see a squadron of Army and Navy planes passing low over the city and out to sea. Straggling behind was a tiny biplane trailing a banner reading ALOHA LURLINE. Who the hell was Lurline and how did she rate a welcome like this?

At the harbor Rachel was astonished to see an even larger crowd at Pier 11, where the Royal Hawaiian Band was playing. The music was nearly drowned out by whistles and sirens from a flotilla of tugs, sailboats, yachts, all making the loudest racket they could as their flags saluted in the breeze. Rachel at last understood what everyone was waiting for as the most enormous ship she had ever seen steamed into port — planes buzzing it in greeting, boats circling and blaring their horns. The ship was as long as an entire city block and from the waterline to the tip of its smokestacks it was as tall as a five-story building! And she laughed to see that, like so many people here, the steamship sported a colossal orange *lei* around its bow.

The crowd cheered as the SS *Lurline,* flagship of the Matson Line, arrived at the end of its first passenger voyage from San Francisco since service as a troop ship during the war. From her vantage point Rachel couldn't make out all the ceremonies going on — a *kahuna* performing a blessing, the governor greeting the ship's captain — but it didn't matter. The ship itself commanded her attention, seized her imagination — a seafaring city out of Jules Verne, one of his "floating islands" like the *Nautilus.* It was hard to imagine anything so massive staying afloat; she was as impressed as she had been when waiting with Mama at the docks for Papa's ship to arrive.

Over the next few days Rachel would discover how much had changed, and how much had not, in this new Honolulu. Kapi-'olani Park was no longer laced with canals but was still quite beautiful, and there was an aquarium and a zoo nearby now. Love's Bakery had moved long ago from Nu'uanu Avenue to industrial Iwilei, but the company's delivery trucks — emblazoned with the Love's logo and the motto BLUE RIBBON BREAD — crisscrossed the city, and it pleased

Rachel to see them. Kaumakapili Church had burned to the ground in the great "plague fire" of 1900, as officials attempting to burn buildings contaminated by bubonic plague inadvertently wiped out most of Chinatown, and Kaumakapili as well. Another church bearing the name had been built uptown, in Pālama.

Gone too was Kapiʻolani Girls Home, its doors closed in 1938, its remaining orphans placed in foster homes or with relatives. Rachel had hoped the sisters there could help her locate her daughter, but now all she could think to do was go to the offices of the Board of Health in the Kapuāiwa Building. "Oh, no," the Chinese woman at the front desk told her, "only records we have here are birth, death, and marriage certificates. No adoption papers."

Rachel thought a moment and asked, "Could the adoptive parents have filed for a new birth certificate? Maybe I could find out their names that way."

The clerk shook her head regretfully. "Sorry. Three years ago, they change the law — all adoption records sealed now. You gotta go family court, ask the judge to unseal the records." She gave directions to the courthouse. Rachel thanked her, started out, then turned back. "Did you say you have marriage records here?"

The clerk nodded. "Marriage licenses and

certificates from 1910 on. Before that they were kept in a ledger, but we type it up and send it to you."

"Could I get a copy of my sister's license? So I can find out what her last name is now?"

The woman looked at her sadly. "Daughter, sister . . . you lose a lotta people, huh?"

"Yes. A lot."

"You know where she got married?"

"No, I'm sorry."

"Okay, no problem." The woman reached under the desk, took out a form, slid it toward her. "Fill this out, give your name, address, one dollar fee, we mail you a copy of the certificate." She gave her a pen and watched as Rachel methodically filled out the form in block letters with her left hand. The clerk's gaze slid down to Rachel's other hand and her eyebrows arched a little. When Rachel had finished the woman scanned the form. "Rachel Kalama Utagawa," she said; and then, "You out on T.R., Mrs. Utagawa?"

Rachel nodded, steeling herself. "Yes."

But the woman just smiled. "Good for you," she said. "You got the address for Vineyard Street Clinic, where you go for check-ups?" She scribbled down an address and handed it to Rachel. "We'll mail you your sister's marriage license, if we got it."

"Thank you."

"Good luck, Mrs. Utagawa."

Rachel then made her way to the U.S.

District Courts Building, where she was asked to put in writing her request for Ruth's adoption papers to be unsealed. The formality of it all, the sober granite face of the building, gave her pause. Did she really want to do this? What if Ruth didn't want to meet her birth mother? A thousand questions presented themselves, a thousand reasons not to do it. But there had also been hundreds, maybe thousands of patients at Kalaupapa who had died without ever having the opportunity to see their children again. Rachel had a chance now at something they would have killed for; could she just throw that away?

She handed her written request to the court clerk, was told that a court date would be set to hear her petition, and hurried out before she could change her mind.

Inevitably, Rachel found herself staring up at a two-story stucco apartment building two blocks from Queen Emma Street, which now stood on the lot where her childhood home had once been. There was not a trace left of the house in which she'd spent her happiest years; Filipino and Japanese children played just as happily upon its grounds, but not a reminder anywhere of little Rachel Kalama, her family, or the life she had led. And she grieved to realize that the home she had so loved existed now only in memory, as distant and insubstantial as the kingdom in which she'd been born.

It was thirty years since Papa had told her about Kimo selling shoes at McInerny's, but she hoped someone there might know where he was today. At the corner of Fort and King, McInerny's Shoes seemed to Rachel a palatial store, with polished mahogany walls, stained glass windows, and expensive Chinese rugs on the floor. The plush upholstered chairs in which customers sat to try on shoes were nicer than any Rachel had ever seen in anyone's home! But when she asked if James, Kimo, Kalama still worked here, no one in the store recognized the name; and one older gentleman went so far as to assert that he couldn't recall anyone by that name ever working here.

She had even less to go on in tracking down Ben. Papa had said he was a boatbuilder in Kaka'ako, but a walking tour of the docks there yielded no shipbuilder who had ever employed or apprenticed a Benjamin Kalama.

Broadening her quest beyond the immediate family she combed the telephone book for Mama's brother Will or his son David. She found neither, but did stumble across a familiar pair of names: *Kiolani, Elijah and Florence, 1901 Ulewele St.* Her pulse quickened at the discovery: Aunt Florence — Papa's sister — and Uncle Eli! It was a different address than the one she remembered, but it had to be them, it *had* to be. Excitedly she sought out Ulewele Street and was soon standing on the doorstep of a neat little saltbox house with the name *Kiolani* stenciled on the mailbox. Beside herself with anticipation, Rachel rang the doorbell and waited as, inside, footsteps shuffled slowly to the door. It was opened by a woman in her eighties, white hair stark against brown leathery skin. Rachel gasped. It was *her,* it was Aunt Flo who made the best *haupia* pudding anyone ever tasted, smiling pleasantly as she said, "Yes?"

"Aunt Florence?" The woman looked at her blankly. "Aunt Florence, it's me — Rachel. Henry's daughter."

The smile vanished from Florence's face, replaced by a scowl. "Not funny. Rachel dead, long time ago."

Rachel laughed. "No, I'm not. Look at me, Auntie, it's Rachel, I'm back from Kalaupapa!"

At that word, the old woman flinched.

"Rachel?" she said. Her voice was soft, and the realization in her eyes not a dawning but a darkening. "Oh my God, baby. Oh my God."

"They released me, Auntie. I'm cured!" She felt tears running down her cheeks. "I can't believe I found you! I'm so happy to see you!"

Florence's gaze swept up and down the

571

street, then back to Rachel. She took in Rachel's clawed hand and a look of distress spread across her face. "Why do you come here?" Florence asked, and now even Rachel could see the black blossoms of fear in her aunt's eyes.

"You're my *'ohana,"* Rachel said as if it were the most obvious thing in the world — and Florence flinched again because it was.

"Baby," she said softly, "you know after my brother Pono got sent to Kalihi, we took in his family; you know?"

"I know," Rachel said.

"The Board of Health, they send people out all the time to check on Margaret and the *keiki.* Bring 'em to Kalihi to test for *ma'i pākē.* Then they start testing me and Eli and our *keiki.* They tell our neighbors, 'These people have relatives with leprosy.' Nobody wants to go near us anymore. People break our windows, they say, 'Go Moloka'i where you belong!'

"Somebody from the Board of Health goes to Eli's job, tells his boss that Eli's brother-in-law, his niece, are lepers. He loses his job, just like that." The memory was still vivid enough to make her wince. "Never once any of us tests positive for leprosy. Never once! But nobody cares. Eli gets a new job, then somebody tells somebody else about you and Pono, and no job anymore. Soon we can't afford to take care of Margaret and her *keiki.*

They go leeward side, where nobody knows them. Never come back to Honolulu. Margaret dead now."

Florence reached out, touching her hand gently to Rachel's cheek. "Took years before everybody forget about the *ma'i pākē*. Nobody here knows. Nobody." She glanced around as if afraid people were watching even now, watching and judging. "Go 'way, baby," she said softly, sadly. "I'm sorry. Please, go 'way."

Slowly but firmly she closed the door on her niece.

If with a thought Rachel could have ended her life in that moment, she would have gladly done so. Denied that mercy, she was forced to walk away from her aunt's house with an even heavier burden than she had arrived with.

Somehow she managed to find the bus stop and stagger home, if that was the word, and into bed, where she cried herself to sleep as she had that night aboard the *Mokoli'i,* her family having been left behind on the shores of O'ahu.

She made no further attempts to contact her family for weeks, instead bearing down on the unpleasant but necessary task of finding a job. But the difficulties were similar to those she encountered looking for an apartment. If she listed her work experience at the Kalaupapa Store and Bishop Home she was announcing herself as a Hansen's disease patient, and the employers inevitably hired someone else. But if she didn't list them, she seemed to have no prior work experience and that didn't help her prospects either. She applied for positions as a grocery store clerk, waitress, hotel maid, cook, seamstress, and cleaning woman; but she was competing in a crowded postwar job market and failed to land any of them.

Her room was nowhere as nice as her cottage in Kalaupapa, but after a few weeks of hard work and some new curtains, it had become quite livable; even cozy. And it had one thing the house on Moloka'i didn't: a world outside its doors. Within walking distance there were movie theaters, concerts, museums, bookstores . . . already Rachel had found two Jack London books she didn't have for a mere 25¢ apiece! She was getting to know her neighbors and the local merchants, starting to lay the foundations for a new life; and if this wasn't the Honolulu she'd grown up in, it was the only Honolulu she had.

Two separate but similar pieces of mail arrived within days of one another. The first was from the United States District Court, family division, notifying her that a date had been set for the hearing regarding her daughter's adoption papers and that she should show up at nine A.M. on the morning of June 9, 1948.

The second envelope also bore a government address, this one from the Territorial Department of Public Health. She opened and unfolded a pale photostat of a marriage certificate.

How could such a simple document — a standardized form, an artifact of *haole* bureaucracy — engender such awe and terror as Rachel felt now? She had not a doubt that this was her sister's marriage certificate; her parents' names jumped out at her. The document went on to note the name of the person issuing the license, as well as the witnesses to the ceremony, including one Dorothy L. Kalama.

Almost before she realized she was doing it, Rachel's left hand had picked up the phone and she was using a pencil held in her crabbed right hand to dial the operator. She requested a phone number for a John and Sarah Kaahea on the island of Maui; and when the operator replied, "I have a Sarah Kaahea on Waine'e Street in Lahaina," Rachel thought her heart would burst. She cradled the receiver between chin and shoulder and with her good hand scribbled down the number — LAH 7939 — and asked the operator for the address, jotting down *633 Waine'e* Street, Lahaina.

She hung up, staring at the address and phone number for so long that they nearly lost their meaning, becoming a set of random

TERRITORY OF HAWAII
RECORD OF MARRIAGE

PLACE OF MARRIAGE

City
and
County of ___Maui___
Township of
or
Village of ___Lahaina___
or
City of _____

MALE

Full name of groom *John L Kahea Jr.*
Residence ___Lahaina, Hawaai___
Age at last birthday _30_ Nationality _US_
Bachelor, Widower or Divorced ____
Birthplace of groom _Maui County_
Length of Residence in Hawaii _30 years_

FATHER

Full name ___John L. Kaahea Sr.___
Race ___Hawaiian___
Birthplace of father _Honolulu, Hawaii_

MOTHER

Full name ___Bethel E. Hohu___
Race ___Hawaiian___
Birthplace of mother _Hilo, Hawaii_

```
┌─────────────────────────────────────────┐
│               FEMALE                     │
│  Full name of bride Sarah L. Kalama      │
│  Residence    Lahaina, Hawaii            │
│  Age at last birthday 26 Nationality US  │
│  Maid, Widow or Divorced___              │
│  Birthplace of bride Honolulu, Hawaii    │
│  Length of Residence in Hawaii 26 years  │
│                                          │
│               FATHER                     │
│  Full name    Henry W. Kalama            │
│  Race    Hawaiian                        │
│  Birthplace of father Hilo, Hawaii       │
│                                          │
│               MOTHER                     │
│  Full name    Dorothy L. Puua            │
│  Race    Hawaiian                        │
│  Birthplace of mother Kaneohe, Hawaii    │
└─────────────────────────────────────────┘
```

letters and numerals signifying nothing. Should she dial the number? What if it wasn't her Sarah? Almost as bad — what if it *was* her? The two of them had hardly been close. Perhaps, like Aunt Florence, Sarah would prefer not to be found.

She thought of nothing else for the rest of the day, and when the weight of it became too much to bear she took herself to the new Bob Hope picture, *Sorrowful Jones,* playing at the Hawai'i Theatre. She lost herself in laughter for an hour and a half, then browsed in the shops along Kalākaua Avenue before strolling home; and by the time she woke the next morning she had made her decision.

If she called her sister on the phone, it would be too easy for Sarah to hang up; too devastating for Rachel if she did. Perhaps if Sarah saw her, saw the lengths to which she had gone to find her, she wouldn't be as quick to turn her away. Perhaps she might even invite Rachel inside to talk for a little while; to reminisce. That was all she wanted really — some touchstone to her past, her family. And if Sarah did turn her away, as Aunt Florence had, at least she would have seen her sister, however briefly.

But what if by some wild chance the Sarah Kaahea in the phone book *wasn't* her sister? Making one concession to practicality, Rachel took a deep breath, picked up the phone, and carefully dialed LAH 7–9–3–9. It rang twice, and then a woman answered.

"Hello?"

Rachel dropped the receiver into the cradle as if it had become electrified. There was no doubt in her mind: she had just heard her sister's voice. And she knew for certain now that she could never be satisfied just to hear that voice; she had to see her, no matter if Sarah wanted to be seen or not.

Airfare from Honolulu to Puʻunēnē Airport

on Maui was sixteen dollars, and Rachel's purse bulged with another fifty for incidentals. The Hawaiian Airlines DC-3 was a larger aircraft than she had flown on from Moloka'i, and a good deal noisier; but you couldn't beat the flight time, barely an hour and a half from Honolulu. From the air Maui appeared to be everything that Honolulu no longer was: lush, green, sparsely populated. It almost appeared to be two islands, connected by a narrow isthmus — one capped like Kalaupapa by a dormant volcano caldera, the other ridged by some of the most magnificent mountains Rachel had ever seen. Terraced farm fields covered most of the island; a sprinkling of towns clustered along the coasts. The plane banked over one of these on its way to Pu'unēnē a short way down the narrow neck of the isthmus. The DC-3 touched down at what used to be a naval air station; abandoned by the military after the war, it now serviced commercial flights.

Rachel carried no suitcase; she expected to be back here by five P.M. to catch the last flight back to Honolulu. Looking for a bus she was told the only one on Maui ran only within Wailuku, and she would have to rent a car or hire a taxi to get to West Maui. Car rental was out of the question — she had no driver's license, none being needed at Kalaupapa — so she approached one of the few taxis dawdling at the airport. "I want to go to

Lahaina," she told the Filipino driver, who whistled and said, "Helluva trip, rental car cheaper," but finally quoted Rachel the dizzying fare of fifteen dollars to West Maui.

"I flew here for sixteen," she noted in mild protest.

He asked her, "You ever drive the Pali Road before?"

"No."

"After we drive it, you think fifteen is too much, I'll knock it down to ten. Fair enough?"

She agreed and got into the cab.

"No bags?" the driver said, puzzled. She shook her head. He shrugged as if to say, *Not my business,* and pulled away from the curb.

Soon they were making their way down a two-lane road winding lazily through fields of spiked pineapple crowns and jungles of tall green cane stalks.

"You a tourist?" the driver asked, curiosity apparently getting the better of him.

"No," Rachel said.

"Been here before?"

She shook her head. "I've come to see my sister."

The driver nodded, satisfied now. "Makes more sense. Maui don't get enough tourists to field a softball team."

Near a sugar mill on their left a column of brown smoke twisted like a *maile* vine in the gentle wind; Rachel inhaled the sweet pungent smell of burning cane almost as a treat. "It's beautiful here," she told the driver.

"Yeah, nice. My father came over in nineteen-nine to work for Wailuku Sugar. Didn't pay worth a damn, but he liked the island; left the mill, worked the docks at Kahului, after a few years bought a cab. Mine now." He laughed, gestured to the outside. "This don't pay worth a damn either, but hey, look at the office I got."

When they reached the base of the isthmus and turned right onto the Pali Road, Rachel understood why there were no buses to Lahaina. The Pali Road was a narrow single lane clinging to a sheer cliff. On their left was a steep drop-off, a view both hair-raising and spectacular: ocean surging around black lava coastline. The road on which they traveled was paved, and wider than the *pali* trail at Kalaupapa, but Rachel still anticipated it crumbling under them, the cab plunging down the *pali* to be impaled on lava daggers. And it was just as switchbacked as the one she'd climbed years before. Rachel stopped counting the zigzagging curves after she'd reached a hundred, and for the first time in her life started getting carsick.

"They call this the Amalfi Drive," the driver said, " 'cause the view's supposed to look like Amalfi, Italy."

"Stop the car," Rachel blurted.

The driver hit the brakes. Rachel opened

the rear door on the driver's side and sent her lunch hurtling down the steep face of the *pali* just half a foot away.

"Whoa," the driver said, looking down, "plenty of food for the fishes today."

When she'd finished Rachel closed the door, wiped her mouth and said, "You don't charge enough for this trip."

The driver laughed and continued on.

They drove for close to an hour, encountering only one other vehicle, a truck for which the cab had to back up two hundred feet and squeeze itself into a narrow turn-out as the truck passed. Rachel provided lunch for the fishes a few more times. Then, sometime after the car passed a sugar mill at Olowalu, scattered houses began to appear on either side of the road.

"Lahaina," the driver announced. "What was that address again?"

In minutes they were pulling up in front of a small white bungalow standing in the green shade of a banyan tree, its garden aflame with helliconia and anthuriums. Rachel gave the driver a nice tip — "Combat pay," she said — and asked hesitantly if he would wait here a minute. "I might need a ride back sooner than I'd like." He asked no questions, just said "Sure." Rachel worked up her courage and walked up the narrow footpath to the little house. She took the porch steps slowly, trying to extend the moment as long as possible . . . then stepped up and knocked on the door.

Thirty seconds later the door opened and a woman in her sixties, wearing a bright floral sundress, looked at her pleasantly and said, "Yes?"

Rachel stared at Sarah, completely recognizable even beneath a patina of age and distance.

"Sarah," she said softly.

One word, and Sarah's whole body jerked as if shot. One word and she knew.

She whispered, "Rachel?"

Before Rachel could respond, Sarah's eyes rolled up in her head like a snapped windowshade, her knees gave out — and she fainted, collapsing in a heap on her own doorstep.

Oh, God! Rachel thought, dropping to her knees. *I killed her!* "Sarah! Sarah!" She cradled Sarah's head with her bad hand and fanned her face furiously with the good one. "Don't you dare go and die on me, Sarah Kalama!" she cried. "*Oh,* this is so like you!"

The cabbie had gotten out of his car and was hurrying to join Rachel, but now Sarah's eyes fluttered open and she found herself staring up into Rachel's panicked face.

Her eyes registered shock, then disbelief. She whispered again, "Rachel?"

Suddenly unable to speak, Rachel nodded.

In a hushed voice Sarah said, "You're *alive.*"

Exploding into sudden laughter, Sarah

583

reached up and looped her arms around Rachel's neck. "My God! Rachel! You're alive!"

She squeezed Rachel in a bear hug, her laughter now joined by tears of obvious joy. And all the tension, all the fear that had been building in Rachel since seeing Aunt Florence — all of it melted in a moment's laughter, and she returned Sarah's embrace just as fiercely.

"Sarah," she said, tears flowing down her own cheeks. "Oh, God, Sarah." She held fast to the warmth of her sister's body, and realized happily that she might not be taking that five o'clock flight to Honolulu.

The cab driver had figured this out as well, and with a smile and a wave he returned to his car and drove off. Rachel and Sarah laughed and cried another minute, maybe two; then Sarah drew back to take in Rachel's face.

"But how is this possible?" she said softly.

"They found a cure."

Sarah said, "But I thought you were dead! When I saw you just now, I thought at first you were a ghost!"

"Maybe I am," Rachel laughed. She had more trouble getting up than Sarah, who offered her a hand and found herself holding the question mark at the end of Rachel's right arm. Sarah said nothing, but her eyes reflected a compassion Rachel had never glimpsed in them as a child.

"Come on," she said happily, "come in."

Inside the cottage, late morning sun streamed through a lattice of green foliage — the banyan tree on one side, the feathery branches of a date palm on the other — dotting the living room with a bright speckling of sunlight. The furniture was simple rattan but with striking wood-carved tables and burnished calabashes decorating the hardwood floor. "Sarah, this is beautiful. What are these floors made of? *Koa?*"

"No, it's monkeypod, like the calabashes. My husband did the woodworking."

"Is he home?"

Sarah said sadly, "Not for a while. He passed away two years ago."

"Oh, I'm sorry. My husband's gone too." Hopefully: "Is Mama —"

But Sarah's sober look told the tale. "Fifteen years ago. I'm sorry."

Rachel had half expected as much, but it still hurt.

"She's buried not far from here," Sarah said. "We can go there later."

"I'd like that."

"I have a million questions for you! Would you like some tea?"

Rachel said that she would, and as Sarah puttered around in the kitchen Rachel wandered about the living room. "How long have you been out? Of Kalaupapa?" Sarah called to her.

"A few weeks. I've got a room in Honolulu." She paused in front of a wooden bench plumped with big inviting pillows; atop the back of the bench were a dozen framed photographs of children at various ages and a handsome, smiling man in his fifties. "Is this John?"

"Yes, how did you know his name?"

"It's how I found you. Your marriage license." She picked up one of the photos, smiled. "And this must be — don't tell me — Charlie, Miriam, and Gertie?"

Sarah entered with a tea tray. "Who?"

"Your children. Papa told me their names — Charlie, Miriam, Gertrude. Or am I misremembering them?"

Sarah put down the tray, looked at her sister oddly. "Papa told you," she repeated.

"Yes, not long before he died."

"Their names are Eleanor, Dorothy, Jack, and . . . Rachel."

Surprised and touched, Rachel couldn't help a grin. "Does this mean you finally forgave me for what I did to your yellow felt hat?"

"You would bring that up. I'd just gotten over it." She poured Rachel's tea. "What about you? Do you have chil—"

She stopped, suddenly aware of what she was saying, but Rachel just nodded. "One daughter. I'm trying to find her." She looked at Sarah with delight and amazement. "I still can't believe I found *you*. I went looking for Kimo at McInerny's, where he used to work, but no luck; Ben too, I couldn't find either of them in the phone book —"

Rachel suddenly noticed that Sarah's face had gone ashen. "What?" she said. "What's wrong?"

Sarah said slowly, "Ben's living near Hāna, but . . . what do you mean, Kimo working at McInerny's?"

"That's what Papa told me."

Sarah hesitated a moment, then said quietly, "Kimo never worked at McInerny's. He never worked anywhere."

"But Papa said so. 'Kimo's selling shoes at McInerny's,' and I laughed because he always hated wearing 'em, and now to be —"

She broke off when she saw the sad, somber look on her sister's face. Sarah said, "Papa . . . either told you what he thought you'd want to hear, to spare you, or . . . maybe he didn't know himself."

"Know what?"

Sarah looked away, avoiding Rachel's eyes as she seemed to gird herself. "You know that Mama and Papa separated," she said finally.

"Yes."

"She blamed Papa and Uncle Pono for your getting sick. She was kind of *pupule* about it." Sarah met Rachel's gaze again. "Then less than a year after you were sent to Kalaupapa . . . Kimo started showing the same

587

symptoms."

Rachel cried out. A wordless, inchoate cry, like that of an animal in pain.

"Small rosy spots on his skin," Sarah said quietly, "insensitive to pain . . . the same as you." She shook her head. "Mama was numb at first. We all were. But after she'd had time to accept it, Mama knew one thing for certain. She told us, 'I won't send another child to Moloka'i. Not like my baby Rachel.'

"So she quickly sold the house to a land developer, and packed us all off to Maui. She had cousins here, and they told her there were places upcountry, near Kula, where people had hidden other lepers and nobody ever found out."

Sarah took a sip of her tea, then blanched as if it had turned bitter. "Mama left Ben and me with her cousins here in Lahaina. We wanted to go with her but she wouldn't allow it, wouldn't risk us getting leprosy too. She found a little house outside Kula, far away from the nearest neighbor. It was a pretty place, she said, on the edge of a guava grove; and there was a stream nearby. A good place for a boy to play.

"Mama would go into Kula to buy food and to take in work as a seamstress, but she never brought Kimo into town; no one there even knew she had a son. And for the next year she took care of him" — her voice broke and her eyes filled with tears — "as he got sicker

588

and sicker. Sores opened up all over his body and she cleaned them, rubbed in ointment, applied fresh bandages each day. She watched his face swell up, but kissed his cheek every night when he went to bed. She played with him when she felt like crying, told him stories when he was too weak to play —"

For a moment she couldn't continue, and Rachel took Sarah's hand in hers.

"And then a bad cold turned to pneumonia," Sarah finished sadly, "and Mama buried him on the edge of the forest. She came back for me and Ben, and we settled in Lahaina. Neither Ben nor I ever came down with leprosy. Or Mama, for that matter. Isn't it odd, how some members of a family get it, but others don't? Isn't that —"

She broke down tearfully, in her face an anguished contrition. "We thought you were dead, Rachel! Because it took Kimo so quickly, we thought surely you were gone as well. I'm so sorry, Rachel, please forgive me!"

Rachel wrapped her arms around her sister and wept along with her. When Rachel was able to speak again she managed to ask, "Papa never knew?"

"We never saw him again after we moved to Maui. Maybe Mama wrote and told him, but I doubt it. I tried to find him after I'd grown up; I wrote to him in care of every steamship company in Honolulu but I never got an answer."

Rachel sat there, battered by a welter of emotions. She grieved not just for Kimo but for Papa too, alone all those years except for his daughter, a world away over the horizon. But before she could think of anything else to say Sarah said, "I'd like to show you something," and Rachel, too numb to think, nodded her acquiescence.

It was a little red clay cemetery at the southernmost tip of Kā'anapali, a few yards in from one of the loveliest white sand beaches Rachel had ever seen; and it looked out on a view no less spectacular, a vista that took in the long curve of the Maui coastline to the south, the cloud-topped island of Lāna'i in the middle distance, and the hazy silhouette of Moloka'i to the north.

Rachel gazed down at the granite marker on her mother's grave as Sarah said, "She asked to be buried here. She told me, 'When I die I want to see to Moloka'i. I want to see my baby Rachel every day.' " Sarah smiled. "To the day she died, she never stopped thinking about you."

Rachel knelt at the foot of the grave, but the tears that came to her were only partly tears of grief. After all the years of anger and abandonment, now she knew the truth. Now she knew: her mama loved her. She didn't forget her; didn't reject her. She loved her. Rachel leaned forward and placed her hands on the warm red earth of her mother's grave, the closest she could come to an embrace, and said happily, "I love you, too, Mama." The ache she'd felt for fifty years was gone and she could feel again what life was like without it: sweet, like a slice of cake from Love's Bakery, or a cold glass of Tahiti lemonade on a hot day.

CHAPTER 22

Lahaina was a long dream, a leisurely ramble through a landscape both new and familiar. With its wooden storefronts shaded by broad awnings from the "cruel sun" that gave the town its name, it had the charm and intimacy of Old Honolulu — Front Street could easily have been Nu'uanu Avenue in 1893, each merchant greeting Sarah by name as Mr. Tinker and Ah Leong had once greeted Mama. Sarah had grown up to be a decathlon shopper, and the first event was a stop at Gladys's Beauty Salon, where over Rachel's protests Sarah treated her to an expensive hair styling. After this a little browsing at Emura's Jewelry Store, then a visit to Sarah's dressmaker, Mrs. Nakai, where they each tried on half a dozen outfits — laughing like little girls playing dress-up — and Rachel purchased a new Sunday dress to wear at her court hearing.

After lunch at the Liberty Restaurant, they strolled down Front Street, several

592

boarded-up shops testimony to the effects of the tidal wave two years before. Rachel asked Sarah if Lahaina got hit hard by the *tsunami*.

"A lot of property damage, but thank heaven only one fatality. Hāna got the worst of it — twelve people died, Ben almost lost his home. We were blessed here in Lahaina. God was looking out for us."

The shops on the *makai* side of the street gave way to a low sea wall; beyond it was a rocky slope of shoreline and a magnificent view of the Lahaina Roadstead, a thriving port back in whaling days but far sleepier today. A Kona wind played with Rachel's newly cut hair, much as Kenji used to twist and turn it in idle caress, and Rachel recalled how Haleola had spoken fondly of these tradewinds off Lahaina. They had an abundance of names depending on direction and mood: the gentle Ma'a'a, the destructive Kaua'ula . . . if a soft breeze blew at night it was called the Uluoa and it was *kapu* to go onto the beach for fear of encountering the marchers of the night.

And now Rachel remembered something else Haleola had told her, something that made her quicken her pace as they approached the big plantation-style Pioneer Hotel. "Sarah, over here! Let me show you something!"

"Show me what? You've never been here before!"

Rachel hurried past the Pioneer, found the end of the low stone wall fronting the harbor and peered down the rocky slope. A rock formation glistened blue-black in the lapping waves; it looked something like a chair, with a low shelf backing a smooth, worn hollow, even a smaller rock serving as a kind of footrest. "Do you know what this is?"

Sarah ventured, "A rock?"

"A sacred rock! Legend has it that in the old days, in order to protect a young girl named Hauola from her enemies, the gods turned her to stone."

"Sounds awfully drastic," Sarah said lightly. "Couldn't they have just hidden her somewhere instead?"

"For centuries *kahunas* brought sick patients here, sat them down with their legs dangling in the water, and the patients were supposed to be cured of whatever ailed them."

With a touch of the old Sarah her sister said archly, "Oh, you mean like leprosy?"

Rachel frowned. "Well I didn't say it always *worked.*"

Sarah regarded her sister dubiously. "You know if Mama could hear all this pagan superstition coming out of your mouth she'd tan your hide, but good."

Rachel suspected no amount of persuasion would convince her devout sister that this wasn't idolatry, it was history; so she shrugged and let it go. They stopped at Kawa-guchi's Fish Market, picked up some fresh *ulua* for dinner, and spoke no more of *kahu-nas* and mystic stones.

When not shopping or sightseeing, Rachel was content to sit outside in the lee of the West Maui Mountains, so close they seemed almost to be in Sarah's backyard. Though not as tall as Kalaupapa's *pali,* they were their equal in beauty: jagged green peaks, graced by clouds, rising above sloping cane fields. Rachel heard the distant whistle of the Pioneer Mill's locomotive and breathed in the bittersweet scent of a cane fire. There was something serenely comforting about these mountains; Rachel couldn't imagine ever growing tired of the view. In the old days, ac-cording to Haleola, Lahaina had been a "city of refuge," a place where those who'd broken *kapus* could come to find sanctuary. Now Rachel found refuge as well, the corruptions and *kapus* of her disease seeming to melt away, dissolved by the "cruel sun" that was actually quite kind.

Then the serene silence was broken by a burst of tinny music and a voice announcing the start of Sarah's favorite radio show, *Queen for a Day,* and Rachel had to plug her ears to keep from hearing the bathetic life stories of contestants vying for a new washing machine or Frigidaire. Had these *haoles* no shame?

She stayed on Maui for ten days, long enough to meet Sarah's grown children and to make the long twisting drive to Hāna to see Ben — forty pounds heavier and as happy and amazed to see his baby sister as Sarah had been. Staying overnight in Hāna, Rachel saw in Ben's children and grandchildren not merely the faces of their parents but those of their grandparents as well: a ten-year-old's smile that seemed an echo of Henry's; a toddler's scowl that for all the world looked like Dorothy in a bad mood. And gazing at cranky, two-year-old Betty, Rachel felt the loss of Mama a little less.

The next day, on the long drive back along the Hāna Road, Sarah broke a comfortable silence. "Rachel? Why don't you stay?"

"Oh, I don't want to wear out my welcome. You know what they say, *ulua* and visitors stink after a week."

"No," Sarah laughed, "what I mean is, why don't you move here, to Maui? Move in with me?"

Rachel was surprised — and touched. "That's a lovely offer, Sarah, thank you," she said wonderingly.

"It's a selfish offer. I could use the company; so could you. Two widowed sisters sharing a house and bickering over religion, doesn't that sound grand?"

They both laughed.

"I don't know what to say," Rachel said.

"Everything's happened so fast. And I have this hearing coming up —"

"Yes, of course. Just something to think about." She paused, then added, "I'm only sorry I wasn't a better sister to you when we were little."

"Well, I did ruin your yellow felt hat."

"Will you stop about the hat?" Rachel laughed, but Sarah went on soberly, "I was always a little jealous of you. I wanted Papa to love me like he loved you."

"Sarah, Papa loved you! He loved all of us."

"I know. He just loved you in a different way . . . maybe because you two were so alike, because you both loved the same things . . . and I was jealous of that. I'm sorry."

She slipped her free hand over Rachel's gnarled fingers and gave them a tender squeeze. "Go back to Honolulu. Find your daughter. Just as long as you know . . . you'll always have a home here."

Rachel held back tears. "Thank you, Sarah," she said softly. "I can't tell you how much that means to me."

Home. She thought of her vanished home in Honolulu, all the years and memories razed for an apartment building. But now she had new homes, around which new memories could be forged: Sarah's cottage in Lahaina; Ben's house in Hāna. Her old family made new, except for . . .

She found herself thinking of another

home, one she had never seen. She turned to Sarah and asked, "Isn't Kula somewhere around here?"

Her sister glanced at her, seeming to know at once what Rachel was thinking. "About twelve miles upcountry."

"You know the way?"

Sarah nodded tightly. "I know the way."

They turned off the Hāna Road and onto a narrow mountain lane twisting through thick woods and small upcountry towns: Ha'ikū, Makawao, Waiakoa. A mile north of Kula, Sarah turned onto an unpaved road. A jolting five minute ride brought them to a tumbledown old house, surrounded by thickets and edging a forest pungent with the smell of ripe guava. It was little more than a shack — one room, two windows — no running water but a clear stream meandering through the trees and past a wide meadow of *pili* grass, tall enough for a child to lose himself in.

Sarah paced off a hundred feet as Mama had told her, leading Rachel to a mound of grass and weeds. They knelt and weeded the plot until the rich red earth could be seen, as well as a small wooden cross with a name carved neatly into the lateral beam: not *James Kalama,* surprisingly, but *Kimo.*

"Mama did this?" Rachel said, and Sarah nodded. "She was reading Ecclesiastes when she came across: 'A good name is better than precious ointment; and the day of death better than the day of one's birth.' She said she thought about all the love Kimo, *as* Kimo, had received, and decided that was the name God should know him by, on that day 'better than the day of his birth.' "

A bird, perhaps a Maui parrotbill, warbled from somewhere deep in the forest. The stream chuckled to itself; the wind rustled the *pili* grass. It was a good place for a boy to play.

United States District Court Judge Walter Birch — a stern-looking *haole* in his fifties — slipped on a pair of spectacles and scanned the documents in front of him. Rachel, in her new Sunday dress, stood nervously before the bench. This courtroom was several degrees of magnitude more intimidating than the one at Kalaupapa. Despite the summer heat, the room felt cold and formal, and not warmed any by the judge, who seemed to have a permanent scowl engraved on his face. In a flat voice he asked Rachel, "You gave up your daughter for adoption in — 1916, Mrs. Utagawa?"

"Yes, sir," Rachel said. "Though not willingly."

He glanced up. "You were given the option, weren't you, of having your family on Oʻahu *hānai* her?"

"Yes, but I couldn't locate them at the time.

And my husband's family wouldn't consider it."

The judge made a grunt of acknowledgment and glanced at another document. "So your daughter would be . . . thirty-two years old now?" He rolled his tongue around inside his cheek as he read, then asked without looking up, "And what exactly do you hope to accomplish by establishing contact with her at this late date?"

"I . . . don't know what to expect from it, Your Honor."

He looked up, a bit sharply. "Not expect — *hope*. What is it you *hope* to gain? A daughter? A place in her home?"

"No, that's not why I'm doing this."

"Because you can't assume, you know, that she'll have the same interest in you as you do in her. Adopted children are often quite content with the number and quality of parents they already have."

Now the courtroom felt very warm indeed, and Rachel was acutely aware of the perspiration trickling down her neck and under her arms.

"I just want to see her," Rachel said. "The woman she's become. I want to hear her story, know that she's happy. And if I have to walk away from her . . ." She was wilting under the heat and the cold of the judge's stare but managed to finish, "If I have to walk away, I want to do it because of what we are, or aren't, to each other . . . and not because I have leprosy."

The judge took that in, removed his spectacles. "Do you have anything else to add?" he asked.

"No, Your Honor."

Judge Birch nodded and lifted his gavel. "The court will take the matter under advisement." He rapped the gavel and the hearing was over. Rachel stumbled out into bright sunlight with no idea how the court might rule or how long it might take.

To occupy herself in the interim, she renewed her efforts to find work, applying for jobs — bank clerk, maid, flower shop girl, nanny — all along the bus route and as far east as Kahala. After a month she was finally offered a position, as a cashier at a gift shop on the corner of King Street and Ward Avenue. The store offered the usual miscellany of snacks and souvenirs: macadamia nuts, guava jelly, pineapples, flower and feather *leis.* It was easy work, and if the owner suspected that Rachel was a Hansen's disease patient, he neither acknowledged it nor seemed to care. Then, a day into Rachel's third week, as she gave a quarter's change with her left hand to a man buying some Kona coffee, the customer caught a glimpse of her other hand. She saw his blink of surprise, his chill of recognition. He gripped the quarter by the edge — as though it had just turned hotter than the sun — and dropped it into a wastebasket on his way out. No doubt he would seek out the nearest washroom and scrub his hands raw.

A few days later Rachel was let go with no explanation from her employer other than, "I'm sorry, this isn't working out." He at least gave her a week's severance pay.

David and Helen were among the new parolees who'd followed Rachel to Honolulu; over dinner one night David complained of how old friends and former employers seemed reticent to offer him work. "We may have to move out of town, maybe a neighbor isle — someplace where no one knows us, and people don't look at you as if you're —"

"Dirty," Rachel said.

"Unclean," Helen agreed. She told of getting back her old job as a bank clerk only to be informed a week later that her fellow employees had gone to the branch manager and threatened to resign en masse if "that leper girl" continued to work there. "At least in Kalaupapa you had your dignity," she said, "and you could work an honest job like anyone else." The territorial legislature was considering changing the official designation of leprosy to Hansen's disease, but they couldn't legislate the fear and ignorance from people's hearts.

That week Rachel was notified that Judge Birch would rule on her petition the following Monday. When Rachel appeared on the appointed day the judge's stern gaze swept over her as he announced, "In the matter of the adoption of Ruth Dorothy Utagawa, the court finds that petitioner has demonstrated good cause to unseal the court records in case number 45601." He rapped his gavel, dust motes flying up from the bench as if startled. "Next case."

A dazed Rachel was taken by a court clerk to the records division, where he brought out a musty sheaf of documents stamped with the case number and smelling of the past. "You may inspect these as long as you wish," he told her, giving her pencil and paper to make notes, and Rachel slowly began sorting through the file.

On top was a sheet bearing her own signature as well as Kenji's: the form they'd signed legally relinquishing "custody and control" of their daughter. It hurt to look at it. This was followed by pages and pages of medical records from Kapi'olani Home; and when at last Rachel came to the adoption papers her hands began to tremble.

TAIZO AND ETSUKO WATANABE
216 S. KUKUI ST.
HONOLULU, T.H.

In pro per

UNITED STATES CIRCUIT COURT
— TENTH DISTRICT
COUNTY OF HONOLULU

In the matter of the Adoption   No. 45601
Petition of:
PETITION FOR ADOPTION
TAIZO AND ETSUKO WATANABE
Adopting Parents

According to the petition and adoption application, dated June 7, 1921, Mr. and Mrs.
Taizo Watanabe of Honolulu — a former
plantation worker at Waimānalo, now a
general contractor, and his wife — were
Japanese nationals who had resided in the
islands for eight years, presently with three
sons. The application listed questions about
the Watanabes' religious background, their
economic status, their family health history;
all answered innocuously enough. In addition
to the petition there were other court papers,
pleadings and court transcripts, that Rachel
read in their entirety, as engrossed as if she
were reading Jack London or Conan Doyle.
At the end of which she saw:

604

WHEREFORE, petitioner prays that the Court adjudge the adoption of the child by the petitioners, declaring that the petitioners and child shall henceforth sustain toward each other the legal relation of parents and child, and have all rights and be subject to all the duties of that relation; and that the child shall be known as RUTH DAI WATA-NABE.

Rachel's sadness at the words "shall henceforth sustain . . . legal relation of parents and child" was mitigated by her pleasure that her daughter's name was still Ruth.

Finally there was a new birth certificate, asserting that Ruth Dai Watanabe had been born in Honolulu on January 8, 1916, thus sparing her the stigma of having Kalaupapa as a birthplace.

The current telephone book had no listing for a Taizo or Etsuko Watanabe on O'ahu, or any of the other islands. Nor was there a listing for a Ruth Watanabe, though surely she would have married by now. The clerk helped Rachel search voter registration files, but this just confirmed the bad news. "Sometimes, you know," the clerk told her, "Japanese plantation workers would fulfill their contracts, then take the money they'd made and move back to Japan." The thought was a dull ache in her heart; if they had taken Ruth to a foreign country there was virtually no chance of Rachel, with her limited resources, locating them.

She took a bus to 216 E. Kukui Street and went door to door, inquiring of the neighbors whether anyone had known a Japanese family named Watanabe who'd lived here in the Twenties. Most hadn't; a few recalled the name but had little else to offer. There were, however, a number of Japanese families still in the neighborhood, and remembering something Kenji had once told her, Rachel asked about the *Yakuba,* the neighborhood archive of family histories. It was from this she learned that the Watanabes had moved out of the neighborhood in 1923. But there the trail ended, with no record of a new address.

In desperation Rachel called Sister Catherine, who, she hoped, might know someone who had worked at Kapi'olani Home at the time, someone who might be of help. Catherine in turn called Sister Mary Augusta, now retired after years of service at both Kalaupapa and Kapi'olani Home.

Sister Augusta knew nothing of the Watanabes, but did recall that Ruthie had been a favorite of Sister Mary Louisa's, now also retired and living in Honolulu. This eventually yielded a letter, in a woman's flowing cursive, addressed to Sister Louisa and dated September 12, 1923:

606

Dear Sister,

This is to let you know that we have all arrived safely and are settled comfortably into our new home. Horace and Ralph got seasick on the voyage over but Stanley and Ruth were fine. It took Mr. Watanabe a few months to find an appropriate lease but we are now settled on a hundred acres raising strawberries and Tokay grapes. It is very beautiful here, we are very happy.

Thank you again for the kindness you have shown for our Ruth. She still talks of her "Sister Lu." Please know how grateful we are to have her, and for everything you have done for us.

With warmest regards,
Etsuko Watanabe
R.R. #2, Box 12
Florin, California

Rachel's hopes sank on reading of the "voyage over," but rose again at the return address: California! If her daughter was on the mainland at least Rachel had a fighting chance to locate her. The long-distance operator informed her that Florin was in Sacramento County, but there was no telephone listing anywhere in the county for a Taizo, Etsuko, or Ruth Watanabe. Rachel was under no illusions: Ruth could be living in Idaho or New York or Timbuktu by now. But if her adoptive parents had owned a farm, it was possible they were still there — maybe they just didn't own a telephone. Lacking a better idea, Rachel sat down to write a letter which would take her two full days to compose.

August 13, 1948

Dear Mr. and Mrs. Watanabe:
  My name is Rachel Kalama Utagawa. You may recognize my name. I am Ruth's mother by birth.

Dear Mr. and Mrs. Watanabe:
  My name is Rachel Kalama Utagawa. I gave Ruth up for adoption.

Dear Mr. and Mrs. Watanabe:
  My name is Rachel Utagawa. My husband and I gave Ruth up for adoption.
  I am living in Honolulu again and would like to contact Ruth. I mean no disrespect to you. I just want to talk to her.

Dear Mr. and Mrs. Watanabe:
  My name is Rachel Utagawa. My late husband and I gave Ruth up for adoption.
  I am living in Honolulu now and would very much like to contact her. I intend no disrespect to you. I would just like the

opportunity to talk with the little girl I

Dear Mr. and Mrs. Watanabe:
My name is Rachel Utagawa. My late husband and I gave Ruth up for adoption.

A day has not gone by since that I haven't thought of her. I wonder how she is. Is she married? Does she have children of her own?

Sister Mary Louisa Hughes has told me what good people you are, and how much you love Ruth. I'm happy to know she had such good parents.

I would give anything in the world to hear her voice or see her face, even once. It is a longing, a setsubō which has never gone away.

I intend no disrespect to you. I am her mother by blood, but you are her parents by law and by love. I hope you will look kindly on this request. Thank you.

Sincerely yours,
Rachel Utagawa
1726 S. King St.
Honolulu, T.H.
ph. HON 68412

She read it over at least a hundred times, then stamped an envelope and placed the letter inside. It sat like that on her kitchen table for another day before she scraped together

609

the courage to seal the envelope, walk it to the end of the block, and drop it in the mailbox.

She told herself it would probably be returned as undeliverable, but at least she'd tried; at least she'd honored the memory of those who had never been able to try.

She wrote a thank-you to Sister Catherine, and a week later received a letter back — smelling as usual of formaldehyde from the fumigation to which all mail was subjected before leaving the settlement.

Dearest Rachel,

I'm happy to have been of help. I hope it bears some fruit. But even if it doesn't, you can be comforted by the knowledge that our Ruth was raised by loving parents. Not every child in this world is lucky enough to say that.

Kalaupapa seems so lonely without you and the others who have been released. But it's a loneliness I celebrate; each empty house represents another life regained. Superintendent Judd continues his reforms. His latest brainstorm: he's going to allow patients to take sightseeing flights of the neighbor islands on one of the little planes that service Kalaupapa. Maybe even meet with family members at airports on Maui or Kaua'i. Who would ever have dreamed of such a thing, when you and I first saw that little biplane over Kalaupapa forty years ago?

As for me, I had a nasty bout with influenza a few weeks ago, but Dr. Sloan pulled me through. Still, when you come that close to an unexpected reunion with the Lord you think of everything you never did, everything you never said but should have.

I have no regrets, Rachel, about the life I chose. The one thing I lacked, you have in part given me. Thanks to you I know a little of the joy a mother must, the pride in a child well grown. I pray you shall know it too. God bless you and keep you, Rachel.

All my love,
Catherine

Late in August and early on a Sunday morning, Rachel's phone rang, jolting her out of lazy dreams. She answered it groggily and a little out of sorts, no friendly "Hello," just an irritated "Yes?"

In someone's hesitation she heard the hiss of long distance and then a woman's voice. *"Is this — Rachel Utagawa?"*

The voice sounded so much like Rachel's own, she was momentarily disoriented — was this real or was she dreaming?

"Hello?" came the voice.

"Yes," Rachel said quickly, "this is she."

Another moment of hesitation, then, *"My name is Ruth Watanabe Harada."*

Rachel tried to pull a sound up out of her throat, but found that she couldn't.

The voice, so eerily similar to her own, seemed to float suspended in space, like something out of a radio drama, tinny and faintly unreal. *"It's three hours earlier in Hawai'i, isn't it? I must've woken you up."*

"That — that's all right," Rachel said finally. "I'm sorry, I . . . wasn't quite . . . prepared for this."

"Well, that makes two of us."

"Are you calling from — California?"

"Yes. San José. Your letter went to my parents' old farm," the voice explained, as if eager to fill any anxious lull with words, *"and the current tenants sent it back. But a girl at the local post office went to high school with me, and —"*

"I named you Ruth," Rachel suddenly exclaimed — to her own surprise, and a startled pause on the other end of the line.

"Did you?" Ruth said at last.

Rachel couldn't tell whether she sounded intrigued or alarmed. "Did you speak with your . . . parents before you called me today?"

"My father passed away several years ago. My mother's very frail, I didn't want to possibly upset her." A small note of annoyance crept

612

into her tone. *"Anyway, it was me you wanted to talk to, wasn't it? Though isn't it a little late to decide you want to get to know me?"*

Rachel sighed.

"Ruth . . ." Despite what she had to say, she thrilled to speak the name. "I gave you up for adoption because I had to. Because I was forced to . . . by the government."

Ruth seemed completely nonplussed by that. *"What?"*

"Have you ever heard of — Kalaupapa?"

"Kala . . . no."

"It's on Moloka'i. Where Father Damien died."

There was a stunned silence on the line; all Rachel could hear was the static of Ruth's breath as it traveled across the transpacific cable.

Finally, in a small, shocked voice: *"You're a leper?"*

Rachel flinched.

"They call it Hansen's disease now. And I've been paroled." She instantly regretted the choice of words; it made her sound like an ex-convict. "They found a cure. A treatment. I've been released, I'm no danger to anybody."

This was followed by another silence, almost as long as the last. *"Hansen's disease?"*

"It's not hereditary. It doesn't pass from mother to child unless the baby remains with

613

the parents for an extended time. That's why we had to give you up."

Rachel hung on the silence that followed; then in a strained voice her daughter said, *"I . . . think I'd better have a talk with my mother."*

Of course that's not what you're having now, is it, Rachel thought with a trace of bitterness. "Yes. That's a good idea."

"I'll call back tomorrow. Or the next day."

Rachel's stomach knotted. She said, "Ruth —"

"I'm sorry. I can't talk right now. I'll call back, I promise."

The connection was severed, and Rachel couldn't help wondering if this would be the closest she would ever come to her daughter — a disembodied voice without face or form, a phantom child she would never see nor hold.

There had been so many days in her life when she had told herself, Nothing could ever be worse than this. The day she was sent to Moloka'i; the day Ruth was taken from her; the day Kenji died. And now this. The waiting, and wondering, and hearing again and again the horror in her daughter's voice. *You're a leper?* She prayed that from this day forward no more parents would live to hear that word spoken by their own children.

She called Sarah, who reassured her and counseled patience. That night she saw David and Helen, who were sure Ruth would

614

call back. "She just needs time to digest it all," Helen said. For days Rachel never left her room for fear of missing Ruth's call; but it didn't come on Monday or Tuesday or Wednesday. By Thursday she was going stir-crazy and took herself out to dinner at Tomo's, a little neighborhood eatery — then regretted it, staying home all of Friday in case Ruth had tried to reach her the night before. But by Saturday she could no longer keep her hopes up, and consoled herself with the memory of that one brief conversation with the girl whose name was still Ruth.

On Sunday morning, as it had the previous Sunday, the phone rang early.

Rachel snapped it up before the first ring had faded, hearing again the hiss and pop of long distance.

"Hi. It's me again."

Rachel's heart pounded in her chest like the sea heard in a conch shell. She shut her eyes and thanked whatever God, god, or *'aumakua* had granted her this.

Simultaneously they said, "I'm sorry —"

Simultaneously they laughed.

"You first," Ruth said.

"I'm sorry if I alarmed you. I'm sure it was enough of a shock, hearing from me, much less the rest of it."

"I'm sorry it took me so long to call back," Ruth apologized. *"I guess I panicked a little. My first thought was for my children; what it*

615

might mean to them."

Rachel thrilled to know she was a grand-mother. "How many children do you have?"

"Two. Peggy's eight and Donald is ten."

"That's wonderful," Rachel said, tears coming to her.

"My doctor says you're right, leprosy isn't hereditary. But that children are more suscep-tible to it."

Rachel asked, "Did he also tell you that you don't get it from casual contact? From touching someone, or breathing the same air they do?"

Her daughter hesitated. *"Yes. But he did say that children are more susceptible."*

Rachel weighed her words carefully: "Ruth, it's you I want to see. I'm willing to do it under any conditions you name. If you don't want me near your children, I won't go near them."

After a moment: *"How . . . bad . . . is your leprosy?"*

"You mean, am I disfigured?"

"I didn't say that."

"My right hand is deformed. And my feet. Other than that, my main complaint is neuritis."

"I'm sorry. I didn't mean to sound — tactless —"

"It's all right. Not many people know much about leprosy. Even in Hawai'i it's something

616

most people would prefer not to think about."

There was a long silence, and then Ruth said, *"I used to wonder about you. Who you were. Why you . . ."* She paused. *"I think it's only fair to tell you. I love my* okōsan, *my mother. I loved my father."*

Rachel felt a pang of loss at the words, but said, "Of course you do. They raised you. Raised you well, to judge by what I've heard. I'm not trying to replace anyone in your affections, Ruth."

"Then what do you want from me?"

"Just what I said in the letter. To see you." Her voice broke. "You were the only baby I ever had, and you were taken from me after less than a day. If someone had taken Peggy or Donald from you right after they were born — if you hadn't seen them in thirty years — what would you want?"

The distance between them crackled in Rachel's ear, then Ruth said, *"This is so strange. Listening to you, it's almost like listening to my own voice."* There was a hint of pleasure in her tone. *"I never looked or sounded like anybody in my family."*

She hesitated a moment, then said, *"We're not rich. I can't afford to come to Honolulu."*

And at that, Rachel smiled.

"I don't expect you to," she said.

She was going through her savings at an

617

alarming pace, but couldn't think of anything she would rather spend it on than this. Round-trip airfare from Honolulu to San Francisco was a bracing $270 plus tax, but a cabin-class steamer ticket ran about the same price. And in the end she couldn't resist the lure of the majestic *Lurline* — the prospect of finally being one of those boarding a ship bound for distant ports, and not just one of the crowd seeing them off. Now, as she and some seven hundred other passengers crowded onto the bow of the luxury liner, stewards handed out gaudy streamers which the passengers let fall in a blizzard of color, to be caught by friends or family on the pier. Rachel threw hers to strangers, even waved at them, and laughed when they waved back. The Royal Hawaiian Band bid them sweet farewell with "Aloha 'Oe," the ship's horn returning the sentiment in a deep basso — three long blasts as the ship pulled anchor. The *Lurline* slipped its berth and was soon heading for open sea, the band's music becoming faint as a fading radio signal. As O'ahu receded from view, Rachel felt a rush of excitement headier even than her flight out of Kalaupapa. San Francisco! The name resonated with memories of her father, the rag doll he'd bought for her back when California had been a place in another country, an exotic land called America. And as the last of the Hawaiian archipelago disappeared from sight Rachel realized that she had gone over the horizon, just as Papa had. The salt air tasted strangely sweet.

She had booked the cheapest cabin available — a tiny room with a couch that converted into a bed — but spent most of the next five days outside anyway, lounging in a deck chair while reading a book, strolling the promenade deck, sunning herself at the pool. She didn't go into the water for fear of revealing her deformed feet, but perhaps no one would have cared if she had; the other passengers seemed far too intent on their own recreation.

After dinner she liked to linger in the aft lounge on "A" deck, listening to music and watching couples swing dancing. She would have given all the rest of her life to be on that dance floor with Kenji, feeling his arms around her as he held her close, followed by a long walk in the moonlight with nothing but ocean and freedom in every direction. As the orchestra played "Autumn Serenade" Rachel shut her eyes and could almost imagine Kenji *was* here, and for a moment she could feel his strong fingers entwined with those of her good hand.

On the fifth day the California coastline crept up from below the horizon, the red towers of the Golden Gate Bridge appearing like devil's horns on the forehead of the sea. It was the largest man-made creation Rachel had ever seen: a flaming necklace strung between brown hills and a city of towering concrete *pali*. She couldn't have been more excited if she'd been transported by whirlwind to the outskirts of Oz.

She would have loved to take in the sights, but instead caught a train that carried her south to San José, which was closer to her conception of a mainland American city — modern and a bit nondescript. From the Cahill Street Station she took a taxi to the Hotel Sainte Claire, a six-story brick colossus that occupied the better part of an entire block. She had considered getting a room at the YWCA, or at a less pricy hotel like the unfortunately named Letcher House, but chose the Saint Claire because she didn't want her daughter to think her indigent; that Rachel had any financial motives in contacting her.

Her comfortable room looked out on Plaza Park across the street. Shaped somewhat like a lopsided arrowhead, the park was an island of California redwoods, date palms, and oak trees surrounding the Victorian spires of City Hall. She freshened up, then lay down on the bed, noting the time: a little after three in the afternoon. Ruth would be here in less than an hour and Rachel found herself growing anxious, restive. The person dearest to her in the world was also, she knew, a total stranger; Rachel reminded herself that the need here was hers, not Ruth's.

As she seemed to do whenever she checked into a hotel she promptly fell into a doze, only to be startled awake by a knock on the door. She sat up, disoriented to see the hands of the clock now poised just after four. My God, she thought, she's here, Ruth's here! "Coming!" she called, terrified the knocking would stop and her daughter somehow vanish like smoke; she smoothed the wrinkles in her skirt, took the brass doorknob in her left hand, twisted and pulled.

A tall, pretty young woman with amber skin and almond eyes stood in the doorway. Her face was as round as Rachel's, but her features were finer, like Kenji's. She wore a yellow dress and her hair fell to her shoulders.

"Hello," she said, smiling nervously. "I'm Ruth."

Something sang inside Rachel, and everything she had endured paled in the bright light of this moment.

"Ruth," she said, less a greeting than a confirmation. She felt tears in her eyes, didn't try to check them. "Oh my baby, you're so beautiful." Ruth blushed, as her mother once had at similar words.

Rachel embraced her, unable to do anything else. For the first time in thirty years she felt her daughter's skin against hers; rejoiced to feel her heartbeat, and each nervous breath she took.

But she also became aware of the tension in Ruth's body, the unease she was probably feeling, and reluctantly Rachel let go of her. She took a step back, wiped at her eyes.

"I'm sorry," she said with a smile. "I'm a blubbering old woman. Take me out and shoot me."

But this did not elicit the expected laugh. Rachel realized that Ruth was staring at her right hand — the wrist that ended so suddenly, the harrowed flesh pulled tight over a stump of bone. The young woman appeared shocked and queasy, suddenly unsteady on her feet.

"May I — sit down?" she asked. Rachel stepped aside to admit her. Ruth teetered a bit on her high heels as she hurried to the bed and sat.

"Can I get you some water?" Rachel asked. Ruth shook her head. She sat there a long moment, taking deep breaths, then finally looked up at Rachel. When she did her face showed less fear than amazement.

"You — really do have leprosy," she said softly.

Rachel was puzzled, to say the least. "Well, yes."

Strangely, Ruth started to laugh.

"I know how weird this sounds," she said, "but . . . part of me didn't quite believe you." Her laughter was so much like Kenji's that Rachel found she almost didn't care what

622

had prompted it, she just enjoyed hearing it.

"I'm sorry. I shouldn't laugh, but . . ." Sobering, Ruth explained, "When my parents first told me I was adopted, I asked them why you'd given me up. All my mother said was, 'Don't judge her, Ruth. She had no choice.' Later I took that to mean you were . . . unmarried, underage. But I couldn't help it, I'd still wonder . . . how you could have given me up. Why you didn't . . . love me enough . . . to keep me."

"Oh, Ruth," Rachel said, sitting down beside her.

"Please don't be offended by this," Ruth said, "but in a strange way . . . it's almost a *relief* to learn that you have leprosy. To know that you gave me away because you had to, because you really *didn't* have any other choice."

Rachel assured her, "Nothing else in this world could have made me give you up."

Ruth looked pleased, but also a little embarrassed at having shared this much, this soon. She stood up, smiling self-consciously. "Why don't we go downstairs to the restaurant and get some coffee," she suggested. "Or maybe something stronger."

Within the hotel was an atrium restaurant roofed by palm trees that made Rachel feel more at home. She and Ruth took a table beneath a large umbrella where Rachel ordered coffee and a Danish pastry and Ruth

— she wasn't kidding — a vodka tonic. A stray shaft of California sunlight fell across the tawny skin of Ruth's arm and Rachel couldn't help touching her, her fingers grazing her daughter's wrist, affirming that she was real.

"So your parents" — Rachel wanted to show she wasn't afraid of the word — "adopted you when you were five?"

Ruth nodded. "Mama always wanted a daughter, but after my brother Ralph was born she learned she couldn't have any more children. So they decided to adopt a girl."

"Do you recall anything of Hawai'i?"

Ruth shook her head. "I'm afraid not. My earliest memories are of Florin, our farm there."

"What brought your parents to California?" Rachel was quite proud of herself, calmly asking questions like a quizmaster on a radio show.

"Well, Papa always wanted his own farm. And in Hawai'i, I guess, there weren't many opportunities of that kind for an *Issei*. You know what that is?"

Rachel smiled and nodded. "My husband was Japanese."

Mortified, Ruth shaded her eyes with her hands. "Yes, of course he was. You had no idea you'd given birth to such an idiot, did you?"

Rachel laughed. "No, you've just either had

624

too much to drink or not enough." She sliced off a piece of pastry with her fork. "You were talking about your father?"

Still chagrined, Ruth said, "Yes, well . . . I'm told we left Hawai'i in '23. Papa got a three-year lease on a thousand acres in Florin, which was predominantly Japanese. Lots of towns had *nihonmachi* — Japantowns — but all of Florin was one big *nihonmachi*! I lived on our farm 'till I was eighteen, when I met Frank."

She opened her purse and in moments had spread a fan of photographs on the table. Pointing to a smiling young *Nisei* she said, "That's Frank."

"He's very handsome."

"And this is Donald, and Peggy." A ten-year-old boy in a cowboy hat straddled a sawhorse and twirled a lariat, and an eight-year-old girl posed shyly in a candy-striped blouse. Their complexions were fairer than Ruth's, closer to their father's. "As you can see, Donald wants to be Roy Rogers when he grows up. Peggy wants to grow up, period."

Rachel asked, "May I — ?" At Ruth's nod she picked up the photos and smiled as she examined them. Even if this was the closest she would ever come to her grandchildren, it was worth the trip to see these faces . . . to be sitting here like any grandmother listening to any daughter go on about her children. "They're beautiful," she told Ruth.

"Thank you. I think so too, when they're not driving me to drink." And then Ruth surprised Rachel by asking, "Your husband. What was his name?"

Rachel looked up. "Kenji. Charles Kenji Utagawa."

"Do you have a picture?"

Pleased, Rachel took a snapshot from her purse and handed it to Ruth, who studied it with some fascination. "He loved you so much, Ruth. He called you his *akachan.* The day you left Moloka'i he told you, 'Papa loves you. He'll always love you, and he'll always be your papa.'"

Her voice broke a little as she said it. All at once she was afraid that her use of the word "papa" could have offended Ruth; but Ruth's gaze as she stared at Kenji's seemed almost tender. "He looks . . . very kind."

"He was. A very kind, sweet man."

Ruth glanced up. "So he's not —"

Rachel shook her head and reluctantly told her the circumstances of Kenji's death. Ruth winced a little and said softly, "That makes two fathers I lost to the war."

"What do you mean?"

"My papa died at Tule Lake." When she saw the blank look on Rachel's face, she added, "The relocation camp."

Rachel felt a chill, cutting as a winter wind at Kalawao.

"Relocation?" she repeated, only dimly

comprehending.

Ruth stared at her incredulously. "You don't know? Where have you —" She stopped, realizing too well where Rachel had been. "But — you had them, too, didn't you?"

You're an old fool, Rachel told herself. You're a blithering idiot, not to have realized! She shook her head. "I don't think so. Not in Hawai'i." She thought back to newspaper accounts of relocation she had read during the war, which had seemed to scarcely concern her at the time. "I . . . believe the Japanese made up too large a part of the workforce."

Now Ruth was flabbergasted. "That sure didn't stop them here! All those farms, no one to work them —"

Dreading the reply, Rachel said, "You went, too?"

Ruth's black eyes flared at what to her must have been an annoyingly dense question.

"Of course I went!" It was perhaps louder than she intended. At adjacent tables heads turned, diners glared. Ruth flushed in embarrassment or anger or both.

"We all went," she said, lowering her voice. "The signs went up on May 2, and we were evacuated on May 9."

Her anger still seemed freshly minted. Rachel said, "One week? They gave you one week?"

Ruth nodded. "Seven days to sell everything you owned or put it in storage. We owned a restaurant — ten thousand dollars in inventory. We had to sell it all for a tenth of that. My parents," and her voice still trembled to speak of it, "were evicted from the farm they'd spent twenty years building. Ownership was 'transferred' to a Caucasian — one of the local farmers who'd lobbied for internment, because the Japanese were giving them too much competition. Worked out nicely for him." She sighed heavily. "You don't really want to hear all this, do you?"

Rachel didn't, not really, but had to. "Where did they take you?" she asked.

Ruth took a swallow of her vodka tonic. "Tanforan Racetrack outside San Francisco had been turned into a temporary Assembly Center. Our 'apartment' was an old horse stall, ten feet by twenty feet. The dirt floor was covered with linoleum but it still stank of horse manure, no matter how much you cleaned it. We were given old Army cots and told to stuff burlap bags with hay for mattresses. We had to use communal latrines, with commodes side by side, no stalls — you'd sit there trying to relieve yourself with someone right next to you straining to do the same. The horses had had more privacy!

"We were there a year before we were transferred to a permanent relocation camp. In Oakland they put us on a train, the windows blacked out, I guess to spare the populace from seeing so many Japanese. Two soldiers in each car, armed with rifles and bayonets. We got off at a train station in Lone Pine, in Inyo County.

"The first thing I remember seeing was the mountains — the eastern wall of the Sierra Nevadas. Mount Whitney rising almost two miles from the desert floor. We were put on buses and taken to our new home. Manzanar."

She stared into space and frowned, as if seeing it again in a mirage. "Barbed wire fence, guard towers along the perimeter. Machine-gun nests pointed *inside,* not out. Seeing those guns pointed at us as we entered the camp was when even the *Nisei* — who thought of ourselves as Americans, not Japanese — realized we weren't 'evacuees,' we were prisoners. Criminals who'd committed no crime.

"The Sierras were like bulwarks between Manzanar and the rest of California," Ruth remembered. "Every day you'd look up at them and be reminded of how the world needed to be shielded from the likes of us."

Rachel asked numbly, "What happened to your father?"

Ruth sighed.

"Question 28 happened to him." She looked as if she'd rather not elaborate, but did. "At Tanforan the authorities circulated a questionnaire to determine whether you were a loyal American who might be eligible for

629

'parole' — to work farms in the Midwest or go to school back East. Question 27 asked, 'Are you willing to serve in the Armed Forces of the United States?' Question 28 asked, 'Will you swear unqualified allegiance to the United States of America, and forswear any form of allegiance or obedience to the Japanese emperor, or any other foreign government?'

"Now, my father was a foreign national — legally prohibited from ever becoming a naturalized American! This question seemed to ask him to renounce his Japanese citizenship, but without becoming an American, either. Papa feared he'd be a man without a country. And he was almost sixty years old; he couldn't possibly have served in the Army. So he answered 'no' to both questions.

"But to the War Relocation Authority, anyone who answered 'no-no' to those two questions was disloyal, a potential threat. So they were segregated — sent to a high-security camp at Tule Lake, California."

Ruth glanced down, as if the sunlight were too bright or too hot and she couldn't bear to look into it. "My father was sent there in '43. Conditions were bad — overcrowding, poor food, virtually no health care. No antibiotics. Papa caught pneumonia. He died without ever seeing any of us again."

When after a moment Ruth looked up again, Rachel was in tears.

She could no longer stop them, the emotions that had been building up inside her finally venting: pain, horror, despair, anger, all fused into one terrible alloy. She tried to hold it in but found she was little more than a broken vessel, ruptured by sorrow, released of grief.

Ruth instinctively reached out and took Rachel's hand, her right hand, trying to stem her tears:

"I'm sorry," she said, "I shouldn't have told you all this — it's okay, *we're* okay, really —"

"It's not right," her mother said, the words almost lost in between sobs. "It's not fair."

"It wasn't right. But it's over."

Rachel shook her head. "No. No." She reached deep inside and found the words:

"You were supposed to be free," she said in a whisper. "You were never supposed to know what it was like to be taken from your home — separated from your family — to be shunned and feared." Then, so softly Ruth could barely hear, "That was all I had to give you."

She wept even more fiercely. Ruth went to her without hesitation. She folded her arms around her, holding her as she would a frightened child, rocking her like the baby Rachel had not been able to cradle. And in cooing, consoling tones she told her, It's all right. Everything's all right. It's all over, she said. I'm free. You're free. It's all right,

Mother. Everything's all right.

Ruth called her Mother, but didn't mean it; not yet. As she took the shaken Rachel back to her room, her mind was a jumble of emotions: pity for this woman's tragic life; pleasure at seeing herself in Rachel's face and voice and complexion; and guilt that by taking any pleasure at all in Rachel's presence she was somehow betraying her real parents, the ones who'd raised her. Unable to reconcile her love for them with her growing, traitorous affection for this woman, Ruth invented somewhere she had to be. After reassuring herself that Rachel was all right she made her apologies, started to say her good-byes . . .

"Wait," Rachel interrupted her, a bit desperately, "just a minute. Please. I . . . have something for you."

She took a suitcase from the closet, lifted it up onto the bed, and asked Ruth to open it.

With some trepidation — as if she were opening an inverted Pandora's Box that might suck her and her love for her parents forever inside — Ruth opened the suitcase.

Whatever it was she expected to see, it wasn't this. The suitcase was filled with gift boxes — dozens of them, in a diversity of shapes and colors. There was one the size of a pillbox, wrapped in pink and crowned by a bright red bow almost bigger than the box itself; a rectangular package, in lavender wrap, ornamented with a yellow ribbon teased and curled into something resembling a flower; and a large box wrapped in light blue foil that shimmered like the sky on a hot August day. Too many to take in all at once. Christmas had never been celebrated in her parents' home, but Ruth imagined this must be what it would have felt like, sneaking downstairs on Christmas morning to be overwhelmed by a glittering pile of gifts under the tree.

Rachel seemed to take great pleasure in saying, "Happy birthday," and when Ruth could manage no coherent reply she prompted, "Open them, if you like."

One by one Ruth opened them. How could she not? Each gift, she discovered, was modest yet chosen with impeccable taste: a baby's rattle that might have captivated her attention as an infant; a Raggedy Ann doll she would surely have loved when she was three; an elegant fashion doll that a six-year-old Ruth would have proudly shown off to her friends; a set of combs and hair brushes for a thirteen-year-old's vanity table; and more. Thirty-two years, thirty-two presents.

Ruth unwrapped the last one — a copy of *Tales of the South Pacific* by James A. Michener — and held it in hands that were suddenly trembling.

On every birthday since she had learned, at

the age of eight, that she was adopted, Ruth would find herself wondering whether there was someone, somewhere, thinking of her. Now she was presented with proof that there had been, and she was speechless with emotion. She told herself not to cry, and her eyes filled with tears.

She did not leave for home. She stayed with Rachel in her room, listening to a life's story that was, she discovered, richer than it was sad. She heard of her birth father, Kenji; her grandfather, Henry, and grandmother, Dorothy; learned of Rachel's *hānai* aunt, Haleola; Uncle Pono and Catherine and Sarah and Leilani and the rest of Rachel's cherished *'ohana*. She learned what *'ohana* meant, and that she was part of it. She began to understand that none of this could replace or usurp the family she had always known, but enriched what she already possessed. With wonder and a growing absence of fear she realized, I am more than I was an hour ago.

The next day, after consultation with Frank and an explanation to Donald and Peggy, Ruth brought Rachel home to their two-story house on Fifth Street, where Rachel met two bright, lively youngsters delighted at the notion of having a third grandmother — and one from far-off Hawai'i, no less. Frank Harada was affable and easy-going, but most gracious of all was Ruth's *okāsan,* Etsuko, a

634

woman of great charm who put Rachel immediately at ease with her questions about Hawai'i and what it was like these days. She reminisced about her days in Waimānalo and Honolulu in the early years of the century, and turned what could have been an awkward afternoon into a delightful one. It was Etsuko who solved a nagging problem of nomenclature by inquiring of Rachel, "What is Hawaiian for Mother?" — and henceforth as Etsuko was *Okāsan,* Rachel was *Makuahine.* This pleased Rachel for many reasons.

She stayed in California for two weeks, playing Go and other games with her grandchildren; Ruth, watching them play, caught hints of the mother she might have had, even as Rachel glimpsed, not without some pain, the mother she might have been. One day Ruth packed everyone up and drove to San Francisco for some sightseeing: they corkscrewed down Lombard Street, strolled along the Embarcadero, ate fish and chips on the Wharf, and rode cable cars not so different than the trolleys of Old Honolulu. It was a grand day, one of the grandest in Rachel's long life.

Soon Donald and Peggy were asking their parents when they could go to Hawai'i to visit their new grandma. Frank smiled and said, "Several thousand dollars from now," and as quickly as Rachel's hopes fell they were kindled again by Ruth, who told the children,

"If we can't get to Hawai'i, maybe Grandma Rachel can come visit us again." Rachel happily assured her grandchildren that she would.

At the end of the two weeks Ruth helped her *makuahine* aboard the *Lurline,* tipping the porters and making sure she was properly settled in her tiny cabin. They walked the length of the ship together until fifteen minutes before the scheduled departure time of four o'clock, when the ship's horn sounded two blasts — final call for all visitors. Ruth hugged Rachel, kissed her, and said, "Thank you. For giving me life, and health, and freedom."

Rachel cried and held onto her for as long as she could. She watched as Ruth walked down the gangway and onto the dock, waved to her as the *Lurline* backed away from the pier and into the bay, and kept on watching until long after the pier had disappeared from sight and the Golden Gate was only a red gleam on the horizon.

On the return voyage Rachel had ample time to consider her future, and what shape it might take; and as she neared Hawai'i she now discovered something else that her father must have felt on his many voyages. As the green palisades with their white skirts of sand appeared in the distance, Rachel could not imagine there was any place on earth more beautiful, any sight more welcoming, than these magnificent islands. And like Henry she knew that no matter how far she might roam, she would always come back to them.

In Honolulu she gave notice to her landlord and began boxing up the belongings she had only just unpacked; and within the week was setting to sea again, this time aboard the interisland steamer *Hualālai.* She watched Oʻahu recede again into the distance, saw the angry waters of the Kaiwi Channel off the port side . . . and watched with satisfaction as they too receded from her view. The western flank of Molokaʻi was visible but never close, and soon it was joined on the horizon by the tall Norfolk pines of Lānaʻi, and then by the terraced slopes of the West Maui Mountains.

At Lahaina Harbor, Sarah happily embraced her sister and arranged for a stevedore to load her belongings into Sarah's old Ford. Together they wrestled the bags and boxes out of the car and into Sarah's driveway, from which they would be unloaded, piecemeal, over several days. In celebration they dined that evening at the Midnite Inn; and then, exhausted, Rachel fell into bed by nine o'clock, her books already neatly shelved around her in the bedroom once shared by Sarah's daughters, including Rachel's namesake.

Sometime after midnight she woke to the touch of a gentle breeze billowing the curtains and knew at once that it was the Ulola. And blown in on the wind was a sweet floral scent unlike any she had ever known. On an impulse she pulled on a robe, slipped into a pair of shoes and out of the house — making her way *makai* down Dickensen Street, the sweet fragrance growing still stronger. Front Street was empty at this hour and now she stood alone at the sea wall, looking out at dark waters stippled by starlight. In the harbor boats slept rocking on gentle swells, waves lapping at the wharves with a rhythm like drumbeats.

Some bold, reckless voice impelled her to climb over the sea wall and down the rocky slope to the water's edge. Maybe this was *kapu,* but she no longer cared what was *kapu.* She kicked off her shoes, cast off her robe, and as she'd done so long ago in Kapi'olani Park, waded into the water. She had not been swimming in the ocean for many years but it felt as if she had never left. Her feet were fairly useless so she relied on her hands to backstroke out some ten or twenty feet from shore. Here she bobbed and floated and laughed with delight as the swells rolled gently under her, a tender reminder from Namakaokaha'i of the way Rachel once exuberantly rode the waves. It all came back in a rush, a floodtide of exhilaration.

As she floated like a leaf on the water she looked down the coast toward Mala Wharf, and saw lights which seemed to hover along the shore before moving out to sea. Fishermen? Torch-fishing, did they still do that? Or perhaps they were the marchers of the night, even as the sweet fragrance might have been the rare bloom of the silversword her *makuahine,* Haleola, had often spoken of. She smiled: if Ruth had two mothers, so did Rachel, and they were both here with her on Maui. She drew in a breath, holding the sweet scent of the silversword in her chest as she held Haleola in her heart; weightless with joy, home at last.

ENDNOTE

1970

The twin-engine Cessna was gliding low over the grassy meadows of what was still the Meyer Ranch in Kala'e when the ground abruptly fell away and the plane dove into two thousand feet of air — leaving Ruth's stomach, she was quite certain, behind. The aircraft then banked as if its specific purpose was to exacerbate her vertigo, the view outside the windows rotating a good forty degrees; she had the sickening and unwanted epiphany that this must be what it felt like to be on the inside of a kaleidoscope.

"Mom," came a voice next to her, "are you okay?"

Ruth glanced at Peggy and said, "I may have to throw up on you. I hope that's all right."

Peggy, now a willowy thirty-year-old, smiled indulgently. "Sure. Better me than a stranger."

"That was my thought as well."

Peggy said suddenly, "Oh my God, look!"

Ruth reluctantly followed her gaze. Despite her queasiness she couldn't help but be impressed by the sight of the lofty green *pali* thrusting up from the peninsula below — like an enormous headstone, she thought, on a tiny grave. But a headstone thriving, oddly, with life and movement: the scudding shadows of clouds across the *pali,* waterfalls storming down clefts in its green face, even the switchback trail zigzagging down with a kind of motionless motion. It was all quite lovely, Ruth thought, but it was also making her quite nauseous.

Then the plane banked away from the cliffs and toward a tiny airport on the western shore. Now the broad plain of the peninsula loomed large in the windows, sudden blustery crosswinds adding to the thrill quotient of the ride, and when the little puddle-jumper finally touched down on the short runway Ruth exhaled in relief.

"Wow," Peggy said, "was that a trip."

"Yes. Stimulating," her mother agreed. In moments the plane had taxied to a stop beside another light aircraft. The pilot opened up the cabin and the four passengers — Ruth, Peggy, and a young Caucasian couple here for a tour of the settlement — wobbled out onto the tarmac.

Inside the open-air terminal pilots chatted with one another as stray cats preened or

641

dozed on plastic seats. A Hansen's patient —
one of two here, Ruth would learn, who operated tours of the settlement — collected the
tourists, as Ruth and Peggy were approached
by a smiling, fiftyish gentleman in a bright
aloha shirt.

The face above that smile sent a little shiver
of adrenaline through Ruth's body: the man's
nose was very nearly flat, the merest of ridges;
his toothy smile gave him the skeletal grin of
a skull, or a jack-o'-lantern.

"Mom," Peggy whispered.

"Quiet," Ruth said firmly. But despite her
tone she felt flustered: she didn't want to
stare, but was afraid to look away, lest he be
offended by that as well.

The man said cheerfully, "Ruth Harada,
right?"

He extended a hand to her. Both were
gnarled and deformed, even more than her
mother's had been, but Ruth clasped the offered hand without flinching, smiled, and said
only half-seriously, "Yes, how could you tell?"

"Aw, I'd know Rachel's daughter anywhere!
I'm Hokea. Your mom and me, we go way
back."

His handshake was soft and gentle, like the
brushing of a leaf.

"You're the painter," Ruth recalled. "She
spoke very highly of your work."

He seemed pleased by that. "Good lady,
your mama. Always came back to see us, at

642

least once a year. Never forgot. Everybody's very sorry."

"Thank you." Hokea's natural ebullience was becoming more noticeable than his disfigurement. Ruth introduced Peggy, whose nervousness was hardly concealed by her smile.

Hokea took Peggy's hand. "Ah, such a beautiful girl! Rachel always said how pretty you are, but eh, face it, what else grandmothers gonna say? 'My daughter's *keiki,* she sweet but ugly'?" Peggy laughed at that, and her mother could see a little of the tension leave her face. "You two want to come with me, I'll take you into town."

As they followed him to the parking lot he explained, "Rules say you can't go nowhere by yourself," then with another smile, "except maybe to the potty."

"Now there's a welcome exception," Peggy laughed.

"You know we even used to have separate potties here? Not men and women — patient and *kōkua.* Big signs posted everywhere. No more though. No more quarantine either."

"Yes, we heard," Ruth said. "Since when, last year?"

He nodded, pointing them toward a '57 Chevy sitting alone in the lot. "Nobody ever has to come here if he don't want to, ever again. It's over, done, *pau.*" He spat out the word with no small satisfaction.

Ruth and Peggy got into the back seat as Hokea slipped behind the wheel. Ruth was a tad apprehensive at the thought of him driving, but his clawed hands had no difficulty operating the gearshift and he effortlessly steered the vehicle onto the narrow road to town.

As Hokea and Peggy chatted, Ruth gazed at the landscape rolling past. She had been to Maui, of course, to visit Rachel, but never to Kalaupapa, and she was surprised at how beautiful it was, how vibrant the colors: the rich green mantle of the *pali,* the black lava coastline shadowed against a tourmaline sea. She remembered Manzanar as nearly colorless: steel gray barracks and the dun of the desert sand, the frequent dust storms leeching even the sky of color. But the *pali,* though not as tall as Mount Whitney, was nearer to the village than Whitney had been to Manzanar, and loomed as an even more forbidding barrier than the wintry peaks of the Sierras.

Equally forbidding was the large number of cemeteries they passed on the way to town: a seemingly endless garden of crosses and headstones overrunning the shore. But eventually it did end, and then they were in a sleepy little village of cozy cottages sprouting TV antennas, neatly trimmed lawns, white picket fences. There were cars in every driveway, all without license plates, and people out weeding in their gardens. They passed a fire station, a general store, a gas station, even a bar. It all seemed perfectly normal.

And all at once it dawned on Ruth: I was born here. This is where I was born!

"It's so lovely," Peggy said softly.

Hokea nodded in agreement. "I know people on the outside, they say, 'Times are tough.' Hard to make a living, you know? We don't have to worry about that here. Or about people giving us the stink-eye. Most of us, we've been here all our lives; this is home." He added, "Now we only hope we get to stay."

"What do you mean?" Ruth asked.

"I'm on the Kalaupapa Patients Council, I hear things. The legislature swears we can stay here the rest of our lives, but you can't tell me the State of Hawai'i wouldn't love to move us all to the hospital in Honolulu. And the minute they do, you bet your sweet behind they'll sell alla this land to Sheraton or Hilton for a big resort. Been talk about it for years. The land's too valuable.

"To them it's just real estate, but to us it's a lot more. The government forced us to come here, and now that it's the only place we know, now that it's home, they want us to give it up?" He shook his head. "We won't go without a fight, though. Not this time."

Ruth was touched by the passion in his voice, but apologetically he said, "Eh, listen to me! Running off at the mouth when you're here to bury your mama. I'm sorry, you want me to take you to her?"

"Can we go to her house first?"

"Oh, she gave that up when she moved to Maui. Six weeks ago, when she come back to Kalaupapa, she went straight into the hospital, she was so sick. Lotta patients here die of kidney trouble, you know; the drugs we take for leprosy, they're hard on the kidneys."

"I know." Ruth remembered her last conversation with her mother; with Sarah gone, Rachel wanted to spend her final days here among her Kalaupapa *'ohana*. Though Rachel had only just been to California, Ruth offered to fly her back again so she could care for her in San José; but Rachel had been adamant. This was where she wanted to be buried, and this might as well be where she died.

"I got all her stuff at my place," Hokea said. "Except for the books, she gave those to the library here."

Hokea's house was impossibly, magnificently cluttered. Ruth and Peggy were astonished by the hundreds of canvases hung, stacked, and stored in every nook and corner: oils and watercolors and sketches of Kalaupapa and Kalawao, the rugged coastline, Father Damien's church, Baldwin and Bishop Homes. "You must've painted every square

646

inch of this peninsula twice over," Ruth marveled.

Hokea chuckled. "Yeah, and I painted over plenty more 'cause I couldn't afford new canvas."

"Excuse me for asking," Peggy said, "but how do you paint with your — hands like that?"

"Oh, no problem." He reached for a device lying on a table, slipping his right hand through a metal loop that Ruth now saw was attached to a brush. "One of our people, Kenso, came up with this for forks and spoons, so if you've got no hands you can wrap it around your wrist and use it to eat. He made me one for my brushes."

He slipped it off again and took them into the living room, where three large cartons were neatly stacked: "Here's your mama's stuff, all except the books. And her Sunday dress, she wanted to be buried in that."

The first carton contained clothing that Ruth and Peggy decided to donate to Goodwill, with the exception of one particular dress that Ruth now set aside. In the second carton were photographs and the accumulated bric-a-brac of a lifetime, which Ruth would keep; while the third box held Rachel's treasured doll collection. Some of them, like the Chinese mission dolls and the *sakuraningyö,* were so tattered and worn they seemed as if they might fall apart at a glance.

647

Others were newer: a papier-mâche folk doll from Mexico; a wooden *kokeshi* bought in Tokyo; a stuffed koala bear from Australia; and others purchased on Rachel's various travels over the past twenty years. These would occupy places of honor in Ruth's home as well as in Peggy's and Donald's . . . all but one.

Tenderly Ruth took out an old, handmade doll with cloth "skin" the color of Ruth's own, a round face and black hair, wearing a miniature *kapa* skirt. The tiny shell *lei* around its neck had long since broken apart, but it still wore a pin where a note had once been affixed.

"Is this the one?" Peggy asked.

Ruth nodded. She turned to Hokea.

"I'm ready now," she said.

At the funeral home, Ruth and Peggy were left alone with their mother and grandmother, laid out in her Sunday dress in a casket she had selected herself. Rachel's face showed the scoring of time, certainly of tragedy, but also of a life well lived: of laughter and adventure as much as grief and ill fortune. Even now, in the lines around her mouth, Ruth saw the ghost of a smile haunting her mother's face. She touched her cheek, and she and Peggy sat and visited with her again, one last time.

After Ruth finalized the funeral arrangements, Hokea took her and Peggy on a walking tour of Kalaupapa, starting with the grave of Mother Marianne near the convent where a handful of Franciscans still lived and worked. On the grass nearby Peggy was amused to see a pair of painted lava rocks. One bore a bright yellow happy-face, while its companion urged the passerby, SMILE — IT NO BROKE YOUR FACE! And automatically Ruth did smile, thinking of Manzanar and how even there children had laughed and played, people had danced and made love, babies had been conceived.

Along the way Hokea introduced everyone they happened across. Ruth and Peggy met Kenso Seki, the resourceful tinkerer who'd invented the fork-and-spoon device as well as special hooks that allowed fingerless hands to button shirts and open flip-top cans. Lively and charming, he wore clip-on sunglasses perpetually tilted up like a blackjack dealer's visor and gave them a tour of his workshop. They stopped for soft drinks at Rea's Store — actually more of a saloon — owned and operated by Mariano Rea, who, Hokea told them later, used his profits to fund college educations for scores of nieces, nephews, and cousins in his native Philippines.

When Hokea first entered Rea's with Ruth and Peggy, someone cried out, " 'Ey, Hokea! What, you robbing the cradle again?"

"Ah, piss off, same to you." Hokea laughed, then explained to Ruth, "My last wife, she was ten years younger'n me, and nobody ever lets me forget it."

"Hokea, how many wives have you had?"

"Only three. My first one died, second we get divorced but still friends, third left me for an older man." He laughed again. "True story."

Ruth smiled. Love, marriage, divorce, infidelity . . . life was the same here as anywhere else, wasn't it? She realized now how wrong she'd been; the *pali* wasn't a headstone and Kalaupapa wasn't a grave. It was a community like any other, bound by ties deeper than most, and people here went to their deaths as people did anywhere: with great reluctance, dragging the messy jumble of their lives behind them.

That afternoon most of Kalaupapa's remaining residents clustered around an open grave in the Japanese cemetery along the coast. It was a bright, clear day, the tradewinds brisk, the surf lapping up nearby Papaloa Beach, where, Ruth knew, her mother had spent many happy hours riding the waves. She would have paid good money to have seen that! A Buddhist priest chanted a *sūtra,* and toward the end of the ceremony, when the time came for eulogies, of which there were many, Ruth chose to speak last.

"My mother Rachel was a remarkable woman," she told the crowd, her voice quaking a bit with stage fright, "but you've all known that even longer than I. I've been privileged, these past twenty years, to discover just how remarkable. I'm lucky, you see: I had two mothers. One gave life to me; one raised me. But they both loved me. You know, some people don't even get that once.

"It took me a while to say the words 'I love you' to my *makuahine*. It was a different kind of love than I felt for my *okāsan,* but founded on the same things. I cherished my adopted parents for the home, the love, and the past we shared. I cherished Rachel for the love she showed me, the past she opened up to me, and the home I never knew: this place. The people she cared for. All of you.

"There's only one disadvantage, really, to having two mothers," Ruth admitted. "You know twice the love . . . but you grieve twice as much."

She paused to collect herself, trying to order her thoughts, to remember all she needed to remember. She took a wrinkled slip of paper from her purse and studied the words written on it. She glanced down into the casket, and in halting Hawaiian she said:

"Pono, Haleola, 'eia mai kou keika hanauna, Rachel!"

Some of the mourners were puzzled, but one old-timer recognized the words and repeated the call to ancestors: *"Pono, Haleola,"* he said, his aged treble sounding quite clear and strong, *" 'eia mai kou keiki hanauna, Rachel!"*

Now Peggy spoke, her voice as resonant and proud as her mother's *"Henry, Dorothy, 'eia mai kou kaikamahine, Rachel!* Henry, Dorothy, here is your daughter, Rachel!"

A few more mourners picked up the chant, some in Hawaiian, some in English.

"Kenji-san, 'eia mai kou wahine male, Rachel," Ruth said. "Kenji, here is your wife, Rachel." She gazed into her mother's face, beautiful in eternal repose, and struggled a bit with the next words: "O Rachel, here you are departing! *Aloha wale, e Rachel, kaua, auwē!* Boundless love, O Rachel, between us, alas!"

As the mourners repeated that last word, Ruth heard for the first time the resonant Hawaiian wail of *"Auwē! Auwē!"* which sprang from every heart at once, and she was moved because it so precisely echoed the grief in her own.

Peggy handed Ruth three things: a small dish of *poi;* the dress Rachel had been wearing that day at the Hotel Saint Claire; and the cloth doll in its *kapa* skirt which Henry Kalama had painstakingly fashioned for his little girl, seventy-six years before.

Ruth tucked them all in the casket beside her mother.

"Here is food, clothing, and something you

loved," she said. "Go; but if you have a mind to return, come back."

She leaned over her mother, tenderly kissed her wrinkled forehead, and told her again that she loved her.

Peggy did the same, bidding *aloha* to her Grandma Rachel before she was overcome by tears.

The casket was lowered; within twenty minutes an earthen blanket had covered it and Rachel Aouli Kalama Utagawa slept again beside her beloved Kenji.

Ruth thanked each guest for coming, listening to their memories of Rachel with the same fond fascination as she'd listened to her mother's stories; then, when only she and Peggy and Hokea were left, Ruth asked him if they might be alone for a moment, and Hokea obligingly walked down to the adjacent Mormon cemetery. Ruth and Peggy sat on the ground facing the two graves and Ruth took her daughter's hand in hers. Except for the metronome of the surf a calm silence surrounded them, tranquil beyond words. The air was moist and sweet. The ocean was pale green shot with blue, cresting white. The blue vault of the sky was bright and sheltering. For a long while they sat serenely in this most serene of places, gazing out at waves rolling in from afar to break gently on the peaceful shore.

AUTHOR'S NOTE

On December 22, 1980, the Kalaupapa peninsula was designated a National Historical Park and its residents were, as per Public Law 96–565, "guaranteed that they may remain at Kalaupapa as long as they wish." As of this writing, there are approximately thirty-one individuals with Hansen's disease living there in quiet dignity.

A novel is by definition a work of fiction, but this particular novel is set in a real place where real people lived and died — people to whom I felt accountable as I tried to tell a story that would also be true to their stories. By interweaving real-life patients and caregivers with my fictional cast of characters, I sought to blur the lines between fact and fiction; but now I think it's important to redraw those lines, however briefly, in order to acknowledge a few of the people whose lives have inspired and enriched this book.

Some are known to us today only as names in the superintendent's annual report: the storekeeper George Kanikau, the baker A. Galaspo, nursery matron Lillian Keamalu, and her predecessor Mrs. Kaunamano. Some still speak to us from correspondence long buried in the files of the Board of Health. J. D. Kahauliko, in a letter dated February 1, 1866, wrote, "An opportunity has been afforded me to inform you how we are getting along in Molokai," and who notes "we are in great need for a water calabash . . . therefore we the patients at Kalawao do hereby beg that you will give us a water-cask for us, do not refuse, but give it to your servants the Lepers." Other residents have found some small posterity in accounts by the journalists who occasionally visited Kalaupapa, for example Annie Kekoa, "a half-white telephone operator from Hilo, on Hawaii, daughter of a native minister . . . without blemish, and very charming — educated and refined, with the loveliest brown eyes and heart-shaped face," in the words of Charmaine London, wife of Jack London.

Ambrose Hutchison's life is better documented. Born at Honomā'ele, Maui, in 1856, he arrived at Kalaupapa on January 5, 1879, where, he later wrote, "we were left on the rocky shore without food and shelter. No houses were provided for the likes of us outcasts." What Haleola saw on her first day at the settlement — a sick man in a wheelbarrow dumped on the threshold of a "dying shed" — was what Ambrose saw on his first day. Much of his life was dedicated to the welfare of the community to which he had been exiled: he served as chief butcher, then manager of the Kalawao Store, and finally as either resident or assistant superintendent over a period of fourteen years. He helped improve the quality of health care and nutrition at the settlement and did his best to assure that newcomers to Kalaupapa were given, upon arrival, a place to live and (as Dr. Arthur Mouritz observed) "hot coffee and warm food." He spent nearly fifty-four years in Kalaupapa.

In real life Samson "Sammy" Kuahine's song, "Sunset of Kalaupapa," was performed on bandleader Harry Owens' television show in November of 1950 and was probably composed earlier that year. I sacrificed chronological accuracy for what I felt was the greater truth of including this only known musical composition by a Kalaupapa resident.

Some fictional characters in this book are based on real people. The artist Hokea, for example, was inspired by resident Edward Kato, also a painter of churches (as well as the rock that exhorts visitors to SMILE — IT NO BROKE YOUR FACE!), though there the resemblance ends. Like Rachel, after quarantine was lifted, Edward Kato enthusiastically traveled the world, visiting nearly every

657

continent on the earth long denied him. And one of the Franciscan Sisters of Charity did in fact suffer a nervous breakdown and was forced to leave Moloka'i — but since much of my character's psychology and background had to be created from whole cloth, I elected to call her Sister Victor instead of the woman's real name.

Ernie Pyle's book *Home Country* recounts his visit to Kalaupapa in 1937–38. Though not without errors — he repeats a baseless claim that Hansen's disease causes "feeble-mindedness" — it is nevertheless a spare, honest, compassionate account by a fine writer. Movingly, he recounts a conversation with the then-manager of the Kalaupapa Store, Shizuo Harada, who was diagnosed with Hansen's just sixteen days after he graduated with a degree in economics from the University of Hawaii. "He was lonely," Pyle writes, "because there was no one in Kalaupapa that he could really talk with as he was capable of talking. He apologized for saying what he did, and explained that he didn't feel himself any better than the rest, but there was a difference." When after several hours of lively conversation Pyle had to leave, Harada told him, "You have given me the happiest day I have ever had since I came to Kalaupapa. Thank you. Thank you." Later I found, in the Bishop Museum Library, self-published annotations on Pyle's work by a settlement physician, Dr. Eric A. Fennel: "Harada is not only a mentally keen man; he is a man of substance and solidarity. He has *not* been denied a career; he has had and is having one. As if the burden of his disease were not enough, Fate decreed that one brother go to Italy with the famous 'One Puka Puka' Battalion, made up of Americans of Japanese ancestry, and that the other one became almost hopelessly ill. So this substantial man, with his salary as Storekeeper, is the sole support of his parents, now aged seventy, and a great help to his semiwidowed sister-in-law and her two children. Hansen's disease has *not* robbed him of a noble career."

And so Charles Kenji Utagawa was born, in conscious tribute to Shizuo Harada.

Rachel Kalama is entirely a fictional creation, but what she experiences as a Hansen's patient is very much based on the real-world experiences of many such patients. I consulted numerous oral histories and biographies, distilling them down to their common elements and from these forging the armature of Rachel's life. To interested readers I highly commend *The Separating Sickness: Excerpts from Interviews with Exiled Leprosy Patients at Kalaupapa* by Ted Gugelyk and Milton Bloombaum; *Quest for Dignity: Personal Victories over Leprosy/Hansen's Disease* by The International Association for Integration, Dignity, and Economic Advancement (IDEA); *Olivia: My Life of Exile in Kalaupapa* by Olivia Robello Breitha; *Margaret of Molokai* by Mel White; *Miracle at Carville* and *No One Must Ever Know* by Betty Martin, edited by Evelyn Wells. In addition I drew upon interviews and articles published in *Beacon Magazine, Honolulu Magazine, Kalaupapa Historical Society Newsletter, The Honolulu Star-Bulletin, The Honolulu Advertiser, Paradise of the Pacific, The Maui News, The Hawaiian Gazette,* and *Aloha Magazine.*

Equally valuable were *Holy Man: Father Damien of Molokai* and *Shoal of Time: A History of the Hawaiian Islands* by Gavan Daws; *Pilgrimage and Exile: Mother Marianne of Molokai* by Sister Mary Laurence Hanley and O. A. Bushnell; *News from Molokai: Letters Between Peter Kaeo & Queen Emma 1873–1876,* edited by Alfons L. Korn; *Exile in Paradise: The Isolation of Hawai'i's Leprosy Victims* and *Development of Kalaupapa Settlement, 1865 to the Present* by Linda W. Greene; *Kalaupapa National Historical Park and the Legacy of Father Damien* by Anwei V. Skinsnes Law and Richard Wisniewski; *Defamation and Disease: Leprosy, Myth and Ideology in Nineteenth Century Hawai'i* by Pennie Lee Moblo; *Yesterday at Kalaupapa* by Emmett Cahill; *Kalaupapa: A Portrait* by Wayne Levin and Anwei Skinsnes Law; *The Path of the Destroyer* by A. A. St. M. Mouritz; *Under the Cliffs of Molokai* by Emma Warren Gibson; *The Lands of Father Damien* by James H. Brocker; *Leper Priest of Moloka'i: The Father Damien Story* by Richard Stewart; *A Tree in Bud: The Hawaiian Kingdom, 1889–1893* by M. G. Bosseront d'Anglade; *Unwritten Literature of Hawaii: The Sacred Songs of the Hula* by Nathaniel B. Emerson; *Lawrence M. Judd and Hawaii* by Lawrence M. Judd and Hugh W. Lytle; *Hawaiian Mythology* by Martha Beckwith; *Reminiscences of Old Hawaii* by Uldrick Thompson, Sr.; *Hawaii Goes to War* by DeSoto Brown; *Hawaii's War Years: 1941–1945* by Gwenfread Allen — among dozens if not hundreds of other texts I lack the space to notate.

I have used Mary Kawena Pukui's *Hawaiian Dictionary,* co-authored with Samuel H. Elbert, and *Place Names of Hawaii,* with Elbert and Esther T. Mookini, as the standard for Hawaiian spelling and orthography in this book, departing from it only on the few occasions when I felt clarity demanded the use of an English "s" for pluralization. As for terminology, I am keenly aware of the disdain that most people with Hansen's disease feel for the word "leper" — a word that objectifies and stigmatizes them — and have used it only in historical context, in the dialog or point-of-view of characters living in a time when the term was regrettably in wide use.

To do otherwise, I felt, would have been inaccurate and dishonest.

For their assistance, expertise, and *aloha,* I am indebted to Patty Belcher and B. J. Short of the Bishop Museum Library; Geoff White and Allen Hoof of the Hawai'i State Archives; Helen Wong Smith of the Hawai'i Medical Library; Victoria Pula of the Maui Historical Society; and the able and helpful staffs of the Honolulu Public Library and the Hawaiian Historical Society. My editor, Hope Dellon, and my agent, Molly Friedrich, each took on this book as I did, as a labor of love, and I thank them for believing in it. Holly Henderson generously shared her insights into adopted children and their birthmothers. Robert Crais has been just as generous with his advice and advocacy for me and my work. For criticism and encouragement I must also thank Carter Scholz and Amy Adelson, as well as my first, best reader, my wife Paulette.

ABOUT THE AUTHOR

Alan Brennert is a novelist (*Time and Chance*) as well as an Emmy Award–winning screenwriter (*L.A. Law*). He lives in Southern California, but his heart is in Hawai'i.

The employees of Thorndike Press hope you have enjoyed this Large Print book. All our Thorndike, Wheeler, and Kennebec Large Print titles are designed for easy reading, and all our books are made to last. Other Thorndike Press Large Print books are available at your library, through selected bookstores, or directly from us.

For information about titles, please call:
(800) 223-1244

or visit our website at:
gale.com/thorndike

To share your comments, please write:
Publisher
Thorndike Press
10 Water St., Suite 310
Waterville, ME 04901